Copyright © 2025 by – Dennis G. Smith – All Rights Reserved.

No part of this book may be reproduced or transmitted in any form by any means, whether graphic, electronic, or mechanical, including photography, recording, taping, or by any information storage or retrieval system without prior written permission from the author.

Other books by Dennis G. Smith

- Missouri's Secret - Historical Fiction
- Night Light - A Chance Jackson Detective Novel
- The Man In The Van - A Chance Jackson Detective Novel
- War Is Hell, A Love Story - Historical Fiction
- One Day At Willow Tree - A Chance Jackson Detective Novel

Author's Comment

One Tough Son Of A Gun, Is a fictional novel. In parts of the story, actual places, historical figures, military units, and real events are referenced to relate the story to actual dates and times that affect the character's lives. A few of these events or similar ones actually happened in my life, but this is not a biography. The old adage *truth is stranger than fiction* might apply. The story itself and all main characters are purely fictional as created by me, the author, and any resemblance to real people, living or dead, is purely coincidental.

Dennis G. Smith
Leawood, Kansas
March, 2025

ONE TOUGH SON OF A GUN

Dennis G. Smith

CHAPTER 1

Wednesday, July 14, 2022
Kansas City VA Medical Center
Kansas City, Missouri
United States of America

Ray "Wildcat" Reynolds has anger Issues. They were probably due to the fact he was drafted way back when, or the fact he was sent to infantry training at Fort Polk, Louisiana, the armpit of the Army. He thought he was smarter than that. Maybe it was the way the Vietnam veterans were treated when they came home. Or it could have been the fact that we were in the war in southeast Asia in the first place. Or the things that happened to him there. We didn't belong there, halfway around the world. It wasn't our problem. It was the stupid politics of it. Like people said - "*If the politicians had to send their children off to fight, the war would be over in no time*". And, from what he knew, he thought a lot of the Vietnamese were okay living under communism. Or they were just too afraid to say or do anything. But why should we try to change that? It's their country.

Besides all that, over 50,000 young Americans died, and countless more still bearing the scars of their wounds, like him. Only many of the wounded were a whole lot worse than he was. Then, to top it all, we give up and pull out without winning the war! Us, the U.S., greatest military might in the world and we let little Ho Chi Minh SOB and North Vietnam win! What the hell? And somewhere he read that Ho Chi Minh said, before he died, "*If the U.S. had only known how close they were to winning the war, they would never have left. We were down to sending 14-year-olds south to fight the war.*" Yeah, Ray knew about that! And he had anger issues. But he worked hard to keep the anger under control.

It's possible that 'survivor's remorse' could have exacerbated his problems. That had been suggested by some of his friends. *Why did I live through it?*, he often wondered. He should just be happy to be alive.

Then again, just last year, the politics of war won out over a military victory in Afghanistan. After twenty years, President Biden ordered an immediate withdrawal of all troops, leaving behind equipment, helicopters, vehicles, weapons and pallets of money for the Taliban - victors without winning the battle. Although they had to get in one last suicide bomber before we gave the country back to them. No wonder his anger wouldn't go away.

It wasn't just Vietnam, and now Afghanistan bringing it all back, and the PTSD, it was also the September 11th attack with the hijackings and the World Trade Center twin towers coming down. That was personal! He certainly had a right to be angry about that! He wanted to re-enlist, but knew he was too old and probably wouldn't pass the physical. He really struggled with keeping his mouth shut at work when these topics came up because he knew his language, cowboy slang and soldier's words would be outside the bounds of reasonable and probably get him fired.

Whatever it was, whatever it is, it's always the same spiel that pours out of his mouth every time he goes to the V.A. meetings to talk with the "counselors" and the other PTSD sufferers. Why does he feel like he is the only one that speaks out with such anger? Why can't he just listen? He used to be able to do that. At least one day out of every month, he has an outlet for his pent-up emotions. That helps. It's almost a joke now. They all laugh when it's his turn to speak, but no one disagrees with him. There's no argument from the advisors, and the other veterans just nod their heads in agreement and sympathy. He even laughs sometimes when he starts in because he knows they all know what he's going to gripe about, so he tries to make it more interesting each month by adding some new legitimate complaint. Lately, it's been the current administration's decision to pull out from Afghanistan, and the issue of Covid 19 and wearing masks. Nobody ever proved the masks actually worked. The others all nodded in silence.

For almost forty years, once a month, he's been seeking help with PTSD. He'd lost count of the number of meetings with the Veteran's Administration years earlier. At first, he thought he was fine, but the problem with nightmares started. Then it got worse. He liked his V.A. doctor, but there didn't seem to be a cure. Drugs were suggested but he didn't like the idea. Too many fellow veterans were suffering from drug abuse and he didn't want to go down that road. He realizes the only thing that will cure him, and probably most of the others in the room, is dying. He just has to live through it. He's been lucky to have these sessions, two supportive wives, and a wonderful doctor available that have helped him keep his sanity.

Maybe he was lucky. At least he can control his anger and his mouth most of the time. If he could only control the nightmares. Staying busy helped. He felt sorry for the veterans who didn't have jobs. That too made him angry. He just had to avoid situations with political discussions and anything else that might get him started.

CHAPTER 2

Thursday, May 9, 1970
Near Cu Chi
Republic of South Vietnam

Sergeant Reynolds, second in command of the First Platoon, is leading his men as part of a search and destroy mission in the flat plain grasslands just outside the north perimeter of the 25th Infantry Division's base thirty miles northwest of Saigon. The mission was to find and destroy any bunkers, foxholes, tunnels and boobytraps. Over the previous two weeks, nighttime movement had been detected in the area both by sound and by sight, although some of the visual evidence was not always clear and could have been animals or tall grasses blowing in the wind.

The area around the Cu Chi base camp was about as flat as you could want in a war zone. The only better position would be to occupy the top of a hill with a clear view in all directions. However, the top of a hill was not always ideal for a landing strip, especially for large planes. The 25th Infantry had been placed in this strategic location to protect Highway 1, a major route leading north out of Saigon, and as a secure outpost for protecting against an invasion of Saigon, the capital city of South Vietnam.

Now, due to President Richard Nixon's new political policies and efforts towards "Vietnamization", most ground troops had been ordered to step down and simply provide defensive assistance and training to the ARVN's (The Army of the Republic of Vietnam). The U.S. military units were providing key supplies, air and artillery support, but not seeking any aggression towards the North Vietnamese forces unless provoked or as necessary to defend themselves. So, search and destroy was about as aggressive as it got at that time. Consequently,

First Lieutenant Johnson, the First Platoon's leader and a recent ROTC (Reserve Officers' Training Corps) college graduate, remained inside the perimeter at the base camp, feigning illness as his protest for the way the war was being handled. This left Sergeant "Wildcat" Reynolds in charge of the First Platoon.

Reynolds received the nickname Wildcat shortly after arriving in Nam, when one of his platoon buddies from Lincoln, Nebraska, Bill Williams, a "Cornhusker", discovered Ray's home was in Kansas and learned that he had spent some time at Kansas State University, the Wildcats, a Big Eight conference rival . They talked football a lot. Ray wasn't the only one to put up with nicknames in the service. Ray's pal, Specialist Fourth Class Bill Williams had learned to live with two first names a long time before the Army. Even in grade school kids called him Bill Bill.

The First Platoon of Charlie Company had the lead responsibility for the search part of this mission. They would either destroy any booby traps as they found them or drop grenades down small tunnels after sending a 'tunnel rat' down to check for the enemy or enemy supplies. When he first arrived in Vietnam as a Private, Ray was grateful that he was six feet tall and too big to be considered for tunnel rat duty. He was surprised by the fact that certain smaller guys were willing to accept the order to go down there without protesting. He didn't know how they did it. He didn't realize he was claustrophobic until he thought about what tunnel rats had to do. Down a hole like a rabbit with nothing but a flashlight and a .45.

The plan for the day was simple. Alpha and Bravo Companies would line up parallel to the perimeter fence line about thirty meters out. No one believed there would be anything to find that close to the perimeter. Once those companies were lined up, almost a half-klick long, Charlie Company would start a search from east to west, perpendicular to the base camp's fence line. Charlie Company's three platoons would scout the area with their men walking five feet apart, looking for anything suspicious. If a hole, a booby trap, or a punji pit was found, the line would stop until that particular obstacle was cleared or destroyed. Once they passed the appropriate length, Bravo Company would advance from their position to crisscross the area just inspected and doublecheck the surface. Then, once Alpha Company's area was cleared, Charlie Company would turn around, move further north and start back the other direction. It was almost two klicks away from the base camp fence line to the nearest tree line in that area and the search was expected to last most of the day.

Part of Alpha and Bravo's duties were to keep an eye on the tree line and high grassy areas for any movement to keep Charlie Company's men safe as those men focused on the ground in front of them. Halfway through the second sweep, when Charlie Company had turned back to the east and Alpha and Bravo had moved north about forty meters, a shot rang out from the tree line.

Charlie Company was at the north end of the surveying crew and closest to the tree line, but still over half a klick away. The First Platoon was close enough to hear the shot and everyone immediately hit the dirt. The rest of the company witnessed the reaction and followed suit. No more shots were heard and all eyes were scanning the tree line in the distance but no movement was detected.

In those first brief seconds following the sound of a single shot, everything was eerily quiet. The first platoon's Radio Telephone Operator had been trailing close behind Sergeant Reynolds. Like everyone else, he was lying face down in the grassy plain waiting to see if any more shots were forthcoming. When he heard a moan nearby, he glanced around and realized his Platoon Sergeant had been hit. The silence was quickly broken by the RTO's shout of "Medic". By the time the medic rushed over, Bill Bill had been close behind the RTO and had already applied pressure to the sucking chest wound and was trying to stop the flow of blood. It didn't look good.

A medevac chopper was called and a dustoff completed in less than ten minutes because of their proximity to the base camp and Ray "Wildcat" Reynolds, a short timer with less than three months to go on his tour of duty in Nam looked like he'd be going home early. Hopefully alive and not in a body bag.

The last thing Sergeant Reynolds heard as he was placed on the chopper was Bill Bill's voice saying, "Hang in there, Wildcat! I'll see you back in the Midwest." Ray was too weak to respond and didn't remember a thing after his litter hit the deck of the chopper.

CHAPTER 3

Spring 1968
Flint Hills
Chase County, Kansas, USA

About eighty miles southwest of Topeka, the state's capital city, is the County Seat of Chase County, Kansas - Cottonwood Falls. That county registered its peak population back in the late 1890's when it had over 8,000 residents. Now it has less than half that number with Cottonwood Falls being the largest population center, barely large enough to be considered a city at less than 900 people.

The only other sizable center of activity for the county was Strong City, just one mile north of the County Seat. For outsiders, the two towns are almost always talked about in the same conversation. Side by side, you can't have one without the other. It has been interesting to note that while Cottonwood Falls is the County Seat and with twice the population of its next door neighbor, Strong City has both U.S. Highway 50 at the northern side of town and the railroad passing through along the south side. Strong City is also known for hosting the longest continuous running rodeo in the state of Kansas. The Flint Hills Rodeo is held the first weekend of June every year since it was started by the Emmett Roberts family in a pasture beginning in 1937. With the town's population hovering around 400, that three-day rodeo event would eventually build an arena big enough to seat 6,000 on the north side of town.

Ray Reynolds grew up on his parents' ranch just three miles outside of Strong City, not far from the field where the Roberts family started the rodeo. Ray's father was a rancher on the same ground his father had ranched and his father's father before that. You just knew that was understood. It was never talked about that Ray was expected to conti

-nue the tradition, but somehow Ray was active in just about everything that went on in and around Chase County. He helped with wheat harvests. He competed in barrel racing and roping events at the annual rodeo. He was the Bulldogs' quarterback, and a guard on the school's basketball team. In the spring, he threw discus and excelled in the high jump by taking third place in the state. There wasn't much going on that didn't include Ray.

Ray liked to follow both K-State and K.U. sports and he was excited to see K-State get a new football coach, Vince Gibson. He thought he would like being coached by him and had decided Kansas State was where he wanted to go to college. He hoped he might qualify for a scholarship. But coming from a Level 4 school, that was probably just a distant hope.

With all of his activities and a winning personality, he was a natural to be elected his high school class president. Serving with him on the board as class secretary was Marilyn "Mari" Key who Ray had known since the start of his high school days at Cottonwood Falls, home of the Bulldogs.

Mari was the daughter of the local realtor, Ralph Key, and his wife Jennifer. An elderly Aunt of Ralph's, a former high school teacher living in Iowa, had spent her retirement years tracing the family's ancestry and determined there was a direct link to Francis Scott Key, writer of the Star Spangled Banner. Ralph was a bit of an entrepreneur and was always looking for additional ways to make money. One example was adding a key making machine to his realty office. Made sense to him, not only because of his name, but also because new property owners always wanted new keys to their property. He also carried a small inventory of various sizes of U.S. flags and special-order flag poles. On the wall behind his desk he had a 13-star flag and an enlarged copy of a family tree extracted from his aunt's book, "I Am A Key", plus a framed copy of the Star Spangled Banner.

Ralph was well known in the county and everyone who bought property in the area knew Mari, who started helping out in the office with answering the phone and filing papers at the early age of 14. In addition, she was on the school's cheerleading squad and participated in Drama Class and many school plays. Her pretty face, blonde hair, and sweet smile were well known by most people in the county, especially those who also had children in high school at that time.

Ralph and Jennifer Key couldn't be any prouder of their daughter.

Ray and Mari were the obvious leaders of the senior class that just graduated from Cottonwood Falls High School. Everyone knew Ray as a star athlete and Mari graduated as the valedictorian of her class. She had been a whiz at math and if other students had problems with any math subject, their teacher would often tell them to go see Mari Key for tutoring.

The previous fall Ray and Mari were voted homecoming king and queen, and both were displayed in their senior high school annual as being voted "Most Popular". Mari was also listed as "Most Likely To Succeed". Her plans were to attend Kansas University on a scholastic scholarship where she would major in Finance and Accounting in KU's School of Business. Ray planned to follow some type of agricultural studies, most likely farming or ranching at Kansas State. He would know better when he went to register later in the summer.

Ray and Mari had started dating their junior year in high school. It seemed only natural that these two would end up together since they were both so active in school and civic activities. That, and their overall personalities, made them known and respected by everyone. Of course in a small town, like Cottonwood Falls and Strong City, miles away from any big city, everyone knew everyone and they took pride in seeing their young people grow up. But, like most small towns with dying populations, they all wondered if once they left for college, would they ever come back to live in Chase County?

CHAPTER 4

Thursday, August 30, 1968
Kansas State University
Manhattan, Kansas, USA

It was the first week of school at K-State and Ray already missed Mari. He missed his mom's cooking and his bed. He also missed his horse Gabby and his dog Rex. He couldn't believe he was so severely homesick after only a few days away and he was determined to get over it.

His roommate wasn't so bad. Tom Johnson, a sharp kid from Overland Park, a suburb of K.C. on the Kansas side of the state line. Overland Park was the fastest growing part of the metro area and was located in Johnson County, known for having high quality schools and cities with strong real estate values.

Unfortunately, Ray and Tom had very little in common, except for being the same age and both starting their freshman year in college. They talked about two things, their interest in K-State and football, both the Wildcats in the Big Eight and the K.C. Chiefs in the NFL. Both young men had played key positions in their high school's football program, but both were overlooked for a possible position on Vince Gibson's squad. During that first week they did agree on one thing; they would go to the first football home game together.

It was three weeks into the season before the first home game, when K-State played number two ranked Penn State at KSU Stadium. Even before the game began that Saturday, Ray felt funny and uncomfortable in the crowd. He tried cheering along with all the others in the student section, but his heart wasn't in it. But he noticed Tom was really going in whole-heartedly. Then the National Anthem was played and sung by a senior student and everyone stood with their hand over their heart. All Ray could think about was Mari's relationship to the songwriter. When the anthem was over, the cheerleaders started leading the crowd to get the team fired up. Then it finally hit Ray. He didn't belong up here in the stands, he should be down there with the team on the field. He tried to remember if he had ever watched a football game with the crowd before, up off the field, in the stands. Then he remembered when he was twelve or thirteen, his dad, uncle and cousin all took a trip to Kansas City to watch the brand new team, the Chiefs. He didn't remember who they played, but thought it was Houston. He did remember the Chiefs won.

After the K-State game, walking back to their dorm, Ray asked Tom, "Did it feel strange to you being off the field and watching the game from the stands?"

Tom thought for a bit and then replied, "Yeah, sorta. It certainly did feel different."

"Well, it didn't help that we lost, especially after winning our first two road games. I actually thought we might have a chance against the Nittany Lions."

Tom laughed and simply said, "Really?"

Being from a really small town and being the star quarterback, starting point guard, senior class president, and so on, he had often heard the expression of being a "big fish in a small pond". He usually laughed it off, or simply shrugged and nodded in agreement. But now, after less than a month away at college in Manhattan, Kansas, often referred to as "The Little Apple", Ray really understood the meaning and he realized the opposite side of that phrase. He actually felt like a little fish in a big pond.

CHAPTER 5

January, 1969
Reynolds Ranch
Strong City, Kansas, USA

Four months later, Ray was back home after the first semester and announced to his family that he wasn't going back. He'd been thinking he could, or would, enlist in the Air Force to avoid the draft. Now, back south at the ranch just outside little old Strong City, he would have to figure out when and where he should go to enlist. Why he didn't do that when they had recruiters right on campus in Manhattan, he didn't know. In the back of his mind, he probably did know, and it was the fact that there were so many anti-war protestors on campus that he was afraid someone might see him. He wasn't real sure why he let that bother him.

According to the evening news, the war in Vietnam appeared to be winding down after the Tet offensive the year before failed to achieve the North's goals. Supposedly, the U.S. was going to revert to being primarily advisors to the ARVN's. Ray didn't know what any of that meant to him, but he hadn't heard any news that said the draft was over. The evening news still showed firefights and talked about "hot spots" and KIA's. He also knew that being out of school put him at risk with the Selective Service System. He could receive his draft notice any day. Each night, before he fell asleep, he would tell himself he had to do something about getting enlisted in the morning.

Now that he was back home, his father treated him like always. Up early, quick breakfast, and then out to help with some of the chores. It wasn't vengeance because his son dropped out of school. It was simply a matter of life and the requirements of getting things done on a ranch. Besides, Ray liked nothing better than the days he would get on Gabby and ride out through the Flint Hills and over the tall grass prairie to check on their herd of cattle and their miles of barbed wire fence. Rex would usually leave the ranch house with him, no matter how cold it was More often than not, the Siberian Husky would lose interest in trailing along behind the horse, especially when the prairie dogs were hibernating, and would turn around and head back to the house or barn. Ray thought there was nothing wrong with being back in the small pond. He kind of liked it. But, he still missed Mari.

Ray couldn't believe how quickly time got away from him. He had dropped out of school in the middle of winter, and now the mornings were smelling like spring. The weather was warmer and the grasslands were turning green. Rex would stay with him longer on his treks out into the pastures and loved to threaten prairie dogs back into their dens. Ray still hadn't found time to go to Topeka or to Wichita to find an Air Force recruiting office. The most he had done was ask older people he thought would know and they all gave the same basic reply, "Oh yeah, they'll have a recruiting office there, especially in Topeka."

Mari was home for spring break and Easter and she and Ray were together almost every evening professing their love for each other. Their relationship continued to be strong even though Mari worried about what Ray was going to do now that he quit college. And, like Ray, she worried about him being drafted. She didn't have anything against him wanting to stay and continue working on the family's ranch, but she had bigger visions for her life. She liked Lawrence, but thought bigger places like Kansas City or other larger cities were in her future. That was a worry for her with their relationship.

Ten days after April Fool's Day, !969, Ray still hadn't found his way to Topeka, but the dreaded letter from the people at the Selective Service System found its way to him. His orders were to report for duty in Topeka on Monday, May 19, 1969. So there was no more choice of Air Force, Navy, or Coast Guard. It would be an Army uniform for Ray Reynolds.

CHAPTER 6

Monday, May 11, 1970
Camp Zama, U.S. Army Hospital
Sagami-ono, Japan

Three days after arriving by Medevac chopper at the base hospital of the 25th Infantry at Cu Chi, Ray had been considered stable enough to make the trip to a recovery hospital in Japan. First, he was choppered to Tan Son Nhut Air Base in Saigon along with another wounded soldier from the 101st Airborne unit. From there, they were loaded on a C-141 with more wounded soldiers on litters than he could count, primarily because he wasn't able to lift his head to look left, but he knew there were many more like him on board. That flight took them to Tokyo where some were transported by helicopter and some by waiting ambulances to Camp Zama, just over twenty miles from the Tokyo airport.

Camp Zama had a long history as the earliest military barracks in Japan and was the former base for the Imperial Japanese Army Academy until the end of World War II. Following the Japanese surrender to the U.S. in September of 1945, the U.S. Army immediately moved in to take over command of Camp Zama. In the early 1950's, the location was perfect as a stopover for U.S. soldiers on their way to and from the Korean conflict and it also served as a supply station and hospital. During the Vietnam war the hospital increased in size and capabilities and often saw as many as 200 to 250 new admissions per day.

Ray was just one more statistic. He not only had to recover from his lung penetration, but also had other internal bleeding that had been slowed but not completely stopped, and there was fear of infection.

He also had some paralysis on his left side from the bullet clipping his spinal column. He was due for at least one more surgery, possibly two, and then would require physical therapy to restore full movement of his leg, arm and head on his left side. The doctors told him they weren't sure how long the PT would take, it all depended on him and how well his body would respond.

His days passed very slowly, laying in a hospital ward with over thirty other soldiers in his area alone. He wondered how many were there total and asked a nurse one day. She smiled at him and asked if he really wanted to know, and Ray replied, "Yeah, I'm curious."

Again the nurse smiled back at Ray and said, "I don't know an exact figure, it changes daily. But, I know we're well over a thousand in this surgery and recovery unit alone. Then there's the burn unit, the eyesight ward, and the critical care unit. I don't know those numbers."

As a polite small town young man, Ray said, "Thank you! That'll give me something to write home about. Just the thousand or so in this building is twice the size of my hometown."

"Oh my, where is home?" the nurse asked.

"I'm sure you never heard of it. Strong City, Kansas. We're about eighty miles south of Topeka."

CHAPTER 7

Sunday, May 10, 1970
Kappa Alpha Theta House
University of Kansas, Lawrence, Kansas

It was going on 11:00 p.m. when Marilyn Key quietly opened the door to her room in the sorority house on Tennessee Street just east of the KU campus. As a sophomore sorority sister pledge, she had the assigned duty to supervise three freshmen pledges cleaning up after a birthday celebration for one of the senior members. She didn't want to wake her junior roommate, but discovered Julie was still awake and studying for her biology final coming up the following week. Julie put her textbook down and they had just begun to visit when there was a knock on the door. It was the housemother, Virginia Swanson in her bathrobe, who said she had a phone call for Mari down in the office. Mari quickly slid back into her suede Hush Puppies and followed their housemother down the hall to the stairs.

"Did they say who it is?" she asked.

"It's your mother."

"Oh no. It has to be bad news."

Mari's mother had been calling her quite often that spring as 1970 turned into a pivotal year on the KU campus with anti-war demonstrations and the local news carrying stories out of Lawrence. It wasn't all just about the war. There were demonstrations about racial discrimination, women's rights demands, and other topical issues. Just two nights before, on May 8th, there was a university-wide convocation that led to proposed alternatives to many of these issues. She was sure that her mother had seen that on the news. Maybe that was what she was calling about, even though she had assured her mother many times that she, and her roommate Julie, both stayed away from the demonstrations and avoided the fracas. Yeah, she *could* be calling about that, but down deep, Mari knew it was something else. This call was later in the evening than her normal calls.

Mrs. Swanson stopped at the office door and turned to face Mari and said, "You shouldn't jump to conclusions. Wait until you know what she's calling about." But, inwardly, even the widowed Mrs. Swanson knew that it wouldn't be good news for a call coming from home close to midnight.

"Mom?" she cautiously inquired into the mouthpiece.

"Mari, I'm sorry to call so late, but we just heard from Ray's mother, and . . ."

Before she could finish, Mari dropped the receiver and let out a scream. She collapsed into the chair beside the desk and immediately started to weep. Mrs. Swanson picked up the receiver and spoke to Mari's mother who said, "Tell her he's okay. Wounded, but okay. I need to finish letting her know what I know." The house mother spoke to Mari and then handed the phone back. This was the third time Mrs. Swanson had experienced a call like this since the Vietnam war had escalated five years earlier. Fortunately, this call did not include a death notice like the other two. Mari stifled a sob and took a deep breath. "What happened?" she asked.

"Ray was wounded two days ago and was taken by helicopter to the base hospital. He's been stabilized and is going to be sent to Japan for surgery and recovery. That's all we know right now. Thank God, he's probably already in Japan. Mrs. Reynolds said she would call me immediately when she learned anything more. Or, she said you could call her at anytime and she would let you know whatever she knows. But, right now, it's probably not worth the call since I just told you everything," She paused to take a breath and let the news sink in. "Honey, I'm so sorry, but I'm pretty sure he's going to be alright. And, it's good to know he's going to be out of that horrible country."

Mari was still sobbing silently, but her mother could hear the sniffles. She told her mother that she had seen part of the evening news earlier and Walter Cronkite had said the war was winding down for the Americans but that the south and north Vietnamese were still battling it out. "They were showing helicopters picking up the wounded and I had to think of Ray. I think of him all the time over there. He must be hurt bad if they have to send him to Japan for surgery. Why can't they just send him home?"

"Oh, Mari, I'm so sorry for you. And for Ray. I know he loves you very much. We love him too! I wish I could be there with you right now."

"Yeah, me too. I miss you, and dad. Especially now, with this."

"Honey, I'm going to let you go now. You try to get some rest."

"No, I'm going to try to figure out how I can get to Japan to see him."

"Oh!" There was a long pause as Mrs. Key hadn't thought about that. "Well, I'm not sure that's a good idea right now, But we can talk more tomorrow."

Mari hung up the phone. Mrs. Swanson immediately gave her a hug. As a gentle, loving housemother, Mrs. Swanson walked Marilyn back to her room and gave her another hug at the door. She said, "It's good to know that he's being treated and is on the road to recovery. Remember that. Okay?"

"Okay," Mari replied, She paused, not knowing what else to say and then gave her another hug and said, "Good night."

"You try to get some rest. And let me know if you need anything."

"Thank you."

CHAPTER 8

Sunday, June 7, 1970
Camp Zama, U.S. Army Hospital
Sagami-ono, Japan

Marilyn Key had never flown before. In fact, she had only been to an airport twice. Once when she rode with her father to pick up her grandparents when they returned from a vacation in Europe, and again when she rode with Ray and his parents to Wichita to send Ray off to Infantry Training at Fort Polk, Louisiana. Now she had just completed her first series of flights, over 6,000 miles to arrive in Tokyo, Japan. She had her mother with her and it was only the second time her mother had taken a trip by air, the first being a round trip to Hawaii with her husband celebrating their twentieth wedding anniversary just a few years earlier.

Ushered into a cab at the airport, they began to experience their first problems with a language barrier. Although the driver could understand some English, they had to repeat almost everything. They finally showed him an itinerary that listed Camp Zama as their destination. "Ah so, Zama!" he said and nodded his head decisively to show that he understood, and off they went.

They were relieved to pull away from the hustle-bustle of the busy airport, but quickly discovered the city streets around the airport were just as busy. Small cars, motor bikes and bicycles along with rickshaws, and pedestrians were everywhere. Car horns, bicycle bells, and rickshaw pullers yelling something began making both women nervous. Their taxi driver tried to assure them everything was fine, but they had no idea what he was saying.

After almost an hour through traffic, they arrived at the gate entrance to Camp Zama. Their driver said something in Japanese about Americans, the only word the women understood, and the security guard went back inside his gate house. Another Japanese uniformed guard came out and walked up to the back window of the taxi. "How may I help you?" he asked the two passengers in the back seat.

They were relieved to have someone who spoke such plain English. "We're here to visit a wounded soldier, Sergeant Ray Reynolds, United States Army."

"Give me a minute," he said, and then mumbled something in Japanese to the taxi driver who nodded in return. After the security guard stepped back inside the guard house, the driver pulled over to a waiting area just beyond the gate.

The car's air conditioner wasn't keeping up with good air flow to the back seat as the car idled in the sunlight. It was almost 2:00 p.m. in Japan and both women had serious jet lag, but they were anxious and excited about being so close to seeing Ray. The heat was getting to them and they rolled down their windows. There was a slight breeze and it helped. Mari pulled her compact out of her purse and used the small mirror to check her hair and make-up. She took a tissue and dabbed at her forehead and cheeks. Her mother decided to do the same.

Finally, after about five minutes that seemed much longer, the guard returned to their taxi and spoke to the driver in Japanese, He then smiled at the two women in the back seat and said, "Welcome to Japan!"

They returned the smile and Mari gave him a polite wave and mouthed, "Thank you."

Two minutes later, the driver pulled up to a building labeled 'Building C'. The driver turned and pointed to the entrance and said, "Here."

Mrs. Key looked at the meter and had no idea how much she owed. She pulled out a ten dollar bill and displayed it to the driver who looked at it and shook his head. She didn't know if that meant he didn't take American money or if that wasn't enough. It didn't seem like that far of a drive from the airport, but the traffic jams, lights, and congestion had taken them almost an hour. She took out another five dollar bill and as soon as the driver saw the two bills together, he smiled and nodded. She handed him the fifteen bucks and he offered no change. She looked at her daughter and they both wondered if that was right or if they just got scammed.

When they got out of the cab and retrieved their suitcases, they again looked at each other. Mrs. Key said to her daughter, "Oh well, I guess we did owe him a tip."

Mari replied, "We've got to talk to someone about the exchange rate."

Inside the building, there was a very small lobby with a uniformed receptionist behind a short counter and they almost felt guilty asking if there was a place they could leave their luggage temporarily.

The young Japanese lady responded, "Yes, I show you in a minute. You here to see Sergeant Reynolds?"

"Yes," they both replied and Mari nodded enthusiastically.

"I.D.'s please!" It was a command, not a request.

After reviewing the driver's licenses and jotting down a couple of notes on a log, the uniformed receptionist said, "You get I.D.'s back when you leave. Okay?"

Both women nodded.

The receptionist slid off her stool and came out from behind the counter. "Come this way please."

Mother Jennifer and daughter Marilyn looked at each other and shrugged their shoulders, picked up their suitcases, and dutifully followed the young soldier in charge. Two doors down the hall and the receptionist stopped and turned to face the visitors. "Toilets," she seemed to shout and pointed to two doors on her left. She then pointed to an open doorway on her right and commanded "Here," and motioned them inside. "Sergeant Reynolds will see you here." She gestured to some space behind the door and said, "Nimotsu. Oh, excuse me, luggage, or suitcases, which word you say?"

They were in a small visitor's room with a sofa and three other comfortable cushioned chairs. In one corner there was a small table with a full coffee pot and cups, a pitcher of ice water and several cans of soft drinks in a plastic bucket of fresh ice. This had to have been set up after the security guard had called from the gate. The receptionist left them there and returned to her duty station. They put their luggage where they had been instructed behind the door.

Upstairs, on the third floor, a U.S. Army nurse came through the ward pushing what appeared to be an empty wheelchair. She stopped at the foot of Ray's bed and reached down to the seat of the wheelchair. She pulled up a framed mirror, a washpan with hot water, a face cloth, shaving cream and a razor. After sitting all of this in Ray's lap, she reached back and pulled up a towel. "Come on now Sergeant, it's time you started looking like a soldier again. I'll make you a deal. If you shave off that growth on your face, I'll take that IV out of your arm."

Ray had no idea what was going on, but he was so ready to have the IV gone that he quickly began the process of shaving. The only reason he still had an IV was to continue fighting off the possibility of an infection in his lung. The wound was healing nicely and the next step in his healing was to begin physical therapy to restore movement on his left side. Originally, the doctors had only detected partial paralysis in his left arm and neck area. But, after a few days of recovery and the need to get him out of bed and moving, they also discovered he walked with an awkward limp caused by some additional paralysis in his left leg. He said it didn't hurt, but he also couldn't move his knee and ankle normally.

As he finished shaving and was drying his face, the nurse was back with a clean hospital gown and brand new olive drab colored boxer shorts. She disconnected the IV from the port in his right arm and then pulled the curtain around his bed to allow him some privacy while changing his underwear and gown.

When he was done and realized the nurse was still right outside the curtain, he said, "Hey, what's the deal? You said you would remove the IV. You just disconnected it and left the port."

She pushed the curtain back open and said, "I know, I'm waiting for the doctor's approval, but at least you have some more freedom of movement right now. Okay? Come on," she added and motioned to the wheelchair, I'll take you for some change of scenery."

Ray hoisted himself up to a sitting position with his right arm and slid off the bed and over into the wheelchair. There was a pair of slippers waiting in front of him. "Where we goin'?"

"Oh, you know, you need some fresh air, out of this ward for awhile."

Downstairs, the two Key ladies were waiting impatiently and wondered what was taking so long. The door to their room was standing open and every time they heard someone coming down the hall they assumed it would be Ray. Most of the people who walked by glanced in and smiled. The women realized there was an elevator further down the hall and could hear the bell ding every time it stopped at their floor level. After the sixth ding, they were beginning to get tired until they heard Ray's voice talking to someone. He was getting louder and closer.

Then, there he was. A nurse pushed his wheelchair through the open door. Ray couldn't believe his eyes.

The nurse exclaimed, "Isn't this a breath of fresh air?" Then she quietly left the room.

Tears welled up in Ray's eyes. As soon as Mari saw his eyes, she started crying too. That triggered her mother and then all three people couldn't see through their tears. Mari couldn't get out of her chair fast enough and Ray threw his right arm up and open, really glad he didn't have an IV tube restricting him.

After an incredibly long hug Mari backed off, stood back to smile at Ray and then said "Surprise!" They both laughed and Mari moved aside to let her mother step in for a quick hug. Ray hugged her back and as she moved away, he reached up with his right hand to wipe away the tears.

"You don't look wounded," Mari said, "You look good, but you sure could use a haircut!" She laughed and Ray laughed with her.

"Here," he said and reached up to pull his hospital gown loose from around his neck. Then he pulled it down to expose the healing scars from his lung surgery.

"Oh my," Mrs. Key exclaimed.

"Oh shit," her daughter exhaled trying not to be too loud. She quickly stepped forward again for another hug. "But that will heal and you'll be fine. Right?"

"I guess. That's what they keep telling me. It's this that's bothering me." He used his right hand to pick up his left arm off the armrest of the wheelchair to show he had no movement in his left side. He placed it back on the armrest and his left hand dropped down beside the wheelchair. He again used his right hand to pull it back up and placed it in his lap. Then he nodded and twitched his head to get their attention and turned his head to the right and back to straight forward but continued his eye movement to the left as far as he could. "That's it, as far as I can turn it to the left."

Mari and Jen were now both looking at him pitifully and he wished he hadn't shown them that. He quickly added, "They say they can fix all this movement stuff with physical therapy. It might take awhile, but I'll be fine, they say. The doctors don't think it's permanent paralysis."

Mari smiled at him and said, "That's good to hear. Have they started any therapy yet?"

"No. They want to make sure my lung is properly healed because all the physical stuff will be on the same side and they don't want to put any unnecessary stress on the wound site, or my lung itself."

"Time, it just takes time," Mrs. Key said. "You're gonna be fine!"

"I know, or I think I know. I just have to believe the doctors. Instead I lay awake and think of things like not being able to drive if I can't turn my head. I can walk all right but I have trouble lifting my left leg. What if I can't ride Gabby? I worry about that. Life won't ever be the same."

Mari wanted to change the subject. "Oh, it's so good to see you! I've been worried sick about you. We got the news and it was the week before finals. I told mom I wanted to come see you and she offered to come along. Thank God! I would never had made it by myself. It's my first time to fly anywhere, and then it's halfway around the world."

"How did you manage to get through your finals and all that?" Ray asked.

"Mom called me back the next day. She had only flown once before and dad put all that together with a travel agent. She had called her sister, you know, my Aunt Betty. She does travel plans for her boss all the time."

Her mother looked at Ray, shrugged her shoulders and smiled.

"Anyway, when she called me back, she told me to concentrate on my finals and she and Betty would get everything put together for the trip. I even got to see Hawaii. We had to refuel there."

"Lucky you! We refueled in Guam."

"And L.A.. I used to think Kansas City was a big city, but I had a window seat and started seeing Los Angeles. Well, I'm sure it was suburbs for a long time before I saw downtown Los Angeles. Then we circled out over the ocean before we landed. It was awesome!"

"You'll be a jet-setter before we know it." Ray laughed.

Just over an hour passed before the nurse returned to pick up her patient.

Mrs. Key addressed her while she was adjusting the wheelchair making it ready to move. "I imagine they keep you pretty busy here based on what we see on the TV news?"

The American nurse looked up at her and rolled her eyes. "It's pretty much twelve-hour shifts, six days a week, until we tell them we can't take it anymore." She forced a smile and laughed. "Then they just cut us back to eight-hour shifts for two weeks before we get back to the longer grind. Now, I've got to get this character back to his comfort station. Right, Ray?"

Mari quickly spoke up, "Thank you for all you do. I'm sure all the patients here appreciate it. I have a quick question."

"Okay, I'll try to give you an answer."

"We'd like to come back tomorrow, but we'd like to be here when it works best for you, or for Ray's schedule."

"I'd suggest early afternoon, right after they all have their lunch, probably 1:00, 1:30."

"Oh good. We've got some serious jet lag and it will be nice to sleep in."

"Are you staying here on the base? They have visitor's rooms."

Mrs. Key jumped in. "Yes. My sister booked the trip for us and she discovered that there were rooms available here when she called to check on Ray's condition. I planned to ask the girl out front where we go from here."

"She'll be glad to help and she can call for transportation."

The next morning Mari and her mom both slept quite late. Almost

10:00 a.m. Japan time, fourteen hours ahead of their home in Kansas. No wonder they were tired. They discovered they missed breakfast in the small cafeteria downstairs, but there were vending machines. They bought a small packet of six powdered sugar donuts and each got a cup of coffee.

They went back to their room and tried to watch some TV, but almost everything was in Japanese. Mari picked up the itinerary Aunt Betty had prepared and was looking it over to see what time of day they had to be at the airport the following day. They had only planned on staying three days since they didn't know what to expect of Ray's condition, and they really weren't there to vacation or shop. She was reading the notes below the scheduled items and suddenly spoke up. "Hey, Mom, Betty's sheet says right here, 'Taxi fare from airport to Camp Zama should be about $12 US.' So we weren't screwed!"

Her mother looked up and seemed surprised that they had that piece of information. "Well, good!", she said..

With time to kill, they went for a walk around the base. It was a beautiful day with the sun highlighting the dark red of the Japanese Red Cedar trees scattered throughout the garden areas of the campus and contrasting with the Boxwood shrubs and evergreen trees. The grounds were perfectly manicured. They talked about the fact they never imagined an Army Base would look so nice.

Precisely at 1:00 p.m. they were back at the reception counter of Building C. The receptionist smiled at them and said "Mata kon'nichiwa." She paused then added in perfect English, "That's 'Hello again' to you."

They both responded in unison, "Hello."

The neatly uniformed Japanese girl said, "I'll let them know you're here. You can wait in the room where you were yesterday, if you'd like."

Mari and her mother moved down the hall and took a seat on the sofa. It was almost ten minutes before the familiar American nurse showed up, but this time she was without Ray. She expected the startled look on their faces, and quickly said, "Please, come with me." She turned back out the door and headed down the hall past the elevators, past the stairway, and opened the exit door. There, two steps down, was a beautiful sunken garden with more Japanese Red Maples, some evergreen shrubs, and beautiful pink Wisteria hanging from a trellis on both sides of a winding flagstone pathway. In the center of the area set between two buildings there was a black iron bench on one side of the pathway across from two matching chairs. Ray was seated on the bench with room for Mari beside him. His empty wheelchair was set off to the side out of the way. Mari quickly took the position next to her boyfriend and gave him a long hug.

"Oh, I'm not hurting you, am I?"

"No, not much." he replied, but then coughed and seemed to tense up a little.

Mari's mother reached over to take Ray's hand for a minute and then took a seat in one of the chairs opposite the young couple.

Someone had gone out of their way to set this up. Ray had on a navy blue kimono with a matching sash over his hospital gown. His hair had been washed and looked better than the day before but still was in need of a haircut. It was displaying curls in the back and slightly over his ears, long by Army standards.

After visiting for about fifteen minutes, Mrs. Key stood and stretched and said, "I'm going to wander about this garden and then step back inside and see if I can get us something to drink." She was really just wanting to give the couple some time alone. She disappeared down a garden path behind them and five minutes later, they heard the door to the building close when she went back inside. The young couple wasted no time hugging and kissing while she was gone.

When she returned with soft drinks for all of them, she also had a tri-fold brochure of the camp that included a layout of the grounds.

She showed it to Ray who acknowledged he had seen it before. She pointed to Building C on the map and showed her daughter that there were six buildings in this cluster and more further away.

Ray started to explain that each of the six buildings had their special services. He was lucky to be in "C" because it was for the least serious patients, mostly like him, recovering from minor surgeries. "Next door," he explained and pointed toward Building B at the other end of the garden, "is eyesight injuries, and then 'D', is the burn unit."

"Oh," Mari exclaimed, "I'm so glad you're not in there, I could never imagine anything worse than burning to death. Every time I see a car accident on TV where the car's on fire, it makes me sick."

"Well, fortunately, the guys in 'D' didn't burn to death. But, now they've got to live with their scars. And, I agree with you, it would be horrible. Some of them probably wish they had died."

It was going on an hour and Mari noticed Ray was glancing toward the door at the end of the garden walkway. She turned to look too, wondering what he was seeing.

"Nurse Jane told me it would be like yesterday, I can only be off the IV for an hour, so, dammit, I'm thinking she'll be coming to get me anytime now."

"Well, dammit is right!" Mari responded and stuck out her lower lip.

Just then the door opened and instead of Nurse Jane coming down the walkway, there was a lieutenant doctor in hospital scrubs coming to visit. "Are you the Reynolds family?" he said to the two women.

"No, we're just close friends." Mari responded and her mother nodded accordingly.

"This is Doctor Johnson," Ray said to introduce him. "And this is my best girl Marilyn and her mother," he added.

"Nice to meet you. and thanks for coming all the way over here.

We seldom have the pleasure of meeting families, or friends."

"Nice to meet you," Mrs Key responded.

"I thought I'd give you an update on Ray from my perspective. I don't know for sure what he's told you so this may be redundant. Anyway, he's doing great. He's probably one of the best conditioned soldiers we have in Building C. He had a chest penetration and collapsed lung from a single bullet, and he's responded well to that surgery. He developed some infection at the surgical site and that's just about cleared up. I don't know if he showed his 'battle scar', but the infection is what caused the redness and makes it look so angry. That should go away in the next week or two. So, we're waiting for that to heal and wanting to make sure the lung is healthy before we release him from here. The other unfortunate part of his injury is the bullet nicked his spinal column and has caused some paralysis on his left side which I'm sure you've noticed. We'll want to show him the therapy he'll need to do before he leaves here and make sure it doesn't interfere with the healing process of his wound. So, that means he'll probably be here another three to four weeks, and then he can go home where he can do PT as an outpatient."

"Wait, what does that mean?" Ray asked.

"PT, that's physical therapy, the exercises you'll need to recover from the paralysis."

"No, the 'outpatient' thing. What's that?" Living in a small town and having never been seriously ill or injured, 'outpatient' was a foreign word.

"Well, that simply means you're no longer required to be hospitalized. You can simply set up an appointment to see a physical therapist who will work with you on your exercises and monitor your improvement."

Ray turned to Mrs. Key and said, "I'll probably have to go to Topeka for that. Eighty miles one way." He looked back at the doctor and asked, "How often? Every day?"

"Oh no. They can work with you on a reasonable schedule. Maybe twice a week to start. They'll instruct you on what you can do to improve at home."

"Do you think I'll be able to ride my horse?"

"Well, maybe not at first, but I'm sure you are young enough and strong enough that shouldn't be a problem long term."

They all thanked the doctor for what he was doing for Ray and for serving the wounded soldiers at this special camp as Nurse Jane came walking up to the group.

Ray stood and motioned for Mari to give him a hug and then settled back into the wheelchair Nurse Jane had rolled up behind him. The two Key women had one more day to spend with Sergeant Reynolds before catching their late evening flight to start their journey home. That next day was pretty much a repeat of day two, only without the doctor visit. Another beautiful hour in the garden and then their final goodbye telling their hero they would be seeing him soon back in Kansas. Tears were shed as they said their goodbyes, but both Ray and Mari managed a smile as they exchanged kisses before Ray was wheeled away. In the taxi on the way to the airport, Mari turned to her mother and said, "You know what's bothering me?"

"What's that?"

"We saw Ray stand to kiss me, but we never saw him walk. I wonder if he can?"

"Well, honey, that's what the physical therapy is all about. I don't think the doctor said anything about his inability to walk. And, he certainly didn't say he wouldn't be able to ride Gabby. I think he'll be fine."

"I sure hope so!"

CHAPTER 9

Monday, July 6, 1970
Over the Pacific Ocean

Ray's flight was a late afternoon departure from Tokyo. It included a one-hour layover in Hawaii and a late evening arrival in San Francisco on the same day. He had trouble rolling this over in his mind but finally realized the twelve-hour time zone difference was making the gain possible. He had picked up a couple of paperback books at the airport and had fallen asleep before getting through chapter two of *Lord of the Flies* by William Golding. He remembered hearing about both books in English class, but couldn't remember if it was in high school or college.

He awoke and tried to continue reading but was too excited about heading home. He reached under the seat in front of him for his canvas bag with his hospital discharge papers, and everything he owned right then. Included in the bag was his other book, *Cat's Cradle* by Kurt Vonnegut, Jr., a fresh change of underwear and socks, a shaving kit with a toothbrush and toothpaste, and some snacks he picked up at the airport.

He wanted to review his flight itinerary to see what time he would be arriving in Kansas City. He would call Mari from San Francisco to let her know, and wondered who all might be there to greet him at the airport. Probably just his parents and his younger siblings, and of course, Mari. That would make for a full car on the drive home. His dad would probably drive the Suburban that could hold six comfortably, or maybe his brother Chip and his sister June would stay home.

When he read his itinerary he thought there had to be a mistake. It showed his scheduled arrival in San Francisco at 9:18 p.m., but his flight to Kansas City didn't depart until 6:10 a.m. the next morning. What was he supposed to do for over eight hours in an airport in the middle of the night? He wondered who put this together for him back at Camp Zama. He pressed the call button to see if he could get some coffee. The stewardess came and listened to his request, nodded and disappeared down the aisle to his left where he couldn't turn his head to watch. She hadn't spoken a word, just a nod. It was several minutes later, but she did return with the coffee and asked if he needed cream or sugar.

Ray replied, "No. And, thank you."

She turned and left without another word. Ray thought that she seemed unfriendly, and then, as he thought about it, he realized no one on the plane had been overly friendly, or displayed any kind of friendly hello's or other conversation. He was lucky to have a window seat on his right and an empty middle seat. When he spoke to the stewardess, he had to position his whole upper body turned left so he could see her standing in the aisle.

The man next to him had nodded when he took his seat on the aisle, then read a newspaper and fell asleep. He was awake now and reading a book. Ray turned on his overhead light and started to read again. He had lost his place earlier when he fell asleep so he started chapter two again, *Fire on the Mountain*. The book couldn't hold his attention. He continued to glance out the window and then when he turned back to the book, he found himself re-reading the same sentence again. He shut out the light and returned to his thoughts, very wide awake.

Earlier on the flight, he thought the food service was okay, but again, he realized there was no friendly exchange between him and the crew or the man in his row. He was sure this was due to his Army uniform. He could hear other friendly conversations going on around him.

Before he was injured, when he was starting to consider himself a short timer, he had heard some conversations from new recruits about how bad it was getting in the states, especially after the news reports started a daily update on the My Lai massacre and the trial of Lieutenant Calley. Guys were saying they heard of uniformed soldiers being called 'baby killers' and being spit on or spit at when they were out in public. Now those conversations came back to him, and he also remembered how angry people had been over the National Guard shootings at Kent State University just a couple of months earlier. They had seen the news on CNN in the recreation room of the hospital. The incident had resulted in the killing of four and wounding nine other anti-war demonstrators. Was this what he had to look forward to in San Francisco? Probably there, but certainly not in Kansas City, he hoped.

Ray stared out the window. Nothing below him but the darkness of the Pacific Ocean and the dark sky above. A whole world out there but nothing to see. He continued to look for signs of life, but there was nothing except the blinking glow of the plane's wing light. Somewhere, out there, in all that blackness, his mind crossed over a line, whatever the line was, while his anger began to build.

Is this the price I pay for serving my country? What the hell did I do wrong to deserve this? My mistake was getting shot, right out in the open. We all should have known better. Over 300 people in the field that day and I get singled out. Probably me because of the RTO right behind me. Some asshole sniper figured I was some sort of big shot. Me, a cowboy from Kansas. If First Lieutenant Johnson hadn't chickened out, it would have been him with the RTO. I hope he knows I saved his live. Protesting son of a bitch!

Oh, what the hell! I don't want to wish my bad luck on anybody else. It just happened to be my lucky day! At least now I'm on my way home.

I just don't think I did anything to deserve being shot. Sure, I shot at some enemy soldiers, but I don't believe I ever hit one. You never know in this war. They disappear down a tree line or into a tunnel, and they drag off their killed and wounded. We just see a blood trail and call it a body count. Who knows whose bullet hit them?

I know we fired a barrage back into that village when someone shot at us after we left. I suppose some of our shots could have hit some civilians, maybe even children. But they were probably all safely in their bunkers before the commie shooter fired at us. The shots were probably fired by the same guy we saw out tending to his rice paddies earlier that day. An innocent farmer by day, enemy by night. Is God punishing me for that? At least we didn't go back and murder the whole village and burn it to the ground like that Lieutenant Calley fiasco. We just moved on.

I should just consider myself lucky that I'm alive and close to being well again, especially compared to most of those guys at Zama. My wounds were not very serious. At least not after the initial surgery. It's just this damn paralysis that's going to be a pain in my ass.

What was I doing in that country anyway? In the Army? Serving was my duty? Yeah, maybe, but who was I serving? What are we there for, so we could pat ourselves on the back and say we saved a country from communism? Were we there so our country could be proud of us? Sure doesn't seem that way now. Nobody seems very proud of me on this plane.

I know, I know, I know, it's so we can keep the first domino from falling. How many times have I heard that? Why should we be the ones responsible? Over half way around the world - let someone else do it! Oh yeah, the French tried and they gave up and went home. Not their problem. Let America do it. Crap! Look what that got us.

It's my own fault. This is what I get for dropping out of college. I should have enlisted in the Air Force. I wonder if they're being treated like this? There's over a hundred people on this plane and I've never felt so alone. It's a giant black hole outside and that's where I feel like I am. I'll bet the Air Force guys are still respected. They should have given me a blue uniform before I left Camp Zama

When I get back to Strong City I may never leave again. What if the folks in Kansas all think I'm one of those My Lai guys, part of the massacre? What if they think all of us in the Army are like that? Crap!

Oh God, I can't do anything to change any of this. It all happened. It's history now and I'm part of it. I'm stuck with this for the rest of my life.

At least I still have Mari, and her mother. They came to see me when I really needed it. I know they will be there to welcome me home. And my family, of course! That's it! That's the best part of my life right now.

I hope my parents don't think I was involved in anything like My Lai. How do I explain stuff like that? What the war was all about and how we were conducting it? The news features 'body count' all the time. Those were our goals every time we went out on an operation. I can hear our commanders asking, 'What was your body count?' like it was a baseball statistic. It's the score of the war - U.S. 202, North Vietnam 46, every day, every week, something like that. At least, last I heard, we were ahead!

I've got to stop thinking like this. Now I'm blaming my parents for things that haven't even happened. Maybe I should start reading my other book. Kurt Vonnegut is supposed to be funny. I've got to get my mind on something else!

He closed his eyes, forcing himself to stop staring out the window into total darkness. it was a total waste of time. Too many negative thoughts, too much time with nothing to do. He reached down for his canvas bag and then up to his overhead light.

He opened Vonnegut's book and turned in a few pages to the beginning and saw the chapter title, *The Day the World Ended.*

Oh shit, can I read this now? Right now, after all these thoughts bouncing around in my head? Maybe I'll find he thinks like me. That might help. At least everyone that I know who's read his books like him.

Over two hours later he was still reading, engrossed in the craziness of Vonnegut's work. He rested his eyes for a moment and then stretched his right arm and tried raising his left up to shoulder height for a few times. When he opened his eyes, he was surprised the sky was turning light again, and then the pilot announced their approach to Hawaii.

During the re-fueling stop, Ray chose to stay in his seat while most passengers de-planed for the one hour break. Ray took advantage of the nearly empty plane and limped back to the restroom. After relieving himself he splashed some cold water on his face and ran a comb through his freshly cut hair. The Camp Zama barber was always there to freshen up the soldiers before they left for home.

On his way back to his seat, he noticed a small gray-haired lady who resembled his grandmother on his mother's side. She was turned in her seat like she was watching for someone to come down the aisle. When he reached her row, she held up her hand as if she had something to say. She did. She looked up at the young Sergeant and said quietly, almost a whisper, "Thank you for your service!"

Ray immediately replied, "Thank you. I appreciate that!"

"I'll bet you do. Good luck to you!"

"Thanks again!"

That very brief conversation improved Ray's attitude, although it upset him that she felt like she had to whisper it, afraid someone else might hear her. He thought to himself that he would watch for her exiting the plane in San Francisco and thank her again. If for no other reason than to show the other people that someone actually appreciated his service to America.

CHAPTER 10

Monday, July 6, 1970
San Francisco International Airport
United States of America

The plane touched down and taxied. Sergeant Reynolds remained in his seat as his row mate and all the other passengers were departing. Ray waited because he didn't want to slow people down who were eager to get off the plane. The gray-haired grandmother smiled as she passed him and offered to let him out into the aisle in front of her, but he waved her on. He hoped he didn't look funny with his whole body turned sideways in his seat, but he did want to wave her another 'thank you' as she passed. Actually, he thought his body language may have appeared as being ready to get up and depart, but not one other passenger offered to let him into the aisle.

He really didn't care, He was already pissed and he didn't want anyone thinking it was that stupid baby-killing soldier with the limp that made them miss their connection. Besides, he had almost eight hours to kill (time, not babies) before they would start boarding his Kansas City flight with one stop in Denver. As he finally limped his way into the terminal building, he passed two stewardesses and a pilot. Only the pilot said "Welcome home" and smiled. Then he paused and added, "I was in the Air Force and served in Nam a few years ago. I know what you're going through. Good luck to you! Thanks for your service."

Ray really appreciated that, but also noticed that the Captain had looked around to see if anyone was close enough to hear before he paused and added those extra comments.

Just outside the gate area was a bank of pay phones. Ray had his back pay from Japan where he never needed to spend any money on anything so all his money was in bills with no change for the phone. He figured he should only need a dime to get an operator and have the charges reversed. He popped into a restaurant that was slowing down since it was well past the dinner hour, but the bar was busy. He pulled out a twenty dollar bill and asked the bartender if he could get some change for the pay phone.

The bartender just glared at him and said, "You have to buy something."

Ray was slow to respond to that comment, wondering if this was part of the anti-war mentality or if this really was some kind of restaurant rule. He thought it must be the war attitude towards soldiers because if it was a job requirement, the guy would have been nicer and would have apologized for the rule. Not this guy.

Ray had plenty of time and said, "No thanks!" even though he thought a beer sounded good right about then. He walked out and tried to loosen his stiff left leg. The PT in Japan had made a noticeable difference and he could get around fairly well, although slow and with a slight limp. He saw a Japanese lady closing up a news stand and he asked her if he could still buy a newspaper. While in Japan, he had learned a number of useful phrases and added the Japanese words for please, "Do ka onegai shimasu." She smiled and stopped what she was doing and said, "Sure". As he stood at the register he looked down and saw Kit Kat bars and picked one up. He couldn't remember the last time he had a candy bar. She rang that up on the register and said, "Kit Kat very good!"

He quickly picked up a second one and motioned with two fingers to add one more.

She rang up the second candy bar and began making change for his twenty. When she handed him the change, he said, "Arigatou gozaimasu" (Thank you). Then he handed her the second Kit Kat and said "For you!"

She smiled again and said, "Arigatou gozaimasu". Ray noticed that it sounded more natural when she said it.

He returned back down the concourse to the bank of pay phones and held out his handful of coins. He placed his call to the Reynolds residence and asked the operator to reverse the charges. While he was waiting for the operator to finish placing the call, he wondered if he should also call Mari, or let his mother call the Key residence to let them know he was almost home. He knew if he called Mari, he would have a tough time getting off the phone, and he kind of wanted to surprise her at the airport and have all their next conversations in person.

After four rings, his dad answered "Hello" with a rough voice wondering who would be calling so late in the evening. He had glanced at his bedside clock before he stepped in the hallway to answer the phone and saw that it was almost 11:00. "Of course," he replied when the operator asked him to accept the call. "Ray, where are you?"

"San Francisco. Sorry for calling so late."

He could hear his mother in the distance through the phone, saying, "Is that Ray? Where is he?"

His father replied, "San Fransisco," as his mother's voice became louder the closer she got to the phone on the wall in the upstairs hall.

After all the 'I love you's,' the 'It's so good to hear your voice,' and 'I'm so happy you're back in the states,' Ray finally got a chance to tell them his plane was due in K.C. at a little past 12:00 noon. It would be a United flight out of Denver. He asked them to call Mari first thing in the morning and coordinate their plans to meet him.

With that task complete, he still thought a beer sounded good, but he had to worry about the server checking his I.D. Still only twenty, but old enough to fight and die for his country, he would most likely be turned down at the bar. Besides, he wasn't about to go back to the bar where the bartender wouldn't give him change. '*Asshole*', he thought to himself.

He only had a light canvas bag to carry, so he wandered slowly down the concourse, remembering the therapist's instructions to concentrate on controlling his left leg so that his foot didn't turn inwards making his limp worse. He thought about finding a comfortable spot to sit and continue reading *Cat's Cradle*, but that thirst for a beer kept him walking and thinking. *What's the worst that can happen? I get turned down. Big deal.* Plus, he began to think about a good ol' American cheeseburger and French fries. He then began to realize how hungry he really was.

He came to another bar that wasn't too busy. It was getting late. There was a menu posted on a stand just outside the entrance. A cheeseburger and fries were right there on the menu and so was beer.

He was still reading other options on the menu when he felt the presence of another person behind him. He glanced over his right shoulder and saw a pudgy man in his sixties dressed in a wrinkled white shirt and an oversized cardigan sweater reading over his shoulder.

"What sounds good, Sergeant?"

"Oh, um, I'm thinking a burger and fries. Been awhile since I've had a good one."

"That does sound good! Come on, I'll buy."

"Really? That's not necessary."

"Always glad to help out a soldier. You on your way home, or on your way to the war?"

"Coming home."

"Good for you! Even more reason to buy you a meal. My way of saying thanks."

They headed for a table and the stranger turned and stuck out his hand. "Name's Rudolf, Rudolf Wanderon. You're Sergeant, um?"

Ray reached out to shake his hand. "Sergeant Reynolds. Call me Ray."

"Okay, Ray. This table okay?"

"Yeah, fine by me." He pulled out a chair and took a seat.

"I'm sorry, couldn't help but notice your limp. Is that a war injury?"

"Yeah. Sniper fire, punctured a lung and clipped my spine. Partial paralysis. Could have been a whole lot worse."

"Sorry to hear that. What's the prognosis?"

"Doctors tell me I'll recover from it with a few months or so of physical therapy."

A waitress walked up and asked, "What can I getcha?"

Rudolf responded in a boisterous voice, "Cheeseburger, fries for me, and I think that's what the sergeant here wants also. Right?"

Ray nodded.

"And bring us a pitcher of beer with some cold mugs!"

The waitress finished jotting down the order, then took a quick glance at Ray but didn't say anything.

When she left, Ray said, "I appreciate you joining me. It's been a long, quiet flight from Japan."

"Oh, I enjoy visiting with servicemen. Hell, I enjoy visiting with everyone. You said Japan, I figured you had been in Nam."

"Well, that's where I got wounded. The Army has a surgery and recovery hospital in Japan. It's called Camp Zama. It's a pretty large place. I think they said there's over a thousand soldiers recovering there now. Some of them are in really bad shape."

"That's horrible, but I can believe it. It's such a stupid war. All politics, stupid! I'm lucky I missed it. Too old, too fat! That's how I got my nickname."

Ray leaned back and gave him a questioning look.

"Oh, I've got several names - Broadway Fats, New York Fats, Chicago Fats. It all depends on where I'm playing. But I'm probably best known as Minnesota Fats. You've probably heard that one."

"Yeah, I have." Ray stuck his right hand out across the table, and Rudolf, Mr. Fats, reached out to shake it again. "Nice to meet you!" Ray paused, then asked, "So you don't have a California Fats nickname?"

"No, I mostly go by the Minnesota name. They had that movie a few years ago that made me famous. Jackie Gleason played me."

"Yeah, I remember seeing that. Wasn't Paul Newman in it?

"He was. Willie too. He played himself."

"Willie?"

"Yeah, Mosconi. That's why I'm here tonight. I just finished playing a tournament against him. Straight pool. We played almost twenty-seven hours straight, only two breaks for meals. I'm beat! And then I get here to catch a plane and they've got mechanical problems. Might be another two hours. I'm ready for the red-eye to New York so I can get some sleep,"

"You win?"

"Well, you know that Willie. He's pretty quiet, but he's good. I don't always lose to him."

The waitress showed up with a pitcher of beer and two frosted glasses and she set both glasses in front of the older man. Ray thought maybe that allowed her to say she didn't serve the young guy.

"Look, Sarge, you can make a lot of money hustling pool, but you gotta be good at the hustle. Mosconi is just really good at shooting pool. I've beat him before, but usually only because I wear him down with all my chatter. I've actually seen him wear ear plugs when he plays me."

One Tough Son of a Gun

"Really? That's funny."

"So, what about you, kid? What's in your future now?"

"I don't really know. I'll get medical discharge papers after I get home. I've been thinking about it all the way across the Pacific. And all the time I was laying in a hospital bed. Haven't figured it out. I should go back to college. I'll have the G.I. Bill to help pay for it."

"Good idea. Whatever you do, don't do like me. Hustling pool can be a pretty rough occupation. Some of these people don't like being hustled and you'd better be prepared for them. When you figure out that's who you're playin', it's best just to let them win a little and then walk away."

Their food was delivered and the conversation stalled while both men seemed overly hungry and started stuffing food down their throats.

Once the eating slowed down, the conversation picked up again. Ray told Fats all about Strong City and Cottonwood Falls and his family's generational ranch out on the tall grass prairie. He also talked about Mari and the fact he knew that one of these days, probably after she finished college, they would get married and start a family. He seemed especially excited about that.

As tired as he was, Rudolf listened intently. He was surprised to hear that this young man was an experienced rodeo contestant. But then, he thought that out there in the middle of nowhere Kansas, that's probably what they do. Just like almost everyone in Minnesota has snowmobiles or boats. In outback Kansas, it's horses and dogs.

Ray finally got around to asking, "What's it like having a movie made about you?"

Rudolf reached for the beer pitcher and emptied it equally into the two mugs on the table. "Okay, I'm tired, so I'm not going to hustle you on this one. The name 'Minnesota Fats' came from the novel *The Hustler* written by Walter Nevis. I sort of stole the name and claimed he wrote the books based on my life. Nevis always said that his books were pure fiction. Could be. But, there are some interesting similarities to my life and his fictional character. You'll have to read the book and make up your own mind."

The waitress came by and dropped the check on the table next to Rudolf. "Pay me when you're ready, no hurry," she said.

"Look kid, I'd better get down and check on my flight status." He paused while he reached in his pocket and pulled out a wad of money rolled up and held in place by a thick rubber band. Ray had never seen so much money come out of any man's pocket before. Rudolf started his conversation again as he peeled off a twenty and a five and laid them on the table. He placed the twenty on top of the check and stuck the edge of the five under the corner of his plate as a tip

"I think you have some hard choices to make. You've got a great family there in Kansas and a long family history on that ranch. You've also got a sweet sounding girl in the middle of her college career that sounds like she's going places. Pretty, and smart. Didn't you say she was valedictorian?"

Ray nodded with some pride.

"Yeah, she's going places. You've also got a golden opportunity to return to college on the government's dime through the G.I. Bill. How can you pass that up? You can't beat having a degree. Believe me, I know. That's from a guy who doesn't have one. But I've been married and divorced and seen friends marry and divorce. I'm married again, great lady this time I think it'll last. But here's what I think about your situation. If you think you can marry this gal and keep her out there on the ranch, I don't think it's ever going to work. You've got to be honest with yourself. So I think your best choice is back to school and study hard and be prepared to follow her wherever her career takes her. She's your mealticket. That's my advice, kid! Good luck to you Sergeant!"

He stood, shook Ray's hand, patted him on the shoulder as he walked by, and was gone.

Ray tried to watch him leave but couldn't turn his head in that direction. He looked at the table in front of him and still had a half glass of beer. He downed it, and two minutes later was back wandering the concourse. He decided his best course of action would be to find the gate where his flight departs in the morning and then find a comfortable place nearby to wait. He surely didn't want to fall asleep and miss that flight.

He checked the schedule board and headed to the designated gate for the Denver flight continuing on to Kansas City. The gate seating area was completely empty. He took a seat at the end of a row along the back wall and set his canvas bag on the adjacent table. He pulled out *Cat's Cradle* and began reading again. He was just over halfway through it and found Vonnegut's imagination and humor refreshing, unlike anything he had read before. It was all about Bokononism and the son of the man who created the atom bomb. And all kinds of other weird things.

It didn't take long but he was finding it tough to concentrate on the book. He was tired and now had a full belly including half a pitcher of beer, and then the comments from Minnesota Fats kept coming back to him. He kept trying to put them aside because they were simply a stranger's suggestions, or one man's opinion, but Ray knew in his gut that most of what the man had said was true, or very likely to be true.

He laid the book in his lap with his index finger marking the page and the paragraph where he had given up trying to read. It was the end of a chapter with the last sentence reading, *"'Son', my father said to me, 'someday this will all be yours.'"*

Was that another prediction, just like Fats', bound to be true? It sure seemed like it.

There was still a moderate procession of travelers and airport personnel passing by his gate area up until about midnight, the last time he looked up at the clock on the wall of the concourse. He had tried closing his eyes to see if he could sleep sitting up. It wasn't going to work. He unbuttoned the brass buttons of his Army dress green coat and then loosened his tie and undid his top shirt button. He knew the rules were "out of uniform" for doing this in a public location, but piss on 'em. He was tired. He was very annoyed about having this overnight layover, and, he was basically out of the Army now anyway. *What are they going to do; court-martial me?*

He awoke around 4:15 a.m.. His book was back in his canvas bag and he had positioned the bag atop the back of his seat, wedged against the wall, behind his neck to serve as a pillow, and to keep it from being stolen. Now, he discovered that he couldn't turn his head left or right. Sleeping in such an awkward position left him stiff, sore, and uncomfortable. He noticed three other people were asleep in the gate area with him. Two of the three, had actually laid down across several seats but looked equally uncomfortable.

After sitting there for ten minutes, he decided to try to walk it off and see if that helped. Besides, he needed a bathroom. Once he looked in a mirror, he realized he should shave before boarding another flight. He then remembered he had clean underwear and fresh socks in his bag. He went into a stall and changed. He came out of the stall holding his dress shirt, coat and tie which he hung on a wall hook. Then he shaved and tried drying the wet collar of his t-shirt with paper towels before donning his only dress shirt. He tied and tightened his tie and buttoned up his green jacket. He almost felt like a new man. Well, maybe not 'almost', but certainly better than before.

When he came out of the restroom, he noticed the gate area was beginning to fill up with passengers. He turned his whole body to look behind him at that wall clock, not quite 5:00 a.m.. He wondered what kind of people would book a flight this early in the morning? He headed down the concourse to find some coffee.

CHAPTER 11

Tuesday, July 7, 1970
Cottonwood Falls, Kansas
United States of America

It was 6:05 a.m. when Walt Reynolds, Ray's father, dialed the number for the Key residence in Cottonwood Falls. Walt didn't know the Keys that well, but did know that he had good enough news that they wouldn't be upset receiving such a call so early, even if they were still sleeping, which he doubted. Most working people that he knew in the midwest would be up by 6:05 a.m. Now Mari, that was a different story, but he was sure after hearing about her trip to Japan she would be very excited to hear about this phone call. Her father, Ralph, answered with a crisp "Good morning" as though he was used to these early morning calls.

Walt replied, "Good morning to you, Ralph. Walt Reynolds here. Have you had your coffee?"

"Drinking it now. How are you, Walt?"

"I'm good! Can you guess who's coming home?"

"Well, considering it's you calling, I would guess it's Ray. When?"

"Today! At noon in Kansas City!"

"My God! I'd better go kick our daughter out of bed and tell her to get her face on so she can saddle up. She's got places to go today. If I was a gamblin" man, I'd certainly bet she'd be happy to go along with you to the airport."

"That's why I'm calling."

"I figured as much."

"Okay, so here's what's up. I'm gonna finish my coffee and I'll go tell my ranch hand what he needs to be doing today, and then me and Beverly will figure out our plan for the day and we'll call you back. Right now I'm thinking we'll need to leave here about 9:00 and then we can stop and have some breakfast in Topeka. So we'd probably want to pick up Marilyn at about quarter of. But I'll call you back in about an hour and confirm that. Okay?"

"Works for me! I'll go yell at the young lady. Plane's due in at noon, right?"

"Yeah, a little after."

"Okay, okay, that's great news! Way to start our day. We'll await your call. Oh, and hey, when you decide on the time, Jen or I will drive Mari up to the rodeo grounds and meet you there. Save you some time."

"That'll be great! Talk to you again in a little bit."

Mari answered the phone after only one ring thirty-five minutes later. "Hello."

This time it was Beverly, Ray's mother

"Good morning Marilyn. It's Bev. I imagine you're as excited as we are!"

"Yeah! Isn't it great!"

"Okay, here's what we figure. Walt says the airport in K.C. is just about two hours from here. Then he's allowing an extra half hour to make sure we don't get caught in city traffic. We haven't been there for awhile. Then, he wants to add an extra hour for a breakfast stop in Topeka, so that means we should be out of here on the road no later than 8:30. Does that work for you?"

"Sure! I'm alnost ready now. Did he tell you we'd meet you at the rodeo entrance?"

"Yes, he did. We'll see you there in a couple of hours."

"Okay. I can hardly wait!"

Bev hung the phone back up on the kitchen wall and went to wake up Ray's brother and sister. Chip's bedroom was right at the top of the stairs and he had heard the commotion and what sounded like excitement and was already awake. Besides, he was used to getting up early to help his father around the ranch ever since Ray left.

The not-quite ten-year-old June was still sound asleep when her mother peeked in her room and asked if she wanted to go welcome her brother home. She blinked her eyes several times to make sure she wasn't dreaming and asked, "Are you kidding?"

When her mother said, "No, we're heading for Kansas City."

"Ray's home?" she exclaimed.

"Noon today. You need to get ready."

June had witnessed so much on the local news about the Vietnam war being fought so far away almost every night, but that stopped once she found out her brother was wounded. Then, June had learned to leave the room, or to at least mentally tune it out. Prior to that, she watched every chance she got thinking she might see her brother on TV. Now she was excited to get the chance to see him again, live and in person, a phrase she often heard on TV.

CHAPTER 12

Tuesday, July 7, 1970
Kansas City Municipal Airport
United States of America

The flight from San Francisco with the stop at Denver Stapleton Airport was uneventful, and landed on time at 12:05 p.m.. Unfortunately, Ray had an aisle seat on the left side of the aircraft and didn't have a chance to enjoy any views of Kansas from the air. He had hoped he might be able to spot Strong City and maybe even their ranch as they flew across Kansas, but that didn't happen. Even if he had the window seat, he would have had a hard time looking out the window to his left. But he did manage a lucky break as the plane banked sharply to the right for its final approach. He happened to glance across the aisle and out the far window at just the right time to get a quick view of downtown Kansas City and the Missouri River before landing at the Municipal Airport.

As bad as he wanted to see Mari and his family, he still continued his habit of being the last one off the plane so he wouldn't slow down any of the other healthy, eager passengers. When he finally ambled up the aisle, he concentrated on two things - keeping his left foot straight so it minimized his limp, and forcing his left arm to swing in a natural motion instead of just letting it hang there. Those are the two things, along with exercising muscles on his left side, that the rehab nurses had him working on.

Right before he stepped through the doorway onto the mobile stairs platform, he paused and took a deep breath and switched hiscanvas bag to his left hand so his right arm would be free to hold the handrail while descending the stairs. He was determined to concentrate even harder on making his movements look natural, but he knew, however, that once he saw his family, and especially Mari, his concentration would be lost.

Just inside the terminal at a large picture window near the doorway to the tarmac stood five anxious people who were beginning to wonder if Ray had missed his flight. As other passengers departed the plane down the stairs and entered the building, many paused to look for family or friends, or signs on where to pick up their luggage. Now there was just one family group left and they had inched their way forward with every passing passenger. They all began to look at one another when Ray's brother Chip saw the sleeve of an Army green uniform reach out of the plane's door to grab the handrail.

"Here he comes," he shouted, even before he actually saw his face. Had to be him.

They all moved forward with their faces almost pressed against the glass. When Sergeant Reynolds stepped off the stairway and saw the group inside the terminal, tears immediately came to his eyes.

Inside, the airline gate agents had moved on to another gate or other duties. Since there was no one there to stop her, Mari reached over to the glass door, pushed it open and ran outside to greet her boyfriend with a hug, but June beat her to him and threw her arms around her brother's waist.

"Hey Jude!" Ray muttered. He had always kidded his younger sister June that the Beatles' song *'Hey Jude'* was about her.

Mari hadn't really stopped her momentum forward and threw her arms around Ray's neck and pretty well squeezed June aside. Next was his mother Beverly, then his dad Walt. Fourteen-year-old brother Chip was last and stuck out his hand to shake. Ray grabbed his hand and pulled him in hard and gave him a hug also. "Hey Buddy, good to see you. You been keepin' this group in order?" He was trying to avoid close eye contact because he didn't want his brother to see the tears in his eyes.

"Yeah, sort of, but they never listen," Chip replied.

"Oh yeah? Well, we'll fix that now that I'm home." He released the hug and gave his brother a right-hand fist into his shoulder.

The group all stood back to admire their soldier hero except for Mari. She stayed right beside him holding his hand. They all shuffled their way back inside the terminal building in a group huddle.

Walt asked his son, "We need to go get your bags?"

Ray tried hard to use his left hand to hold up his canvas bag with the name Camp Zama and the military hospital logo on it, but didn't get it much above waist high. "This is it," he said.

"Really?" his father was astonished. "Well, okay. Let's head for the car."

The family took off together through a set of glass double doors and turned to head for the parking lot. Walt turned to ask Ray, "How's it feel to be back in Kansas?"

June piped up and said, "Dad, we're in Missouri!"

Then they both turned to see Ray's reaction and realized he hadn't heard them. Ray and Mari were still inside the terminal building holding hands and walking slowly. That was the first sign that made Walt realize how serious his son's wounds were. He quickly said to the rest of his family, "We've got to walk slower."

Ray and Mari caught up and they all walked leisurely across a pick up and drop off roadway toward the short term public parking lot. Walt turned down the second aisle and stopped at a new white Chevrolet Suburban. When Ray noticed his father unlocking the new vehicle, he asked, "What happened to 'Black Jack'?"

"It was dying. It was time, ten years old and somewhere over 120,000 miles. The odometer quit two years ago."

Ray responded, "Wow, well this is nice!" as he climbed awkwardly into the middle row of seats beside Mari. His younger siblings were in the back behind him.

When they all got comfortable and quiet, Mari said, "Who was Black Jack?"

Ray laughed and said, "That was our nickname for the old black station wagon. It was a Suburban, like this. Somewhere along the way, the first 'U' fell off the tailgate so it read 'S BURBAN'. So, we named it after Jack Daniels, my dad's favorite drink. And, since it was black, well, you remember it don't you? 'Black Jack'."

Fourteen-year-old Chip piped up from the back seat and said, "Yeah, but that's *not* how you spell bourbon!"

His father yelled back to him from the driver's seat and said, "How is it that you know that?"

"I've seen your bottle sitting on the bar more than once," his youngest son replied.

By then, Walt had backed out of the parking space and had revved up the V-8 engine for Ray's benefit before he slipped the oversized station wagon into low gear and let out the clutch.

For some reason, Ray thought of Vonnegut's words that he had just read the day before. *'Son,' my father said to me, someday this will all be yours.'*

CHAPTER 13

Tuesday, July 7, 1970
West of Strong City, Kansas

The two-hour ride home was full of questions and conversation for the first forty-five minutes. Everyone in the Reynolds family wanted to know about Ray's wounds, how he got shot, how he was treated at the hospital, and so on. Then there was a short lull in the conversation and Ray fell asleep with his head on Mari's shoulder. She couldn't be happier. When the others in the vehicle realized Ray was asleep, they all shut up.

He awoke as his father slowed down to pull into their ranch driveway. It was like his inner body instinctively knew he was home.

Ray's mother had invited Mari to stay for dinner and when they got inside, she asked Mari to call her parents and invite them to join the party. She told Walt to not get too comfortable because she was going to need him to run back into town to pick up a few groceries.

It was going to be a wonderful family homecoming that night. Break out the Jack Daniels.

Walt called their butcher in Cottonwood Falls that afternoon and asked him to cut up eight t-bone steaks from the Reynolds stock on hand. "Make 'em at least an inch and a half thick," he instructed. When he got there an hour later to pick them up he also grabbed a fresh bag of charcoal briquettes. Then he noticed a rack of white butchers' aprons that claimed, "Cottonwood Falls Top Chef" in bright red letters and he picked one off the rack. But that exposed another apron behind it that read "Strong City's Top Chef". He put the first one back and took that one.

Beverly got busy making a large bowl of lettuce salad with grated carrots, tomatoes, diced celery, green peppers, radishes and a small batch of green onions. When Walt got the charcoal going in their homemade large steel barrel grille, Bev stuck a dozen potatoes wrapped in foil on the top rack at least an hour before Walt would be grilling any steaks. She also whipped together two bowls of scalloped corn ready for the oven later. Then she got busy making dinner rolls. When she had them covered with a damp dish towel to rise, she worried about a dessert and then remembered she had an apple pie in the freezer. She hoped that could thaw near the west window and would be enough for everyone. She figured most people, except the kids, would probably be too full to want dessert.

Meanwhile, Ray had changed into some old Levi's and a Strong City Rodeo t-shirt. He and Mari had wandered out to the barn to see Gabby who was very happy to see Ray. Rex, the Siberian Husky, wouldn't leave Ray's side now that he was home and June had tagged along talking a mile a minute.

On the way to the barn, June asked Mari, "So, are you going back to college now, or are you going to stay here and take care of my brother?"

Ray looked at his sister and said, "June, what kind of question is that?"

"Well, I just wondered."

Mari cleared the air by answering the question. "I'll be leaving Monday morning to head back to K.U.. I'll be a Junior this year and I have some duties as a teaching assistant where I'll be tutoring some athletes on math courses this summer. I think your brother looks well enough to take care of himself, don't you?"

Ray shot his sister a look, and he noticed she seemed disappointed at the response from Mari. But, if he was being honest, Ray would have to admit he was even more disappointed.

Once Mari's parents arrived, Walt fixed cocktails for anyone who wanted one, except for the two youngest, Chip and June.

After dinner on their patio in the shade of the old oak tree, almost everyone skipped dessert, except Ray and Chip. "Ala mode, please," when asked how they wanted it. Then Ray added, "This is the best meal I've had in over eighteen months!"

Before the evening was over, Ray had told the story of how he got shot two more times. Once when the three adult men were watching the steaks on the grille and Mari's dad asked, and then later at the dinner table when Mari's mother asked. Ray went into the same detail of getting hit out in the middle of an open field and figured he was selected by a sniper because he had an RTO right behind him, and then he had to explain what an RTO was. To keep the story short, he always ended it with the fact that he didn't remember anything after being loaded in the Medevac chopper and hearing his buddy Bill Bill say he'd look me up back in the States.

During that last story, he added an explanation about everyone having nicknames. "'Bill Bill' was called that because his name really was William Williams, or Bill Williams for short, so Bill Bill was just a natural. And, ol' Bill Bill started calling me 'Wildcat' when he found out I had gone to K-State. And Johnny, our radio operator was 'Shorty' because he was only five foot five. Our M-60 machine gunner was called just that, 'Gunner'. And, then our company clerk was called 'Twiggy' because he was thin as a rail."

June made a funny face and said, "Eww! Wouldn't a guy hate it to be called 'Twiggy'?"

Ray responded, "Nah. Well, I don't think so. It was all in good natured fun. He never acted like it bothered him. Some of us wore our nicknames with pride, although I didn't tell most people that I only attended K-State for one term."

When the Key family got ready to head home that evening, Mari hugged Ray and gave him a kiss and then said, "Goodnight, Wildcat."

One Tough Son of a Gun

It was almost 11:00 and Ray was exhausted. His parents had the Tonight Show with Johnny Carson on and Ray had admitted he missed that. He was trying to watch and visit with his folks, but he could barely keep his eyes open. He was really looking forward to flopping onto his old bed and finally said, "I can't do this anymore. We'll have to talk in the morning. I'm goin' hit the hay. Goodnight!"

"Goodnight son. It's so good to have you home!" His mother got off the couch and stood to give him a hug.

His father gave a slight wave and said, "See ya in the mornin'."

Sometime in the middle of the night, Ray was dreaming that he was back at Camp Zama. *The nurse was there at his bedside changing his IV bag. He looked up and noticed the bag was filled with a dark fluid instead of the clear antibiotic he was used to seeing. He asked the nurse, 'What is that?'. She replied, 'Don't worry, you'll be fine,' and then she laughed as she walked away. Ray didn't understand that, especially the laughter and he yelled after her, 'Nurse, hey, nurse!' Mike, the guy in the bed to his right yelled 'Knock it off!' Ray turned to see why he was upset and it wasn't Mike in the bed at all. It was an NVA soldier in full uniform laying on top of the sheets and holding an AK-47.*

Ray yelled again, 'Nurse, help!'

Then the guy on his left yelled 'Knock it off' and Ray realized he'd never seen the guy on his left because he couldn't turn that way, but he knew his name was Bill. In his dream it was his buddy Bill Bill and all of a sudden he had no problem turning left and saying 'Bill Bill, I need your help.' Only it wasn't Bill Bill, it was another NVA soldier in full black uniform with an AK-47. Then he heard another chant of 'Knock it off!'. Everywhere he looked there were more North Vietnamese Army soldiers, some in beds, some just standing around. The nurse was long gone.

Then another chant of 'Knock it off!' came from the far end of the room, followed by 'Dirty rotten Commie!' and another shouted out, 'Yeah, dirty rotten Commie bastard!' followed by more chants.

In his dream, he knew he had heard that saying before and it scared him. *Something awful was about to happen, he was sure.*

Then he woke up, and sat straight up in bed. He could feel sweat on his upper lip and on his forehead. Some of the details of the nightmare disappeared instantly except that he remembered he was dreaming of Camp Zama and he couldn't shake those last phrases being shouted at him, '*Dirty rotten Commie bastard!*'.

He laid back down, but was wide awake. That phrase kept running over and over through his head. It didn't take long for him to remember very vividly where he had heard those exact words.

In January of 1970, his Charlie Company was on patrol near the Boi Loi Woods looking for signs of the enemy when they suddenly encountered automatic weapons fire coming from a nearby tree line. Immediately, he and all of his fellow soldiers hit the ground to take some cover in the tall grass, and he heard shouts of 'Medic' coming from two different directions. The soldiers of the First Platoon were closest to the tree line and started firing back. 'Gunner' returned fire with a vengeance, spraying the trees with a constant barrage of rounds. Ray could see leaves and small branches exploding off the trees.

When the two wounded men were evacuated and the enemy fire had stopped. Charlie Company moved into the hedgerow to see if they could determine a body count. They came upon some blood trails where it was obvious that a wounded enemy had been dragged from the area. Then, not far from there, they found an obviously dead NVA soldier laying in a ditch, face up, eyes frozen in a stare at the bright sun above. The First Platoon's leader, First Lieutenant Johnson, walked up to the group of his soldiers standing around looking at the dead enemy. Johnson pushed his way through and took a quick look at the North Vietnamese soldier, pointed his M-16 at him and pulled the trigger putting a hole in the middle of his dead head just above the eyes and said, "*Dirty rotten Commie bastard!*". Then the platoon leader walked away. It was a scene Ray would never forget.

CHAPTER 14

Wednesday, July 8, 1970
Reynolds Ranch
West of Strong City, Kansas

'Dirty rotten Commie bastard!' The words kept echoing in Ray's head. He laid there in his bed flat on his back staring up at the dark ceiling trying to think of something else. He remembered the soldier's dark empty eyes staring up at the sky. He *needed* to think of something else. Here he was back home, in America. Safe. No longer fearful of being ambushed, stepping on a booby trap, or being singled out by a hidden sniper some fifty yards away.

He turned to his right to look at the digital clock radio and saw the red numerals flashing 12:00. Apparently the power had been off at some time and the clock never reset. He realized he needed a watch, but then remembered the old battery powered alarm clock on the nightstand and briefly turned on the lamp. A little after 4:30 a.m.. He shut the lamp off.

He couldn't think of anything else. As he laid there fully awake, remnants of his nightmare kept coming back. The vision of all the NVA regulars in his hospital ward and the nurse walking away laughing. He wondered what the joke was. *'Dirty rotten Commie bastard!'* He wondered what the NVA's said when they killed an American - *'Dirty rotten Democrat!'? 'American Asshole'?* He was sure those NVA's had probably shot a dead corpse many times, or worse, but still. Then he remembered he had heard stories where Americans had been beheaded, or their ears cut off as a souvenir, but he had no proof of that, but still. He knew they were mean, sneaky bastards. He had witnessed that with all the trip- wire explosives, punji pits, and leaving dead civilians behind with a booby-trapped grenade set to explode when the body was moved. Yeah, they may have deserved the title, but that one guy didn't deserve Lieutenant Johnson's final chapter and verse, *'Dirty rotten Commie bastard!'*, with one more bullet in his already dead head. It was a lousy war, but still. He needed more sleep!

Ray remembered the day they were about to search a small village and the Commanding Officer called the platoon leaders for a quick meeting. Ray was standing within fifteen feet of where the CO was gathering the lieutenants on a trail that went past the edge of the village. As the third platoon leader came by to join the group, a young private standing on the trail just opposite Ray, stepped back into a bamboo hedge out of the lieutenant's way and immediately lost his right foot to a hidden grenade booby trap. *'Dirty rotten Commie bastards!'* No boot, no foot, no ankle, all gone. Amazingly, no one else near him was wounded; the blast had gone straight up. A medic had been called and rushed over. New in country, he took one look at the shattered leg, saw nothing left below the shin, and he ran off. The CO sent someone after him and found him tossing his cookies further down the trail. They called for a second medic and then they had to wait for a dustoff. Ray really had to think of something else.

As he remembered that incident, he wondered why he thought of it. It certainly wasn't the worst. Maybe it was just that it happened right next to him and there was absolutely nothing he could do about. No one to shoot in retaliation, no getting even. That was the NVA's equivalent of 'body count'. Send another *American Asshole* home to live the rest of his life in misery. *Dirty rotten Commie bastards!*

He thought he heard something down the hall from his bedroom. He tried the lamp and clock routine again and saw that it was now going on 6:00. He had laid there over an hour trying to get back to sleep. He was sure that what he heard was his father getting up to start the day. He needed the distraction. He knew he wasn't going back to sleep. It was Vietnam's fault! *'Dirty rotten stupid fuckin' war!'* That's it! He knew it, he was getting up to have coffee with his dad.

He grabbed the canvas bag from Zama and dumped the contents on the bed. Deodorant, a small bar of soap, a razor, his dirty underwear and socks from changing in San Francisco, a manila folder with paperwork, boarding passes, his two books, and finally what he was looking for, the toothbrush and toothpaste. He went across the hall to brush his teeth and could hear water running in the master suite on the other side of the wall so he knew his father was up. He was always up before 6:00 as long as Ray could remember. He wanted to beat his father to the kitchen and have the coffee made for him.

It worked, just barely. Ray had filled his cup with coffee and had just taken a seat at the kitchen table when his father came down the steps and into the kitchen. Ray glanced up at the clock on the wall and saw that it was 5:58 a.m.. It was the routine down on the ranch.

"What are *you* doing up?" his father asked.

"I wanted to have coffee with you."

"Oh, bullshit."

"Naw, really! Couldn't sleep any longer and thought I heard you, so I decided to make you coffee."

"Man, I figured you'd sleep til noon."

"I think it's the jet lag. Too many time zones yesterday and day before. I've even lost track of what day it is."

"Well, I'm pretty sure it's Wednesday. I think it's supposed to be a nice day, but hot. This hot spell we're having is another reason I got rid of ol' Black Jack. I wanted one with air conditioning!"

"Good move! That new one you got is really nice." Then Ray added, "We seldom heard what the temperature was in Nam, but during the dry season it got really hot!"

"It's probably too early to ask you this, but have you thought about what you're going to do now?"

Ray kind of shook his head, then took a sip of coffee to stall with his answer. The words of Minnesota Fats started coming back to him, and he didn't want to hear them right then. But he took his time with his father's question, another sip of coffee, and a pause, "I've been thinking a lot, and I'm not real sure yet." The words of Fats were haunting him - *'If you think you can marry this gal and keep her there on the ranch, it's never going to work.'* something like that. *'You've got to be honest with yourself.'* He remembered that part clearly. *'Your best choice is back to school and follow her. She's your mealticket.'* Ray wasn't sure how that would work.

Walt got up and went for the coffee pot. "Another one?", he asked Ray.

"Sure."

Walt filled his son's cup. "What was it like over there? Did you constantly worry about getting hit, wounded, or worse?"

'Be honest with yourself.' Those words were still resonating in the back of his head. "I'd be lying if I said I never thought about it, but honestly, it wasn't like it was always there, always in the back of my head. Like, the day I was shot, it was probably the farthest thing from my mind. We're out in an open field, just outside base camp, simple search and destroy operation. I don't think anyone expected to be shot at that day. I was just the lucky one."

"You're probably lucky to be alive. We're lucky you got out of there and back home. So are you fully discharged now?"

"I don't know. I guess so. They told me I'd be getting paper work in the mail when I left Camp Zama. They also gave me a list of VA facilities in the State of Kansas. I guess that's part of my answer to you about what I'm going to do now."

"How's that?"

"Well, I need to continue my physical therapy program and my exercises so I'll know what I'm going to be capable of. That's probably my first order of business."

"Yeah, that sounds right," Walt agreed.

"I'm thinking I'd be foolish to not take advantage of the G.I. Bill and not go back to college." Again, Minnesota Fats words in his head, *'You can't beat having a degree.'*

"Makes sense. Look," Walt continued, "I know you and Mari are like this," and he held up his hand with the index and middle finger side by side, "and I want you to know that your mother and I could not be prouder if she becomes part of the family some day. But, I just sort of hope you don't make that decision and go down that path too soon. Does that make sense?"

Now another thought was creeping into his mind. Is this leading up to the words spoken by the character Julian Castle in *Cat's Cradle*, *'Son, . . . someday this will all be yours.'*? He hoped not. He wasn't ready for that and he knew if he heard those words right now, it would only add to his confusion about what to do. There was already a sort of unspoken family understanding that the ranch would some day be his, but having that spoken out loud by his father could influence the rest of his life. But living the rest of his life on this ranch didn't seem like such a bad idea.

Ray glanced over his father's shoulder out the kitchen window and noticed the first rays of sunlight shining over the Flint Hills and starting to crawl down the cupola on the barn's roof. He looked up at the kitchen clock, 6:45. He was surprised his father wasn't already outside tending to chores, but then he knew that Juan, their ranch hand, didn't usually start his duties until 7:00 a.m.. He heard a rustling sound behind him and turned to see his mother in her bathrobe and slippers.

"I thought I heard voices." She looked at Ray and said, "What are *you* doing up?"

"I just wanted to make the first pot of coffee."

"Oh, that's a laugh!, Beverly giggled at her own comment.

Walt looked up at the clock, picked up his cup and swallowed the last of his coffee and said, "Gotta get busy. I can't let ol' Juan out there in the bunkhouse out work me!"

Bev commented, "You always say that, and then you give him more work to do."

Before Walt could get to the door, June walked into the kitchen all sleepy-eyed in her pajamas. "How come I wasn't invited to the party?"

"Hey Jude," Ray teased his sister, "Did you know you're my favorite Beatles song?"

"Hey, it's *June*, buddy! And don't you forget it!", she smiled and went to Ray's chair and gave him a hug. "I'm gonna start calling you Sergeant Pepper!"

Walt had to laugh at that and then he was out the door. He had equipment in the barn to work on.

Ray realized he had managed to escape any commitments on his future plans, but he also knew he was going to have to commit to something soon.

At 10:00 a.m., Mari called to see if Ray was up yet. They visited briefly and then she asked him how he felt about going to Emporia for a movie and dinner later. She told him "Blazing Saddles" was playing. He hadn't heard of it, but then, he hadn't heard much in the way of Hollywood news while overseas. It didn't really matter to him. After all he'd been through he knew a day with Mari would be a great day.

She picked him up at 1:00 so they could get to Emporia early. She wanted to shop for some new shoes and sweaters for the school year. Ray discovered that shopping for women's clothes is both time consuming and extremely boring.

Later at dinner at the local Pizza Hut, they discussed a number of topics, but Mari focused on her upcoming school year and the courses she would be taking. That led her to ask Ray if he had decided what he was going to do about school. Like he told his dad, he admitted he would be foolish to pass up the G.I. Bill opportunity. Mari agreed with that and encouraged him to plan on it.

On the drive home, they had a lively discussion about the movie. Ray thought it was hilarious and exactly what he needed. Mari went along with Ray's assessment, but actually thought some of the humor was childish and not really *that* funny.

When Mari dropped him off at the ranch, they talked about plans for the rest of the summer, but realized they were mostly just dreams of things to do. Maybe a day trip to Topeka, or Wichita, or Kansas City when she was home on weekends. They even talked about an overnight trip to any of those places but knew their parents would have a fit. Ray especially knew it would set a bad example for his younger siblings. He mentioned his need to follow up with the VA and figuring out how his outpatient status was going to work. They decided they would just have to see what turns up.

Before she kissed him to say good-bye, she invited him to have dinner at their house Saturday night.

Ray paused, as if in thought, and Mari wondered if he was going to turn her down. Then he said, "You know I'm not sure I'm ready to drive. I can't see stuff off to my left."

"Oh, I'm sorry. I didn't think about that. I can pick you up."

"No, that's fine. I was just thinking my mom or dad could bring me over, or, I was thinking maybe I could ride Gabby."

"Well that would be neat. I bet you'd enjoy that!"

"I would. One way or another, I'll be there. Around 4:00, okay?"

CHAPTER 15

Saturday, July 11, 1970
Cottonwood Falls, Kansas

Ray did ride Gabby that afternoon. His younger brother Chip helped him put the saddle on the roan mare and told him, "You gotta tell Mari I wish she had some younger sisters." Then he added, "Wait a minute, I'm gonna ride with you part way." Chip saddled up his horse, Ranger.

They crossed US Highway 50 just east of their ranch driveway and then followed the railroad tracks to the south side of town. There they stayed on the shoulder of the two-lane Kansas Highway 177 to the city park in Cottonwood Falls and across the old stone arch bridge over the Cottonwood River. Chip stayed on Ray's left to watch for traffic. Once they reached the park and were in the town's limits, Ray was amazed that three different cars slowed and stopped to yell at him, not in anger, but in surprise to see him and wish him well. "Hey Ray, welcome home!"

He was happy to hear those words from the locals. Happy to be back in Kansas, back in the small towns where there were no demonstrators against the war or anything else. He felt good. It felt right to be back on Gabby's back, *'back in the saddle again.'* He could hear those words of Gene Autry and wanted to break into song but couldn't remember any other lyrics, except that he knew it had something to do with friends.

After the bridge, Chip said, "Okay, you're on your own. I'll see you later, probably tomorrow sometime," and he turned to head home.

Just after 6:00 p.m. Mari and her parents and Ray all gathered in the dining room and took a seat for dinner. Mari's father listened as

Ray described his horse ride and the cars that stopped and he suddenly thought of it and said, "*Out where a friend is a friend.*" He laughed and said, "Remember that song? I think it was Gene Autry, *Back in the Saddle Again.*"

"Yeah," Ralph said, "Good ol' Gene! Have another stick of Doublemint. Remember that?"

Ray continued his story about the ride and the cars that stopped. "One was Jimmy Clark's folks, but I really didn't know the other two. I've seen them before but don't know their names. I just smiled and waved, and said thank you."

Ralph said, "That doesn't surprise me that people knew you. You've been the main topic of discussion all day today in town. Everyone wanted to know how you were. And they were all glad you made it back in one piece."

They had a great meal of ham balls, mashed potatoes, green beans, and fresh homemade bread. Ray especially enjoyed the pecan pie that Mari's mother Jennifer had made for dessert. The phrase 'Home Sweet Home' came to Ray's mind, probably partially influenced by the picture on the Norman Rockwell calendar on the wall behind Mari's head. He looked back at her across the table and smiled. It was good to be back in Kansas.

CHAPTER 16

Saturday, August 22, 1970
Cottonwood Falls, Kansas

Later that summer, Ray was back at the dining room table in the Key house for breakfast. His father had driven him over and dropped him off. It was 9:00 a.m. Saturday morning and shortly after breakfast, Jennifer was going to drive her daughter back to Lawrence for the fall semester. Ray had ben invited to ride along. Ralph wasn't there for the send-off, he had already left to open Key Real Estate because he had an early morning meeting with a prospective client who was anxious to get his business on the market. Saturdays were always a busy day in downtown Cottonwood Falls.

News out of KU's Campus had continued during the summer and Mari's parents had tried to talk her into changing schools because of all the ruckus. Mari insisted it was just a small faction of the students, and oftentimes it was outsiders stirring things up and she was safe at the sorority house and inside the classrooms. There was nothing to worry about.

It was less than a two-hour drive to Lawrence and it gave the Key women plenty of time to quiz Ray about his future plans and give their opinions on what he should be thinking about doing with his life. He really liked Mari, a lot, and he thought highly of her mother. She had always treated him well and with respect. Jennifer Key had maintained her youthful good looks and some people had accused the mother and daughter of being sisters. Ray was pleased to be invited along and would have offered to drive Mari himself if it wasn't for the lingering paralysis on his left side. He was, however, doing better after weeks of exercise. As it was, he thought going along for the ride with no responsibilities sounded like a great day, but by the time they got to

Lawrence, he wasn't looking forward to the ride home. Whenever he mentioned the College of Agriculture at K-State, they would ask if he ever considered other areas of education like engineering, architecture, or maybe construction management. "You'd be good at any of those," said Mari.

He tried to be polite and kept responding, "Yeah, I'll think about that," or, "I'll have to look into that."

Then they would try a different tactic like, "Maybe you could do a smaller school at first to get used to college. Just a thought." Then Jennifer suggested veterinary school. "Yeah, you love animals," Mari added. With those comments he really began to think they were just trying to help him sort things out in his mind. Before that, he was pretty sure they thought he should be studying more professional courses that could lead to bigger city occupations and get him away from the small town ranch living.

He was relieved when they pulled up in front of the Kappa Alpha Theta House and he could help carry things in from the car without having to listen to anymore opinions on *his* education. But he still had the ride home looming ahead of him.

All the time they were in Lawrence and around Mari's sorority sisters, Ray concentrated hard on minimizing his limp. Before he and Jennifer left town, they took Mari and her roommate Julie to a late lunch.

After kissing Mari goodbye, Ray and her mother got back in the car to head back to the Flint Hills and home. Before hitting the highway, Jennifer took a different tone. "I don't know about you, Ray, but if Kansas would let us have liquor by the drink, I'd be ready to stop at a bar and down a couple."

Ray was totally surprised by that comment, and it immediately made him think of Mrs. Robinson in the movie *The Graduate* he had seen a few years back, before he was drafted. He began to wonder if she was going to reach over and put her hand on his leg? But then she continued to explain her feelings.

Ray had to turn his whole body in the car seat so that he could see her face. He leaned back against the passenger door.

"You know it's really hard to realize your only child is grown up and has already partially left the nest. All you can think about is wanting her to have the best, to be the best, and wishing her success and love and happiness and all that's good in this crazy world. When you grow up and live your whole life in a small town, it's scary to think your child is probably going to end up in some big city, and you hope it's okay, you know, safe, and that she'll be all right."

Ray listened, not sure where this conversation was going, but figured it was somehow going to be a continuation of the talk they had on the way to Lawrence. Now he had to expect another hour and a half of the same on the way back home. But to his surprise, the tone was different.

Mrs. Key continued talking, but started to apologize to Ray. "I have to confess," she began, "Mari started a conversation with me this morning about you, before you got there. She told me how crazy she was about you, but that she was also going crazy not knowing what was going to happen to the two of you. In my mind she's trying to rush things since you got wounded and now you're home, but her real concern is that you're a small town guy, kind of like me and Ralph. You're a rancher type, different in a way, like your family. She's pretty sure she'll wind up in some city as an accountant or in some financial position and hates having the thought that might mean leaving you behind, 'cause you wouldn't be happy with that.

Ray's conversation with Minnesota Fats again came back to him. He was surprised he hadn't forgotten it. *Why are all these people trying to give me advice?*

"Anyway," Jen continued, "she had me convinced that we should try to pick your brain and figure out what you're thinking so that she could start making plans accordingly. And I'm sorry, by the time we got to Lawrence, I think we had gone way overboard. We were on the verge of being aggressive!

I'm surprised you didn't just jump right out of the car and start hitchhiking home. You've got your life to live, and if it works out that, well, you know, you and Mari are part of that life, so be it. Ralph and I won't complain. In fact, we'd be thrilled!"

There was a slight pause and then she continued, "Next time I talk to my daughter, I'm going to tell her I thought we really picked on you too hard. You're too nice a guy to be berated like that. Especially now, just home from the war. I hope you'll accept my apology? And, we don't need to tell Mari about this little talk. It'll be our little secret." She reached over and patted her hand on Ray's knee.

And here's to you, Mrs. Robinson

Jesus loves you more than you will know

Whoa, whoa, whoa

Now he couldn't get that song out of his head.

Ray is thinking that everyone is getting too serious too soon about him and Mari, and he needs to find a way to stop all the speculation. He needs more time to think things out. He realized that Mrs. Key had apologized for the way they treated him on the ride over, and he also now realized that she had stopped talking and he should probably say something, but he didn't know what. Then he remembered the comment from Minnesota Fats and repeated it verbatim, "You can't beat having a degree."

Jennifer Key looked over at him and smiled.

God bless you, please, Mrs. Robinson

They rode along in silence for a few miles and then Mrs. Key added, "You're right about the degree. But, it isn't everything. It should really be something *you* like. You know? Don't you agree?"

"Yeah. I've been thinking about that ever since my first semester at K-State. Most of my classes were interesting, but I wasn't really *excited* about them. Does that make sense?"

Then there was a lull in the conversation and after a few minutes when Mrs. Key looked over to say something to Ray, she noticed his eyes were closed. Whatever it was she was about to say, she let it go. It wasn't that important. Her daughter's veteran hero needed his rest.

Ray dozed for almost thirty minutes and woke up shortly after they passed through Emporia, headed west on US Highway 50, just in time to see the beginning of the five faded red and white Burma-Shave signs. He could recite them in order since he had passed them so often. Although the Burma-Shave company had been sold to Philip Morris in the early sixties and their commercial signs disappeared from the nation's rural roads after that, somehow this set of five still remained, each sign a hundred feet apart.

DON'T LOSE YOUR HEAD
TO GAIN A MINUTE
YOU'LL NEED YOUR HEAD
YOUR BRAINS ARE IN IT
Burma-Shave

Ray motioned with his hand to catch Mrs. Key's attention and pointed at the signs as they passed by. He said, "Do you remember that there used to be another set of those signs on the south side for people driving east? It was closer to Strong City. I remember when I was learning to read and my dad pointed them out to me and asked me to read the signs. After that, I read those to myself every time we went to Emporia. I still remember what they said because I didn't know what the last word was and I had to ask my dad. I was really disappointed several years ago when we went by and the signs were gone."

"What was the word?"

"Well, it went like this . . ."

> DON'T TRY PASSING
> ON A SLOPE
> UNLESS YOU HAVE
> A PERISCOPE
> **Burma-Shave**

"I was really interested in periscopes after that. I wanted my dad to buy me one." He laughed at the thought. "I wonder how much Burma-Shave they sold using those signs?"

CHAPTER 17

Monday, August 31, 1970
Reynolds Ranch
Strong City, Kansas

Ray was up early again, making the coffee for his father. When asked what he was up to, he said, "I'm making a list of stuff I need to get done so I can prioritize things and get on with my life."

"Like what?" his father asked.

"Well, like today, I want to start calling these V.A. Hospitals to find out where I can go to continue my physical therapy. And I want to find out if there's other alternatives, like the hospital over in Emporia. It'd certainly be a lot closer than Topeka or Wichita."

"Good plan! So, that's priority number one?"

"Right now, yeah. I should have done this several weeks ago. Then I want to start calling for information, or maybe mom can drive me over to the library in Emporia so I can research colleges and programs under the G.I. Bill and see what I have to do to qualify."

He continued, "Oh, and I don't know where to start, but I need to call somewhere to find out when I will get all my back pay since when I was wounded. They told me in Japan it would be mailed to my home address."

"Ahh!," his father piped up, "I think your mother has two of those checks. They came in the mail. She stuck them away somewhere and apparently forgot about them."

"I think there should be at least one more. I hope."

"Sounds like you're going to have a full day."

"Probably, but I have to find time for my exercises, and I want to ride Gabby and take Rex out to tease the prairie dogs."

"We've got one colony out there that's really grown since you left. I'm guessing there's at least fifty in that town. If you go out along the north fence, you'll see 'em, about half a mile out."

"Maybe that should be a place for target practice one of these days?"

"Yeah, I've been thinking of suggesting you and Chip could have a heyday out there sometime before winter. Just make sure you bury 'em all. I don't want the cattle finding 'em."

"Then, last night when I was talking to Mari, she said her father wants to see me at his office. He's got some sort of idea for me."

"Wonder what that's all about?"

"Don't know. Mari didn't either. I'm hopin' mom can drive me over tomorrow or Wednesday."

CHAPTER 18

Wednesday, September 2, 1970
Key Realty
Cottonwood Falls, Kansas

"Hey! Good morning, Ray." Ralph stuck out his hand to shake. "Hope I didn't take you away from anything important?"

"Nah. I got caught up on a bunch of stuff yesterday and on Monday. I think I'm officially out of the service now, except they still owe me a check. And, I'm waiting on what the V,A,'s goin' do for me for compensation"

"I wish you well with that. And, I think I keep forgetting to say this, but thanks for your service!"

"I haven't heard that very often since I got home, and when I do I'm not sure if I should say 'thank you' or 'you're welcome.' Anyway, thanks!"

"C'mon back here with me. I want to show you what I'm about to do." Ralph started towards the back of his real estate office in the old native stone building on Broadway. Ray limped along behind him. "Do you know the Hanson Brothers from over near Emporia?"

"Can't say I do."

"Well, they've got a small construction company and they do odd jobs to keep busy. They're scheduled next week to knock out this wall."

Ray noticed the area that used to hold old fashioned wooden file cabinets and an antique rolltop desk had been cleared out. "Hey, what happened to your old antique office display?" he asked.

"I always thought that made your office interesting, especially in this old building."

"Yeah, built in 1889. Over eighty years old. Just sixteen years younger than the county courthouse and made of the same stone, supposedly by the same mason. This used to be a mercantile when it opened, sold all kinds of goods. After World War One, this became the telegraph, telephone office for about twenty years or so. Not sure when it changed, but there was a small cafe in here back in the '50's, mainly a coffee shop and bakery type place with deli sandwiches. I don't think they ever had a grill. Then it sat empty for about five years before I bought it. Some of that furniture you're wondering about is in the back room where I found it when I bought the place. Anyway, I'll bring it back out for display after the work is done."

"Good. I bet your customers like it."

"Yeah, some do. Well most, I guess. Every so often, people want to know if I'll sell any of it. Anyway, have a seat." Ralph pointed at the short sofa across from his desk and asked Ray if he'd like some coffee.

"No thanks. I think I've had my fill for the day."

"Anyway, I've got plans for this space. And maybe you'd like to get involved with it and help me get things started?"

Ray was curious as Ralph unrolled a drawing laying on his desk and turned it to face Ray. My office area here is going to get a little smaller, and I'll lose some of the storage space I have in the back. It just collects junk anyway." The wall to be removed was shown on one plan with a series of notes about light fixtures, electrical outlets, and ceiling tile to be revised. Next to that plan was a new layout of the space, about six feet deep and twelve feet wide, again with notes about a new ceiling, lights and outlets, and floor repairs.

Below that plan, on the same sheet, was a layout for a new kitchen with refrigerator, dishwasher, and a space marked *'future microwave oven.'* Ray was wondering what all of this had to do with him.

"So, I'm sure you're wondering why I invited you over? And what's all this got to do with me?"

"Well, yeah, kind of."

"Let's talk big picture stuff first. You probably know, if you've ever thought about it, I'm the only active real estate agent here in the Falls and Strong City. At least the only one with an office here in town. Everyone else that deals over here has their office in Emporia. And, if you've noticed when you go through Emporia, there's lots of new homes and other development going on over there. All due in part to that new Interstate 35 being finished one of these days. Emporia's almost exactly halfway between Topeka and Wichita. Less than two hours to Kansas City when that interstate's done and we can drive like we're going somewhere. Emporia's a good stopping off spot. Motels, gas stations, restaurants, and so on. And there's other new development offering jobs. Not so much here."

"Yeah, I noticed some of that coming back from Kansas City."

"Well, I still have faith in our little towns. A lot of folks just like it out here away from the big cities. And I've always considered myself somewhat of an entrepreneur."

Ray acted like he understood, but wasn't real sure what an entrepreneur was. He nodded in agreement.

"You know what I hear almost every time I show a home here in Cottonwood Falls or Strong City? The wife is almost exclusively the one to say it, 'I wish the kitchen and bath was updated,'. Almost always. Or the husband says, 'I'm gonna have to remodel that kitchen, so will they take a little less for the place?'"

Ralph continued, "You know, there hasn't been a significant new house built here since the early '50's. Oh there's been a few, self-built low-end houses, but nothing that amounts to much. Strong City's even worse. So every time somebody buys, that somebody almost always gets started with a kitchen or a bath remodel. Or both. And, guess what? Both of those rooms require cabinets."

"That's for sure." Ray thought of some of the older homes he'd been in.

"I'm taking on a line of kitchen cabinets. Good company, old established firm out of Ohio. We'll display their top of the line cabinets along the walls and then have the island made out of four less-expensive model base cabinets with a variety of door styles. One end of the island will have a countertop extension with room for four barstools. Did you notice there'll be a refrigerator and a sink and dishwasher, and a space for a microwave? I'm waiting on the price to come down on those as they get more popular."

"Yeah, I saw the note on the plans. My folks have been wanting to get one, but they're waiting until they talk to someone who has one."

"Don't want to be the guinea pigs, huh?"

"That, and like you, they think the price is a little steep."

"Anyway, for now, I'll get a commercial coffeemaker. And I think I'll even start carrying a line of coffee and feature different flavors of the week for customers to try. So then, when Jen's in here doing paperwork, or Mari's working in the summer, maybe we can entice housewives in here to try and buy some coffee. And when they're here, they'll see our line of cabinets and some ideas for remodeling their kitchen or bath."

Ray nodded like he understood all of that, but was still wondering what this had to do with him.

"I'm sure you're wondering why I'm sharing all this with you?"

Ray's eyebrows went up and he nodded.

"I'm gonna need some help kicking off this program. I don't really expect to sell that many cabinets, but If someone in Chase County wants to re-do their kitchen or put in a new bath, I want to at least have a chance at selling them cabinets and maybe even some appliances. Look, I've got very low overhead here. This place is paid for and taxes are low. The

Dennis G. Smith

Hanson Brothers said they'll work with me to get customers a very competitive price for installation and, well, it's kind of an experiment, but I think a lot of customers here will prefer to be loyal to the local hometown guy, especially if my price is reasonable."

Ralph continued, "So that's where you fit in. If I understand what's going on with you right now, you're going to be going back to college next term, starting in January, and you probably have a few things around the ranch you may be wanting to help your father with. I know you're still recovering and will have some physical therapy sessions, but I think you could fit in here on a flexible part-time basis for the next few months to get this new cabinet program going. And I think you're perfect for the role to help attract local customers, you know, local high school sports star, prom king, now an Army hero. You're very well liked around these parts. People might have a hard time saying 'no' to you."

"But I don't know squat about kitchen cabinets. And I'm no Army hero! I'm just a veteran."

"That's the beauty of the timing on this. When I started thinking about this a few months ago, I had no idea you'd be back home. But here you are, and then I thought about your situation and the timing, and well, I think it's perfect. The cabinet manufacturer has a three-day seminar they put on twice a month. I went through it back in June when I agreed to sign up for their program. While this work is getting done, you could go to Ohio for a few days, all expenses paid, and then you'll be ready to go when we have a grand opening on 'Cottonwood Cabinets' or 'Key's Kitchens,' whatever we decide to call it."

Ralph still wasn't finished with his pitch. "You'll be the initial sales person, trained kitchen design 'expert,' and free to set your own hours, make appointments, go out and measure people's homes, help them with their layouts, etcetera. When you go back to school, you could probably still make some calls and help people on weekends if you want. I'm not going to press you on that part. I'm mainly concerned about getting this program kicked off big these next few months."

"This really sounds interesting, but I need to think it over a bit. I've never thought about being a 'salesman'. Can I let you know early next week? I might have a better idea about my physical therapy by then."

"One more thing for you to think about. I'm thinking, when we launch this with a two-week grand opening, I'd want you here as many hours as possible during that time. And it might get pretty boring so I'll pay you four bucks an hour. After that, it will be a straight commission position, five percent on every job you sell. A $4,000 kitchen remodel could put $200 in your pocket. If the Hanson Brothers do the install, you'll get another three percent on their work. Usually, they tell me, the labor on cabinets is about equal to the material cost, so that could be another $120 for you with hardly any additional effort. Well, except for signing the contract. And come the end of the year, first of January, you can be right back on your schedule to go back to college."

Ray didn't know what else to say. He looked back at Mr. Key and finally said, "I guess you've covered everything. I don't know much about selling stuff, but I can learn." Then, once again, he felt it was right to add those words he heard in San Francisco, "You can't beat having a degree."

CHAPTER 19

Monday, September 14, 1970
True Dimensions Cabinets
Findlay, Ohio

Ray was met at the Toledo airport by a young female representative of the True Dimensions Company. She walked him out to the company van where another seminar attendee was waiting. Ray really concentrated on his left leg as he walked beside her. He didn't want her to notice his limp.

Miss Julie Clark explained the schedule during the forty-five minute drive south to Findlay. There would be eight 'students' attending the seminar. The other six were driving from their hometowns to Findlay. The sessions would begin that afternoon after a group lunch with several TDC executives.

She went on to explain the schedule for the following two days and said she would be their driver to and from the motel each day unless they ended up riding with the other students who had cars. "But," she added, "don't hesitate to call on me if you need anything. I'm in the front office. Just tell the receptionist, Gladys, you need to speak to Julie. She'll know where to find me. I'm the Marketing Assistant so that means I do just about anything except making cabinets."

The sessions went well. Ray learned that all the cabinets were made out of the same materials on the sides, top and bottom and back. Particleboard. Only the face frame and doors were different, made of select woods or Formica veneered in a variety of colors. He also learned that base cabinets were a standard two-feet deep - True Dimensions - and wall cabinets were one-foot deep, standard in the industry, with widths in modules of four inches. They all had three ring binders with color brochures and pages with diagrams showing ideal kitchen layouts using the 'kitchen triangle' as a basis for planning. It was important in the layout of the sink, refrigerator, and stove.

On the final day of the training, the company's National Sales Manager came in to speak to the group. He started off by saying, "I know some of you have no experience with kitchen cabinets or bathroom remodels and some of you have no experience with sales." Ray felt like he was talking specifically about him. "When I started my career, I was somewhat like that, but I found out that if you believe in your product, and if you believe that the services you offer are as good or better than anyone else, then it's easy to sell. If down deep in your heart you aren't so sure, then you'll have a tough time convincing buyers to buy from you. They can sense sincerity. We want you to leave here believing, like I do, that True Dimensions offers cabinets that are as good as, or better than, any cabinets around, and we offer them at very competitive prices. Have we convinced you of that?"

The group of trainees wasn't sure exactly how to respond. Some nodded their heads in agreement and some shouted 'Yeah!' Then a couple began to applaud so the rest joined them.

"Okay," the Sales Manager continued, "then you're now equipped and ready to go out and make a living making people happy with their new kitchens and baths. You've got the brochures, you've got the planning kits, and you've got the ability to use your creativity to solve people's remodeling needs. Don't ever think you're not a 'salesman'. How many of you are married?" Most of the hands went up. "You were most likely using your very best sales skills when you asked your wife to marry you. Or was there a shotgun involved?" That drew laughter.

"Remember the first time you asked your father for the family car to go out on a date? You were applying sales skills you didn't know you had, just to convince him that you were old enough, mature enough, and experienced enough as a driver to take that girl out and bring his car back in one piece. As you go through life, you will find more often than you think, that you are constantly using your sales skills. When you get back home from this session and you tell your wife you want to go out for a nice juicy steak, and she hems and haws and talks about having a rough day and being tired, what are you going to do? You're going to tell her, 'Oh, honey, I'm so excited about everything I've learned and I just want to tell you all about it over dinner. You won't have to do a thing! No cooking, no dishes, just you and me and a nice t-bone.' Try it, I know you'll know how to sell her!"

"One more thing to keep in the back of your mind when you're trying to close a deal. If you sense that your customer may not be sure that a kitchen remodel is the right thing to do, ask them this question: When friends or relatives come to visit, where's the first place in the house they always gather? Kitchen, right? You offer them a drink, they'll follow you to the refrigerator. You go to put out some chips and dip, they're gonna be in the kitchen with you. Present your case and you'll see people nodding in agreement. If you can get that nod, you're just one step away from a signed contract.

When the course was finished and Ray was on his flight back to Kansas City, he felt he had absorbed a lot and thought it might be fun helping people plan their new kitchen. And, he believed that trying his skills as a salesman sounded like a good challenge. If it didn't work out, he'd be back in college in a few months; nothing like a degree! What he hadn't thought about was the problems with older homes and understanding load-bearing walls, plumbing vents, electrical service, and gas lines. He had been warned by True Dimensions Cabinets to always get the installer involved early so that problems with those types of things could be resolved before the cabinets were ordered. Being a good salesman might have other advantages. If he ends up following Mari in her career, he should be able to find a sales job wherever they land. *Maybe it's selling cars, carports, or carpets. The secret was letting people know they were about to buy the best that money could buy! Gotta make them believe!*

CHAPTER 20

Friday, October 2, 1970
Key Realty / Key Cabinets - Grand Opening
Cottonwood Falls, Kansas

A week before Ray left for his training session in Ohio, the Hanson Brothers had already knocked out the wall and had done some floor repair in the area where the new 'kitchenette' would be. The day before he left, twelve large boxes from True Dimensions had arrived and were stacked in the back room.

Six days later, two days after his return, Ray headed over to see his new boss and possible future father-in-law to report on his training session. He was surprised to see the cabinets all in place with floor tile being installed. Formica countertops were scheduled to arrive the next day. All that would be left was installing the new ceiling tile, some light fixtures, and the tile backsplash along the wall in the renovated floor space. It was close to being finished and looked great, ready for the grand opening over the upcoming three day weekend.

Ray was there early Friday morning and was placing stacks of brochures with his business cards in three different locations. He helped Ralph replace the 'Coming Soon' sign with a much larger 'Grand Opening' sign in the front window. There was another smaller sign in the other window that said, 'Register To Win $200 Savings.' That gimmick was obviously there to get names and phone numbers of people who are interested in remodeling their kitchens or bath.

Just before 9:00 a.m., Ray asked Ralph how to make coffee in the new commercial coffee pot. He also wanted to know what flavor he should brew. They decided on a French Vanilla and the brewing produced a nice aroma in the eighty-year-old building. Ralph's wife Jennifer showed up right at 9:00 and asked Ray for some help unloading her car. Ray's mind immediately went to *'Here's to you Mrs. Robinson'* as he followed her out the door. She had three trays of homemade brownies, four bags of cookies, some store-bought hard candies, and mints in grocery sacks.

At 10:00 a.m., the three of them were sitting on the bar stools around the brand new kitchen island wondering when the first prospective customer was going to arrive. Ralph said, "Suppose this was a mistake? I can't believe this, considering how many people told me this was a great idea and that they were really looking forward to seeing what I was going to offer."

Jen offered a comment, "I hope these brownies don't go to waste. I probably should have frozen some of them. Otherwise, Mari can take them back to K.U. and share then with her sorority sisters. Those girls will eat them!"

Ray was still a novice to this entrepreneurial business and said, "Hey, it's still early and only Friday. Wait 'til Saturday when people don't have to work."

"That's a good point. I just halfway expected a handful of housewives would be really curious what a new kitchen might look like and would be waiting to knock down the door," Ralph replied and then got up to get another cup of coffee.

Just then his phone rang and he switched directions to get to his desk. When he hung up the phone, he came back to the island and said, "Well that makes me feel a little better."

Jen looked at him and raised her eyebrows, "How's that?"

"That was Mrs. Bean over in Strong City and she said she had just got home from the hardware store where everybody was wondering what time we were going to open. Said she couldn't wait to come see but nobody seemed to know when. I don't remember, but guess I didn't list a time in the ads. Didn't think that would make a big difference."

A shadow passed by the sign in the front window followed quickly by another. The door swung open. It was 10:10 a.m.. The show was on!

At 6:15 p.m., there were still a few stragglers hanging around checking out the cabinets and looking through brochures. Ralph showed Ray the sign-up sheets stuffed in the glass fishbowl, leads he had for follow-up. "Twenty-nine names," he said as he finished counting, "and this is only Friday! But, I noticed more than one couple where both the husband and wife filled out a form. People really want to win that $200 discount!"

Ray chimed in, "One lady brought in three Polaroid pictures of her kitchen and said, 'What can you do with this?' I told her it has lots of possibilities but before we get too carried away, I should bring my installer over to look at the structure of your house and see where load-bearing walls are, and where we can access water, drain lines, gas, and so on."

"That makes sense," she said, "Can you start tomorrow?" Then she laughed. Ray set up an appointment. Before the day was over, he had two appointments for Monday and four more later in the week ahead.

Ray was beat, totally spent. He hadn't been on his feet this long since he left Vietnam. His left leg was aching and he found himself looking for a chance to sit whenever he could. On top of that, the best part of the day for him was when Mari showed up just after 4:00. He knew she was coming home for the weekend and they planned on going out for pizza in Emporia, but now he was thinking they should find something to eat right there at home.

At 6:25, Ralph was turning out lights and thanking his 'team' for their hard work. Mari said they were heading to Emporia to eat and asked her folks if they wanted to come along. She would drive, she offered. She had convinced Ray he was hungry and all he would have to do was sit in the car and choose what kind of pizza he wanted. That sounded good to him!

By Saturday afternoon, business slowed down and Ralph commented that he thought everyone in Chase County that owned a home had been in to see their display by then. But then another couple would wander in and seem really interested and that kept Ray busy. By four o'clock, the front door had stopped moving and Ralph and Jennifer were at his desk having a glass of the champagne they had available for customers during the grand opening. Ray waited dutifully over at the kitchen island. He was thumbing through the chain with all the color samples of Formica, trying to memorize the names.

Just before five, the door opened and a familiar shape walked through. With the late afternoon sunlight shining in the open doorway, Ray couldn't see the face but the silhouette was recognizable. Ray dropped down off his barstool and shouted, "Hey, Buck!" They met in the middle of the office and shook hands and hugged briefly.

"How ya, doin' cowboy?" Buck said.

"I'm okay. Glad to be home."

"I'll bet you are!"

Ray turned toward the Keys watching from the realty office desk, and asked, "You guys remember Eugene Rogers? We call him "Buck". He was my center when we played football."

Ralph stood to shake hands and said, "Oh sure. Your folks still farming out south?"

"Yup. Been there almost thirty years now!"

"Tell them we said hello." Then Ralph realized that's one couple that hadn't been in to see his new venture.

"So, what's up, Buck?" Ray asked. "We haven't seen each other in, what, well over two years?"

"Yeah, probably." Buck replied. Then he turned toward Mr. and Mrs. Key and said, "I had to stop by, I figured this guy misses putting his hands on my ass."

Both Keys laughed and Ray slugged Buck in the upper arm, and said, "You are the only guy that I would automatically recognize bent over from behind." And Ralph and Bev laughed again.

Buck looked at his watch and asked, "Is it quittin' time? I tried to time it right. I brought ol' cowboy here a cold beer out in the truck."

Ralph looked at Ray and said, "Git out of here. You gotta be beat!"

Ray turned to Buck and asked, "You going to drive me home?"

"Well, I can. But you gotta keep your hands to yourself!" Everyone laughed.

"Okay, I'm gone!" Ray grabbed his coat from the hook by the door and the two young men were gone.

Out in Buck's truck, before he turned the key, he opened the small cooler on the floor next to the gearshift and handed Ray an ice cold Old Milwaukee. "Hey, It's not the best beer, but It's cheap." He drove north through Strong City, across the highway and then west towards the cemetery and off on a side road near Fox Creek. He parked facing southwest so they could see the highway and the setting sun. "Man, I'm glad you're home!"

"Same here. It's good to be home!"

"So, what was it like over there? You kill any of those commie assholes?"

'Dirty rotten commie bastards' immediately came to Ray's mind. "No. Well, not that I know of for sure. I certainly shot at some."

"Hey, how could you miss? I always remember you as a real sharpshooter. You'd knock off those prairie dogs right and left."

"Well, those commies were pretty shifty and good at dragging off their dead and wounded, so we didn't always know how many we might have actually hit." He paused, and then, like when he was in

Nam, he added, "But we always came up with a body count."

"So how are you? I heard you got shot up pretty bad."

"Where'd you hear that?"

"Oh, you know, small town. It's been, what, four, five months ago. Word travels."

"I'm getting better. Still got physical therapy to work out. You see how I'm sittin'? Can't turn my head to the left, but I'm working on it."

"That sucks. You were always in such good shape, rodeo, football, basketball."

"Doctors say I should recover completely, *if* I work at it."

"That's good to hear."

"Yeah, I'll be okay again, one of these days."

"You score any of those slant-eyed chicks over there? Remember Will? He came home last year and said the prostitutes were all over the place. Especially in Saigon."

"I really didn't spend much time in Saigon, just flying in and again later when I left. But I wasn't in very good shape flying out and don't remember much about that. Besides, I stayed away from that crap. I had enough trouble wanting to stay alive. I didn't need any diseases to complicate my life."

"Yeah, smart move. I guess that's why you were the quarterback, smarter than the rest of us, huh?

"I don't know about that. So, how'd you avoid getting called up?"

"Flat feet, man! I thought you knew that. That's why I was the center; I can't run for shit. Besides my weight, I just wouldn't make it very far if I had to run. When I got called in by the draft board for a physical, I was prepared. I even had a letter from my podiatrist!"

"So what are doing to keep busy?"

"Helpin' my ol' man run the farm. Our neighbor down there, Wilkerson, gonna retire soon, probably next year, and my dad's gonna buy his farm, or rent it, I don't know. But then Sandy and I can live there, You knew we got married, didn't ya?"

"No, hadn't heard that. Congratulations!"

"Yeah, we're living in that little house on the south side used to belong to that Richardson guy. He worked on oil wells all over the state. Anyway, when my dad gets Wilkerson's place, that'll be mine to manage. I'll have to pay him so much of my profits though, but that's fair."

"Sounds like a good deal."

"Yeah. How about you? I heard you're still goin' with Mari."

"Yup. She was waiting patiently for me to come home. She even came over to Japan to see me when I was in the hospital."

"Wow, that's cool! Good thing you didn't mess with any of those Vietnamese cuties."

"Hey, that reminds me of a funny thing that happened over there. We would get gift boxes every so often from the Red Cross or some kind of charity. And one day we got one from some ladies church group in Illinois or Indiana, can't remember. But it was full of things like stationery, envelopes, decks of playing cards, crackers, and cookies. There was this one small brown paper bag, like a lunch sack with something in it, but it was folded closed and taped shut and someone wrote on the outside, 'To keep your cigarettes dry'. It seemed weird and I think there was four or five of us all gathered round to see what the hell this was all about. We opened it up and it was a box of condoms! Couldn't believe it! We all got a chuckle out of that."

"Man, that's strange! Did anybody actually use them for their *cigarettes*?"

"Don't know, can't remember what happened to them."

Ray and Buck went on reminiscing about their days on the football team, the time Silver Lake really kicked their butts, and the time they almost beat Smith Center. Buck remembered that night because he was really sick, but he still got out there and played and knocked some of those Smith Center guys on their asses. Ray didn't remember that Buck had been sick that game.

When the six pack was gone, Buck slipped his truck into gear and headed for the Reynolds ranch. He said, I'd best be gettin' home to Sandy; she'll have dinner waitin'."

On the short drive to the Reynolds ranch, Ray asked, "So who else is still around?"

"Well, Mick's still here, farming with his dad. Chub Johnson's in Emporia working for a contractor. He still lives here, built an apartment above his parents' garage. Vicky Willis, remember her? Big boobs, she's working down at the courthouse, engaged to Ronnie Fritz. He was a couple years ahead of us. Remember him? There's a few others."

As he got out of Buck's truck, Ray said, "Gosh, it's been really good to see you. We need to get together and take the girls out to dinner sometime over in Emporia."

"Sounds good. I know Sandy would like that."

"Okay. Stay in touch!"

By the end of the weekend, Ray had secured a total of eight good leads from people who said they *definitely* wanted to re-do their kitchen, and they wanted him to come out and put together an estimate. He also found seven more possibles on the sign-in sheets where people had checked, "Call in the next 6 months." Ralph said he had three more people who told him they would be back after they talked things over.

Ray was also surprised at the number of people who had recognized him. Almost everyone said things like, "We're glad you're home," "Good to see you back," "Thanks for your service," and so on. He recognized the faces of some of those people, but for the most part, they knew him as the Bulldogs' quarterback and basketball star.

As he lay in bed Sunday evening, both exhausted and excited about his sales prospects, he realized he had lived a privileged life his first twenty years. Not like a spoiled rich kid, but this was the first time, unless you count the Army, that he had ever worked for a paycheck. Growing up on a ranch, there were always chores to help with, and that started at an early age, not because he was forced to, but because he wanted to be like his father. In the summer, as early as he could remember, he would try to follow his dad around and ask if he could help. During the school year, as soon as he hopped off the school bus and greeted his dog, King, a German Shepard (prior to getting Rex years later), he would run into the house and ask his mother where his dad was. If his father was anywhere close, he would be there with him seeing what he could do to help.

He never got a paycheck for his work on the ranch because it was his duty as part of the family. But he couldn't remember a time that he had to ask for money, or that he wanted something important that he couldn't have. His parents were his biggest supporters. When he turned 16, they let him have the old Ford pick-up to drive to school. No more school bus. But they did make sure he kept up with chores around the ranch so he would have gas money.

It wasn't like he never had to work. It was just different work. Besides helping with the chores and odd jobs around the barnyard, he worked hard at staying in shape for football, often running down the side of the highway to the rodeo grounds and back, a little over six miles round trip, sometimes at 5:00 a.m. before he started his chores. He worked hard before basketball season shooting baskets at his hoop on the side of the barn. When he was a freshman, his father moved the backboard to the front of the barn above the sliding door and had a twenty foot square concrete pad put in to give Ray a better practice area. Some days he would shoot baskets from the time he got off the school bus until he was called for dinner. He often worked on free throws and counted the number he made out of one hundred shots. His best was the day he made eighty-six. That day he had to apologize to his mother for being late to dinner. He was on a streak, he told her, couldn't stop.

So, Ray knew what hard work was all about.

Now, he lay there worn out from standing on his feet most of the three-day grand opening. *There's something wrong with this,* he thought to himself. *I just got out of the Army. I'm only twenty years old. I shouldn't be worn out like this. Yeah, I was wounded, but I'm mostly healed, and I know what exercises I need to be doing. I've got to get back in shape!* He realized the single shot wound and the months of recovery had taken more out of him than he thought. *Time to get back to work!*

Once again, Ray lay there awake thinking how that one bullet from an unseen sniper had nearly ruined his life in a war that he really wanted no part of. But politics drove him there. He knew he was much better off than so many others who were wounded, or killed, and thinking of them pissed him off even more. He wanted to do something, but what? He wished he could do something, but what? *You have to live with what life gives you. Play the cards you're dealt.* 'Dirty rotten Commie bastards!'.

CHAPTER 21

Monday, October 12, 1970
Reynolds Ranch
Strong City, Kansas

A week after the grand opening, the afternoon mail included two government envelopes addressed to Ray Reynolds. One contained two checks, one for his last month of service in Vietnam, and the other for the three months of 'duty' served at Camp Zama in Japan. That was a pleasant surprise. The other was a letter that said he would be receiving his Purple Heart commendation within the next few days. It arrived the following day.

He also received mail that week from the Veterans Administration which included specific instructions to show up for a follow-up evaluation at the Veterans Administration Medical Center in Topeka, Kansas on November 12 at 0930 hours.

He told his mother about the two checks and said, "Maybe I should buy a new car, except I can't drive!" *'Dirty rotten Commie bastard!'* he thought to himself. He still had the old Ford pick-up parked in the barn. Then he told her about the appointment with the V.A. and asked her if she'd be able to drive him.

"Of course. What day is it? I'll put it on our calendar." She pulled a pen out of the kitchen junk drawer and turned the wall calendar to November when Ray gave her the date.

Then Ray had an idea. "Maybe we could make a full day of it. If I can get an appointment with a counselor at K-State for that afternoon, could we drive on to Manhattan?"

"Sure," she replied without hesitation. "So you're getting serious about going back to school? Good for you. Any way I can help, I will."

CHAPTER 22

Thursday, November 12, 1970
Veterans Administration Medical Center
Topeka, Kansas

Ray and his mother arrived at the VA Medical Center a half hour earlier than Ray's appointment. That gave them ample time to find a place to park and locate the registration desk. After checking in, they waited in a large lobby until Ray was called back to a separate internal waiting room. He told his mother he had no idea how long he'd be, and she nodded and said, "I know, Ray, I know!"

According to the large round government clock on the wall, it was almost thirty minutes after his appointed time before they called Ray's name. This time he was taken into a small exam room where he waited again. No clock on the wall and Ray wished he had a watch. He decided then and there that he would use some of his Army money to buy one. Maybe one of those new digital watches that had just come out a year or two earlier. Then he remembered that they were priced somewhere around $2,000 and that idea went away real quick. He'll get a Timex that *'takes a licking and keeps on ticking.'*

The more he stared at a blank wall and thought about time, the more pissed he got. He never liked waiting. During his days as quarterback of the Bulldogs, he was quick to call his signals and only waited when they wanted to try and pull the opponents offsides. When he barrel raced at the rodeo, he waited right up to the last few seconds to mount Gabby because he didn't want his horse to sense his tension, or to get bored waiting to run. Now he's stuck just sitting and the only magazines in the room were some medical journals. He also felt sorry for his mother. He should have told her to go shopping.

Finally, after what seemed like another half-hour, a doctor walked in with, presumably, Ray's report in his hand. Ray said, "What time is it?"

The doctor looked at his watch and said, "It's just past 10:45."

"Yeah, I thought my appointment was for 9:30?"

The doctor didn't respond at first and was still looking at Ray's records, but then said, "Sorry, we can't control the needs of other patients before you. Please remove your jacket and shirt." After looking at both the entrance and exit wounds, he examined the scarring from the surgery site and then asked, "How's the paralysis? Have you been doing your therapy exercises?"

Ray responded, "Not as often as I should, but I'm getting back to helping around the ranch and that gives me plenty of exercise."

"Let's see you lift your left arm."

Ray grimaced a little as he raised the arm up even to his shoulder level.

"Is that as high as you can go?"

"Pretty much. It's better than when I left Japan."

"I think you should be doing better than that by now."

"I was shot!" Ray retorted. *'Dirty rotten Commie bastard!'*, He didn't say it, but he thought it!

"Let's see you stand." Ray stood and Dr. Gordon opened the door since there wasn't room for more than two short steps inside the room. "Take a short walk down the hall for me."

Ray wasn't sure if he should concentrate and do his best not to limp, or just relax and let the doctor decide. He started by walking as straight as possible, but when the doctor said, "Okay, come back," Ray relaxed and let his left foot turn in slightly and his limp began.

"Well, that could be better, too!"

Ray said, "It depends a lot on how tired I am."

"It's still morning. Did you get a good night's sleep last night?"

"Yeah. It was okay. But then I've just been sitting here for over an hour!"

The doctor motioned for Ray to sit up on the table and he began a series of reflex tests on his knees, ankles and feet. Then he checked Ray's neck and asked him to turn his head, first right and then left. When Ray couldn't do more than about ten degrees to the left, the doctor said, "That's a concern!"

Ray replied, "I know. I can't *drive* like this! Pisses me off! Dirty rotten Commie bastard!"

The doctor scribbled some notes on the report sheet he had on his clipboard. "Wait here. Someone will come get you."

There he was, waiting again. His poor mother.

About five minutes later, a nurse in slacks and a smock opened the door and said, "Hi, Sergeant Reynolds, I'm Jane Sutton, a physical therapist. I'm here to see what we can do for you."

Ray was anxious to get out of there, and said, "I know the exercises I'm supposed to be doing, and I really don't want to drive up here very often just to have someone show me what I already know. So, is there anything new that you can do that I can't do on my own?"

"Probably not. I got a couple of sheets of exercises to show you with notes on how many reps you should be doing. This is information that came with your files from Camp Zama." She handed him the pages.

Ray glanced at the sheets of paper and the diagrams of the exercises and thought it looked a whole lot like the pages he got with his discharge papers from Japan. "I'm already doing most of these, just not as often as I should."

"Well, let's do this. Considering the distance, my information and contact number is on the first page. If you find you're having trouble or not seeing the improvement we expect, please give me a call and we'll set up an appointment. Otherwise, according to the analysis from the doctors at Camp Zama, they expect you should heal up in time as the nerves in your back get better, but you have to keep up the exercises so your muscles will cooperate with your healing timetable. Fair enough?"

"Fine by me. Thanks for your help."

"Good. Wait right here. Dr. Gordon wants you to be seen by one more doctor before you leave."

"Really?"

"Yup, really!"

Oh crap!

It wasn't a long wait this time. After only a few minutes, a young nurse with a pretty smile showed up and said, "Sergeant Reynolds?"

Ray reacted to her smile with a quizzical smile of his own and said, "Not anymore. Just call me Ray now."

She said, "Well, you'll still show up as a Sergeant in our records. Thanks for your service, and, I'm sorry you were wounded."

She led him down two different hallways to a different part of the hospital to another small room with a desk and two chairs. "Doctor Gordon wanted you to see Doctor Zehr before you go. She'll be with you shortly."

"Okay. Thank you." They exchanged smiles.

Now he was waiting again. He wondered what time it was. It had to be going on noon. If it got to be much later, he'd be late for his appointment at the university.

He started counting to sixty so he'd realize how long a minute was without a clock, and then he wondered if that would allow him to guess how long he was left sitting in this tiny cramped office. He wondered what would happen if he just left. Could he find his way back to the main lobby? Surely there were signs that would guide him. His letter from the V.A. didn't say anything about seeing two doctors. Just as he was about to get up enough nerve to leave there was a light knock on the door. A good looking woman with Farrah Fawcett hair and wearing a white lab coat entered the room.

Oh well, guess it was worth the wait! Ray wondered what she would be doing to examine him. *Do I need to remove my shirt?*

She stuck out her right hand, "I'm Dr. Zehr. I typically like to interview veterans to see how they are adjusting mentally after leaving a war zone. Dr. Gordon noted that you may have some latent anger issues. How are you feeling now that you're home?"

"Oh, I'm feeling okay, pretty good actually. I think that doctor realized I was pretty upset over sitting around waiting so long. I was supposed to have a 9:30 appointment. What time is it now?"

"It's five til noon. You have been here a long time. Unfortunately, that's the nature of our business these days. There are so many wounded veterans. Both physically and mentally. Do you feel like you are suffering from any mental fatigue?"

"No." It was hard for him to respond negatively to this pretty woman. Whatever anger issues he was having, they went away, and he wasn't going to discuss them with her anyway. "It's just that my mother has been sitting out in the lobby now for almost three hours," he exaggerated.

"Sleeping okay?"

"Yeah, pretty much."

"No nightmares?"

"Oh," he hesitated. "Not since I left Camp Zama in Japan. Do you know that place?"

"Yes, we get lots of veterans who have been processed through there. How did you like it there?"

"Oh, it was okay, considering. They treated everyone good. As good as could be expected under the circumstances."

'What did you mean, 'considering'?"

"Well, considering what we were there for, it was okay, nice, really, for a hospital."

"Why do you suppose you had the nightmares?"

"Only one. It started out about the sniper who shot me, but then another incident from Nam entered in. Something my platoon leader said. And, ah, wait," This woman's presence made him stutter. "I remembered wrong. It wasn't, or no, it didn't happen at Camp; no wait. Let me start over."

"Sure, go ahead."

He paused, took a breath, and began again. "The dream was *about* Camp Zama, but I had the dream the first few days after I got home. I dreamed I was back there but then all the beds were full of North Vietnamese Army soldiers and they all started criticizing me for talking about the guy who shot me. I guess I had referred to him as some kind of rotten Commie. That was something I heard my platoon leader say after we had killed one of them. All the people in my dream started calling me that, dirty rotten Commie bastard. It woke me up. But it hasn't happened since."

"How do you feel about the war now that you've experienced it and been harmed by it?

"Well, I *never* liked it. Even before I went over there. But I felt I was doing my duty, you know, serving my country." He looked at her and smiled. "Just like you."

"Yes, but have your thoughts about that changed?

"Yeah, now I *really* don't like it. To see all the battles and the guys carried off in the medevacs. I don't remember mine after they loaded me up and my buddy Bill said something about seeing me back stateside. I hate that war. We shouldn't be there. We have no business there!"

"You don't believe we should try and stop communism?"

"Have you been there? I don't think the South Vietnamese worry about it that much. At least that's the way they act most of the time. Maybe it's cause they're too afraid of losing their life if they say something negative about the North. I don't know, but it's a little country halfway around the world. And we're losing guys right and left to try and defend people who don't really give a shit. There, that's how I feel now! Sorry, pardon my French."

"That's okay. Listen, Ray, I'd like to see you again in a few months, maybe after the holidays sometime in January. Here's my card which gives you a direct line to my office and my assistant will help set up an appointment. Will that be okay with you?"

"Yeah, I guess." He couldn't say no to this woman, but he added, "I'm planning on going back to college on the G.I. Bill starting in January. Actually, my mother's waiting out there to take me up to Manhattan when we leave here. I can't drive because of my neck and that's the worst thing that's bothering me." He reached over the desk and took her card.

"Sergeant Reynolds, you stay healthy, okay." She glanced down at the reports on her desk and thumbed through a couple of pages. "Do your exercises. It looks like your prognosis is good and your arm and leg are both better than when you left Zama. It just takes time."

"Dr. Zehr," he asked as he looked at her card, "Why am I seeing you? A psychologist?"

"Two reasons. The V.A. really wants to know the effects war has on soldiers so we have to ask questions from the guys who experienced it first hand. And the other reason, we want to try and help the ones who experience negative effects from the war. That might include you.

We won't know until we check with you over time."

"Shouldn't that include everybody? I really can't imagine too many people who don't experience negative effects from war."

"Well, you're right. However, we have limited resources. So, we have to pick and choose to get a broad spectrum of those who have been there, done that, and we want to talk to people who will be bluntly honest with us about what's going on in their lives after they come home. I think you'll be a good candidate."

"Really?"

"Yes, you seem very open and honest. I'm also worrying that your one nightmare could just be the beginning. I hope not. Let me give you a brochure so you can read up on PTSD."

"PTSD?"

"Yes. Post Traumatic Stress Disorder. I'd like you to read up on this and you don't have to participate in the study if you don't want to, but I'd really like to see you at least one more time in January. All right?"

"All right. I hope I can drive by then."

"Me too. Good luck! Don't forget your exercises."

CHAPTER 23

Thursday, November 12, 1970
Kansas State University Office of the Registrar
Manhattan, Kansas

Despite all the delays and reviews at the V.A. Medical Center in Topeka, Mrs. Reynolds still got her son to the university in Manhattan on time. The difference was that they didn't have time to stop for lunch. As they arrived in Manhattan, she pulled into a gas station and Ray used the restroom and bought a Payday salted nut roll candy bar and a Dr. Pepper to tide him over. Ray knew where the building to register was from his previous time there. When his mother dropped him off, he told her to go get some lunch and pointed to a parking lot where he would look for her later.

Inside, he announced his name to the receptionist and said he had an appointment with a counselor. The receptionist pointed at a seating arrangement and said, "He'll be with you shortly."

While he was waiting again, he thought about the conversation he had with his mother on the drive to 'The Little Apple.' He purposefully brought up the fact that while he had only a small exposure to doing sales work with Mr. Key and the kitchen cabinet program, he found it interesting and exciting to think that he felt like he was going to close two sales, if his intuition was right. He felt good about them.

He also told her that the short training session he had in Ohio actually inspired him to try his best at selling cabinets, or anything, as far as that goes. He didn't quite have the heart to come right out and tell her that he was going to talk to the college counselor about studying Marketing. He figured that after his session with the counselor, he would be better able to break that news to her and then let her tell his dad that the college plan only included some elective courses in agriculture or ranching related courses like cattle feeding and breeding. As he was formulating this plan, the comment from Vonnegut came back to haunt him, *'Son', my father said to me, 'someday this will all be yours.'* He didn't want to be the one to break this news to his father. He was hoping he could make it make sense to his mother and she would understand. Then she could tell his father in her own way. Maybe for this first term back, he could say he was taking a variety of courses just to get back in the groove and see how things developed from there.

On the other hand, Ray had thought about this before. Maybe his folks had three kids for a reason. It could be Chip, or maybe even June, that ends up taking over the ranch. As he considered that, something inside felt funny. He vaguely remembered thinking about the future of the ranch before and when he did, he thought about Chip and June. He now recognized the same feeling, sort of queasy, upset, but not really sick. Could it be jealousy? Surely not. He'd always only wanted the best for his younger siblings. But then. The ranch?

On the ride home, his mother wanted to know how his meeting went and if he was excited about returning to school.

Ray really wasn't prepared to break the news about planning a degree in Marketing, so he kept his comments simple and said, "It went okay. I don't know if I'd say I was excited, but I'm kind of looking forward to getting a degree so I can get on with my life."

"Did you select any classes for your first term back?"

"Yeah, just kind of some general stuff to get me started again. You know it's been three years since I last opened a book to study."

"So, what type of general courses will you be taking?"

Ray thought this might be the easy way to break the news, but chose instead to just downplay it for now. He actually led with what he figured she would most like to hear. "Oh, there's a course on basic Animal Science. I think it leads into breeding and diet and stuff like that."

His mother quickly picked up on that. "That sounds interesting and right up your alley!"

"I was told I have to have so many credits in English and I already have four from three years ago. I didn't really like English 101 and the counselor talked me into a Creative Writing course. And again, for general subjects, I need so many credits in sciences so I signed up for Chemistry class. Just for fun, and what I think will be an easy course, I enrolled in Marketing 101." There he said it.

"Oh, that sounds interesting, and quite a variety."

"Yup. That's me - variety!"

CHAPTER 24

Friday, November 13, 1970
Key Realty - Key Cabinets
Cottonwood Falls, Kansas

Ralph had called Ray at home just before 8:00 a.m. and told him he would be attending a breakfast meeting but would leave the back door unlocked for him. He also shared that he had some good news. He left him a note on the new kitchen counter display for Ray to call Mrs. Johanson. They are ready to order a full kitchen remodel but want to meet with you again to make a couple of minor changes. "Looks like you've got your first sale! Congratulations, Ray!"

Ray's mother dropped him off and he opened up the back door to the Real Estate / Cabinet Sales office just before 9:00 a.m. and began turning on lights.

Then he started to brew a fresh pot of coffee. He selected a Vanilla Hazelnut and dumped the beans into the grinder, then into the brewing filter. He wondered what the hell a 'hazelnut' was, but knew he liked vanilla. There was a crazy teacher from grade school named Hazel and Ray figured the coffee could easily have been named after her. He'd have to ask his mother if she knew anything about a hazelnut, and if there was any possibility that it was named after Hazel Watson. His mother would get a laugh out of that!

Once the coffee was brewing, Ray looked for the note with Mrs. Johanson's phone number but couldn't find it. He went to Ralph's desk and looked there. Nope. Back to the kitchen area where he circled around the island. There it was on the floor. He guessed that when he turned on the display lights, the ceiling fan came on and the note blew off the counter.

Dennis G. Smith

He went to the spare desk up front used occasionally by Mrs. Key and Mari when she was home for more than a weekend, and dialed up the number. What a nice lady. Ray guessed she and her husband had to be in their early fifties. Mr. Johanson was a vice president of a bank in Emporia but they preferred living in Cottonwood Falls for the peace and quiet of the country.

Ray was asked if he could come by the house, anytime today would be fine, so Mrs. Johanson could show him the two items they wanted to change. "Then," she said, "my husband will be ready to sign a contract."

Ray explained his situation that his boss was at a breakfast meeting and he would need to stay in the office until he returned but thought he could be over to her house by 10:30 a.m. Actually, Mr. Key had told Ray he could leave whenever he needed to, just use the sign in the window that says '*Will Return By* ____,' and fill in the time. However, Ray was still not driving so he would need Ralph to drop him off at the Johanson residence. He had been using Ralph, Jen, or his mother to ferry him back and forth to various appointments at potential clients' homes. Usually, depending on the location, he would get dropped off at the designated time; then, when he was finished gathering information and taking measurements, he would walk back to the office. He needed the exercise and Cottonwood Falls wasn't that big. Strong City was even smaller and the two towns were just a mile apart.

He met with Mrs. Johanson and pulled out the sketch he had made of their new kitchen. The two things they wanted to change included making the wall cabinet above the refrigerator a 24" deep cabinet instead of a standard 12" depth. Mrs. Johanson said she'd have to drag out a step stool to use that shallow cabinet above the refrigerator, and that didn't make sense. Ray noted that there was no cabinet currently above the refrigerator so he was a little surprised that she thought of that. He told her he would have to look into that because he didn't recall True Dimensions offering anything but 12" deep wall cabinets.

"But," he told her, "we can always order a custom cabinet, or Hanson Brothers can modify a base cabinet to make it work. We'll figure it out."

The other request was to move the dishwasher to the left of the sink and switching the cabinet that was there to the right of the sink. "Just the old switcheroo," she said. "That shouldn't be a problem, should it?"

Ray looked at his notes and then pulled out his tape measure and took a quick measurement.

"Well, there is a problem," and he showed her the kitchen layout plan. "That cabinet is a 20" cabinet. The dishwasher requires 24", so the sink cabinet will have to move 4" to the right."

"Is that a problem?"

"Your sink will not be centered under your window."

"Four inches, is that gonna be noticed?"

"Where the faucet comes up might make it noticeable. The sink we have planned is pretty big. We could just get a slightly smaller sink. Then the only issue would be the sink is not centered in the cabinet, but I doubt many people would notice that."

Mrs. Johanson thought for a minute, trying to picture it in her mind.

Ray asked what he thought was the obvious question. "What's your reason for wanting the 'switcheroo'?"

"Oh, it's silly really," she said. "I'm left handed and I'm afraid it will feel awkward to me loading the dishwasher with my right hand. I was hoping we could change that. I've never had a dishwasher before. I'm so excited."

Now Ray was at a loss for solutions. She would need to make a decision. So what he thought was going to be his first sale was hung up on two decisions. He hadn't told Mrs. Johanson yet, but he was worried about too much weight in a 24" wall cabinet could pull it loose from the wall. He needed to talk to one of the Hanson brothers. The decision was ultimately up to her, or them, depending on how much say her husband has on the kitchen design.

Damn! He was hoping to have a signed contract by evening along with a deposit. Or at least a positive verbal agreement that he could report back to Ralph.

Mrs. Johanson said the words he was expecting. "Let me talk this over with Bob tonight when he gets home and I'll give you a call in the morning."

Double Damn!

As he was heading out the door, Mrs. Johanson thanked him for coming and then added, "I sure hope you continue to heal all right. It's so good you're home. We need more nice young men like you here in our little town. I'll be praying for you."

Walking back to the office, Ray sensed a car slowing down behind him. When he heard the sound right beside him, he had to turn his whole body to the left to see who it was. He didn't know her first name, but recognized her as Patty Wilson's mother. Patty was one of the cheerleaders in his high school class, and her mother attended all the basketball games.

"Oh, hi Mrs. Wilson," he said as she reached over to roll down the passenger window.

"Hi, Ray. It's so nice to see you back home. Would you like a ride?"

"Well, actually, walking is part of my physical therapy exercises. I'm trying to get back where I can maybe jog once in a while."

"Oh, come on Ray. I'm going right uptown anyway. Hop on in here. It's cold out there!"

It was hard to say 'no' to a nice lady's invitation, so Ray climbed in, and the heater felt good. It was a short conversation before she pulled up in front of Key Realty / Key Cabinets, but she managed to fill Ray in on Patty's updates. It seemed like one long continuous sentence.

"You know Patty's up at K.U. where Mari's at, but she's not in one of those sorority houses, she's in the dorms and she likes it there with a good roommate, the same one now for her third year, neither of 'em has a steady boyfriend so they go out a lot together, football, basketball and so on, you know how good the Jayhawks are at basketball, it should be a good season. I really hope you're doing well. It's so good to see you!"

"Yes, same here. Thanks for the ride!"

"Oh anytime. Let me know if I can help you out."

Ray crossed the sidewalk and entered the old stone building. Something was really bothering him about that short conversation. He went inside and filled Ralph in on the upcoming purchase from the Johanson's.

Later that afternoon, Bev Reynolds popped into the office and asked her son if he was ready to go home. She looked over at Ralph to see if that was okay. Ralph shrugged his shoulders and said, "Up to him."

Ray had been making some follow-up phone calls in order to get appointments and he was working on a kitchen layout for the widow Lydia Swanson. Lydia's husband had left her with a nice life insurance settlement. No one in town knew how much, but everyone talked like it was 'a lot!'. It seemed like that rumor may have slipped through the lips of the pastor at the Methodist church, but again, no one knew for sure.

"Yup," Ray responded to his mother. She had just picked up a few groceries and was headed home.

His mother asked him how his day had been and Ray somberly replied, "Okay." She asked about the expected contract and he said,

"Not yet, probably tomorrow. They have to make some decisions and I'm waiting on a call back from the Hansons to see if we can hang a 24" cabinet on the wall."

Beverly didn't quite understand all of that, but she did sense Ray's disappointment. What she didn't know was that Ray was still excited about the pending contract. His quiet mood stemmed from the short ride with Mrs. Wilson. He couldn't quite figure out why that was bothering him, so he thought, *maybe, if I tell my mother about it, I'll figure out what's wrong.*

"Remember Patty Wilson in my class? She was a cheerleader. Kind of short, blond."

"Yeah, I remember Patty. She always seemed happy, even when we were losing the game."

"That's Patty! Her mother picked me up and gave me a ride back to the office today. Talked a mile a minute. So, I'm all caught up on news about Patty. Her mother's nice."

"Yeah, I don't really know her. I know who she is if I see her, but we've never been close. That was nice of her to give you a ride."

That was it. Ray didn't say anything else. His mother didn't have anything to add. But he was still puzzled by the fact something about his conversation with Mrs. Wilson bothered him.

He tried replaying it in his head. It was all one-sided. She did all the talking so he was pretty sure he didn't say anything to embarrass himself, yet that was sort of how he felt. He tried remembering the conversation again. It had been all about Patty. She did mention Mari and the fact Patty lived in the dorms, not like Mari in a *'sorority house.'* Could that be bothering him? He thought about it and remembered she didn't say it like that, it was just sort of matter of fact. It had to be something else. It seemed like it hit him after he got out of the car. The ride had been pleasant enough, and he was okay listening to a woman talk about her daughter, a girl he knows. What was it?

And then, on top of that, he remembered Mrs. Johanson's last words, *'I'll be praying for you.'* Was that part of what was bothering him?

His mother pulled into the driveway and stopped in front of the two-car garage. Ray got out and told his mother he was going to his room and started for the house. Then he remembered his mother had gotten groceries and returned back to the car and grabbed the two bags from the back seat before she could.

"I can get those," his mother said, but Ray already had them. He had to use his right hand to put the first bag into his left hand and then picked up the other bag, again with his right hand.

"I've got 'em, if you'll open the door." The strange feeling was still there and now he felt closer to figuring it out. He set the bags on the kitchen counter and again told his mother he would be in his room for a little bit.

He got to his room and closed the door. He dropped down on the bed and stared up at the ceiling. Now it was what his mother just said - *'I can get those.'* He had been raised on this ranch knowing that he was expected to help with things and he almost forgot to carry in the groceries. But his mother didn't say *'thank you;'* she said *'I can get those.'* It was almost as though she didn't think he was capable, or, maybe she was worried he might hurt himself. So what was it with Mrs. Wilson? *That's it!* He remembered when he got out of the car she said, *'Let me know if I can help you out.'* All of a sudden, he's wondering about a lot of things. *Everyone thinks ol' Ray is a wounded veteran and we have to show our respect and be kind to him. He's walking everywhere and kind of limps and we need to help the poor boy out. Mrs. Johanson is praying for me! Shit! Did Mr. Key have that attitude when he gave me the job? Why isn't my dad asking me for more help around the barn? Why would his mother say 'I can get those?'*

He laid there another five minutes trying to think of other examples that he might not have noticed. He wondered if some of the interested cabinet buyers just came to the grand opening to see the side show - *the former quarterback now a wounded veteran home from the war? They just came to give me some sympathy. They no longer respect me; they feel sorry for me!*

That is what's wrong. I'm going on 21 and I'm back in my hometown and people see me walking everywhere. I used to be the quarterback, and I averaged over 16 points a game in basketball. Almost all of my classmates are gone, moved on, or they've settled in as farmhands and realize that's their destination in life. That's it! I've got to change this. I've wasted too much time not getting well. I've got to do the exercises and even more. I'm going to start driving again. It's silly, I can turn my body to see left when I need to and the pick-up's got outside mirrors. I'm not gonna be nobody's baby, or their war hero! I wanna go back to being the high school quarterback and basketball team captain. Fuck that war shit! I don't need a purple heart medal, it just makes it obvious I'm a cripple! I'm through with the soldier crap! I don't need the V.A.. What the hell are they gonna do? All the thoughts racing through his brain suddenly paused and he felt a slight change in his attitude. *Well, I might go back to see Dr. Zehr.*

Suddenly, he was all upset and determined at the same time. He was going to change things, make them better. He got up and went to the kitchen. "You need help with fixin' dinner?" he asked his mother.

"No, not that I can think of. Maybe you can set the table later, although June usually does that."

"Okay, then I'm gonna change into some sweats and go shoot some hoops."

"Good for you. You sure you're okay to do that? It's cold out there."

There it is again. "I don't know, I'll find out. And I've got to talk to dad about the pick-up when he gets home. Where is he anyway?"

"Said he had some business at the bank. He should be home anytime unless he stopped for a beer and a visit with some of the guys. You know how that goes. I'm making a tater-tot casserole so go work up an appetite. But don't overdo it!"

There she goes again. Now I'm probably going to notice little comments like that all the time. Crap!

Ray had just started shooting baskets when his siblings got off the school bus. June walked halfway over toward the barn and said, "Are you supposed to be doing that?"

"Yes I am! It's my life!"

"Oh. Don't hurt yourself!" And she left towards the house.

Ray heard that and almost didn't believe his ears. *Oh my God, I didn't realize it was this bad. Have I just been overlooking it?*

Chip shouted at him from the back door of the house, "Let me change clothes and I'll come out to play a game of horse."

Ray waved back at him. At least Chip didn't say anything. What Ray didn't know was that Chip figured maybe he'd be able to beat his older brother now that he'd been wounded.

At dinner that night, Ray asked his dad what he would have to do to get the pick-up running again. Walt told his son he had been taking it out for a spin every couple of weeks or so just to keep the battery charged, and when they heard Ray might be coming home, he had it lubed and the oil changed. "Should be ready to go," he said.

"Are you thinking about driving again?" his mother asked.

"Yeah, I'm not sure why I was so afraid to try it. My leg is strong enough to push the clutch so I don't think that'll be a problem. And I can turn at the waist to see left, plus the truck's got good side view mirrors."

"I just hope you'll be careful."

Oh, Jeez, I'm almost 21 and still living at home. I think I'll really be glad to get back in school, away from here for awhile. I love my family, but oh my God!

Ray didn't sleep well that night, constantly tossing and turning. First it was trying to remember something he was going to tell his mother that was funny. Or at least funny to him, but he really thought she'd get a kick out of it. *What was it? It happened that morning at work, early on. It had something to do with grade school. Not Mrs. Wilson or her daughter Patty. I already told her about that conversation. Mrs. Wilson, she's part of the reason I can't sleep - 'Let me know if I can help you out' - Yeah, don't ever offer me a ride again! Up yours, bitch! Ah, shit! Now why am I thinking that way, it's not her fault. She's a nice enough lady. 'Hop on in here. It's cold out there.'*

Then mom has to tell me 'It's cold out there' when I went to shoot buckets'. What do they expect? It's November in Kansas.

Where was I? I'm tryin' to think of something else. I need to get some sleep. 'Don't hurt yourself!' Crap!

Coffee! It was the coffee! Hazelnut! How can I remember to tell Mom about that? When I get my first cup of coffee in the morning I'll think of it. Yeah, that'll work.

I'll have to get even with Chip before dinner tomorrow, I can't let him beat me at horse again. That little shit! He's been practicing since I've been gone.

I've got to get widow Swanson's estimate finished and get with her. If she's got all that insurance money, she'll buy. Her kitchen really does need it. I should get up early and go in. I need to wash the pick-up if I'm gonna drive it. When can I do that?

On and on it went. He couldn't figure out how to stop all the thoughts. Just when he thought he was through and might finally doze off, he'd think of something else or he'd hear a voice telling him something he didn't really want to hear. Like the beautiful Dr. Zehr with all the hair said, *'Dr. Gordon noted that you may have some latent anger issues.' What the hell does that mean, 'latent anger issues'? And what's this PSTD, or PDST, or whatever acronym crap they were talking about? BS, that's one I know!*

Crap, I'll never get to sleep.

Ray finally managed to sleep by forcing himself to think about taking a day's ride on Gabby out to the prairie dogs' towns and just sit at a distance and watch their antics. Sunday, he thought, would be a good day for that. The forecast was for cold, but above freezing by noon and close to forty for the high. He'd dig out his thermals and wear the new hooded K-State sweatshirt he'd bought when they were in Manhattan.

CHAPTER 25

Saturday, November 14, 1970
Key Realty / Key Cabinets
Cottonwood Falls, Kansas

Ray parked his pick-up in a diagonal space on Broadway just a few spaces down from the stone office building. He didn't want to take up potential customer spaces directly in front of the business, but he did want to park out front so people who knew him would recognize that he was driving again. It was a new day. He had noticed the kitchen calendar before he left the ranch and although he wasn't superstitious, he noticed that his bad day the day before had been Friday the 13th.

Driving in, he thought to himself that if someone says something like, *'I'll be praying for you'* or *'Let me know if I can do anything for you'*, he would simply answer, "I appreciate the sentiment, but I'm fine," and he would try not to sound angry when he said it.

After work, he had decided, he was going to start an exercise routine every day, or at least every other day. Initially, he would push himself to last thirty minutes and then build it up to an hour, instead of just doing some exercises when he felt like it. Like it or not, he realized he had to do it!

And he still had his plan to saddle up Gabby about noon on Sunday and go watch the prairie dogs. If it was sunny and bright as forecast, and near forty degrees, they would be out. He needed the peace and solitude for an afternoon.

Mari finally did call and said she wasn't feeling that great and hoped she'd be better later in the day. Ray told her of his plan to go riding and she said, "Have fun."

CHAPTER 26

Saturday, December 26, 1970
Reynolds Ranch
West of Strong City, Kansas

"If you're still not feeling well when I get back," he told her, "there's always college football to watch."

It was almost 11:30 and Ray had gone to his room to put on his thermals and get ready for a ride when he heard Rex barking. He went back into the front room to look outside to see what the dog was so excited about and saw an unfamiliar car pulling up to the house. It had Nebraska plates. Ray went to the front door and stepped out onto the porch. There was a glare from the sun off the windshield and he couldn't tell who was behind the wheel or even if there was more than one person inside. Then the door opened and a tall man wearing a Nebraska cap and a heavy sweatshirt stepped out. He recognized him immediately. It was Bill Bill.

Ray took two quick steps off the porch and ran with a slight limp to greet his buddy from Nam. Rex was enjoying the excitement and continued barking. By then, Ray's mother had come to the front door and looked out and his father was heading their direction from the barn to see who this stranger was.

"I told you I'd look you up!" Bill Williams said to his old pal. "How you doin', Wildcat?"

Ray waved his mother out and as she walked up, his dad had also reached the growing group. "Mom, Dad, this is 'Bill Bill'," he paused, "Bill Williams from Lincoln, my good buddy from the war. Remember, I told you the last thing I heard before I passed out in the medevac chopper was Bill here saying 'I'll look you up back in the Midwest'." Then he turned to Bill and added, "Hey, man, you didn't forget!"

Bill reached out to shake everyone's hand as Chip and June both came out to see what the commotion was all about. Even Rex jumped up on Bill to say hello. Then Bill reached out to Ray to shake again and pulled him closer for a hug, and said, "God, it's good to see you! I have to tell you this was a scary trip down here for me."

"Scary? What? Why?", Ray asked.

"I left home this morning, knowing how to get to Strong City. I remembered that name and all your talk about the place. I'd looked it up in the atlas and knew where I was going. But, I didn't know what I'd find. You were in bad shape the last time I saw you and I never knew if you made it or not. I was worried I'd be coming down here and be bringing sad memories to your folks. But, I can tell now," as his voice cracked and he paused, "you're one tough son of a gun!" He reached over and gave Ray a slap on the back and another man hug. He might have used more colorful 'Army' language, but he had been raised in the midwest and he had just met Ray's parents for the first time, and there were the younger kids, so he kept it polite.

Ray's father Walt said, "Come on, let's go inside. I need to wash up and it's cold out here."

Mrs. Reynolds chimed in, "I can put on a pot of coffee, or we have some soft drinks. You'll stay for lunch, won't you?"

"Of course he will, Mom."

Walt said, "Actually, Bev, these guys might prefer a cold beer. Right?"

"Yeah! We have reason to celebrate."

Bill Bill replied, "Sounds good to me! As long as it's not that Korean beer we used to get in Nam!" Bill and Ray both got a chuckle out of that.

The youngster Chip kicked in a comment, "Yeah, sounds good to me too."

What a happy day, Ray thought.

At lunch, Bill was invited to stay the night and it was determined that he came prepared. "I brought my toothbrush," he said. Actually, he had a small duffle in his car with a change of clothes.

So, shortly after lunch when everyone was in the family room visiting, Ray excused himself and went to the kitchen to make a phone call. He called his buddy and former football center 'Buck' Rogers. He asked Buck if he was available to come over that evening for a party. "Can you get hold of the other guys you said are still around and invite them too? We had an old army buddy show up today and I'd like him to meet you guys."

"Sure," Buck said. "Hey, what about Mari? Is she gonna be there? 'Cause I think Sandy would like to come too. Should I bring her along?"

"That's up to you. I haven't called Mari yet to tell her about the party. She didn't feel good this mornin' so I'm doubtin' she'll be here. And let people know we'll be out in the barn. My dad put in a wood burning stove last year and it heats up pretty good, but you'll still want a warm sweatshirt or a jacket."

"Okay, got it. What time?"

"Oh, let's say anytime after 5:00. We'll have some snacks and maybe my mom can put out a pot of chili."

"Good deal. Need me to bring anything?"

"Yeah. When you know who all's comin', can you pick up an appropriate amount of beer? I'll pay you for it."

"Okay. You know there's a bunch of guys, and some gals, home for Christmas. How many you want?"

"The more the merrier. That's why I said the barn. Plenty of room. And, it's good to be home!"

By 5:30 that evening, there were seven guests' cars in the driveway and Ray's parents looked out their picture window and could see headlights of more vehicles turning in off the highway. Beverly turned to Walt and said, "I'd better get another pot of chili started. Would you look in the pantry and see if we have more crackers?"

Ray had called Mari and she was feeling worse with sniffles and a cough and said she would have to miss it. She told Ray to have fun and she would plan on meeting Bill Bill tomorrow if she was feeling better. Maybe Ray could bring him over for Sunday dinner, she suggested.

Buck had shown up early with the back of his pick-up loaded with a shiny new galvanized cattle watering tank full of beer and ice. Ray looked at it and said, "Holy shit, how much do I owe you?"

Buck responded with, "Hey, it's on me, cause I'm glad you're back, and I'm gonna take home whatever's left over."

Bill Bill looked in the back of the pick-up and said, "Hell, you probably paid more for the ice than the beer!"

Ray opened the large barn door and had Buck back his truck in opposite of Ray's pick-up, not too far from the wood burning stove which was just beginning to heat the open area to a comfortable temperature. With the tailgates down, that provided at least four places to sit and Ray, Bill Bill, and Chip had carried out eight folding chairs from the house. Anyone more than that would have to sit on the bales of hay Ray had spread around the open area in the barn. The four horses all watched the activity with curiosity, and Rex followed Ray and his friend everywhere they went.

By 6:00 the party was in full swing. Besides Buck and his wife Sandy, Mick Washington and Chub Johnson were there from the football team Both men brought their brides, and Ray had to congratulate them on their marriages. Jimmy Williston, the 6'-4" center from the basketball team, was busy introducing his fiancé whom he had met at college. And big boobs Vicky Willis, the former cheerleader, was there with her soon-to-be husband Ronnie Fritz, a man two years older than most of the group who were from Ray's class of 1968. Ray wondered how Ronnie had escaped the draft.

One Tough Son of a Gun

Another half dozen or so former classmates wandered in later. Ray lost count, but was having a good time except for one thing. He kept noting that almost everyone had offered him two sentiments - One, something to the effect of 'It's good to see you,' or 'Glad you're home,' and the other, 'Are you going to be all right?' or 'How are you getting along?' He got tired of the sympathy and had to bite his tongue more than once.

As the evening wore on, Ray and Bill Williams were sitting on the tailgate of Ray's pick-up, letting people come to them to visit. When Ray was introducing Bill as his favorite Army pal to Jimmy, Jimmy said, "Well, I bet you're glad to be home from there!"

Bill responded, "Yeah, I am, but I'm going back."

Ray couldn't believe his ears. "What? You didn't tell me that!"

"I just hadn't got around to it yet."

"Oh my God, why?"

Jimmy stayed right there to hear more. Chub Johnson overheard the conversation and moved in closer. He, too, was curious to know why someone would go back to a war zone.

Bill turned towards his buddy Ray and said, "It's like this. I don't really have anything lined up in my life right now here in the States, and the war is winding down so it's not so scary over there anymore. Matter of fact, you were the last person shot in our company. And by re-enlisting, I got a promotion to Staff Sergeant E-6, so higher pay. Plus we still get hazardous duty pay over there. It gives me some time to sort out what I want to do when I get out, and I'm kinda thinking I just might make a career out of the Army. At least I'll always have a place to stay and food to eat." He laughed at that last comment.

Ray looked at him in amazement.

Jimmy reached out and shook Bill's hand and said, "We appreciate your service. I don't think I could do what you're doing, that's why I'm staying in college. But we do appreciate it." He wandered back to his fiancé.

Chub Johnson took a couple of steps back towards his bale of hay and pretty much stumbled back on to it.

A few beers later, at almost 8:00 p.m., a couple of the married couples decided it was time to head home and worked their way around saying their goodbyes. Some of the conversation had died down and Chub decided it was his time to ask some of the questions in the back of his now drunk mind. "So," he spoke up, loud enough where he thought most of the people could hear, "How many of those gooks did you guys shoot over there?"

'Gooks' Ray thought, he knew the slanderous term was used often and he had probably used it himself when he was in Nam, but now his brain immediately went to *'dirty rotten Commie bastards'*.

He replied to the question, "That's not something we want to talk about."

Chub wouldn't let it alone, "Aw, come on, You musta killed a bunch of 'em. That's what we sent you over there for!"

Ray didn't like the tone of that statement and where this conversation might lead. He asked, "You ever shoot anybody, Chub?"

"Naw, can't say I did, but you musta."

"Okay, then just shut your mouth!"

"Yeah, like who's gonna make me?"

Ray responded, "I will, and I'll throw your ass out of here!"

Chub is thinking this guy has been wounded and has trouble walking straight. He slurred his response, "Uh huh? You and what army?"

Bill Bill didn't turn to look at Ray but stared right at Chub as he slid his 6'-2" Jack Spratt lean body down off the tailgate and planted his feet firmly on the solid ground of the barn floor. He quietly folded his arms across his chest and waited to see what might happen next.

Luckily, Chub was still just sober enough to know that this might mean trouble and hesitated before he said anything else. Then he looked around at the other guests and realized they were all staring at him so he asked, "What about you guys? Aren't ya curious?"

No one said anything, but Ray slid off the tailgate to stand next to his buddy.

Chub looked up at the two of them from his seat on the hay bale and said, "Never mind. I think I gotta go home now."

That night, Bill Bill was given Chip's room to sleep and Chip was relegated to the sofa in the living room. It was after 1:00 a.m. when Ray and Bill finally gave up their conversation. They had talked about everything including the various guests at the party and Ray told Bill about meeting Minnesota Fats. They reminisced about events in Nam and the fellow soldiers they lost over there. Bill Bill again reminded Ray how worried he had been driving down to Strong City and thinking he might learn that Ray never made it out alive. Chip had stayed up with them listening intently, partly because he wanted to and partly because Bill was sitting on the sofa that was to become Chip's bed that night.

Sometime after 3:00 a.m., Ray awoke from another nightmare and almost screamed out loud. It was the same one, only different. He was in the Camp Zama hospital ward and Bill Bill was in the bed next to him. Like before, all the others in that ward were wearing NVA uniforms and they all gathered around Ray's and Bill's beds. They just kept asking, *'How many gooks did you kill?'* Bill tried to get up out of his bed to knock these guys down, but they kept pushing him back. After several tries, Ray tried to get up to help Bill, but the NVA soldiers pushed them back with bayonets fixed on their rifles and Ray saw Bill bleeding from a chest wound. That's what woke him up! *Dammit Fats,* he thought, *your stupid question caused that shit!*

Early the next morning, Mari called to say she was feeling much better and wanted to hear all about the party. She said her mother was preparing a brunch and asked Ray to bring his pal over so she could meet him. Ray and Bill had a cup of coffee with Walt and Beverly and then headed over to Cottonwood Falls.

That evening, after Bill had left for Lincoln, Ray watched some TV with his folks and then went to his room early. He wanted to figure out how he could quit having nightmares and the more he thought about it, the more he thought that thinking about it would only cause more. He was still mad at Chub even though he knew it was Chub's problem with too much beer. He had a reputation of being a mean drunk, and Ray was glad it hadn't escalated into anything worse. But he was still pissed about that and all the sympathy he received from the party guests. All these thoughts were running through Ray's head at the same time, like his concentration was in a blender on high speed.

Why do all these little things piss me off so bad? I'm home, safe, and healing from my wounds. The exercises seem to be doing the trick. Why can't I just forget about all that now. It's over.

Why would Bill Bill want to re-enlist and go back? Four more years, he said. Must make sense to him - meals and housing provided. He's probably done just like me and sent all his government paychecks home to a savings account. Except for buying a few beers, there's no need for spending money over there.

I hope school and studying will force me to take my mind off all these little things that keep bugging me. If I have to memorize the periodic table, I won't have time to think about the NVA. I hope that'll make the nightmares stop. Maybe I can dream about something else.

CHAPTER 27

January, 1971
The Tall Grass Prairie
East Central Kansas

It was a new year. Ray had three things to look forward to, not so much with excitement, but with the attitude it would be a change in his life and maybe that would help him get his mind right. He also had two things to worry about, missing home and being away from Mari so much.

His first priority was getting back in the groove at school. He had to figure out good study habits. He would be moving back in the dorms and he had no idea what kind of roommate he would have. He worried that could be a hindrance. The counselor said they would try to match him up with someone who had similar interests. He hoped to find a couple of guys he liked that might be willing to invest in an off-campus apartment, but he would just have to wait and see.

Then, there was the issue of getting away from home and being on his own. He had that same feeling before when he left for college, and again in the Army, and especially in Vietnam. He was in charge of his own destiny, and that made him feel like a man, an adult on his own. But he wondered, *Why did I quit college before?* He remembered being homesick, missing his family, his horse and his dog, and mainly Mari. But going home didn't necessarily give him more time with Mari. She was always away at school. He had to be careful to not let that loneliness bother him again.

The third thing he was more intrigued by than excited about was having a follow-up meeting with Dr. Zehr with the Farrah Fawcett hair. He certainly remembered her beauty and he looked forward to seeing her again, but he was more interested in the fact she seemed to be smart and was studying soldiers with PTSD. Now he remembered the initials and the name after reading the brochure she had given him. He wanted to find out if that might be part of his problem and could she stop the nightmares?

He also wanted to show the physical therapist at the V.A. his success with the exercises. He barely limped anymore and had started some short jogging when he was out walking for exercise. He guessed he was now able to turn his head to the left about halfway, but he was most excited about the improvement of his left arm. He discovered one day in the shower that when he rinsed his hair he often placed his heels against the back wall and propped his hands against the opposite wall with his head directly under the shower head. When he was finished he would use his arm strength to push himself back upright and he started practicing a version of a push-up from that position, pushing himself away from the wall and then repeating it. His right arm did most of the work at first, but he was now at a point where he had tried real push-ups off the floor. He still couldn't quite do it, but he could tell he was going to be able to in the near future if he kept working at it.

Then there was one other thing, the old proverbial money burning a whole in his pocket. He had almost all of his paychecks from the government from the time he went into the service stashed away in a savings account. After his injury, he began to get correspondence from the V.A. telling him his condition would need further evaluation to determine his level of disability, but until then he would be receiving a 100% monthly disability payment in a lump sum check. That was another reason for a follow-up at the V.A. hospital.

On top of all that, he had sold seven kitchen remodeling projects and two small bathroom remodels. When all of those were finished, he calculated he would have almost $2,400 coming from Key Cabinets and there were still three more contracts that he thought had possibilities of turning positive. All in all, Ray Reynolds was pretty well fixed for a man about to turn twenty-one later in the month.

Naturally, as a guy, he was thinking about a new car but he hadn't expressed that interest to anyone. He figured his parents would tell him to wait until he was comfortable with his school work, or some such reason to wait a while. Still, he wanted to find both the Chevrolet and the Ford dealers in Manhattan or in Topeka so he could pick up brochures on the Camaro and the Mustang. He either wanted the Super Sport or the Mach 1.

A few of his high school friends bought new cars right after they graduated and got a job. He knew some of them were constantly worried about making their car payments on time and complained about the high cost of insurance. Ray didn't have to worry about the cost of the car. He could write a check for the full amount. That felt good even if he didn't go ahead and buy a car. But currently his father was paying for the insurance on his old pick-up and he wondered when that would change and how much that would cost.

In the back of his head, he knew he should wait. There were always unexpected expenses with going to school. He was pretty sure the G.I. Bill would at least cover tuition and the cost of books. His parents offered to help and they would pay his dorm room expense. But, what if he found someone to share an apartment, how much more would that be? And how much would he have to spend on groceries, light bill, gas and so on? It all gets complicated and starts to bug him that life is not simple and he begins to wonder if it's worth it. Then, Minnesota Fats's words came back to haunt him, '*You can't beat having a degree*'. This time, Ray even remembered what he said after that - '*That's from a guy who doesn't have one*'.

Thoughts kept entering his head like cars entering the freeway during rush hour, one right after another. *Yeah, Minnesota Fats, but you made a living shooting pool. How much fun would that be? Then there's Cassius Clay who could control his own destiny just by being a sports star, or Len Dawson of the Chiefs. If I hadn't been shot, maybe I could be like that. I had a lot of wins in high school.* Then his mind would go back to his first semester at K-State almost three years earlier and the realization that he wasn't even

Dennis G. Smith

considered for the football program. That was when he was in good physical condition. *Yeah, I'd better get a degree.* It was always the same conclusion, he couldn't change it. Every time he thought about this stuff, the idea of a new car took a back seat. *'Nothing wrong with the old Ford, and it's paid for. Except it really belongs to my dad.'*

Ray had this terrible feeling that he was being forced into this college situation, but he had no one to blame, no one to point a finger at and say 'No, I'm not doing it!' It was all his own doing and he needed to take responsibility. He knew it was the right thing to do, but still, did he really have to? He wondered if he should discuss this with *'Dr. Farrah Fawce*tt.'

CHAPTER 28

Friday, January 22, 1971
Veterans Administration Medical Center
Topeka, Kansas

Ray had scheduled his follow-up session with the physical therapist at the V.A. for a Friday afternoon followed by a meeting with Dr. Zehr. With that schedule he only had to cut one class and could leave Manhattan around 1:30 and be in Topeka in plenty of time for his 3:00 p.m. therapy session, and then see Dr. Zehr at 4:00.

The only thing he didn't like was that he was skipping a Geology class, which he liked. The professor was interesting and Ray hoped he could learn more about the Flint Hills. Geology was one of his science requirements for a B.S. degree and he knew his father would be pleased with that course. Obviously, it had nothing to do with Marketing, unless maybe he decided to sell real estate, and he thought about that idea as he drove over the gentle rolling hills of the tall grass prairie of east-central Kansas. After all, his short stint as a cabinet salesman proved lucrative and maybe he could learn more about being a realtor from Mari's father.

Those thoughts were interrupted with the idea of stopping at some car dealerships while he was in Topeka, but he decided he'd rather head home immediately after his appointments since Mari was also heading home to Cottonwood Falls for the weekend. He hadn't told her about his appointments with the V.A., but said he would call her the minute he got home and they could make plans then.

The physical therapist was pleased with Ray's improvement, significantly better than his last session. He told her he credited it to the exercise routine and that he was staying loyal to the workouts. There was an exercise room in the dorm and he used it on a regular basis, usually early in the morning since he was used to getting up early. He also liked to shoot baskets when the weather was warm enough. The therapist said she thought his leg strength was nearly eighty-five percent of normal and his left arm was close to ninety. She measured his head turning ability at about seventy percent and told him he needed to keep working on that.

Then he found himself waiting in the same small office-like exam room for Dr. Zehr. When she finally knocked, walked in, reached her warm hand to his, and smiled, he immediately forgot about how impatient he was becoming. He was getting agitated when his Timex watch showed it was after 4:20. A nice smile from a beautiful woman can put any man at ease.

They discussed his school schedule and his exercises and then Dr. Zehr asked him about his anger issues. Ray said that was about the same and so were his nightmares, maybe once a week or every two weeks. He couldn't predict them and didn't know what triggered them. As far as anger, he told her that little things he had no control over would piss him off. He said he tried to control it, and most of the time people didn't notice he was pissed, but he was still pissed. Just having to wait in line at Walmart while someone ahead of him wrote a check always bugged him. "Why couldn't they bring cash, or at least have most of the check filled out in advance?" he said. "They're writing a check for $8.00. My God! And then, the little old ladies who wait to hear how much the total is before they start digging in their purse to find their checkbook. I want to scream!"

Dr. Zehr looked at him and smiled. "Unfortunately, that's the nature of some human beings. You and I may not like it, but you're right, you can't control it or do anything about it. You could always step over in another check-out line, but you already know, you could face the same problem there, or maybe even worse."

Ray shrugged his shoulders. "I know. It's crazy!"

"Well, we know you're not crazy. A lot of people are bothered by similar events. Little things bug them. But, we have to work on controlling emotions so that those things don't become major issues where you find it difficult to cope." She paused, waiting to see if Ray wanted to respond, but he didn't. "What about the war? Do you still think that your anger at being shot, or your issue with being involved in a war could be part of the problem that makes you angry?"

"Uh, yeah! I mean, I guess so. I know I still have that feeling. You know, I've never said this to anyone, and I wouldn't wish what happened to me on anyone else, but," he paused in thought before proceeding, "If Lieutenant Johnson hadn't acted sick that day, the RTO would have been following him, not me, and he would have been the most likely one to get shot."

Dr. Zehr studied his facial expression and could tell he was very sincere about this statement. She responded, "Well, that's something that no one can say for sure. But what makes you say Lieutenant Johnson 'acted sick'?"

"Oh, he was always finding little ways to show that he protested the war. He didn't agree with the way we were doing things, the U.S. I mean, overall. He just didn't like it. And he and the First Sergeant were like this." He held up his right hand with the index and middle fingers pressed tight together. "So just before we boarded the trucks to go out on the assignment, Top, the First Sergeant, looked me up and said 'Johnson's not feeling well. You'll be in charge of the First Platoon.' Hell, he looked fine at breakfast an hour earlier. He even went back for seconds."

"I can understand your frustration. And, I also understand why you wouldn't want to share those thoughts with anyone. But, holding them inside and not letting them go for all this time is probably aggravating your issues with anger. That's like the little old ladies in Walmart, only much worse. You want to put the blame on someone else, even though they weren't the one to pull the trigger. It's over now, in the past, and you can't go back and change it." She looked him directly in the eyes and gave a slight smile.

He looked directly back at her and halfway shrugged his shoulders like saying I don't know how to handle it. At the same time, he was thinking, *Oh my, she has pretty eyes!*

They both sat there quiet for a minute, letting what had just transpired sink in. Dr. Zehr thought this might be a breakthrough for Ray to admit what he had just told her.

Then Ray opened his mouth to say something, but he paused.

The doctor's eyes were still fixed on him and she said, "Yes?"

Again, he opened his mouth, but stopped. Then he said, "The only good thing I can think of about being drafted and going to Vietnam is that I have the G.I. Bill to pay for my college. But, I'm not even sure I want to be in college. I just know it has to be the right thing to do at this point in my life, so here I am."

"I can understand your feelings, and I agree with you that college is the most practical thing to be doing now. It will not only educate you on things that should help make your future life better, but it also gives you time to sort things out in your mind. What do you think?"

He didn't answer right away. He had a response forming in his head that was not really relevant, but he wanted to say it anyway, even if it was wrong. Like before, he started twice to open his mouth and then paused again. Finally, he said, "You know, I said the only good thing that came to me from fighting the war in Nam was the G.I. Bill, but there was one other thing."

"What's that?" the psychologist asked with curiosity.

"I got to meet you."

CHAPTER 29

Tuesday, February 23, 1971
Ahearn Field House, Kansas State University Campus
Manhattan, Kansas

The week before the big 'Sunflower Showdown' basketball rivalry game between the two Big 8 Universities in Kansas, Ray received a short letter from Mari saying that one of her sorority sisters had scored four tickets to the game and she would be coming to Manhattan on Tuesday with her friends. *'Can you save me a seat so I can sit with you?'* she wrote, and, *'Where will we meet?'* Ray quickly fired off a note back to her and hoped she would get it in time before her group left Lawrence. It was too awkward to try and call from a pay phone and wait to reach someone in a sorority house or a dorm, so the postal service was usually the best option. He thought about telling her - *'Look for me, I'll be wearing a purple K-State sweatshirt!'*, but he wondered if she would get the humor or if that would just make her mad.

As it turned out, Ray saved room for her on the bleacher bench next to him by placing his jacket there. He had to apologize several times to people who wanted to squeeze in, and eventually, about ten minutes before the tip-off, Mari found him. She worked her way down the row with plenty of 'Excuse me's' and booing from the Wildcat's side since she was wearing KU's crimson and blue.

When she sat down next to him, Ray could tell she wasn't in her best mood. Something seemed to be bothering her.

"What's up?" he asked.

"Oh, you wouldn't believe the traffic and what caused us to get here late. Right at the exit for Manhattan, there was an RV pulled partially off the side of the road and it was completely on fire. You know how much I hate the thought of fire, someone burning to death. I couldn't stand it. There were no firetrucks there yet, but some cars had pulled off and some of those people had fire extinguishers, but they were no match for the fire. I thought I was going to throw up thinking there might be people inside. As we passed by on the opposite shoulder we saw five KU guys standing in the ditch watching. We decided that the RV belonged to one of them and they all got out okay. But it still upset me. I hate that, just the thought."

During the game, it took Mari awhile to get in the right mood and then she began to cheer every time KU scored, which was often and she again received 'boo's' from those Wildcats around her and Ray. There were some snide remarks about 'go back to your own side', or 'go back to Lawrence', and some comments that made Ray turn around and give dirty looks to whoever it was that called Mari out. He had to constantly bite his tongue since K-State was losing the game and his fellow students were obviously not happy. Mari's presence simply made matters worse.

And if that wasn't bad enough, Ray was having one of his episodes, like at the first K-State football game a couple of years earlier. He felt like he didn't belong there, in the stands, in the crowd, cheering the team. He wanted to be down on the floor, running full speed, making lay-ups, jump shots, free throws and hearing the crowd cheering for *him*. But those days were over and he knew it and that just caused him more agitation. He was having a hard time cheering, especially for the losing team.

It turned out like everyone expected since KU was on a streak and this game's final score of 61 to 48 made it fifteen wins in a row. Ray knew that Mari would tease him about this for a long time. Later in the season, he was kind enough to praise KU's Coach Ted Owens on their eventual twenty-one game winning streak and their success in getting to the Final Four that year.

After the game, Mari and Ray waited in their seats until most of the crowd disappeared. Ray didn't want Mari to be jostled around by a large group of disappointed Wildcat fans. When they finally got up to leave they held hands all the way to her sorority sister's car where the other three girls were waiting and the car was already warmed up. Ray and Mari said their goodbye and exchanged a quick kiss.

Ray stood there in the parking lot in the cold and watched as they drove off into the night. He hoped the burnt out shell of the RV, wherever it was, would be gone so Mari wouldn't have to see it again on the drive back to Lawrence. He knew how much she hated the thought of fire.

Then he began to wonder - *Why was Mari so concerned about those guys she didn't know along the side of the road, It was obvious they were safe. The RV was just an RV, it could be replaced. I've never heard her seem so concerned about me. I was shot and nearly died. Yeah, she was worried enough to come to Camp Zama, but since then? It's like it never happened. Even when she rubs her hand over my scars, she never mentions it. That's weird! She said the fire almost made her sick and thought she was going to have to ask to stop the car. An hour later at the game she was still shaken by it.*

Ray had begun to notice that every time he had one of his little fits of frustration, even simple agitation like not being able to participate in sports anymore, there always seemed to be other issues at that same time that would add to his growing anger. This issue with Mari and her lack of concern for *him*. *Why did that enter his mind?* He always managed to hold the anger inside and not let it show. *Could this be part of the PTSD?* He wondered if Dr. Zehr could explain that. Then he also wondered if he would ever even mention it to her.

CHAPTER 30

Spring, 1971
Flint Hills- Tall Grass Prairie
East Central, Kansas

Ray had accepted the fact that he needed to earn a degree, but not necessarily *why* or in *what field*. However, by midterm, he decided he really did need the B.S. and he thought the initials were appropriate. He would stick with his plan of a major in Marketing and also take some Agriculture electives. He was going to stay for the summer session so he could get his degree quicker and get on with his life. There had to be better things to do than reading boring textbooks and taking pointless exams.

As he learned things in his college courses, he began to categorize them in his head. He had decided there should be two major headings: things I learned in school, and, things I learned in life. Two of the things he placed in the life category were, *'Don't talk to Mari about fires,'* and *'The horse will always find his way back to the barn.'* Every time he had thoughts about the lessons learned in life issues, he thought he should write them down, but then decided who would care. These are just things he knows from experience. But he couldn't help himself. Every time he thought about a specific piece of knowledge he had learned for this category, like, *'Don't let the RTO follow you so close!,'* he would also think of the old Roger Miller song, *'You Can't Roller Skate In a Buffalo Herd.'* That song, of course, added the line, *"But you can be happy if you've a mind to,"* which always bothered Ray. He hadn't figured out how that part worked.

The "lessons learned in school were easier to categorize, but not always easier to remember. Except that he found interesting ones were also the enjoyable ones and that included Geology classes. Maybe it was just the professor, but even though Geology 101 only touched on a few comments about the Flint Hills and the Tall Grass Prairie, Ray found that really interesting and he wanted to learn more. He went to the campus library to find books on the subject and he also signed up for Geology 102 for the summer session. This was a subject that could fall into both categories - the stuff he learned living on the prairie, watching the changing seasons, and studying the prairie dog towns, and then the underground geology stuff he was learning in class.

At one time, back when Columbus landed in what was to become America, it was estimated that more than 30 million bison roamed the prairies between the Appalachians and Rocky Mountains. Some scientists have said estimates could have been as high as 60 million. Ray's high school science teacher, Mr. Cowan, had taught them the proper name for North America's largest land mammal was '*bison*,' not buffalo, and they could '*weigh up to 2,400 pounds*'. Those facts stuck in Ray's head. After the American westward movement and settlement of farmers, ranchers and city people throughout the 1800's, estimates of bison remaining on the prairie plummeted to less than 1,000. Ray hated it when he learned that fact.

The Tall Grass Prairie was an area that extended through fourteen states from Texas to Minnesota and the Dakotas and on into Canada, covering over 179 million acres before modern day generations converted over 90% of it into farmland, cities and towns. One of the largest areas of native prairie land remaining is in northern Oklahoma and eastern central Kansas called the Flint Hills. The Reynolds family's back yard, and their entire ranch lies smack dab in the middle of it. Here the gentle rolling hills are sparse with trees due to minimal layers of soil covering layers of limestone and shale. Over years of drought, fires and herds of bison and now cattle grazing the area, this area of prairie has been preserved by nature itself since the land is just not suitable for plowing and therefore remains as grazing lands, unfit for farming.

Ray was well aware of many facts about the Flint Hills and he knew a lot about the wildlife in the area from observation and hunting with his father and his uncle. He knew about the prairie dogs for sure, and the many species of migratory birds, mallards, snow geese, and Canada geese. Another lesson learned from Mr. Cowan - *'They're Canada geese, not Canadian geese!'*, he had emphasized the correct name. Ray had hunted bobwhite quail and wild turkeys and had seen bobcats and white-tailed deer and antelope. Many migratory animals like the bisons moved on to greener pastures during long periods of drought.

Another life's lesson Ray thought about was that if you were used to being a player, especially a key player on a sports team, it's insanely difficult to simply become a spectator. He kept trying, but kept thinking of Roger Miller's song about a buffalo herd. *It should have been a bison herd!*, and the suggestion in the song that said *'But you can be happy if you've a mind to,'* followed by a chorus that said. *'All you gotta do is put your mind to it; Knuckle down, buckle down, do it, do it, do it.'*.

That required a third category in Ray's head - Things I learned from media. He had started thinking of that chorus as he headed for classes he didn't especially like but knew he needed to take. And when his roommate complained about an upcoming exam or an assignment he didn't like, Ray would repeat it to him - "*Knuckle down, buckle down, do it, do it, do it.*"

CHAPTER 31

Thursday, April 8, 1971
Veterans Administration Medical Center
Topeka, Kansas

Ray had scheduled a follow-up appointment with Dr. Zehr at her request. It was the Thursday before Easter, Good Friday eve, and he would be headed home for the spring break. Dr. Zehr had told him she would be hosting a lunchtime session with a group of veterans, primarily from Vietnam, and most were suffering with some level of PTSD. Dr. Zehr told Ray he might find it interesting and could decide for himself if it might be helpful.

Ray didn't know what to expect, but he knew one thing, maybe related to his growing list of life's lessons. He would not be saying anything to Dr. Zehr about his happiness to see her. He had continued to have thoughts of the last words he had said at their previous meeting and how they might have been interpreted. He remembered seeing Dr. Zehr blush when he said 'I got to meet you.' Since then, he had tried to convince himself that he only meant it as a statement of fact that he thought she was a nice lady and a good doctor, but he was sure she had taken it as some sort of comment on their relationship and possibly his desire to make it romantic. Now he knew he had to be careful what he said and even thought about trying to apologize but thought he might not get his words to come out right and could possibly make matters worse. There was something about seeing her walk into a room that just made him lose control of his thoughts and speech.

At the hospital, he was ushered into a large private dining room off to one side of the cafeteria. There was a young male nurse in a white lab coat with a name badge who greeted him at the door. "Hi, I'm Daniel. I'm a Vietnam veteran like all the guys who will be here today. I work with Dr. Zehr and help her with the PTSD study. We're glad you could be here today." He turned around and pointed at the table with name tags and asked, "Your name?"

"Ray Reynolds."

Daniel picked up the tag with the bold handwritten name 'RAY' and peeled off the backing so Ray could stick it on his shirt. He was told he could sit anywhere. The table had chairs for twelve people and half the chairs were already taken. Ray walked over and took the first chair he came to. "Ray," he said as he stuck out his hand to greet the man next to him.

"Ben," the man said as he shook Ray's hand. "And, this is Jim," he added as he introduced the man next to him. Jim nodded an acknowledgement. Other guys around the table nodded or gave a quick wave. Ray waved back.

Ray looked at his watch, 11:50 a.m.. He noticed that some of the guys were visiting as though they knew each other and others were just sitting quietly waiting for the meeting to begin. Within the next five minutes all the chairs had filled except two, one for the nurse Daniel, he presumed, and one for Dr. Zehr. Daniel came in and announced Dr. Zehr was on her way. A couple of guys nodded and smiled as though they, like Ray, were really looking forward to seeing her again. Ray understood that feeling.

Dr. Zehr arrived and said, "Hello, how's everyone doing?"

There were some "okay's" and some moans, and Ray heard one voice at the end of the table say "Good."

Two servers came through a door pushing a serving cart and started setting salads in front of everyone. Dr. Zehr announced they would go around the room and introduce themselves and say where they were from. Then we will all eat before we begin the meeting.

One Tough Son of a Gun

By the time they finished eating, Ray had learned that the older man across the table, the one that looked to be in his fifties, was a World War II veteran and the guy next to him had fought in Korea and Vietnam.

Ray hadn't really known what to expect, but two hours later when the meeting ended, he realized it was just about what he could have imagined. Almost everyone had complaints about nightmares, or people not understanding them and their feelings. The Vietnam veterans complained about their treatment when they came home. "I didn't choose to fight the war," was one complaint. When it was Ray's turn to speak, he simply said, "I'm new at this, but I agree with the other Vietnam vets." Then he added, "I too have had some strange nightmares. The kind that wake you up at night."

When the session was over, Dr. Zehr stood and walked around the room shaking each soldier's hand and thanked them for coming. She told them they were welcome to stay and visit as long as they liked and she looked forward to seeing them again. Ray looked her in the eyes and said, "Thank you!".

Two of the veterans looked at their watches and left immediately after Dr. Zehr. The others began to visit. Ben and Jim started to chat and Jim asked Ray where Strong City was. He said he had heard the name before but didn't know where it was located. Ray told them about the Flint Hills Rodeo. He also noticed that Daniel, the nurse, never left the room, but did offer to get more coffee or water if anyone wanted some. Even then, he didn't leave the room, but did go to the kitchen door and asked the server to bring more coffee. Ray was sure he stayed around so he could report any activity to Dr. Zehr.

When Ray headed down the long corridor toward the exit on his way to the parking lot, it hit him. He actually felt like a veteran, something he hadn't really given much thought to before. He guessed it was the fact that he could relate to those other veterans in the room. He now knew that others felt a lot like he did about the war, any war. Wounded or not, those guys wished they had never experienced it.

Dennis G. Smith

He told himself he was not going to let being a veteran ruin his life. He thought: *I'm proud that I served my country! Yeah, I'm a veteran. I've got a Marksman's badge, an Army CIB, a Vietnam Service Medal, a Bronze Start for valor, and a Purple Heart for being shot. I'm not ashamed of any of those. My parents are proud of my service, and so are Chip and June. Mari's proud of me. She's said so, and so are her folks. And, I think most of the people in Chase County are too, considering how they act when they see me. Or, is that just because I played football and basketball?*

As for everybody else, they all think we're village-burning marauding raiders, pot-smoking, dope-loving murderers, and baby killers. Well, hell with them!

Another life lesson. Don't talk to strangers about being a Vietnam veteran! Ray thought about that a little more and modified that lesson - Just don't talk to *anybody* about being a Vietnam veteran!

CHAPTER 32

A decade of events

A lot had happened in the 1970's, and now the Reynolds couple had a new challenge to face. A big decision was going to become available to Mari, but it would mean leaving their Kansas families in rural America and moving to a really big city life.

With a few exceptions, primarily in Ray's life, everything after Vietnam had seemed like a storybook for Ray and Mari. It seemed like things had worked out perfectly as though there was a master plan established for them. Ray realized his life of playing football, basketball, and participating in the rodeo were now long ago things of his past and he did his best to put them, and the war in Vietnam, out of his mind. It worked most of the time.

Ray had stayed through summer sessions at K-State so he could get his degree as soon as possible. Mari had completed her Bachelor's degree in Finance at K.U. in the College of Business and graduated summa cum laude and then hung around the university to obtain a Master's Degree. Her father, Ralph, joked that he had to sell a lot of kitchen cabinets and a few large ranches for her to be so successful. He laughed about it, but it was true. Ray had been part of the success with Ralph's cabinet business as he continued to work for Ralph on long weekends and breaks between college sessions to pick up extra cash. He had been consistently successful with cabinet sales.

As it turned out, Ray and Mari both graduated at the end of the 1974 fall session, Ray with a B.S and Mari with her Masters. Both were now free to pursue their careers. Mari may have had her Masters degree, but Ray liked to brag to everyone that he managed to use one single term paper for all three of his last classes at K-State. He had his fourth English requirement in Creative Writing, another Marketing class towards his major, and an American History class. His term paper, modified only slightly for all three classes, was titled:

**WHATEVER IT WAS
WHATEVER IT DOES
THEIR ROAD SIGN PUNS
WERE ALWAYS FUN
Burma-Shave**

He worried a little about being discovered, but ultimately didn't care. It was fun, and it was funny.

By graduation, Ray's father was well aware that his oldest son may not be the chosen one to take over the ranch some day. Walt had been concentrating on teaching both his younger son and daughter, Chip and June, the ways of life on a ranch in the Flint Hills. He really couldn't predict what might happen when he would be ready to retire. The world seemed to be changing too fast. He may one day have another ranch for Ralph Key to sell.

That Christmas, just after Ray's graduation in December, there was a small gift under the Christmas tree for him from 'Santa.' It was smaller than a pack of cigarettes and he held it up for Mari to see and then shook it. It had a light rattle like something solid inside a cardboard container. He unwrapped it and opened the small box. It was a key chain with a single key and a gold colored fob with a 'Camaro' logo on one side. He looked as his mother, then his father, and said, "Are you kidding me?"

His dad responded and said, "Sorry, Buddy. That little package is the only one you get this year. It's both your Christmas and your graduation gift. I'm going with you over to Emporia to let you pick out what you actually want, just to make sure you don't go all out for gold wheels or something." He paused and then he added, "Oh, and I want my pick-up back! Chip needs something to drive."

Ray was still shocked, "I can't believe this! I still think this is some kind of joke. Thank you both!" He got up and went over to hug his mother and shook his father's hand, saying, "Thank you! Thank you! Thank you!"

Richard Nixon had resigned the presidency of the United States to avoid impeachment proceedings and Gerald Ford took over. The Nixon-led peace process had failed and Congress acted to make sure U.S. troops would turn Vietnam over to the ARVN's and leave Vietnam totally. Less than two years later, Saigon had been taken over by the communists, and was soon renamed Ho Chi Minh City. When that hit the local news in Kansas City, Ray's first thoughts were *'dirty rotten Commie bastards'*, and that triggered another nightmare. The kind of wake-you-in-the-middle-of-the-night in a cold sweat event still kept happening years after Ray was shot by the sniper, the bastard!

Ray and Mari had married in the spring after graduation on an early Friday evening, May 9, 1975 just before sunset in the pasture behind the barn at the Reynolds ranch in the Flint Hills. Eugene "Buck" Rogers was Ray's best man and three other football team members served as groomsmen. Ray had first invited Bill Bill to be his best man, but Staff Sergeant Bill Williams was in Germany on assignment. Mari had one of her fellow high school cheerleaders as her matron of honor and three of her sorority sisters as her bridesmaids. Following the outdoor ceremony, there was another large party in the barn, this time with all the doors open to allow the cool evening air in.

The wedding party was a reunion of sorts as both the bride and the groom were now gainfully employed and living in the Kansas City area since completing their education. They had rented a two-bedroom apartment on the west side of the metro area in Lenexa, a suburb on the Kansas side of the state line. Mari had been snatched up by a large regional accounting firm with offices near the Kansas City Country Club Plaza, an area well known for its architecture, its shopping and restaurants and its annual Christmas lights display covering several city blocks. It was a pretty straight forward commute for Mari from their

Dennis G. Smith

Kansas apartment down Shawnee-Mission Boulevard to her Missouri office building.

Now it was a new era, the 80's. America had elected Ronald Reagan as president, a movie actor and former governor of California. The country was expecting a lot. Ray just wanted that nightmare to stop. And, every so often after one of those sleepless nights, he had the feeling there was a different nightmare that kept him awake, but he couldn't explain it. If he tried to recall it, it took him right back to the day of the shooting. One of the best things about his marriage to Mari was that she understood and was always there to calm him down and help him get back to sleep.

After graduation, it took Ray a few weeks before he accepted a job at a big box hardware store as their kitchen cabinet design specialist. It wasn't exactly what he had dreamed of, but he certainly had the qualifications and he knew his stuff about kitchens and baths. Two years later, he heard from the national sales manager for True Dimensions Manufacturing and was told about a new dealer they were adding in Overland Park, a suburb not far from their home. He contacted the owner, was welcomed for an interview and was hired, almost on the spot after displaying his resume of experience. He later learned that True Dimensions had recommended him to the owner long before the interview.

The young couple had their first child. a boy named Matthew, in May of 1980. and three and a half years later, Mari presented Ray with a daughter, Fran, born in September of 1983 and named in honor of her father's distant relative Francis Scott Key, author of the country's national anthem. Once they learned of Mari's pregnancy with Matt, they started looking to buy a home, a three-bedroom minimum.

Ray had an urge to buy a lot and have a custom-built house made so he could design the kitchen and baths. Mari was more inclined to simply find a house they both liked and then buy it and move in, much easier. She, of course, knew all about what it would take to finance the property and what they would qualify for, and she thought their best bet was to use Ray's veterans benefit and get a V.A. mortgage with no money down, even though they had managed to save several thousand dollars since their marriage.

Both young parents had received promotions and raises since starting their careers. Mari was the leading breadwinner which bothered Ray a little, but while he received a smaller salary, he also earned a significant part of his income from commissions on his cabinet sales. After only six months with the new cabinet company, they put him in charge of commercial accounts which led him to lots of opportunities to sell hundreds and sometimes thousands of cabinets to new apartment complexes under construction. Many times, Ray would learn of the developer's plans for new apartments or condos and he would offer to help the architects with the kitchen planning and show the developer how he could save them money with True Dimension cabinets. By year-end and tax time, Ray's salary plus commission checks would often be up there close to Mari's income.

Ray's brother Chip had followed the Reynolds legacy on the hardwood floor through high school. He had a growth spurt his sophomore year and by the start of his junior year, he was 6'-4". The coach switched him from a guard position to center and he quickly became the team's leading scorer. He graduated K-State with a degree from the College of Agriculture in Animal Sciences. Ray wasn't sure, but imagined by now that Chip had probably heard the *'someday this will all be yours'* speech. He hoped Chip would think that sounded good, for his sake and his father's.

June, or Jude, as Ray liked to call her, had met a senior, Jim Sommers, in college when she was just a freshman. Two years later after she had dropped out of college to follow him to Colorado, they were married in a small ceremony on Lookout Mountain, just west of Denver, above Golden, where Jim worked for the Coors Brewery in an H.R. role. Ray didn't feel like he knew that much about Jim, but every time they were around him, he liked him, and he could tell June really liked him. Jim and June started having kids almost immediately, and now had three, two boys and a girl.

Ray continued to receive requests from Dr. Zehr about once a year asking for an update on his life and wanting to know if he continued to have problems that might be caused by PTSD. Her form letter always included a hand written note saying that he was always welcome to come back to Topeka to attend one of their monthly meetings. More than once, especially after a nightmare episode, Mari had suggested that Ray should take a day off work and go to Topeka to attend a session. "It might be good for you. It certainly can't hurt!", she said.

Ray did take her up on the suggestion, once in 1977, and again in 1979. Dr. Zehr seemed very glad to see him, and he was happy to see Dr. Zehr again, although her Farrah Fawcett hair style was gone. She was now a lighter shade of blond with long bangs pushed to one side and shoulder length curls. She still had the nice smile, beautiful eyes, and the warm handshake.

Almost every holiday, Ray and Mari made the trek down I-35 to Emporia and then west to Chase County. During one of those early trips, shortly after Matt was born, Ray thought something was wrong when they got to Strong City. He couldn't figure out why he felt that way, but something was different. After spending a couple hours with his parents, they left to go see Mari's folks. As they reached the south end of Strong City and passed the sign that read 'Cottonwood Falls - 1 mile', Ray realized what was wrong. Maybe he just missed it, but he never had before. He turned to Mari and said, "You know what it is?"

She looked at him puzzled and asked, "What what is?"

"What was wrong with the trip down here?"

"No, I didn't know there was anything wrong with the trip."

"Don't you remember? I said something's wrong when we turned into the ranch driveway. You said 'Really, what?' Remember?"

"Uh, yeah, I guess. So what's wrong?"

"The Burma-Shave signs are gone!" he said loudly. "My God, I was looking forward to showing them to Matt whenever we made this trip and he could read. Now he'll never know."

"Oh, I'm sorry. I know how much you loved those. You use to always read them out loud to entertain me, and then you'd recite the words from the ones that no longer existed on the other side. Something about a periscope."

"It was 'Don't try passing on a slope unless you have a periscope'. And, of course, the last sign always said 'Burma-Shave'."

Now, they had a tough decision facing them. They liked their home they had bought three years earlier in the suburb called Prairie Village, a small city tucked neatly in between Kansas City, Overland Park, and Leawood, Kansas. While they struggled a little at first with the expense of their mortgage, taxes, and their home owner's insurance and the costs associated with raising a family, they had finally adjusted comfortably as their income grew.

Mari had attended a three-day seminar in St. Louis on updates to corporate tax law earlier in the year and sat at a table with two executives from a national mortgage company. She learned that firm specialized in large corporate structures dealing with developers of high rise offices, condominiums, shopping malls and other large finance arrangements like municipal sports arenas and stadiums. She had shown a strong interest in their business and asked a number of questions during breaks in the class. Before the seminar ended, they had exchanged business cards and one of the two executives, Randall Haley, the V.P. of Communications, asked Mari how long she had been with her firm and then told her he looked forward to seeing her again.

She didn't see him again, but he did call. He told her they had an opening in their Illinois branch office in Chicago for an assistant director that could lead to a management position. He mentioned a starting pay range that he thought she would qualify for and it was extremely attractive, along with nice benefits like health and life insurance and a country club membership. She was asked to respond by the end of the week so an interview could be arranged.

Ray and Mari had discussed the opportunity every morning at breakfast and every evening since the phone call. They made a list of pros and cons. She liked her current job and was treated well there. They both liked their new home and they had chosen Johnson County, Kansas because of the reputation of the good schools even though they still had a couple of years before their kids would be starting school.

By Friday, she had made up her mind to say she might regret the decision, but she felt this was just a little early in her career to make such a move, especially with a one-year-old in the family. She added that her husband agreed with her that they would both like to stay where they were right then. She was told they understood, and the H.R. representative on the conference call said, "If it's all right with you, I'll keep your name and number here on file and we may try you again when the time is right."

Overall, that made Mari, and Ray, happy. It was good to know someone recognized your talents and respected your business acumen, and it was also good to have the decision made and over with.

CHAPTER 33

July, 1981
Crown Center
Kansas City, Missouri

Ray and Mari had become good friends with their next-door neighbors, Bob and Suzanne, there in Prairie Village. They were the kind of neighbors that could walk over after work and open your back door and say, "Anybody home?" or "Hey, we're here." They had a daughter, Ruth, just four years old and Mari just loved babysitting her. Bob was a 'car guy' and loved Ray's Camaro. Bob had an older Chevrolet, a 1957 Bel Air convertible, that he and his father had restored, and the two couples often called the high school freshman just down the street on an impulse to see if she could babysit Ruth while they went out for dinner or to a drive-in restaurant in the Chevy with the top down.

One Friday, in the middle of July, Suzanne called Mari at work and told her about the year-old Hyatt Regency hotel just south of downtown in the newly created Crown Center area holding a summer Tea Dance on Fridays after work starting at 5:00 p.m.. It was the hotel's idea to promote the new facility with a live band playing old standards in the large lobby between the hotel tower and attached convention center. Suzanne said she already had the babysitter lined up for their daughter and Ray and Mari could drop Matt off next door after getting him from day care.

Mari said it sounded like fun and they would catch up with them there. "Probably be closer to 6:00," she told her good friend. Then she called Ray, who reluctantly agreed and told her he would swing by her office and pick her up after taking care of their son. They could get her car after the dance and most likely dinner. He pulled up in front of her office building just after 5:30 and jumped out of the car as Mari exited the building. He passed her and said, "Be back in a few minutes, I need a restroom."

"Are you okay?" she asked her husband when he returned to the car.

"Not sure," he said. "I think so. Must have been something I had for lunch."

By the time they got down to the Crown Center, halfway between the Country Club Plaza and downtown K.C., and then found a place to park, it was almost exactly 6:00 p.m.. They entered the lobby from the parking garage and spotted Bob and Suzanne over near the bar. They worked their way through the crowd as the band broke into another song and people began dancing. They ordered a drink and Ray handed Mari a twenty and said, "Be back in a minute."

"Oh no," she said.

"I wonder where I'll find a restroom?"

Just then a waiter walked by and Ray asked. He quickly left the area. Five minutes or so later, he returned. His face looked pale and his eyes tired. He apologized and said, "I'm sorry guys, I don't think I can stay here tonight. Stomach's really acting up!"

"Well, okay," Bob said. "We'll have to try again some other Friday night. I think they're doing this all summer. Look at the crowd! Good God!"

Suzanne added, "You go home and get to feeling better! We'll check on you in the morning."

"Okay," Ray said and grabbed Mari's hand in a rush to get out of there. They had only been there long enough to hear three songs and Ray never felt comfortable enough to dance.

Ray dropped Mari off at her car in the parking garage and wanted to know if he could get in the building to use the restroom. She said she'd have to let him in with her pass key, so he parked and they both headed for the door. When they finally got home it was almost 7:30. Ray went inside to change into comfortable clothes and to look for the Pepto-Bismol.

When he came back downstairs and met Mari and Matt coming in from the garage, she said the kids and the babysitter were out playing in the back yard when I went to get him. Little Ruth wanted him to stay."

Ray feigned a laugh, His stomach told him not to exert himself. He turned on the TV and sat down in his recliner. When the TV warmed up and the picture came on, there was a 'Breaking News' banner on the screen and the news anchor came on and said, "We are cutting live to Michael Mahoney at the scene of a major disaster at the Hyatt Regency Hotel. We understand the sky bridges connecting the hotel to the convention center in the lobby of the hotel have collapsed during a Friday night Tea Dance and there are numerous injuries and presumably many killed underneath the rubble."

Ray yelled at Mari who was in the kitchen about to prepare something for dinner. "Mari, come here. Hurry!"

The TV cut away to a close-up of the reporter who was at the hotel with a cameraman to cover social events in the city. The Tea Dance was one that had gained popularity in just a few weeks and there had been a huge crowd. The camera panned away toward the lobby below the mezzanine and it was dark and dusty with sounds of people yelling and moaning. The report was premature but indicated there were many people buried in the rubble, and emergency crews were just beginning to arrive.

Ray said, "Oh God, I hope Bob and Suzanne are all right."

Mari's legs felt weak and she dropped onto the sofa and began crying.

The TV news anchor was saying that reports from emergency workers at the scene are requesting any contractors near the hotel to bring large equipment capable of picking up heavy concrete slabs as quickly as possible. Mari couldn't help with that, but she could say prayers and started saying them. Ray's stomach was still churning and this news was not helping that situation. He realized one of them needed to go next door and relieve the babysitter, since there was a possibility that Bob and Suzanne might not get home for awhile, if ever. He didn't want to suggest that to Mari, and then thought what he would simply say, "There's no need for the babysitter to keep getting paid. I'll run over and bring Ruth over here. She may have to spend the night." Then he wished he hadn't added that last sentence.

Mari said, "What? Did they say something on TV? What did you hear?"

"No. It's just that it's bad. Even if they aren't hurt, knowing them, they're in there helping dig people out. You know. Or, they may be asked to."

Ray and Mari stayed up long past their normal bedtime. The news station just kept posting updates and they kept watching, hoping they might spot Bob and Suzanne, but it just didn't happen. There were reports of doctors arriving and having to tell people they couldn't do anything for them. Others were having arms or legs amputated with chainsaws so they could get them out. One report came on that said the Life-Flight helicopter pilot that was there said it reminded him of Vietnam, only much worse!

It was after 2:00 a.m. when Mari gave up and went to bed. Ray followed about half an hour later. It was a horrible night! He tossed and turned, looking over at the clock radio several times wanting to turn it on for more news.

Finally, he fell asleep only to have a dream about his first week in Nam. He had been assigned as the assistant machine gunner, designated to carry extra belts of ammunition and a spare barrel for the M60 machine gun. That meant he had to stay close behind the machine gunner and be prepared to take over if ever needed. At the end of his first week in country, their company was eagle-flighted into the Parrot's Beak, a bend in the river between Cambodia and Vietnam. They were immediately fired upon once the choppers took off and left them on the ground in the middle of a rice paddy. Ray's dream recalled him hunkered down behind a berm and seeing tracer rounds flying over his head. His gunner was no more than six feet away behind the next rice paddy berm firing away. Suddenly, Ray noticed the sound of the M60 had stopped and he wondered if Bernie needed a new belt of ammo. He cautiously peeked up over the berm just in time to see his squad leader shove Bernie's lifeless body out of the way and Bernie's body landed right in front of him, his glazed-over eyes staring straight up at the smoke-filled sky. The squad leader was already firing away as the enemy rounds seemed to be dissipating. Ray's dream just kept playing over and over the squad leader's shoving of Bernie. The squad leader took over what Bernie had been doing and what was expected of Ray to do. But it was the first time in Ray's nineteen years that he had seen a dead man, and it left him frozen in shock. He awoke from that dream and looked at the clock. 4:14 a.m.. He wondered how many people at that hotel were seeing a dead person for the first time.

The next morning was a struggle for Mari to make breakfast and to make sure little Ruth was entertained somewhere away from the TV. Matt was too young to understand but she used him to keep Ruthie occupied. All channels were now covering the Hyatt disaster full time and she didn't want Ruth seeing that. Shortly after he got up, Ray went next door to see if Bob and Suzanne were home. He came back and called Suzanne's mother to see if she had heard anything. "No, And I'm worried sick." She was widowed and Ray asked if she'd like to come over and sit with them and her granddaughter. Thirty minutes later she was there and they all waited and watched together to try and learn where the couple might be, in a hospital or in the makeshift morgue set up in a conference room in the hotel.

The following day, a Sunday, names of those killed were being posted on TV pending notification of next of kin. Ray had called in to a number shown on TV earlier to help relatives learn the fate of any family members they hadn't heard from. Ray told them that he was a neighbor and that Suzanne Reese's mother was staying with them at this time and left his phone number. He even commented that he and his wife had been there a half hour before the collapse but left because he had an upset stomach. The operator said, "You should thank your lucky stomach for that!" Neither of them laughed at that remark.

At 10:30, the Reynolds's phone rang and the caller asked to speak to the mother of Suzanne Reese. She was told that they had reached Bob Reese's parents and told them that their son was killed outright in the collapse. She was then informed that her daughter was pulled from the rubble in critical condition after having a leg amputated, but she did not survive the night.

Eventually they learned that 114 people had died and another 216 were injured. The catastrophe affected all of Kansas City and was said to be one of the worst man-made disasters in American history. Ray knew that night from listening to the reports that it was obviously a structural failure and had to be caused by either poor design, faulty materials, or substandard workmanship. As time went on, the reports about faulty engineering began to surface.

For more than two weeks after that night, Ray had nightmares of one kind or another almost every night. Thoughts of Bernie's death in Vietnam and the Kansas City Life-Flight helicopter pilot's comments about Vietnam, *'only worse'*, were the triggers. A couple of times the Camp Zama scene with the NVA's shouting *'dirty rotten Commie bastard'* was part of the nightmare. Some included the young private getting his leg blown off right next to Ray. Other nights it was him getting shot and Bill Bill saying he'd look him up right before Ray lost consciousness. One night there seemed to be another nightmare, all in a similar sequence but different. When he awoke that night and tried to recall it, it was as if it never happened.

But now there was another new scenario that he did remember. Two times, his nightmare included Mari and him returning to Japan to visit Camp Zama with plans to thank the doctors and nurses. After an almost fourteen-hour flight, they arrived fresh and excited in Japan. Time in dreams is fleeting, a fourteen-hour flight might only last a few seconds in a dream. They took a rickshaw to the Camp and were waved right through the gate almost as if there was no one there. The rickshaw runner pulled over in the waiting area just past the gate and helped Mari out. Ray gave him money and he hurried away.

They had to walk the last three blocks inside the parklike setting past the Japanese Maples to a clearing where they could see the A, B and C buildings where Ray had been housed. When they reached the end of the tree line, again only a few seconds later, and looked to the west for the buildings, they saw nothing but rubble and could hear moans and screams and voices uttering *'help me'*. All three buildings, and more beyond them, were just crumpled steel, brick and mortar. But the gardens between them were pristine, gorgeous with the flowers and the benches where Ray and Mari had visited before. Some benches even had people sitting there reading, or otherwise oblivious to the smoky ruins nearby. In the dream, Ray looked closer and was sure the couple on one bench was Bob and Suzanne.

This was another wake-up with the cold-sweat type nightmare. He told Mari he would have to explain in the morning. He got up and went to the wet bar and poured himself a shot of bourbon, swallowed hard, and waited a few minutes thinking about the dream and waiting for his anxiety to dissipate. He poured another shot and then returned to bed to try to get more sleep. He wasn't sure the bourbon would help, but it was always worth the try. He had to find something.

CHAPTER 34

Monday, July 20, 1981
O.P. Cabinets & Hardware
Overland Park, Kansas

Mari called her boss Monday morning and explained the circumstances with her neighbors' deaths and their daughter and the grandmother staying at her house. She said she had some work files in her briefcase and to call her if needed but she would be staying home that day.

Ray went to work just off Metcalf Avenue in Overland Park. When he pulled into his parking space, he realized he didn't remember a single thing about the drive in, his mind was on many other things. His boss, the young receptionist, and the two receiving/warehouse workers all just sat around the front conference table, drinking coffee and discussing the Hyatt news. The others couldn't believe it when Ray said he and Mari had been there just a half hour before the collapse. Then he told them about his good friends and neighbors who had invited them to the dance.

As they talked, one of the warehouse guys said to Ray that he heard the helicopter pilot say it was a lot like Vietnam, only worse.

Ray responded, "Yeah, I heard that too. I didn't sleep well Friday night, and I think that comment, along with everything else, like not knowing if our friends survived, kept me up."

His boss said, "Well, I certainly understand that. I didn't know of anyone there, and I was just simply watching the news and couldn'tquit. I think it was well after 1:00 in the morning before I shut it off and then I couldn't sleep either. I almost got back up to watch more."

Ray realized some of the thoughts he was having on the morning drive to work. He had shut the radio off, because he just couldn't stand the thought of hearing more news. He remembered what Dr. Zehr often said at the PTSD sessions about opening up and talking about your feelings. There was another pause in the conversation, like there had been all morning. It was a hard topic to discuss, knowing so many people had died so unexpectedly. He got up and went to the coffee maker and brought the pot around and filled everyone's cup who wanted some. Instead of sitting back down, he stood behind his chair and began to speak. It started as a continuation of his response to the comment from the warehouse worker about the pilot and Nam.

"You know, you try not to think about it, and most of the time you don't think about it. But when you go off to war, you know in the back of your mind that you will see people die, get shot, blown up, or whatever. It won't be pretty. It's war. Even though that expectation is there, it still startles you when you first see it. I know it did me." He paused, but held up his hand with his index finger pointing up indicating he wasn't through. He reached down for his coffee and took a sip and then began again.

"They warned us in basic training that we needed to watch out for each other's backs, and that you'll become buddies with the guys in your outfit. But, and I can't remember exactly how they said it, but it was something like 'Don't get too close to your buddies and become the *best* of friends because you will really suffer if you see your good friend get killed'. something to that effect." His mind immediately went to Bill Bill, and then he stopped talking. There was a pause while his mind tried to focus on something he just said. Something that he had sensed before but couldn't figure out. Something about that moment of being loaded in the helicopter. He had to force himself back to the conversation at hand.

"I realized in Nam, that you can't just shut off your feelings about people and that, unless you're just some cold-hearted son of a gun, you're going to make friends with those people you hope have your back, and you have theirs." Again, his hand and index finger went up.

"This situation, the Hyatt hotel, was different, and I'm not sure the helicopter pilot thought of it in this way, but," he paused, "when I was in Nam and I was shot, I remember hearing the gunshot in the distance *after* I fell to the ground. It was *war*! Just like that! Out of the clear blue sky, one bullet, one shot from a sniper nearly killed me. No warning!"

"This, this last Friday night, all those people were *not* at war, not expecting anything bad. They were there for a good time. Happy, smiling, drinking, dancing, laughing, and suddenly they hear a loud crack. In the instant they look up towards where the sound came from, it all collapses on top of them. They were not prepared. They had no chance to escape. It was just the luck of the draw who survived. I will tell you I've been learning a lot since Vietnam about PTSD, and the people who survived in that hotel lobby, injured or not, will be suffering from PTSD the rest of their lives."

Ray stood there silent for a few seconds, then pulled his chair back and sat down. Everyone was quiet until his boss finally said, "You certainly have that right. I wasn't even there and it will bother me for a long time. You can't just simply put it out of your mind."

Again, everyone just remained quiet until the receptionist asked, "Ray, what does PTSD stand for?"

"Oh, I'm sorry," he replied. "It's a psychological thing that we humans all react to differently. It's called Post Traumatic Stress Disorder. It's been described as the reason many veterans commit suicide."

"Um, do you have it?" she asked.

The boss quickly spoke up, "Cindy, I don't think that's appropriate."

Ray answered, "It's okay. I attend some sessions at the V.A. once in awhile over in Topeka. They're doing a study on it. I like to think that I don't have it, but if I was totally honest, I'd have to say I have certain symptoms. But, I will add, between my lovely wife Mari, and my V.A. doctor, I think I have everything under control. They have drugs that help some of the guys, but I've never needed them. Of course, losing our good friends and neighbors Friday night," he paused as his voice cracked and he started to tear up, "doesn't help. But I don't think that's any different for me than for any other normal human being. It's tragic!"

Cindy responded, "You have our sympathy."

CHAPTER 35

Saturday, November 7, 1981
Prairie Village, Kansas

When Ray stepped outside one Saturday morning to check his mailbox, he glanced next door and saw a car in the Reese's driveway. He assumed it was another realtor showing the property as the For Sale sign was still in the front yard. Little Ruth had disappeared from their lives to live with her grandparents after that one horrible night. He imagined she still wonders whatever happened to her parents.

As he stepped back inside and sorted through the various first-of-the-month bills, he noticed a letter from the V.A. in Topeka. He again assumed he knew what this was, just like the car in the driveway next door. another form letter from Dr. Zehr. However, when he opened this one, it wasn't the usual mimeographed copy with a handwritten note. This was stationery typed under Dr. Zehr's heading. She was informing him that she would be transferring to the Kansas City VA Medical Center on Linwood Boulevard right after the first of the year and would continue her study of PTSD and her consultation sessions there beginning in February. She said she wanted to personally let Ray know about the move and hoped he would be able to join her and the other veterans in the monthly sessions to be held on Wednesdays beginning February 10, 1982.

Ray showed the letter to Mari and said, "I guess this is good news. I won't need to drive all the way to Topeka." Then he added, "Maybe this will give you a chance to finally meet Dr. Zehr. What's it been? Something like ten or eleven years I've been seeing her. You probably wonder about her." Ray was remembering that first time he saw her and he was all pissed off about all the excessive waiting he had done that day while his mother was in the hospital lobby patiently waiting for him. Then, Dr. Zehr walked in with the Farrah Fawcett hair and that gorgeous smile and he forgot all about being pissed. He was glad he waited and hadn't walked out.

Yes, he thought, *this is good news!*

CHAPTER 36

February 10, 1982
Kansas City VA Medical Center

Ray showed up fifteen minutes early hoping he could catch Dr. Zehr for a few minutes before the meeting, but no such luck. Like in Topeka, there was a nurse to greet the veterans outside the meeting room and give them name tags. He learned later in the meeting, during introductions, that this nurse Diane was also a Vietnam veteran.

During the meeting, Ray remained relatively quiet since it was mostly all new people for him, except for two veterans from Lawrence, Kansas who used to drive to Topeka. Now, like him, they were still following Dr. Zehr here in Kansas City. He spent most of the time admiring Dr. Zehr's beauty. Her hair had changed again, longer, light brown with streaks of blond and pulled back in a ponytail which Ray thought made her look much younger. Her eyes were still gorgeous, her skin smooth and creamy, and she glowed when she smiled.

After the session, as people filed out and shook hands with the doctor, she asked Ray if he could stick around for a few minutes to visit. Of course, he said "Yes" and waited just down the hall from the meeting room.

When she finished saying her goodbyes, she led Ray down a couple of halls and up the elevator to her office. "It's good to see you again," she said. "I hope you'll become a regular at these sessions. I just wanted to catch up a little and see how you're doing. You know, what's new?"

Ray was a little surprised at the casual conversation, but replied, "Oh, not much. Mari and I are doing well. New home, jobs are fine. You know we've got a son, Matt, going on two?" He laughed after that comment, and then added, "He can be a handful, but he's a lot of fun."

"Congratulations on the son. I think you told me that a few months after he was born." She paused, then switched to more serious concerns. "Are you still having nightmares or any other effects of PTSD? I noticed you didn't say much during the meeting."

"Well, I didn't feel that comfortable around this group. They were almost all new to me and I wanted to wait and see how others reacted."

"That's understandable. It normally happens like that, especially for newbies. But you're an experienced veteran. I kind of thought you'd speak up."

"Maybe next month."

"Well, I'll remember you said that. You surely must have some new stories to tell."

While it was impromptu that Monday at work after the Hyatt disaster, Ray remembered his little speech about war and dying and the loss of his neighbors and friends and how all those people had no time to react, just '*Poof*' and they were gone. He recited it to Dr. Zehr almost word for word.

She listened intently and processed it for a minute after he finished. Then she said, "You are exactly right! Those people who were there and survived that night, injured or not, are perfect examples of PTSD sufferers. They might not know it, or might not call it that, but they will be suffering and having nightmares or other forms of problems related to what they experienced that night and won't have a clue how to cure it unless they seek medical or spiritual help. Some may resort to antidepressants or other drugs while some will find themselves using alcohol to drown out the memory. We find there are many different ways that sufferers try to cope. This certainly applies to you since you were there that night just before all hell broke loose. How lucky for you that you didn't feel well! I hope you will remember what you just told me and might be willing to share it at the next meeting."

They visited a little longer and then she wished him well and asked if he could find his way back out.

He remembered their second meeting years earlier when he was so enthralled with her looks and her kindness that he almost said he loved her. So, as they shook hands in her office doorway, he asked, "Remember that one meeting way back when, when I said something that was probably totally inappropriate?"

She looked at him quizzically as though she wasn't sure what Ray was talking about, and he really wasn't sure if she remembered or not, but there was a sly smile.

"Well, I'm still glad I got to meet you!" He smiled and turned and walked out the door.

CHAPTER 37

Over the years, Ray had noticed certain things about his dreams. While his brain was doing cartwheels in the middle of the night just to show Ray how clever it was, once he woke up from a nightmare and calmed himself down, his brain continued to work overtime. Even though he was not a religious person, he would often begin to think he should be. His thoughts would range from prayer and asking God for help to outright cussing and blaming God for what was wrong. That night after the Hyatt disaster and losing their neighbors was a prime example. He figured it was after 4:00 a.m. before he went to sleep, and he was awake again following a bad dream before 6:00. His brain continued to excel at working all hours of the night.

'Oh God,' he thought, *'Stop this! Please! What can I do? If I come to your church, will that help me? Which one? Methodist, Baptist, Catholic? No, please not Catholic, I don't understand it. What if I pray regularly? Will you listen? Why did you take so many lives? Why did all those people have to suffer such horrible deaths? And why an eleven-year-old girl? And the ones who were mangled and torn apart, they now have to live like that, I don't understand. If you do exist, tell me how I can change things, show me what to do. Please, God!'*

Some of those thoughts started way back at Camp Zama. He thought his getting shot was probably retribution for him shooting at them, the gooks. He didn't want to talk about it, and he didn't even want to think about it. But he couldn't help it. It was the boy that caused the nightmares back then and many times since. He didn't even talk to God about that. Maybe he should ask forgiveness, but it wasn't his fault. It was war and he had his orders!

He thought he should tell Dr. Zehr about this. Not just the nightmares, she knows about *most* of those, but the thoughts afterward.

One other thing that he thought was almost always true; the nightmares seemed to occur only, well, almost only, when he was more idle. He had noticed that when he was extremely busy at work, maybe chasing a large apartment complex and excited about the prospect. Or, when he had two major projects with bids due the same week. When his mind was actively involved in key life issues, he didn't recall ever having a serious problem with a jump-out-of-bed-screaming dream. Except that one time. He did recall, however, that several times when he was troubled with sleep, it was when he had taken time off work during the holidays or for vacation. Maybe he should be documenting this. He should bring it up at the next PTSD session. He wondered if others had similar experiences.

But he didn't bring it up at the meeting, and he didn't mention it to Dr. Zehr. It's like the issue with the boy. He'd never ever mentioned that to anyone. Sometimes your inner thoughts are just that, *your* inner thoughts. Maybe he was afraid to expose them. Was he worried about letting others know he wasn't a religious man? Would they think he's strange for not believing in God? He was sure he had heard other veterans say they had a hard time believing, or that they were agnostic, if not a confirmed atheist. Why was he afraid to admit such beliefs? Sometimes his dreams and these inner thoughts made him wonder if he wasn't halfway crazy, off his rocker, one card shy of a full deck, or just plain loony.

Maybe next meeting.

CHAPTER 38

Friday, July 29, 1983
Best Western Motel
Council Bluffs, Iowa

Ray and Mari, along with several others in the wedding party, all had rooms at the Best Western Motel on West Broadway. It was the eve of Ray's brother's wedding. Chip and Erica had arranged for the whole group to have dinner at the Pizza King on the east side of town following the wedding rehearsal at St. Paul's Lutheran Church.

Erica, who grew up in Council Bluffs, guaranteed that Pizza King was the best pizza anywhere and her soon-to-be husband nodded in agreement. They had met at college in Lawrence, Kansas their freshman year and dated for almost the full four years of college and had pledged to marry after graduation, which had been earlier this year. Chip had landed a job with an automotive dealership as the parts manager, which he told the family was only temporary, while Erica was planning on keeping the tradition of working in her family's wholesale plumbing business.

Ray was having some concerns about his brother leaving the nest and now only June was left to hear those words, *'someday this will all be yours.'* This pre-celebration certainly made Ray aware it was a real thing, and maybe it was simply the fact that the Vonnegut comment no longer applied since it would now be spoken to the wrong gender, but something more than that was bothering him. It just didn't seem right. Maybe it was a feeling that it was one more step away from the family ranch - his father's place, and his father's father before him, and then one more father before that who started it way back in the 1800's. Why couldn't Chip stay in *our* family business and let Erica be the one to move to the Flint Hills? *No, it wasn't just that, there was something more.*

Dennis G. Smith

The pizzas hadn't arrived yet, but when the waitress came around, Ray ordered another drink. He wasn't engaged in all the conversations between the Reynolds group and Erica's family. Ray had his hands full with young Matt, now three. Mari wasn't much help since she was now seven months pregnant with their second child..

Ray just kept looking across the table at his brother and wondered. It can't be the fact Chip is leaving the ranch with no loyalty to the family's heritage. That's the exact same thing he had done himself. He can't fault Chip for that. It's a new world. His parents have to understand that. *No, it's something else.*

The pizzas started showing up, eight of them for twenty people in the private dining room. Mari asked Ray why he was so quiet. He shrugged his shoulders and said, "I don't know. Tired, I guess." He ordered another drink and asked Mari, "I'll bet you wish you could have one?"

"No, I'm fine," she said. "That's three for you. That's unusual."

"Yeah," he replied. "I'm celebrating!" He smiled half-heartedly at her as he cut small bites of pizza for Matt.

When the rehearsal party broke up and everyone was headed to the parking lot, Mari reached in her purse and pulled out her car keys and said, "I think I'm driving!"

Ray reacted calmly and said, "I'm fine, but that's okay." Then, as he strapped Matt in the car seat, he added, "Oh, and I'm sorry. Something's bothering me and I can't figure it out. I'm sure it's related to Chip getting married, but I should be happy about that. They've gone together a long time."

At the motel, Mari got ready for bed and got comfortable while she waited for Ray, who continued to sit in the one easy chair in the room staring at the TV with a sleepy Matt on his lap. She finally had to ask him if he would come to bed so she could sleep.

There was a reason he was bothered and he thought he knew what it was, but he didn't want to admit it. It all confronted him in the middle of the night. It was similar to the nightmare he had many times before, starting back at Camp Zama, only this one had a twist.

Back in Nam during his first month there when he was serving as the assistant machine gunner, just a week or so after Bernie had been killed, they were in the field and his squad was assigned to set up an ambush patrol for the night. After dark, they took up positions on both sides of a cart path coming out of a village a little over a klick away. Claymore mines were set up on both sides of the path facing away from their company's nighttime location about forty yards behind them. There were several shrubs and some rice paddy berms for the squad to hide behind, and they agreed on their two-hour watch rotations and took their turns.

At midnight, Bill Bill woke Ray, "Hey, Wildcat, it's your turn," he whispered.

It's hard to wake up at that time of night, but you realize the necessity of your duty and the lives at stake and it becomes easy to stay awake. You also start imagining that you see things or hear things and start watching and listening even closer. Shortly after he heard Bill Bill's breathing change that indicated he was asleep, Ray thought he saw movement in the bamboo thicket about fifty yards from their position. He carefully kept watch and saw it again. Something was moving in the moonlight behind the thicket headed toward the cart path, but was it an animal or human?

There was a break in the bamboo about fifteen yards off the path and the moonlight was shining through. Ray watched that spot intently and sure enough, the movement showed up and crossed the opening. There were three men who appeared to be wearing black pajamas and Ray definitely saw they were all carrying weapons. He was about to wake Bill, but the enemy disappeared. He assumed they would show up on the cart path momentarily and that would be when he would need to wake everyone, especially if they started down the path towards their position. He didn't want to create a false alarm and wake people unnecessarily. But that was it. He didn't see them anymore.

When he awoke Gunner for his turn as watchman, he told him about what he had seen and where they were. He said, "They must have bedded down for the night or they have a tunnel entrance down there because I haven't seen them since."

Two hours later just as Gunner was waking Bill Bill for his second round at watch, they both spotted movement and they woke Ray and the others. The three men were up and had stepped out on the cart path and headed towards the ambush. Everyone grabbed their weapons, and two guys put their hands on the claymore triggers.

Ray took a deep breath, let it out and aimed his M-16 down the pathway toward the men. Someone in one of the G.I.'s positions got antsy and fired a shot before the gooks got close enough for the claymores, so everyone else opened up. Two of the enemy soldiers immediately turned to run back toward the bamboo thicket and tried to fire their weapons behind them as they ran. Ray had fired three quick shots and noticed his second was a tracer round and he watched it appear to hit the man who had been last in the procession and he watched him fall. One for the body count he thought, retribution for Bernie! The other two fell also, right in sequence. The ambush patrol's radio immediately squelched and Lieutenant Johnson wanted to know what happened. They reported seeing three men in black pajamas with weapons. They were ordered to stay put until daylight and then he would be out to inspect. A little after 6:00 a.m., Johnson, his RTO, and the second squad showed up and they all marched down the cart path to survey the damage. Ray heard the platoon leader get on the radio and report a body count of five, almost double what they actually had.

Ray didn't pay much attention after that. He looked down at the body of the man he was sure he had shot. It wasn't a man, it was a boy, couldn't be over fourteen, if that. He thought of his brother, Chip, back home. The body count should have been two and a half.

At the Best Western, about 3:00 a.m., Ray woke up screaming, jumped out of bed and went to run out the door in his boxer shorts. He tried to open it but then had trouble undoing the security chain that kept anyone from coming in. Once he had that undone, he ran out into the early morning air and stopped at their car and leaned on the hood breathing heavily. Mari had grabbed her blouse from the night before and pulled it on over her nightshirt and came rushing out to urge Ray back in. Luckily, there was no one up at the motel at that time of the morning although there were a few cars traveling along on Broadway.

Now, Mari had to calm Ray quickly so she could get back inside to quiet down Matt who was now wide awake and sobbing.

It was one of the worst nightmares Ray could remember. He had many nightmares about that night and he always remembered Lieutenant Johnson reporting the body count as 'five' which always reminded him of seeing the young boy and thinking it should have been 'two and a half'. The boy! It was the boy that had been bothering him all night. The same age as Chip was then. Now Chip was getting married, but that wasn't all that made the nightmare horrible. No, it was worse than all the other times.

He was sleeping and Gunner and Bill Bill woke him and pointed down the cart path. He grabbed his M-16 and got ready, took a deep breath and exhaled. He sighted down the barrel towards the trail just like he did with prairie dogs. It was dark but he could see a prairie dog at the end of his sight. His finger was on the trigger. Bill Bill whispered, I've got the middle man. Gunner said, "Right!" Whatever that meant from a machine gunner.

Ray focused on the third man in line and said "I've got the dog!" He wanted to hurry before the prairie dog ducked back down his hole. He imagined it was sounding a warning to the others. Just as he pulled his trigger the prairie dog face he was sensing at the end of his sight changed to human. Unlike the other dreams, this time the face was Chip. he tried to pull the bullet back. That failed. He saw the body fall. Then he was with Lieutenant Johnson, and Ray looked down at the young boy's body dressed in black with Chip's face.

That's when the screaming started and Ray ran out of the motel. Again, like all the times before, he couldn't tell Mari, just like he'd never told anyone about this one - the fourteen-year-old boy that he killed. Then, years later, when he read Ho Chi Minh's confession about sending boys that age off to war, he was physically sick. Some things you just never get over!

Then he remembered, *It was him who jumped the gun and squeezed off the first round. He almost caused the whole ambush to fall apart. If those farmer gooks had been NVA regulars, they would have dove for the ditches instead of turning to run and then the ambush would have failed. But the kid, the boy, he was down before he had a chance to dive in the ditches. And Bill Bill and Gunner took care of the other two, or four by Johnson's count. What a disgusting war! He hated it!*

Back in Nam, every time after that night, when his outfit engaged in a firefight with the enemy, Ray didn't bother to aim his weapon by sighting down the barrel. He either pointed it high over the Commies' heads, or low into the ground. Mari had coaxed him back inside and picked up Matt. Then she got Ray a glass of water from the bathroom and gave Matt a pacifier. She went back and dampened a washcloth for Ray and brought it out and cooled his forehead. Ray's breathing had slowed back down and he looked at her with tears in his eyes and simply said, "Sorry".

The wedding went off without a hitch later that Saturday and the reception was a fun occasion. Ray shied away from the alcohol except that he did drink a glass of champagne for the traditional toast He slept well that night after losing so much sleep the night before. Mari laid awake for a long time, worried about her husband and wondered if he would ever lose his nightmares. She also wondered if he would ever tell her what they were all about.

CHAPTER 39

Saturday, August 19, 1987
Reynolds Ranch
West of Strong City, Kansas

The Reynolds family from Prairie Village headed to Strong City and Cottonwood Falls for a family visit and a week's vacation in the Flint Hills. Their son, Matthew, was now seven, and old enough to enjoy the drive and seeing the livestock and horses on the ranch. His sister Fran was two months away from her fourth birthday and also liked the animals. Both had learned to love seeing their two grandpas who both teased them and always had candy or some kind of gift hidden away for them.

Driving down, Ray had noticed the wind was quite strong and occasionally rocked their minivan as they came out from passing an eighteen-wheeler. Other than that, the weather was fairly normal for the great plains in August with high's in the upper 80's. The wind, too, was fairly normal, especially for the central plains. The exception this summer was that the Midwest was well into the second year of below-normal rainfall and the start of possible drought conditions, with long-range forecasts that could be as bad as the days of the Dust Bowl. When they exited I-35 at Emporia and headed west, Ray and Mari talked about the darkening sky they could see in the northwest and hoped that might mean some much needed rain.

They passed through Strong City and Ray turned north off US 50 where Fox Creek nears the highway. As he turned onto the long gravel driveway of the Reynolds Ranch, he always liked viewing the large Sycamores standing out among a clump of Silver Maples planted by his grandfather years ago. Along the ditch he enjoyed the sumacs when they turned red in the fall, but now the sumacs and tall grasses past the fence were all dry and brown without a shade of green amongst them. He couldn't help but notice the westernmost Sycamore that had died a few years earlier and remembered his father saying he needed to take it out some day. Ray thought this vacation might be a good time to suggest to his father that he'd help with that.

As the minivan cleared the slight rise and they could see the two-story white farmhouse and the red barn and machine shed up ahead, they were amazed by the stark contrast of the sunlight on the white house with the darkened black shelf cloud behind it. He thought about stopping to take a photo but wasn't sure if they had packed the camera. To the northwest, still miles away from the ranch, Ray could see a virgo, something he learned in geology class, a dry rainstorm where a shaft of precipitation can be seen coming from the clouds but evaporates before it hits the ground.

"Maybe we'll get some rain," he said to Mari.

"Probably, since you washed the van before we left."

Ray laughed and said, "That's what causes it." Then he turned to her and asked, "Did you know that washing your car also causes bird poop."

"You're goofy," she said.

After the greetings and the hugs and all the attention to young Matt and Fran, Ray finally said to his dad, "Have you looked out back? I think we might get some rain?"

His father got up to go look and said loudly from the kitchen, "Boy, can we use it!"

Ray added, "Have there been any tornado warnings?" Always a worry in the summer in Kansas. "Remember Dorothy and Toto?"

"No specific warnings or watches that I've heard. Well, this morning's news said a *slight* possibility of severe weather, but I'd be surprised if we got anything."

Ray had followed his father into the kitchen and watched as Walt looked out through the window in the kitchen door, then opened it and stepped outside. They both felt a gust of wind come through the screen. After a minute of walking out past the oak tree for a better look, he came back in and said, "Well, that dry rain ain't gonna make it to the ground and it appears to be letting up. I think that big dark cloud is at least twenty miles further away and goin' north. What do you think?"

"We were watching it all the way over from Emporia and it wasn't movin' very fast, especially considering how hard the wind's blowing, but yeah, I think it's probably going to miss here."

Walt reached over on the kitchen counter, turned on the radio, and tuned in the weather channel and they heard reports of brief downpours along I-70 and just south of Topeka. There were also high wind warnings to high-profile vehicles.

"Yup," Walt said again, "I don't think we're gonna get anything. Damn! Sure could use it."

They went back into the family room and joined little Matt and the females. Just after they sat down, there was a sharp clap of thunder and they all jumped and Matt looked at his dad with big eyes. A few seconds later the sound of the air conditioner stopped and the one table lamp that was on went dark. Beverly got up and tried the light switch on the wall. The ceiling light and fan did not come on. "I guess tha power's out. Do you think I should call?"

Walt responded, "Let's give it a few minutes and see if if gets corrected. If not, I'll try to call the power company."

Ray had picked up Fran and was bouncing her on his knee and offered her to his father and she was eager to go to her grandpa. Walt took over the entertaining responsibilities. Matt wanted to know when they could go out and pet the horses.

When there was a pause in the conversation, Ray got up to get something to drink and went to the kitchen. He again looked out the kitchen door window to the north and he thought he smelled smoke. It looked like there might be smoke in the air but the wind was blowing so strong it was hard to tell. Then, as he turned to the refrigerator, some movement out the west window caught his eye. He saw Juan, running from the barn through the pasture toward the gate, and the horses were right behind him. Ray moved closer to the window and looked to his left at the barn and saw smoke rising from the back side.

"Dad, quick," he shouted, "The barn's on fire!"

Walt set Fran down on the floor and jumped up. He ran to the front door. It was closer. He stepped out on the front porch and saw the prairie grasses all the way towards the road were blackened and putting off white smoke and the whole south side of the barn was on fire. Juan had let the horses out and opened the gate so they could escape. He then came running toward the house screaming.

"Mr. Walt, Mr. Walt, you gotta get out! Get out! Hurry!"

Walt turned back and rushed inside. "Grab Fran and your purses! We gotta go! Now! Com'n Matt, to the car." His voiced cracked and Beverly sensed that he was crying.

"What's going on?" Mari shouted and just then smelled smoke coming through the front door. When she picked up Fran and stood, she saw the flames out the front picture window way down the driveway near the highway. "Oh, dammit, dammit, *damn it!*" Nothing frightened her more. "Ray!" she yelled and ran for the minivan.

Ray had gone out the back door to head for the barn but then saw Juan and he turned back to the house. He stopped in the kitchen to call 911, but the line was dead. He ran through the house and out to the car where Mari and Fran were already in the front seat. Matt was climbing in the back. She hadn't bothered with the child seat in the back, she just wanted to get out and get out quick. Fran didn't know what was going on but sensed the tension and was crying uncontrollably. Matt also was unsure how to act, but knew they needed to go.

"Shit!" Ray exclaimed, "The keys are on the kitchen counter." He jumped out and ran back in the house. When he came back out, he saw his mother in their car and his father in the smoke-filled driveway waving his arms and communicating with Juan. Apparently, he wanted Juan to ride with them, but Juan was ready to head back to the barn to get the old pick-up out of there. They turned to look back at the barn and the wind had spread the flames all the way across the roof. Juan started to run towards the barn and Walt ran after him and caught his shirt sleeve and pulled him back to their car. When they got there, Walt pointed at the barn again. It was almost completely engulfed. Juan climbed in the back seat.

Ray had pulled part way down the driveway and watched the Walt-Juan battle in the driveway until he saw Juan get in the car and then he took off which greatly pleased Mari. Matt was no longer happy to be on vacation and was a combination of screams with Fran crying and then gentle sobs as his mother held her tight.

When they got to the high point of the driveway, where Ray had wanted to take a picture an hour earlier, he stopped briefly and got out to look behind them. His father caught up and got out and joined him beside the van. Even from the distance, they could see burning embers blowing toward the house and landing on the roof and the porch. Just then, the cupola collapsed into the barn roof and larger embers and pieces of burning wood went flying toward the house. Ray looked at his father and saw the tears in his eyes.

Mari yelled out the open door, "*RAY, we gotta go!*"

Walt looked at Ray and said, "Son, let's get out of here. I can't bear to watch this!"

Ray turned to head back inside his van and said, "I'm going straight to Chase County Fire Department."

His father yelled back, "It won't matter, it'll be too late.'

Less than ten minutes later, Walt caught up with his son's minivan

Dennis G. Smith

in front of the Chase County sheriff's office and pulled in beside him. Ray came walking out with a deputy and reported the fire department volunteers were all on their way. They could hear the truck siren up the street headed north. The women got out and shared a long hug with Matt, now sobbing along with his sister, caught in the middle of a group hug. Walt kept wiping tears from his eyes with the back of his hands. Ray couldn't remember ever seeing his father cry. Juan stayed in the back seat with no idea what he should do now.

Just a few minutes later, Ralph pulled in fast and jumped out of his car and ran to hug his daughter and grandkids. Word travels fast in a small town, especially when the volunteer fire department is called out. Ralph had immediately jumped in his car to try and find the Reynolds family. The sheriff's office was going to be his first place to stop and ask.

They all stood there not knowing what to do next. Finally, it all sunk in with Beverly. They had no home, no belongings, no place to go. Their long family history and all of the photos, keepsakes, antique furnishings, valuable dishes, and everything else was all gone. They didn't need to go back to see it, she just knew. She took two steps towards her husband, put her head on his shoulder and broke down in deep sobs.

Ray tried to remember if he had ever seen his mother cry. He was pretty sure she did when they met at the airport after he returned home from Nam and Camp Zama, but those were tears of happiness. These were ranchers, Kansas Flint Hills ranchers, and they were tough, hard-working folk. They had lived through the depression, the dust bowl, World War II, Korea, and their son in Vietnam, but nothing could have prepared them for this.

Ralph told the deputy they would all move over to his office and asked him to call with any reports from the ranch. When they got to the Key realty office, he put on a pot of coffee and then offered cold drinks from the refrigerator. No one seemed too interested, but the women both accepted a soft drink absent-mindedly. Ray and Juan both took a beer.

Ten minutes later, Mari's mother Jennifer walked in with a box of cookies. She knew better than to walk around the room offering them treats. She simply opened the box and set it on the counter in the cabinet display area and then proceeded to walk around the room giving hugs, starting with Mrs. Reynolds. She could tell by her eyes that she was in need of help.

After long periods of silence, nobody knowing what to say, Ralph finally offered a few thoughts. "You all need to come over to our place this evening. Jenn and I will fix dinner and you can stay there tonight."

"Mari piped up, "Dad, you don't have enough beds. You converted my old room to a den and all you have is the guest room. I think maybe we can all go back to our house in Prairie Village."

It was quiet again, nobody wanted to express their concerns over the gravity of the situation. Finally, Walt spoke up. "I need to stay here, somewhere, maybe a motel in Emporia. I'll have to take care of things."

Juan had finished his beer and was holding the empty can as though he didn't know what to do with it. He opened up with his response to the current conversation. "I have a friend I can call over by the rodeo. He watches over the property and keeps the grounds clean."

Ralph pointed to the phone on his desk and told Juan to feel free to use it. Juan pulled out his wallet and started searching for a scrap of paper with a phone number. Ray got up and went to the refrigerator and took Juan another beer. He also grabbed one for himself and looked around to see if anyone else needed anything.

More silence. Ray wanted to say something to ease some of the pain his parents were going through but he couldn't think of anything that might be appropriate. Instead, he was thinking of some of the things that were in the house that were now lost. His dad's gun collection, the antique desk and chair in the den, his old army uniform and his medals. Then he thought of the barn and his saddle and the old Ford pick-up, stuff that really isn't that important, but now just isn't.

The office door opened and the Reynolds's insurance agent walked in. "Walt, Beverly, I'm so sorry," he said as he approached to shake their hands. "As soon as I heard, I rushed right over. Well, I had to track you down first. But I'm just so sorry to hear the news. How bad is it?"

Walt had trouble answering. "I don't know for sure, but it's bad, John. Ray can tell you."

Ray started in, "Dry lightning. Out of an apparent clear blue sky hit a tree down by Fox Creek. Set it on fire. It also split in two and we saw that it knocked down the utility lines where they cross the creek to come over to our driveway and up to the house. Dad and I saw the virgo earlier and the storm appeared to be north of us, but then we heard a really loud clap of thunder. We all jumped. Had to be the lightning strike. A minute or so later the power went out. I found out that the phone was dead, too."

Ray continued. "But, how bad? Like dad said, we don't know for sure, but I'll tell you what we saw. When I first smelled smoke, I saw Juan chasing the horses out of the barn into the open prairie. Then I looked and the whole south side of the barn was on fire. All the dry prairie grass and the wind, oh my God, the wind, had carried the fire from the creek a half mile up to the barn. By the time we rushed out to the cars with just our clothes on our backs and our kids, the roof on the barn was engulfed with embers flying everywhere.

"We stopped near the rise in our driveway and saw where the tree was still burning but all the prairie grass, by then had been burnt up and blown away. Dad and I looked back just as the roof of the barn started to collapse and pieces of burning wood were landing on the house, the roof and the front porch. We couldn't watch anymore. I just can't imagine there is anything left."

"Oh my, I am so sorry. I'm going to do everything I can to help you guys out. I'm pretty sure your policy covers everything," the agent said.

Walt looked up and directly at his agent and said, "John, we appreciate that, but I want you to know, right now it's not the money that's the problem." His head went back down and he began to sob. Beverly was sitting next to him and reached over and put her arm around his strong back. She could feel his body trembling.

John added one more remark, "Just don't forget to hang onto any receipt now that you might get. Since you've lost your place of residence, motels, restaurants, groceries can all be recoverable expenses."

Walt raised his head again and said, "John, it wasn't just a place of residence. It was our life!"

John stood up and walked over and said, "I know Walt, I know. I'll be back in touch. Keep me informed on how to reach you."

He left and the room again went quiet until the door opened and the sheriff walked in. "Walt, Beverly," he said as he walked over towards the kitchenette and shook their hands. "The volunteers couldn't do much, Walt. You've served with them before, you know. By the time they got there, what, with this wind out there on the prairie, the fire had already spread two or three acres north of your house and was moving quickly. The barn was gone and the roof on the house was too. The whole house was involved by then. You know there's no hydrants out there, and well, that pumper truck only carries so much water. They looked at it all and figured it would be a waste of water trying to stop what was left. And, well, with the wind the way it was, it would have been a waste of time to try to catch up with the fire and put it out. It's natures way with the prairie. You know that."

Walt slid down off his barstool and stepped towards the sheriff.

"Thanks for going out there, Jack. You're a good man. I appreciate it." They shook hands and exchanged a man hug.

The sheriff added another comment, "Let me know if I can do anything, okay?" Then he passed Ray and Mari on the way out and said, "I know it's a sad day, but it's good to see you two. It's been awhile." He looked at Matt and Fran in Mari's lap and said,"Looks like you got two fine young additions to the family there. Congratulations on that."

When the door closed behind the sheriff, Ralph spoke up. "I've got an idea. You all know that widow Swanson passed away a couple months ago. I've got her house on the market and have the keys. Her kids were back here and cleaned it all up before they listed it. I don't know why you couldn't stay there until things get worked out. It's fully furnished." Then he looked at Ray and added, "It's got a pretty new kitchen and bath. thanks to you. Let me call her daughter and check. They'll probably want some kind of rent."

Ray jumped in on that and offered, "It's really a pretty neat house for its age. It's held up well."

Walt looked at his wife and back at Ralph and nodded in agreement.

Ray watched as Walt walked to his desk and then said, "If it's okay with you, when you finish with that call, I need to make a couple of long distance calls to tell Chip and June what's happened."

Ralph nodded, "That's fine. You go right ahead."

When Ralph hung up the phone and walked away from his desk back toward the kitchenette, he started explaining his conversation. "That was Shirley, Mrs. Swanson's daughter. I explained the situation here and the circumstances. She remembers you guys. She's out in western Colorado now. She doesn't want to take the home off the market, but said she had no problem with you guys staying there and said you could move in when it was convenient. I told her it would be tonight and there would be no 'moving in', all you had was the clothes on your back."

"Ralph, that's great! That must be the best thing that's happened today!"

Beverly chimed in behind her husband, "Well, the best thing besides seeing Matt and Fran!"

Matt's ears perked up and he slid off his chair and ran over to his grandmother. Fran noticed and followed along.

"There's a catch," Ralph said, and Walt and Bev's expressions changed. "Shirley said they should probably charge rent to make it legal."

Walt's shoulders shrugged and he said, "That's only right." He was remembering what John, his insurance agent, said.

"Yeah," Ralph said, "She wants a dollar a month."

"Oh crap. You're kidding?"

"Nope. That's it!"

Ray spoke up, "I don't think that would happen in the city."

CHAPTER 40

Week Starting Monday, August 21, 1987
Key Realty - Key Cabinets
Cottonwood Falls, Kansas

Both Ray and Marilyn had called their employers and asked to extend their vacation a few more days while they took care of family business. They said they would be back as soon as possible and were told 'not to worry' and their bosses were sorry to hear the sad news.

Ray had set up a temporary office of sorts back at the spare desk in the Key Realty building. Small town people all knew about the catastrophe and learned where Ray was and where Walt and Beverly were staying. Ray was surprised at how many old friends and even people he didn't know stopped by during the day to offer condolences and to drop off casseroles, cookies, pies and cakes, and even bags of groceries both at the office and at the Key family residence.

In the evening, before his parents arrived for dinner, Ray and Mari talked about it and wondered why so many people didn't go direct to the late Mrs. Swanson's house and deliver their gifts there, where they were needed and would be appreciated.

Mari's father had been listening to their conversation and spoke up. "You know, I've lived in this community all my life and I've been listening to the comments of those people dropping off pies and cakes and I think it's just this. They don't know what to say to your folks. It's easier to ask *you* to give their gifts to them. It's one thing when someone dies and, well, it's a shame, but it'll eventually happen to all of us. And we've all had experience saying 'Sorry about your loss' and 'We're gonna miss him, or her'. But this. This is something else. When a prominent citizen of the community, a well-known hard-working couple with a good family, loses everything they've worked for all their lives. All that hard work and dedication flies out the window and folks just don't know what to say. Your dad said today that a few people had stopped by, and that's exactly what he said, 'They just didn't know what to say', and he couldn't blame them. They mostly just shook hands and gave a hug and said, 'I hope this helps'."

Both Chip and June had been back in town since Sunday with their spouses and kids and staying with old friends and classmates. So the family was gathered to figure out what they needed to do to help their parents.

On Monday, the three kids and their spouses had all driven out to the ranch in Ray's minivan and surveyed the damage. Their parents opted not to go. They really didn't want to see it, not then. It was too soon. The grandkids all stayed behind with their grandparents at the Swanson house. The plan was to see the damage and then head over to Emporia to pick up a few new items of clothing for their parents. After all, they needed everything from shoes, socks, underwear to outerwear and even winter coats, hats and gloves.

When they passed over the rise in the driveway, both Chip and June gasped. The house and barn were completely gone except for the fireplace and chimney. The stone fireplace and grill their father had built on the patio outside the kitchen was still standing as a monument to his work although it was covered in soot and pieces of burnt wood from the house or the barn.. The shell of the 1960 Ford pick-up was there with all the tires burnt off and the interior completely gone. The equipment shed behind where the barn once stood was mostly metal and it looked like a shadow of its former self, blackened and warped out of shape with the tractor and baler shells still there supporting the collapsed roof.

Ray walked over beyond the patio, past the oak tree which looked like it might survive with green leaves still attached to the top branches. He stopped by the old tractor tire filled with sand next to the swing set they had all played on when they were young. His brother and sister and their spouses had followed him.

Ray looked up at the tree and then down at the wooden seats suspended by chains from the wooden supports and said. "These old oaks are tough." *'Son of a gun,'* he thought to himself, remembering Bill Bill's comment there in the driveway years earlier. "Look, these swing seats didn't burn."

June walked up and rubbed her fingers across a seat to see if there was soot that might rub off. It didn't feel dirty and she turned to sit in the swing. She casually pushed with her legs to start swinging gently. There were tears in her eyes. The others all watched.

A slight breeze rustled the oak leaves above them. A meadowlark was chirping in the distance.

Ray began singing, "Hey Jude, don't make it bad. Take a sad song and make it better. Remember to let her into your heart, then you can start to, to make it better." He stuttered and choked on the last few words and couldn't go on. It wasn't just that he didn't know the next verse, but he couldn't go on anyway because he was totally choked up with tears running down his cheeks. He didn't want to turn around and have the others see him like that, but if he had, he would have seen they all were full of tears.

June got up off the swing and stepped over to her brother and wrapped her arms around his waist. "I love you, Sergeant Pepper." she said.

"Love you too, Jude!"

Then they all shared hugs and cried together.

Three days later, Walter Reynolds, third in a line of family ranchers in the Flint Hills of the Tall Grass Prairie, father of three, and a grandfather of five more, with no place left to leave to his kids, died of a massive stroke at 4:00 a.m.. By the time the Life-Flight helicopter had arrived from Emporia, a local retired nurse who lived just four doors away had already tried CPR and told Walt's wife of 43 years he was gone.

The funeral was set for Monday, the 28th.

After only six nights in the Swanson house, Beverly Reynolds could no longer stay there, alone, in the bed where her husband died. Ralph Key moved his desk out of the den and into the garage and called a furniture store in Emporia to have a bed delivered. Beverly moved in with the Keys that Thursday to be where her son, daughter-in-law and two grandkids were staying. Being around Matt, Fran, and of course Ray, gave her some comfort.

CHAPTER 41

Monday, September 4, 1987
O.P. Cabinets & Hardware
Overland Park, Kansas

Back in his office on Monday, Ray had to fill everyone in on the tragedies they had faced on their so-called vacation. All of the people in the small office staff had trouble believing so much tragedy could happen to one family in such a short time-frame. They all wanted to know how Ray's mother was holding up.

"Not so well," he replied. "She went back to Colorado with my younger sister for now. She's not sure where she wants to live. I tried to talk her into coming up here since she's familiar with K.C. and it would be close if she wanted to go back to Chase County and visit. She decided on Colorado just to get farther away for awhile and then maybe come here or go to Chip's next."

After things quieted down, Ray closed his door and called Dr. Zehr. He had to leave a message, but he was surprised when he heard back from her in only twenty minutes.

"How are you?" the psychologist asked.

"Oh, you're not gonna believe all of this."

"Why? What's happened?"

"Well, first, I called just to let you know I'm not coming to the meeting Wednesday. You know and I know that most of the guys, and girls, that show up there have lots worse PTSD than me. Listening to them talk about their problems helps me realize my problems aren't really so bad, just dealing with nightmares every so often and letting little things make me angry all the time. But, the big things, like that Hyatt disaster and losing our good friends, Bob and Suzanne, in the prime of their lives, or me getting shot by a sniper when the war was winding down, all because some chickenshit Lieutenant didn't want to go to the field that day. You know me, I can't let those things go."

"Yeah, I know," she replied.

"We took a vacation two weeks ago to go home to the ranch." Then there was a long pause.

Dr. Zehr finally spoke up, "Ray? You still there?"

"There was a lightning strike out of a clear blue sky above us." Another shorter pause. "We had to run for our lives. The whole place burned to the ground!"

"Oh no!" Now, Dr. Zehr had to pause, not sure what to say. "Ray, I am so sorry!"

"Wait, I'm not done." He was catching his breath from holding back the sobs. "So, my parents are left with just the clothes on their back. Then, later that week, my father had a stroke and died. Obviously, my mother is taking it hard."

"Oh, Ray!"

Neither of them said anything for what seemed like minutes, but like time in a dream, was only ten or fifteen seconds. Dr. Zehr spoke next. "Ray, you know these PTSD sessions are meant to help for any kind of personal stress or loss. It doesn't have to be connected to military or war."

Ray sniffled as he answered, "I know, but it's too soon, and I don't think I can talk about this in front of the others right now. They all have their own problems and I don't want them to be burdened with mine."

"But that's what we're here for, Ray."

"I know, I know. That's exactly why I called you this morning. I felt I could tell you and it might help me, but actually, it just makes me feel weak. I can't handle these things by myself." Again, he paused.

"Actually, I shouldn't say that. I have Mari, and she's wonderful and very supportive. You know that. We've talked about it before. But she's as traumatized by all this as I am. She hates fires! And we had to get out of there in a hurry to escape this one. The wind was pushing the flames from the barn to the house and she saw that and I thought she was going to pass out. She clutched both kids so tight little Matt was crying. I have trouble talking to her about all of this, and I don't want her to know I've called you. She'll think I'm weak. This is life and we have to deal with it. But I hate it!"

"Ray, this will take some time. I wish you'd reconsider coming on Wednesday and maybe just listen to the others. Don't talk about this yet. Give it some time."

"Part of what's bothering me is the fact I haven't had a nightmare now for a few months. I used to write down the dates so I'd know how often, but I've stopped doing that. I'm afraid all of this will be a trigger and they will start again."

"That could be. But, as you just said, with time they do tend to go away. Let's not jump ahead and assume this might trigger something."

"I know, I know."

"Give some thought to coming on Wednesday. And Ray, you really have my sympathy. When are the services for your father? I'll try to be there."

"They were last week, Thursday."

"Oh, I'm so sorry. Your poor mother. Is there anything we can do to help her?"

"I can't think of anything right now. She's gone back to Colorado with my sister to stay for awhile. Maybe, when she comes back here sometime, I could bring her by to meet you. Or, we could have lunch?"

"Yes, I'd like to meet her. She's got to be a strong woman."

Again Ray thought of Bill Bill's words, *one tough son of a gun*. "She is," he replied and then added, "Speaking of strong women, I'd better let you get back to work."

"Thanks for the kind comment, but I haven't been through what you or your mother have. You call me again if you need to. Okay?"

"Okay. Thanks for listening to me!"

CHAPTER 42

Wednesday, September 6, 1987
O.P. Cabinets & Hardware
Overland Park, Kansas

All morning Ray anguished over attending the PTSD meeting at the VA Medical Center on the east side of Kansas City. All kinds of thoughts were running through his head including the dream the night before about a fire at Camp Zama. Everyone had piled into 'Black Jack, the old Suburban, to escape. *'How did that vehicle get to Japan? Only in dreams,'* he thought. He knew what triggered that one. When he hung up the phone, something made him think about the news report he had heard that Ronald Reagan was suggesting a name change for the V.A.. He wondered if it would really make a difference. The concept was to change *Veterans Administration* to the *Department of Veterans Affairs* and make it a cabinet-level department. That word 'Affairs' in the title made him think of something that happened between two people, normally a man and a woman. That took his wandering mind back to Dr. Zehr.

Eventually, he knew he would have to decide. It was close to a half-hour drive to the *Department of Veterans Affairs*, and he appreciated Dr. Zehr's urging him to attend. But he really wasn't ready to face those people. He felt that it would look like he was there for sympathy, and he didn't need it anymore than the rest of them. They all had problems. Like Dr. Zehr said, *'Your poor mother'*. She needs help, sympathy, and time to heal. She could use a PTSD session or two. The only thing the PTSD group could possibly do was send her gift certificates to clothing stores, but Ray was sure that the insurance money and his sister June would be taking care of that. He went to lunch with his co-workers and put the meeting out of his mind.

CHAPTER 43

January, 1989
Prairie Village, Kansas

It was a Monday and a new year, January 2nd, the day after the holiday. Mari received a call from Randall Haley, the V.P. of Communications with American National Mortgage out of New York. She had met him several years ago at a seminar in St. Louis, and this was the second time he had called. That evening, she told Ray about the call. "He just wanted to follow-up with me and see if I was still happy here in K.C.. He asked about the kids and how they were doing in school and so on. I told him about Matt and Fran, and that they were both in school. Seemed he really was interested, not just small talk."

"So, no job offer or anything?," Ray asked.

"No, not really. But, there was this underlying current that you could tell that's what he was fishing about. He ended by saying he just wanted to check in on me and wished me a happy new year. He also wondered if I was attending the tax update seminar here in K.C. later this month and I told him I was. He said he wouldn't be there, but a couple of his associates would be. He said he would send me a note with their names and hoped I would have a chance to meet them."

Ray's nightmares had returned, every couple of weeks it seemed. Only now they were different and almost always included fire. One night was very vivid and he woke up sweating and quickly realized why Mari was so fearful of fire. He had dreamed, *he was lying with a sucking-chest wound in the dried-up swamp grasses of Vietnam and couldn't move. A tracer round had started a grass fire in the distance. The wind was blowing the fire towards him and the wind kept getting stronger. The dust-off chopper was headed in to pick him up but he didn't want it to land because the blade wash would only make the fire stronger and closer to him. Where was everyone? They all ran for their lives when the fire started. The chopper pilot noticed the situation and thought he could put out the flames with the wind from his aircraft like blowing out candles on a cake. It only made matters worse. Ray felt the heat from the flames and it was getting hotter and hotter and making him sweat.* He was soaked when he awoke and sat up in bed.

When he calmed down and cooled off from a wet washcloth with Mari's help, he tried to go back to sleep. Something about that dream was different. Not just the fire, but something else. He laid awake a long time replaying the parts of the dream he could remember, but he couldn't figure out the difference. He finally accepted it *was* the fire and that allowed him to go back to sleep.

Back when he finally returned to attend PTSD sessions, there was a Wednesday the day after one of his dreams. He chose not to speak and just motioned the moderator to move on when it came around to his turn. A couple of the regular attendees sort of laughed. and one said, "What's a matter, Ray? Nothin's new to bitch about this month?"

Dr. Zehr quickly spoke up, "It's everyone's prerogative to choose *when* they want to talk. Let's move on."

As the meeting was ready to close, Dr. Zehr asked if anyone had anything else to add and Ray raised his hand. "Yes, Ray, go ahead," she said.

"Sorry I didn't have my usual complaints this time. Last night was a bad night and I haven't figured out what triggered it. I just wasn't ready to talk about it."

The attendee who spoke up earlier looked over at Ray and said. "I'm sorry, Ray, seriously! I shoulda kept my mouth shut!"

Ray nodded and mouthed the words, "Thank you."

CHAPTER 44

Tuesday, January 24, 1989
Hyatt Regency Hotel, Crown Center
Kansas City, Missouri

Marilyn Reynolds was one of fifty-two attendees at the annual three-day tax updates seminar. Kansas City was one of sixteen locations around the country to host the event during the months of January and February. During the break on the second morning, Mari grabbed a Danish roll and a cup of coffee and walked over to a quiet corner on the mezzanine where there was an empty stand-up table where she could set her coffee cup while she nibbled on her pastry. From where she stood on the third floor mezzanine, looking over a decorative wooden railing, she realized it was the former entrance to the upper most skybridge that had failed years earlier. She felt her stomach start to churn and put her Danish back on her plate. There was a clear view of the hotel lobby and she quickly changed her line of sight to look straight out at the ornamental art consisting of maybe a hundred or more silver balls individually suspended on lightweight chains from the four-story high ceiling to form a perfect diamond shape. As she moved her view from one position to another, she could see the perfectly formed alignment created by the artist. *Simple, but amazing*, she thought. She tried to forget the disaster by concentrating on the artist's work. *A nice addition after the disaster eight years earlier.*

Then she looked down at the lobby floor and the one sky bridge that still existed. She and Ray had been back in the building a few times since the accident almost ten years earlier and they couldn't help but think of Bob and Suzanne whenever they entered. They had noticed before that the remaining long sky bridge had large supporting columns underneath instead of the clear span that it used to have. She was looking down trying to envision what renovations may have been made after the disaster when a young man and an older woman approached.

"Marilyn Reynolds?, the woman inquired, "Hi, we're from American National. Randy, well, *Randall* Haley, told us to look you up and say 'hi'. So, hi, how are you?"

"Oh, I'm fine. Thank you. I was just thinking about. Oh, never mind, I was actually admiring the art work hanging there and wondering what you would call it. Is it a 'sculpture'? Or, what do you think?"

They just got involved in some discussion when the bell rang for the end of the break.

"Maybe we can have lunch," the young man inquired.

"Sounds like a plan." Mari replied.

When the session broke up at 4:00, Mari swung by her office to check on messages before heading home. Her boss stuck his head in the door and asked how it was going.

Mari responded "Fine." Then she asked, "What do you know about American National Mortgage?", and she pulled out one of their business cards and showed it to him. "I seem to keep running into them. They seem like nice people, but I've never heard of them before except at seminars like this."

"Well, *they* should be nice! They're big time. New York headquarters. You've probably not heard of them because they operate at a very high level, much higher than us. Multi-million dollar investments, hotels, shopping malls, major skyscrapers, etc.. But, they also buy up regional firms that are showing big time growth. I've been worried that we might be next, did they say anything about that?"

"No, not a word."

"They usually don't use the ANM name. They buy up these regional companies and continue to operate them under the local familiar name. This new internet's amazing. I've got access to it on my computer. I can show you how to check them out sometime. You'll be surprised!"

"Interesting, I'll have to try that."

CHAPTER 45

It was approaching the turn of the century. In the last decade, if Ray or Marilyn Reynolds had kept a diary, there would have been a number of significant pages. Instead, their memories of those events were in their heads and Ray kept a series of photo albums to capture some of those key memories. He recently began looking at digital cameras to replace his Nikon 35mm SLR, but just couldn't give up the old film camera. Nor did he want to spend the money for a new fine quality camera since he already owned the Nikon, even though they could afford it.

They had now been in their house in Prairie Village for fifteen years and Mari had refinanced the balance on their V.A. loan to a lower fixed-rate, fifteen-year mortgage. She had it figured that they could have the home paid for in another five years by paying double on the principal. Ray let her handle all that financial stuff.

Ray's photo albums were divided into books with the kids pictures through the years and separate books for their vacations and then another for home remodeling projects and one for odds and ends. Their vacations in the past decade had included trips to Disneyland and Walt Disney World, Myrtle Beach, a fall foilage tour of the New England states, and several trips to Colorado to visit June and their mother, and occasional trips to Council Bluffs to see Chip and Erica. Ray never considered Council Bluffs a 'vacation', it was just a family visit.

One Easter trip back to Cottonwood Falls to see Mari's family, Ray was up early and while Mari and her mother Jennifer were planning to start a big brunch, he said he wanted to drive out to the ranch to see it one more time.

There was a fog hanging over Fox Creek as he turned off the highway and he noticed some weeds had started to take over sections of the gravel drive. He had his camera and took some pictures of the landscape which was broken only by the oak tree, the stone fireplaces, and the old swing set. Someone had taken out the remains of the old Ford, the tractor and the baler, and the equipment shed to sell for scrap metal. Sometimes he wished he hadn't taken those pictures. They were always hard to look at. He wished instead he had stopped long enough that fateful day to take the one of the bright sunlight on the white ranch house and the red barn with the distant dark gray storm background, but that picture, too, would have brought back the same bad memories of that fateful day and the ghost storm that killed the ranch.

When the insurance settlements came in, both for the ranch and for her husband's life insurance, Ray's mother Beverly made the decision to stay in Colorado and bought a nice condo near the foothills in the suburb of Lakewood. It was only a couple of miles from where June now lived in Golden. A couple of years later, when the ranch property sold, she offered to split it four ways with her children, but all three of them turned her down, telling her it was hers, not theirs. That was Ray's last chance to maybe hear that phrase *'Son, ... someday this will all be yours'*. He could now, once again, totally wipe that off his bucket list.

The kids had grown considerably with Matt turning 17 and already over 6'-0", taller than both of his parents, as he entered his senior year in high school. He had a serious interest in basketball and spent a lot of time practicing in the driveway at the hoop his father had installed. Fran was entering her freshman year and still under five feet. She was just starting to show serious interest in certain boys and urged her parents to let her date. She also had become an avid reader and loved Harry Potter, possibly sparking her interest in boys.

Both Ray and Mari had done well in their careers. Since areas in the south part of Johnson County had started to expand, there were many new homes, apartments, townhomes and condominiums being built which kept Ray very busy. They had added an assistant who had a design degree from a junior college. There also seemed to be more and more high-end subdivisions popping up with single-family homes in the half-million dollar range and up. Those architect-designed homes required custom-built cabinetry. Ray discovered that some architects and homeowners liked the idea of using a kitchen design specialist. Of course, the standard-sized True Dimensions pre-manufactured cabinets wouldn't work for these sophisticated and wealthy buyers. Ray and his boss got together and looked for a small custom cabinet shop that could produce quality work and made the owner an offer. By 1995, O.P. Cabinets & Hardware had a name change to O.P. Custom Cabinets & Hardware. They rented out a 5,000 square-foot space just across the alley for the woodworking shop and added two more lines of high-end cabinet hardware. Their first two sales were both to homes in the Hallbrook Subdivision, property that was part of the Hall family farm, *the* Hall's of Hallmark Cards.

Ray still pursued the big multi-unit projects but had an estimator to put the bids together with Ray's supervision. They also hired a young woman to work as both receptionist and manager of the expanded showroom. Ray helped out with walk-in customers whenever necessary when he was in the office, But he still found time to mentor the new design associate with the thing Ray enjoyed most - designing kitchens and selling them. The more sales, the more income.

Mari's company had expanded with new offices in both Columbia and Joplin, Missouri ,and they were working on expanding to Topeka in Kansas. Mari's responsibilities now included oversight of the managers of the two Missouri facilities, and she had a new title of V.P. - Mortgage Management. Naturally, this promotion came with a nice increase in her salary.

As life got better, and Ray's tragic events became further in the past, his nightmares subsided to the point that he stopped going to the V.A. meetings every month, and when he did go, he tried to report only positive things. Dr. Zehr had noticed and complimented him on his improvement as he was leaving one day. He thanked her for noticing the change.

With their financial increases, they had kicked around the idea of buying a new, larger house, partly for the prestige and also for the investment, maybe even in Hallbrook. Eventually, Ray considered that to be out of his league and Mary decided Ray was right for the both of them. They stayed in Prairie Village. They needed to continue saving for the kids' college funds.

Ray's good friend from the war, Bill Williams, had come to visit twice during the '90's when he was home on leave. He now had well over thirty years in with Uncle Sam and was serving in Korea the last time he visited. He had been in Kansas City one time during the first Wednesday of the month and Ray invited him to go along to the PTSD meeting at the V.A..

Ray introduced Bill as his platoon-mate and very good friend and then explained the nickname. He was surprised when Bill Bill stood up as though he'd been introduced to give a talk, and he started in, "Glad to be here among all you veterans. And I certainly appreciate your service. Got to tell you a little bit about my pal here. Ol' 'Wildcat', we called him, cause he went to K-State. Of course, Nebraska still beats the Cats in football most of the time. What's the current streak, something like 25 in a row? But, ol' Ray here, he got himself shot by a sniper back in, what? 1970, if my memory serves me well. Sucking chest wound. We all learned about those in basic training. Right?" He paused and saw most of the guys, especially Army vets, nod in agreement and listening intently.

He continued, comfortable in this assumed assignment. "I tried to do what we were taught, you know, apply pressure to the opening, but luckily the medic rushed right over. The bullet passed straight through, puttin' another opening in his back. The dust-off chopper was there really quick cause we was right outside our base camp at Cu Chi. That's probably what saved him. I helped put him in the chopper and told him I'd see him back stateside and then noticed his eyes close and I really thought he was gone. And maybe he was." Ray noticed Bill's hand quickly move to his face to catch a tear before it dripped onto his cheek.

"Well, I came home to Lincoln after Nam and was determined to go down to Kansas and see Strong City which Ray always talked about, and to stop and see Ray's folks. I really never heard whether ol' Wildcat made it or not, so I was worried about meeting 'em. But I found the ranch he always described and I'll be damned, there he was, upright and smilin' big time. I told his folks they raised one tough son of a gun. They just smiled and said they was happy to meet me. I still think he's a hell of a friend! Even though he did go back to K-State to get a degree." He sat back down and the group applauded. They had a new appreciation of Ray, although he hadn't done anything special that day, except bring an active-duty friend to the meeting.

When the meeting ended, several of the veterans came over to Ray's side of the table to visit with Bill Bill. Ray felt good inside that he had invited Bill to the meeting instead of just skipping it because his friend was in town to visit.

CHAPTER 46

Monday, August 27, 2001
Midwest Mortgage & Finance Office
Kansas City, Missouri

At precisely 10:00 a.m., Marilyn Reynolds's office phone rang and she answered to a pleasant sounding female voice asking if she could hold for Randall Haley, president of American National Mortgage. Mari paused from the surprise call and the realization that her acquaintance was now the president, *and* he was calling her. Well, someone else was calling her on his behalf, she thought. Finally, she said, "Oh, sorry, yes, I'll hold."

"Good morning, Marilyn! It's good to talk to you again. How are you?"

"Fine. I'm good. Business is good. And congratulations on becoming president!"

"Oh, thank you. President *and* CEO, actually. It's taken awhile, but I'm finally here. But I still want to stay in touch with people I've met along the way. That's why I'm calling. You know we're in the financial business, but I like to think more than anything, we're in the people business. Wouldn't you agree?"

"I would," she said. "I'm now managing three branch offices along with the home office responsibilities and finding the right people is the key to everything."

"You're absolutely right. And, here in the commercial world, we take that same attitude to the customers we seek. If our corporate accounts don't feel the same way about their people, we take a second look at our desire to finance their projects. It's not all just about the money. We really question whether their poor attitudes about their people will support their goals long term, and long term is very important to us."

"That certainly makes sense."

"So listen, we have some new business opportunities in our middle market sector. Smaller regional companies. You are probably aware from speaking with me and some other associates that we typically pick up regional firms in growing market segments and make them ANM companies. Quietly, behind the scenes in many cases. *Those* people are important to us too. Your boss may not know this yet, but we've been doing our due diligence on your company, Midwest Mortgage and Finance. I know you've never been anxious to leave Kansas City, at least not until your kids finish school. How are they, by the way?"

"Oh, um, Matt's turned 21 last month, a sophomore at K.U., hoping he would be a basketball star. And, Fran just turned 18, a senior. She's spoiled rotten. Her dad gives her anything she wants."

"I understand that. I have two girls myself, and two boys. What a challenge."

"You can say that again!"

"Anyway, do you think we can get you up here to New York to talk about some opportunities that might work for you without having to leave K.C.?"

"Um, well, sure. I'm always happy to listen and explore what's out there. And you just said the magic words, '*in K.C.*'. Let's talk about it!"

"Okay, good! I'll put my secretary back on the phone to make arrangements. She knows my schedule and she'll figure out all the details, but we'd like to see you fairly soon if at all possible."

"That sounds great. I'll look forward to it!" Mari's thinking, *I've never been to New York.*

Randall ended the conversation by saying, "Okay, hold on for Mercedes."

Mercedes! Mari thought, *Now that's got to be a great name for a secretary in New York!* While she waited on hold until Mercedes picked up, she grabbed her Franklin Planner from her briefcase and opened it to her calendar.

"Okay, Ms. Reynolds, Mr. Haley would like me to schedule you here sometime in the next two to three weeks. Do you have your calendar handy?"

"I do."

"What looks good to you?"

"Um, let's see. I'm scheduled out of town the first three days of next week. But after that I can rearrange anything, so anytime after the 6th. I could be there that Friday."

"Oh, that won't work. I don't show anything on his schedule, but Mr. Haley always has me keep Fridays open so he can get out to his club in the afternoon for a round of golf with his friends. Oh, I mean clients," and then she laughed. "What about the first part of the following week? I can schedule you to fly in on Monday and then set aside Tuesday for your meeting."

"That works for me."

"Good! I'll set up your hotel and your airline. Do you have a preference?"

"Ahh, no," and Mercedes could detect a pause, or a 'but' coming.

"Is there a problem? Do you not like to fly?"

"Oh, no, no. That's not it. There's no problem with the dates. They'll work fine. I'm thinking. It's just that I've never been to New York before, and neither has my husband. I'm thinking this might be a nice little weekend getaway for us. Would you mind if I talk to him and then get back to you on the travel arrangements? It may be tomorrow."

"Oh no, that's fine. But do let me know as soon as possible.

Sometimes, if there's an event going on, the best hotels can fill up fast."

"Okay, I will get back to you no later than this time tomorrow. And thanks again."

Mari hung up and immediately called Ray at work. "Can we meet for dinner tonight after work? We need to talk."

Ray sensed her excitement and asked, "Sure, what's up?"

"I just talked to Randy, you know, Randall from American National in New York. He's now the president. They want me to come up for an interview."

"You mean you now want to relocate somewhere? New York? I don't know."

"No. They said I wouldn't have to move. Sounds like there's a couple of different opportunities without leaving Kansas City. We'll see. I think it's worth the trip. And I thought you might like to go along."

"Oh Mari, honey, I'd feel out of place. That doesn't sound right. They want *you*!"

"No. That's not what I'm talking about. I thought we could make a three or four day weekend out of this and have a mini-vacation. That's what we need to talk about."

Ray gave in, "Um, okay. Where did you want to meet?"

"Let's go to that new place, O'Neill's, on Mission Road. I'll meet you there at 6:00. I'll let Fran know."

"Okay, see you then."

Mari spent the afternoon in her office with the door closed. She called her aunt Betty in Oklahoma who was so good at planning the Japan trip years ago and asked if she was still on top of booking travel arrangements for her company personnel? Betty said, "All the time. What do you need?"

Mari explained her situation and told her she was still uncomfortable with doing anything more than looking up company names and phones on the internet. She had gotten used to using accounting processes and software on her new computer, but the internet scared her.

Betty jotted down a few notes and dates and asked if they'd be interested in a Broadway show. Mari asked about seeing '*Cats*' and Betty said she'd check but thought it shut down last year. Betty suggested '*Les Miserables*', and Mari said she didn't think Ray would like that one.

"Are you taking the kids?" Betty asked.

"No, I'm not planning on it. Matt's already back in Lawrence for his sophomore year, but Ray and I are meeting for dinner tonight to discuss this whole idea. So maybe Fran, depends on what he thinks. I'm thinking about asking my mother to come up and stay with her."

"Oh, Jenn will like that."

"Let me find out what's playing and I'll get back to you. I was thinking of '*The Lion King*' or '*Beauty and the Beast*'. Fran would probably like them. How *old* is Matt by now? In college, wow!"

"Twenty-one! And, I think you're right, the whole idea of a Broadway musical would be *gross* to him! One of his favorite words these days."

"Okay, I'll get busy on this and probably call you at home later this evening. It sounds exciting. I'm so happy for you guys."

"Great! Thank you. I'll be anxiously waiting for your call. And thanks again!"

"You're welcome. Talk to you later. Bye."

That evening, following dinner together and talking to Betty again, their plans were set. Mari had called her mother and Jennifer said she would be delighted to spend a few days with Fran, and Matt if he was home for the weekend. Good to get away from Ralph she added jokingly.. Now, Mari just needed to call Mercedes back in the morning to verify everything.

The plan was to depart Kansas City on Friday. September 7th and arrive in New York early afternoon. They were booked at the Marriott Marquis hotel in Times Square through Monday with a flight home late on Tuesday. That gave them three and a half days to shop, sightsee, and tour the city. Betty had recommended they go down to the piers and take the Circle Line Boat Tour around the island of Manhattan and to be sure to do Central Park, the Statue of Liberty, and Ellis Island. She also gave them three recommended choices for shows on Broadway. Ray and Mari agreed on *'Chicago'* at the Ambassador Theater. If that was sold out Friday, Saturday and Sunday, *'Rent'* would be their second choice. Mari didn't want to do a show Monday evening. She wanted to be rested up for the meeting on Tuesday.

AT 9:00 a.m. the next morning, Mari closed her office door and called Mercedes to give her the details. Mercedes surprised her when she asked for their flight number and time of arrival. She said they would have a car waiting to pick them up at the airport; the driver would be waiting in the luggage pick-up area with their names on a sign.

"Oh," Mari said, "I didn't expect that. I don't have the exact information yet. My aunt is going to FAX it to me later today. I'll send it to you then. But you don't have to have us picked up."

"We would have had you picked up if it was just you, and it doesn't cost anymore to pick up two people. Also, we'll have a driver pick you up on Tuesday at your hotel. I'll be sending you those details. Save your receipts. We won't reimburse your whole vacation trip, but *your* airfare and at least one night of the hotel will be on us."

"Oh, I understand. That's very nice. Thank you."

When she hung up the phone, she was both elated and exhausted. It was only 9:30 in the morning, but she was ready for a third cup of coffee, something she normally didn't do. When she went to the break room to get a cup, she noticed someone had brought in a box of doughnuts, something else she didn't normally do. Right after finishing her coffee and doughnut treat, she headed to her boss' office to tell him what was going on and to mention the need for a few days off.

Mari and her boss had always been straight forward and honest with each other. She started by reminding him of their brief conversation earlier about ANM. He nodded. She said, "Did I tell you then that they had been tracking *our* growth?"

"Well, you might have," he replied, "but I already knew. I've had lunch a couple of times with one of their people. I couldn't tell for sure if he was fishing for a job or fishing for more information about us. Either way, I figured we were probably on their list of possible acquistitions."

"One of the guys I met back in St. Louis years ago, Randy Haley, is now the president and CEO."

"Yeah, I saw that in a trade paper about six months ago. He's had quite a climb in the financial world. Nice guy from what I hear. Very smart."

"Well, that's what I need the time off for. I'm invited to New York to meet with him. Not sure if it's to learn more about us, Midwest Mortgage, or possibly a job offer? Maybe both. Besides, I couldn't turn him down; I've never been to the Big Apple."

CHAPTER 47

Friday, September 7, 2001
New York City, New York

Ray and Marilyn Reynolds, a couple of small town citizens raised and educated in Kansas, finally hit the big time. Or, so it felt. Actually, they were just visitors in another world. New York City was pretty much what they had always expected. Hustle-bustle. People everywhere. It seemed like all nationalities and races were represented, and there was something to buy on every street corner - bagels to hot dogs, purses to Rolex watches. They may have arrived from their home in Kansas, but that's right next door to Kansas City, Missouri, which is the 'Show Me' state, and they were having fun with some of the vendors when they asked to see the *real* Rolexes, or the *real* Louis Vuitton purses.

They decided they'd better stop playing with the street vendors after they pissed one guy off who had lowered his watch price from $100 all the way down to $10. "What's a matter you? Ain't you got a lousy ten dolla? I give you fair price. You waste a my time! Get away from me, you sheepskates!"

They enjoyed their first afternoon in the city, wandering in and out of stores and grabbing a late lunch in Times Square. The limo driver had picked them up at the airport just as Mercedes had said and dropped them off curbside at the entrance to the Marriott Marquis. It was too early to check in, but the desk clerk had the bellboy take their luggage to a secure storage area and would have it sent up to their room when it was ready, probably around 4:00 p.m..

By Monday, they had walked through a good part of Central Park in the afternoon, then took a horse-drawn carriage ride around and through the park seeing some of the same areas they had just walked,

One Tough Son of a Gun

but they learned more about the park. The guide pointed out The Dakota apartment building across the street from Central Park on the west side where John Lennon had lived, and died. He showed them where Jackie Kennedy Onassis had lived. He gave them history on Frederick Law Olmsted, America's first prominent landscape architect who designed not only Central Park but many other famous parks and grounds like the Biltmore Estate in Asheville, North Carolina. And he pointed out the Great Lawn where Simon and Garfunkel gave a free concert to an estimated half a million people on September 19, 1981. At that time, according to their guide, it was the the largest concert ever held.

Ray and Mari really enjoyed the relaxed ride and tipped the driver accordingly. They were back at the hotel by 5:00 p.m. and both were exhausted. On their walk, they decided they had checked off everything that Aunt Betty had told them to see and much more. They had been to Grand Central Station, seen the United Nations Building, went to the top of the Empire State Building and rode around on a double decker tour bus. And oh the food! A couple of meals in Little Italy and one dinner in Chinatown, plus a lunch in a Manhattan diner. They decided they had to play down their enthusiasm for the trip when they got home or the kids would be mad because they didn't get to go. Remember, they had told them, it was a *business* trip.

They decided to simply stay in their hotel room Monday evening and order off the room service menu that last night. They were both ready for just a plain old-fashioned cheeseburger and fries. Mari wanted to eat and rest up for her interview the next morning.

Tuesday morning, Mari let Ray sleep in while she quietly got ready for her big day. When she was ready to go, she bent over the sleepyhead in bed and said, "Wish me luck." Ray had been awake listening to his wife's final steps in getting ready.

As she gave him a kiss, he propped himself up to look at her in her new robin's egg blue dress. "You look really good!" he said. "Go get 'em Tiger!"

The limo driver was already there at 8:15 in the hotel lobby ahead of the scheduled 8:30 pick-up. Mari had headed down to the lobby early, not knowing how long the wait might be for an elevator. Since the driver was already there, Mari was anxious to go.

Mercedes had told Mari that Mr. Haley was an early riser and was usually the first one in the office every morning. Marilyn Reynolds wanted to impress, so she asked for an early morning meeting. Mercedes said that Mr. Reynolds had an 8:00 a.m. meeting already scheduled so they settled on 9:00 a.m..

The driver dropped her at the taxi drop-off and pick-up area outside the north building of the World Trade Center. "American National Mortgage is on the one hundred-sixth floor," he told her with a Jamaican accent. She offered him a $5.00 tip, but he refused to take it. "I get my money from the company. They pay me good. They call me when you are ready to go back to your hotel. See you then. Okay?"

"Okay. Thank you!"

She found her way through the crowded hustle-bustle of the lobby where people were entering from below-ground subways, and from city buses, taxis and other limos. It took her a few minutes to find the right set of elevators that would take her to the top floors and she exited on the 106th floor at 8:40 a.m.. She saw the large double glass doors with a side panel etched with the name and logo of American National Mortgage, Suite 10600, and walked through. She was greeted by a young receptionist who said, "You must be Marilyn Reynolds?"

Mari responded, "I am. You can call me Mari, spelled with an 'i'."

"I'll let Mercedes know you are here," as she dialed a number. She replaced the handset on her phone and said, "Mercedes will be here shortly," and motioned towards the sitting area.

In less than a minute, before she had a chance to sit down, Marilyn saw a beautiful middle-aged woman of some kind of mixed descent, possibly a light-skinned black, but there appeared to be some Asian features, with perfect black hair including a streak of grey down one side, perfect make-up and gorgeous blue-green eyes. "Marilyn," she said, as she reached out her hand, "So glad to meet you. Please come with me."

Mari followed her to a large corner conference room with floor to ceiling glass windows facing both the north and east. Mercedes asked if she could get her coffee or water.

"Coffee, please. Black." Mercedes turned on her spike high heels to fetch the coffee. She was back in less than two minutes and walked through the glass conference room doors. Mari had navigated over to the north glass wall of the room and was admiring the view of the Hudson River to the northwest.

When she came through the door again, carrying coffee, Mercedes said, "I forgot to ask if you needed cream or ..." and her voice stopped with a low gasp and Mari heard the coffee cup crash to the floor as she turned to face Mercedes. Mari saw her eyes the size of half dollars. She turned to look east where Mercedes was staring and saw the large American Airlines jet headed straight for them. They could see the pilots faces. The pilots were smiling.

Before either woman had time to react, the plane struck about ten floors below them and a huge fireball erupted past their window. Both of them screamed as the building shook violently, but Mari was sure no one could scream louder than she just did. The air smelled like jet fuel and the fireball was churning from reds, oranges and yellows into a dark black smoke. The roar of noises was almost impossible to describe, and Mercedes had dropped to her knees onto the coffee-soaked carpet and was reaching for a chair to get back up. "This way," she said to Mari as she got back on her feet. She kicked off her stiletto heels and headed towards the lobby. "We can't use the elevators," Mercedes said and started to file into a line of other employees who were screaming and crying. Randall Haley was one of them and he saw Mari and just shook his head and offered a spot in line ahead of him. There must have been twenty-five or thirty people all trying to squeeze through the fire door into the stairwell at once.

Dennis G. Smith

By the time Mr. Haley, Mercedes and Mari got to the doorway, they could hear people moaning and coughing and crying and smoke was coming up from the floors below. Mari stepped out of the line and said, "I can't. No, I can't!" She had always feared fire the most. Randall grabbed her arm and tried to pull her back but she jerked away. "No!" she screamed. She worked her way past the remaining people and into the elevator lobby where some people were actually waiting for a lift. There wasn't as much smoke there yet. She cut through that area into an office on the south side of the building where the air was better. She stopped to gather her thoughts. She was sweating profusely. The temperature in the building was rising fast. She still had her purse on her shoulder. She hadn't removed it since she arrived. She pulled out her cell phone and called Ray. He was still laying in bed watching TV when she left. The last thing he said to her was "You look great! I love you. Good luck."

The phone rang and rang and then went to voice mail. She couldn't know that he was in the shower. She left a message. "Ray, I love you with all my heart. I'm so sorry. I love you. Goodbye."

She put her phone back in her purse and pulled the purse off her left shoulder and put the strap over her head so it wouldn't fall off. She started looking for something that would work and that she could handle. The chairs looked awkward and cumbersome. A desktop computer might work, but awkward. There was a bronze Remington statue on a display table, but it seemed too heavy for her to throw. The display table that held it might be right. It had a metal frame and a heavy glass top. She dropped the statue to the floor and removed the glass tabletop. Then, she picked up the forty or fifty pound designer frame and went to the outside wall of glass and swung that table base with all her might. The glass cracked, but didn't break. One more swing and the large pane shattered.

Marilyn Reynolds was believed to be the first one to jump that day.

Ray showered after shaving and brushing his teeth. He had to wait for the steam to clear so he could see to comb his hair. When he stepped out of the bathroom to get dressed, he could tell by the announcer's voice on TV that something awful had occurred, or was in the process of occurring. He still had a towel wrapped around him, but stopped to watch for a minute before hunting for a clean pair of underwear. There were people running or walking quickly away from something, apparently right there in New York. Then they cut back to the studio of the Today Show and the hosts were all frantic and said they now had video of the plane. Just then, they said, "Hold on, we have another live report," and they switched to a camera apparently on top of their NBC building in Rockefeller Center as a second plane struck the south tower of the World Trade Center.

Ray watched in horror as he realized that's where his wife was going. He looked at the clock on the bedside table and confirmed his thought that she must be there by now. He didn't know which building she was going to, but it didn't matter. Now, both of them were on fire. *God, she hates fire!.*

He dropped onto the edge of the bed right in front of the TV. He didn't want to see this, but he couldn't stop watching. *Phone*, he thought, *Where's my phone? I've got to call her.* He picked up his phone off of the hotel room desk and hit 'Send'. It didn't ring. Instead, he got a recorded message that all circuits are currently busy. He disconnected, then tried again. Same message. Then he saw that he *had* a message. He listened as his eyes filled with tears.

What could he do now? Ray didn't have a clue. He just sat there with a towel wrapped around his waist and watched. It was an attack. It was history in the making. They were part of it. He couldn't stand it. *Dirty rotten commie bastards!* He wanted to scream!

CHAPTER 48

September 11, 2001
Manhattan, New York

The realization of the devastating event that just happened had Ray stunned and crying. All he could do was hope. Hope that somehow Mari escaped that inferno. He couldn't know that she had escaped from a certain fiery death to another more preferred by her.

He continued to try to call someone, anyone to have someone close to him to talk to. He scanned through the contacts in his phone through blurry eyes. He tried Mari's mother in Overland Park. Thank God the kids are in school and not watching this, although he wondered about Matt's schedule at KU. He didn't realize that Fran's high school history class had a TV in the room and they were all watching the same thing Ray was.

The cell towers just couldn't handle the volume. *All circuits are currently busy!* He kept hearing that over and over. He decided to try the hotel phone and dug his AT&T credit card number out of his wallet so he could call long distance. *Your call cannot be completed at this time. Please try again.* Each attempt required dialing seventeen numbers, nine for an outside line, then the hotel code for long distance, then his AT&T card number. Always with the same result. *Your call cannot be completed at this time. Please try again.*

After trying June and his mother in Colorado, Mari's mother Jenn again at his home number, and Ralph, he then tried Dr. Zehr. Nothing worked. Back to his cell phone. He noticed the battery was low and he had to find the charger. Something new was breaking on TV.

He turned back around just in time to see the final part of the collapse

of the south tower.

His hope for Mari still being alive dwindled. He not only didn't know which building she might have been in, but he also had no idea what floor she was on. Perhaps she was on a lower floor and got out early, but then he remembered her phone message. It sounded so final.

He pulled his charger from an outside pocket on his suitcase and plugged it in. While he was at the suitcase he realized he still hadn't dressed and he pulled out underwear and a pair of Levi's, and a KC Chiefs t-shirt. He was thinking he needed to go down there to try to find her, but, it seemed like that would be an insurmountable task in a city like New York.

Now cameras on the street were showing people, blocks away from the buildings, running for their lives to escape the massive amounts of dust and debris raining down on them from the 110-story building collapse.

He sat back down on the foot of the bed to watch the people, their faces, their hair, and their clothes all covered in dust, looking, praying he might see Mari. All he needed to do was pull on some shoes and he could head down there. But he was transfixed, unable to move, somehow knowing he wouldn't be able to find her. No matter what street he went down, there were ten or fifteen more she could be on. It seemed so hopeless. *Oh God, I love her! Bring her back, please!* The sobs started in again.

Exactly thirty minutes after the first building's collapse, the north tower came down. He heard the announcer's voice and watched through his tears. He just couldn't take it and the tears turned into sobs. It was now 10:30 a.m.. He had been watching this whole catastrophe for almost two hours. All alone in a hotel with no one to grieve with. No one would see him cry. He didn't care if they did.

Prairie Village, Kansas

Jennifer had been up since 6:30, fixed breakfast for Fran, and got her off to school. She turned on the Today Show around 8:15 Central Time, after the hijackers had already hit both towers. She couldn't believe what was going on. She was shocked by what she was seeing and surprised that Ray or Mari hadn't called. She knew they were due home that evening, but had no idea what their schedule was other than that. She thought she would try Ray's cell phone number since she would hate to bother her daughter while she was in an important meeting.

Lakewood, Colorado

It was just after 8:30 in Colorado. Beverly was enjoying a beautiful Colorado morning sitting on her deck at her condo. She was reading the morning paper and drinking coffee when her phone rang. It was her daughter, June.

"Mom, do you have your TV on?"

"No, why?"

"Horrible event going on in New York. Are Ray and Mari still there?"

"Yeah. They get home tonight. What's happening?"

"It might be the start of World War III. Terrorists have hit the World Trade Center and the Pentagon using hijacked planes. I'm going to call Ray. I'll let you know what I find out."

Council Bluffs, Iowa

Chip had called his wife, Erica, a couple of times to give her updates on what was happening since her plumbing warehouse didn't have a TV. The automotive dealership where Chip worked had a TV in the waiting area. Chip and some other managers had gathered around behind the customer chairs and sofa to watch, each leaving every so often to check on their work stations, but then quickly returning to see what else was going to happen next.

During one break away from the TV, Chip tried calling his brother's cell phone but couldn't get through. He tried Mari's number with the same frustrating results. He told one of the other managers about his phone attempts and that manager said he had just heard them say that the 911 system plus all the other calls had overwhelmed the network. Most calls were not going through. Plus, they mentioned, there was a key cell phone communication tower on top of the north building that had collapsed. That certainly didn't help anything.

Five of them, and a half dozen customers, were all watching when one of the service workers came inside from a smoke break and elbowed a manager and said, "Ca-mere, ya gotta see this," and he made a motion toward the back door.

That manager and Chip followed the worker outside who then pointed to the west up in the sky. There was a large shiny silver plane on a descent headed south over Omaha. They watched for a minute and then realized it had to be Air Force One with President Bush on board. They had seen the news report that George W. Bush had been reading to a group of school children in Florida when news of the attack was whispered in his ear. In short order, he had excused himself and was rushed to his plane, but then there was no way to know where to go since the Pentagon had been attacked in D.C., and the Capitol or the White House could be next. Newscasters kept the mystery going by announcing they had not been told where Air Force One was going. Now, three guys across the river in Council Bluffs were pretty sure they knew the President was landing at Offutt Air Force Base.

Dennis G. Smith

Cottonwood Falls, Kansas

Ralph was in his real estate office when his wife called to tell him to turn on the news. He had added a small TV in the kitchen cabinet display area a couple of years earlier and left his desk to see what she was talking about. They both expressed their worries about their daughter, and Ralph said he would try to call her. Jennifer told her husband she had tried but couldn't get through, something about all the lines being tied up. He suggested they both needed to pray.

Going on noon, Ralph called his wife back and she could tell by his voice he didn't have good news.

"I finally remembered," he said to his wife.

"What?"

"The name, American National Mortgage."

"Who's that?"

"That's the company Mari was going to meet with in New York."

Jennifer was beginning to sense where Ralph might be going with this and a lump formed in her throat. She didn't say anything. She waited.

"I looked them up on the internet." He paused, wanting to make sure he could state the next sentence without breaking up. "Their headquarters are in the World Trade Center." Jennifer gasped.

"Let's not jump to conclusions, but it gets worse."

"Why? What do you mean, worse?"

"They're on the 106th floor. But, but wait, we don't know *when* she was meeting with them. Maybe it was yesterday, or, or later today. Hell, the kids flew out on Friday morning. Maybe she met with them that afternoon.

"No, she would have dressed different if she was going to that type of meeting on Friday. And why hasn't she called? She has to know we would be worried."

"Hey. I'm sure it's the same problem we're having getting through to her. All those people are trying to call 911 or their relatives to tell them they're safe. And their relatives, just like us, are trying to call them."

"Did you try Ray's cell phone?"

"Yes, both numbers. Multiple times. Same problem."

"Yeah, me too." Ralph could tell she was crying.

"I'll call you if I hear anything. Do you have Beverly's number?"

"I think so. I'll try to reach her."

"Okay. Let me know. Listen, I don't know how you keep this from the grandkids, but try to handle it carefully. They probably don't know anything about where their mother was supposed to be meeting.

"Okay, understand. Love you!"

"You too."

Marriott Marquis Hotel, Times Square, New York City

Ray was still on the edge of the bed. It was going on 12:30 and he remembered they were supposed to check out at noon. *Well, Hell with that!* His mind was racing with all kinds of thoughts. *Mari had this all planned out, which day we would do the Circle Line, when we would do the Statute of Liberty, the Empire State Building, Central Park, all figured out. This was her trip, our trip, but she made it special. She knew what time her meeting was and told me to check out and have our bags secured at the hotel until it was time to head to the airport. There'll be no airport trip today. Flights are all grounded.*

Dennis G. Smith

I've got to hear from Mari. The phones should be working again anytime, She'll call. No, she already called and it sounded ..., No! It sounded so final!

He picked his phone up again off the bed and tried her number. Same result. He pushed the buttons to get to her voice mail message and listened to it again, "Ray, I love you with all my heart. I'm so sorry. I love you. Goodbye."

He was sobbing. He didn't think there could be any tears left. He didn't know what to do. What could he do? He had to watch and wait. The news of the other hijacked planes had begun to soak in. One had hit the Pentagon in D.C. and one went down in a field near Shanksville, Pennsylvania. The reports were now giving the body count of the passengers and crew on board all four flights, but no one had a guess on how many people were killed inside the buildings that were struck. Ray didn't want to know all of this. There was only one person he wanted to know about. Just one!

Ray turned the TV off. He couldn't take it anymore. But as soon as the screen went black, Ray instantly turned it back on. He *had* to watch and listen. He had to know. Perhaps her car had been caught in traffic and she was late getting there. She left early enough, but maybe she waited in the lobby before going up. He didn't know what floor she was on. *She had every chance at being below the crash and then racing down the stairs with other people and getting outside. God, I hope she didn't take the elevator. They always say, 'In case of fire, use the stairs.' I hope she wasn't trapped in an elevator. She will call, any minute. No, the phones still don't work. She'll walk through the door anytime now. Even if she had to walk all the way back to Times Square, she should be here soon. No, she'll call. Oh no,* and he started to sob again. *She did call and it was a final call. Why didn't I answer? I must have been in the shower.*

He flopped on his back and laid there looking up at the ceiling. He prayed. "God, if you're there, please help me find her. Help her come back to me safely, I need her. I love her. Oh God, please help. Have mercy on her soul." *I hope those were the right things to say.*

Just then the hotel phone rang and he jumped. Suddenly elated, he was going to know something. He got off the bed and stepped to the desk to answer. "Hello?"

"Mr. Reynolds?"

"Yes."

"This is Sondra at hotel reservations."

"Yes?" Ray was getting anxious,

"We have you down for checking out today at noon. Are you about ready to depart? Do we need to arrange transportation?"

"No. I can't leave now. I may need to stay another day. I don't know. Can you add that to my bill?"

"Oh, I'm sorry Mr. Reynolds. We're booked up for this evening. We will need your room."

"No!" He was trying to think of the best way to respond. *The truth. Always tell the truth. They'll surely understand and do something.*" You've seen the news, right?"

"Yes. It's horrible."

"We're here because my wife had an interview this morning in one of those towers. I don't know which one, but I can't reach her. I can't leave now."

"Oh, I am *so* sorry!" Sondra said. Then there was a long pause followed by, "Just a minute."

Ray waited. The TV was showing first responders starting to dig in the rubble. Then the network repeated pictures of the people on the street earlier in the morning running for their lives when the buildings collapsed. All the dust and debris and the fear on people's faces. Ray watched again in disbelief hoping to see Mari's face. Ray couldn't know, but her face, her whole body, was out there, but not running, and certainly not suitable for TV.

Then Sondra came back to the phone. "Mr. Reynolds. I am so terribly sorry, but I need your help. We are actually overbooked for tonight, but with today's events, we expect some cancellations. If you could please pack up and vacate your room for now, we have a small conference room where you could wait here on the second floor. I'll send someone up in half an hour to help you. If we still don't have a room for you by 5:00 p.m., then we will help you find one nearby. That's the best I can do right now. Also, under the circumstances, let me know at extension 2220, if there's anything we can do here at the hotel for you. Room service, coffee, let me know. Okay?"

"Can't I just stay here?"

"Mr. Reynolds, may I call you Ray?"

"Yeah, fine."

" I'm sure you understand. We have to try to take care of all of our guests. And if you were flying in this evening and found out you no longer had a room reservation, you would be very upset. I'm really sorry to do this to you, but. . ."

There, he caught her mistake and had a logical argument. "But there won't be anybody flying in tonight! The news reported that all flights have been grounded. I don't even have a way home."

"I understand. You're right. And, that's why I told you we expect cancellations. Probably a lot. There have already been three, but we still are five rooms overbooked. I'll tell you what. You sit tight, for an hour. Please have your belongings all packed and ready to move, and i'll call you back no later than 2:00 to give you an update. My guess would be, like you said about the airlines, we'll have plenty more cancellations. I'm sure people are trying to call but can't get through."

"Okay. Thank you for helping me out." He hung up.

He went back to his position on the edge of the bed in front of the TV. His mind blanked out whatever was being said on television and he started thinking about his predicament.

I'm in a large hotel where hundreds, maybe thousands, of people are staying and just down the street, in a city of millions, people have been killed by terrorists, most likely including my wife. I'm all alone surrounded by tens of millions of people and I have no one to talk to, except maybe Sondra. But she wants to kick me out. Put me out on the street at this time of need. I am so screwed. My poor wife! She hated fire so bad! I hope, if she's really dead, she died quickly with no pain, no burning to death. All these people, all over Times Square, all over New York, I've never felt so alone in my life.

He thought back to Vietnam, the ambush patrols at night. The two-hour watch intervals when he felt all alone out there on the edge of the rice paddies, or deep in the woods. But back then, even though he was the only one awake in his position, he still had Bill Bill or Gunner, Jesse, or Rod sleeping right there beside him. That was lonely and scary, but nothing like this. He just wasn't prepared for this.

As he thought about his predicament, he realized how many others there were out there with husbands or wives, sisters or brothers, mothers or fathers, aunts and uncles, or just close friends who had to be going through the same thing he was right now. Wondering if their loved one survived. Then he heard a news report that broke through his mental blockage of trying to screen out all the bad news. They were talking about all the first responders who had gone into the burning buildings to rescue people or to try to put the fire out. *Maybe that's it,* he thought, *Maybe Mari's been rescued from a lower floor and being held somewhere in order to identify as many people as possible and she can't call cause the phones don't work. Oh God, I love her. Please make that happen!* Then they talked about the first responders who were trapped inside and radioed that they couldn't get out.

He picked up his phone and tried Mari's number again. Same result. 'All circuits are currently busy. Please try again.'

Dirty rotten Commie bastards!

The tragedy continued. The death toll at three of the four locations continued to rise. In Shanksville, they knew how many people were in the plane and no one was killed on the ground because the passengers fought the hijackers before that plane could get to its objective. Ray kept thinking it's like Vietnam, only now it's the enemy who's enjoying listening to the body count. If the known master terrorist, Osama bin Laden is involved, he is surely out there somewhere watching CNN and listening as his squad of suicide pilots succeeded with three-fourths of their missions. *Bastards!*

At 2:20 p.m., Ray's hotel room phone rang. It was Sondra with good news, if there was such a thing that day: Ray could stay in his room, and she told him he could order off the room service menu whenever he was ready. It would be provided by the hotel at no charge. She again told him how sorry she was to hear of his circumstances. She also said, "I know this won't be much comfort to you, but we've found that we have at least three other guests in similar circumstances waiting and hoping for good news of their loved one."

At 4:00 p.m., Ray began an attempt to call the airline to cancel his flights and to ask if they had any idea when they would be allowed to fly again. He couldn't get through, but he didn't get the 'all circuits are busy' message.

CHAPTER 49

Wednesday, September 12, 2001
Marriott Marquis Hotel
New York City, New York

The next morning, he checked his phone and was able to get service. He immediately tried Mari's number and it immediately went to voice mail. He left a message, fully knowing that she was not going to get it, but he had to try. 'Mari, I love you, more than you can ever know. Please give me a call as soon as possible. Love you.' He had to choke back tears on the last two words.

Then, he called home to talk to Mari's mother and to ask if the kids knew anything about what was going on. They cried together on the phone. He said he didn't know when he might be able to get home, but he wanted to stay put until he knew more about Mari. Jennifer told him the kids knew about the attack, and they knew the airlines were shut down so their parents couldn't fly home, but they didn't know their mother had been at the twin towers.

Next, he called June in Colorado and, after filling her in on everything, asked if she could call their mother and tell her about Mari. He didn't think he could do it. It was hard enough talking to Jennifer.

It hadn't been two minutes after talking to June and his phone rang. It was Ralph, and Ray could tell by his voice that he was choked up and had probably been crying. "Ray, I am so sorry we lost her. That's just horrible. I hope the fire didn't get her. She always hated that." Ray sniffed as he responded, "I know. I've been thinking the same thing."

"What are you going to do now? It sounds like you can't get out of there. No flights. And I heard them say this morning that all the rental car companies are reporting all of their cars are gone. I can take off now and drive up there to pick you up. Or, you remember my sister Blair. They live outside D.C.. I'm sure they would be glad to drive up and get you, and then maybe you can get a rental car there."

"Oh, Ralph, I appreciate that. I really haven't figured anything out yet. I keep thinking I'll hear something about Mari and I want to keep waiting. I've extended my stay here a few more days. Let me give that some thought and I'll call you back."

"Okay, son. Just so you know, we're here for you. We'll do whatever we can. Okay?"

"Okay. Thanks for the call. I'll keep you posted now that the phones are working."

Ray hung up and realized he was hungry. He hadn't eaten anything the day before and he remembered Sondra's offer. He called room service and ordered breakfast. He finished eating and had dumped the leftover coffee which had turned cold in his cup, and then filled it with hot coffee from the thermal pot which came with his breakfast. Then the phone rang in his room. It was a gentleman who identified himself as a detective with the NYPD.

"Mr. Reynolds?" he asked.

"Yes."

"I'm sorry to tell you this, but we believe we have your wife's body, Marilyn Key Reynolds. Was she at the World Trade Center yesterday?"

"Yes," Ray responded reluctantly, waiting for the next statement.

"This is not normal duty for me, or for our department, but I'm sure you can understand. Anyway, she's one of the first, maybe *the* first person to be identified from the tragedy. She was pulled off the street before the collapse of the north tower. It was obvious she had jumped. Luckily, she had her purse strapped over her shoulder and we found her I.D. and a Marriott room key. The hotel confirmed she was registered there along with her husband and put me through to you.

Dennis G. Smith

We really need you to come down to the city morgue and identify the body. I know that will be hard, but if you could do that this afternoon. it would really help us."

"Okay," and he began to sob. This conversation had confirmed all of his thoughts from the past 24 hours. Now, he knew for sure. At least she had escaped the fire. "Where do I find the morgue?"

"Are you driving?" the detective asked.

"No, I'll be taking a cab."

"Well, I'll give you the address, but almost any cab driver knows where to find it." He waited for Ray to get a pen and paper off the desk and then gave him the address.

Ray thought about calling Ralph back, but what if it wasn't Mari? *They have her I.D. and she had a Marriott room key. It has to be her.*

CHAPTER 50

It may have been the hardest thing Ray Reynolds ever had to do. Harder than basic training, harder than Vietnam and getting shot, harder than seeing the ranch on fire and his father dying. Identifying the lifeless body of his childhood sweetheart, his wife of 26 years, the mother of their children, seeing the sheet pulled back to expose her badly bruised face and having to say, "Yes, that's her." He couldn't stop crying. He felt like he was about to throw up.

The attendant left him there in a waiting room to allow him time to compose himself. He came back after a few minutes and asked him to sign some forms, and then escorted him back through a couple of long hallways to the exit and the waiting taxi. One of the forms was to authorize release of the body to a family member or a funeral home. Ray said he would call them back with the name of the funeral home when he got back to Kansas City.

When he returned to the hotel, he immediately made the necessary phone calls to family members and verified the bad news they had all expected.

When that was complete, he started calling car rental companies and checking on where they would have cars available to the west of New York. He managed to reserve a car with Avis in Columbus, Ohio, and then started to check on Amtrak to get him there. He realized he wasn't thinking clearly. *Why not just take Amtrak all the way to Kansas City?* Amtrak's website showed everything out of NYC 'Sold Out' but said they were in the process of adding more trains and 'Check back later'. He called back to Avis and cancelled his reservation. *There must be a better way*, he thought.

He was both mentally and physically exhausted. Ray laid back on the bed thinking that he would stay right there until tomorrow and then tackle the task of getting home. He needed to call his boss and update him on when he might possibly be back at work. Then he realized he also needed to call Mari's boss. *Tomorrow*, he thought.

CHAPTER 51

Thursday, September 13, 2001
Marriott Marquis Hotel, Times Square
New York, New York

Ray awoke early and realized he was terribly hungry. Prior to taking advantage of Sondra's comped room service, he wanted to see if he could get in early to see the concierge before they got overwhelmed with other guests. He looked on the hotel's list of amenities and saw that concierge services were available beginning at 8:00 a.m.. It was 7:25.

He rushed through brushing his teeth, shaving, and showering and headed down to the lobby. First problem of the day was ten people on his floor waiting for the elevator. Some were nervously looking at their watch. One well-dressed businessman commented, "It's always like this around rush hour, 8:00 in the morning and between 4:00 and 6:00 in the afternoon. You have to bring your patience when you come to New York."

By the time he finally got to the lobby, he counted twelve people in line at the concierge desk. He noticed that they had added a second person at an adjacent table so perhaps the line would move faster. He got in line, not sure if he wanted to wait or to succumb to his hunger pangs. He gave it a few more minutes, but the line didn't move. Another hotel guest got in line behind him. Hunger won out. He stepped out of line and told the man to go ahead.

Just then, a woman walked up and saw Ray step out of line. She asked him, "How long is the wait? Any idea?"

Ray was surprised by the question. How would he know? He responded by saying, "I don't know. I just got here. I thought I would be early enough to beat the crowd."

The attractive middle-aged woman laughed and said, "That's what I thought. I thought I could accomplish something here and then run up to breakfast, but I guess I might as well do breakfast first."

"That's exactly why I stepped out of line. I'm too hungry to stand there very long. And, I need some coffee."

"Well, let's go to breakfast."

While they stood waiting for the elevator, the woman stuck out her hand and said, "Emma, Emma Strong."

The way she said it with a pause in between, Ray wanted to respond with 'Bond, James Bond', but instead he said, "Ah, I grew up in your town." Then he laughed and added, " Ray Reynolds," as they shook hands. The warm soft skin of a female's hand felt nice. Then he explained the Strong City connection to her name.

As they exited the elevator and headed into the restaurant, Emma asked if Ray minded if she joined him for breakfast. "No, not at all. That would be fine. I could use the company."

Once they were seated and coffee was ordered, Emma said, "I'd be willing to bet $1,000 that anyone else you would meet in this hotel would not know where Strong City is. But I do. Does that surprise you?"

"Yeah, kind of. It's pretty much just a wide spot in the road. I never thought growing up there that I'd someday end up here in New York. How do you happen to know about Strong City?"

"I grew up in Buffalo, Missouri, pretty much straight east of Strong City. My uncle on my mother's side used to do rodeo, bull riding. We all thought he was crazy, and he finally had to give it up after too many injuries, but we made the trip over to Strong City several times in the summer when they had the rodeo. Is it still going '*strong*'?"

"Yeah, first weekend in June, every year. When I was in high school, I did some barrel racing and roping events."

"You gave it up?"

One Tough Son of a Gun

"Yeah, I got drafted. Back in the years of Vietnam."

The waitress came to take their order, then said she'd be right back with more coffee.

The subject changed back to the events of the last few days. Emma asked, "So are you like me, trying to figure out a way out of here?"

"Yup," Ray hesitated before he said anything else, then he added, "I lost my wife in the twin towers Tuesday."

"Oh, Ray, I am so sorry," and she reached over and put her hand on top of his. "I thought I sensed some melancholy in our conversation. But," and she paused before asking, "according to reports, there is so much confusion and possibilities of survivors in various hospitals, are you sure?"

"I'm sure. I may have been one of the first to identify someone from the big mess. My wife was there, um, *we* were here, for an interview with a big national company. She was excited about it. New York, World Trade Center. Times Square. We've been here since Friday. She absolutely hated fire. She jumped. Maybe the first jumper." Tears filled his eyes, and when he looked through those tears at Emma, he saw that she had her own tears.

"Oh, Ray, that's terrible. I am so sorry for you." Emma didn't know what else to say and squeezed his hand.

The waitress showed up with more coffee and said, "Your breakfast should be right out."

Ray said, "I'm just trying to figure out how to get out of here."

Emma asked, "So, where is home now?"

"Kansas City. Actually, Prairie Village, Kansas."

"Maybe I can help you out."

A server came to the table with their food and the conversation stalled for a few minutes while they unwrapped their silverware and got their napkins on their laps. The server asked if everything looked all right. They both nodded and he left.

After a few bites, Ray couldn't stand not knowing what she meant about helping out and asked.

"Well, guess what. You're from Prairie Village and I live in Lawrence. Small world, right? That's another reason I know Strong City. I met you downstairs this morning probably for the same reason you were there. I wanted to know what my options are. I still do. But, I have one situation probably entirely different than anyone else. Who knows?" She paused to pick up a strip of bacon and bit off a chunk.

"What's that?" Ray asked.

Emma took another bite off her bacon strip and laid the remainder back on her plate. "Three of us were here on business. Our company is in the process of a merger with a much larger company headquartered here in, guess what, the World Trade Center. We had meetings scheduled for Monday and Tuesday. I'm in charge of H.R. and we covered all of that on Monday, so I elected to stay here and do some shopping on Tuesday. Our corporate attorney and our sales manager went to the Tuesday session. We, meaning the company back in Lawrence and their families, still don't know their fates, but I know the offices they would have been in were on the 80th floor of the north tower, right where the plane struck, so we all pretty well know what to expect."

She took a sip of coffee. and Ray used the break in conversation to say he was sorry to hear that.

Emma continued, "There's a lot more to the story, but I have to tell you that, if I sound a little cold about this, it's just that these were business associates, not family, not loved ones, and, well, I guess I just lucked out. That still leaves me with a sense of shock. It's nothing like what you're going through."

They both continued with their meals. Ray still wondered what she meant about 'helping out'?

Emma finally spoke up again. "So, here's where I'm at right now. When we, the three of us scheduled this meeting, James, our attorney decided he wanted to spend some time with his older brother who lives in upstate New York. He took a week's vacation to begin on the 12th, after our meetings. He was going to do a road trip and drive so he told us, the sales manager and me, that we would be welcome to ride along. We left on Saturday and got in here on Sunday. I had a flight home scheduled on Tuesday evening, but obviously that didn't happen.

Ray spoke up, "Yeah, we did too! Possibly the same flight."

"Right now, my hope is that I get the i's dotted and the t's crossed with everyone and then I can leave when I'm ready and drive James's car home. It might be the quickest way out of here. I've laid out that plan to our company president and he didn't see any problem, but was going to check with some others. Obviously, he won't be checking with our company attorney. I've left a message with James's family. That's who I think our president is checking with since we'll need his wife's permission."

Ray nodded to show he understood the situation.

"I've checked with the hotel. Marriott needs a family member's approval to collect personal items from their rooms and an authorization to turn them over to me. If I get everyone's approval, we could be on the road, maybe yet today or tomorrow. It would be nice to have some company along the way."

CHAPTER 52

At 11:15, Ray's phone rang and Emma said she would be ready to go in half an hour. If he wanted to ride along then he would need to meet her in the lobby at 11:45. All the details had been checked and approved except for knowing where the car was. When they had arrived on Sunday, they utilized valet parking, but the valet ticket had not been found. James must have had it with him. She had described the car, a silver colored 2001 Chrysler 300M, almost brand new, and the parking attendants were searching for it as she spoke.

Ray gathered up his stuff, threw his shaving kit in the suitcase, closed it and set it next to the other two suitcases. They were Mari's. He thought to himself, *I could just leave them here. What am I going to do with her things now? Matt would probably never notice, but there's a good chance Fran would.* He knew he wouldn't be able to explain that away to his daughter.

It was almost exactly 12:00 noon when the car was loaded and they pulled away from the hotel out onto the side street just off Times Square. Ray had checked online that showed it was a seventeen-hour drive time to Kansas City. He estimated that with pit stops and meals, they could be in K.C. by 7:00 a.m., actually maybe 6:00 a.m. with the time change. That assumes they don't stop to sleep somewhere. They hadn't discussed that. Instead, as Ray looked out the passenger side of the windshield, Emma said, "There's a road atlas in the pocket behind my seat. I need you to help navigate. Here, the hotel gave me these directions to get us down to I-78. We take that west and then cut down to I-70 somewhere in the midwest. I'll let you decide."

Ray thought this sounded like quite the adventure. He hadn't been on a long road trip for years. Any way that took them far away from New York right now sounded good to him. He started thinking about

One Tough Son of a Gun

Mari laying in the morgue and tears started to form in his eyes. He had to think of something else.

"Okay, we're across the river in New Jersey," Emma seemed to be shouting out commands that brought Ray's mind back to the task at hand. "Where do we go from here?"

Ray looked at the photocopied directions and said, "Stay west til we see I-95, then south to Interstate 78." Then he added, "Nice car. Hey, it looks like this has GPS. Why don't we just use that?"

"Fine by me, do you know how to use it?"

"Not really. Let me play with it and we'll see."

The first thing that happened as soon as Ray hit a couple of buttons was a warning sign that popped up saying, 'Navigation cannot be set while car is in motion.' He read that warning to Emma and she said, "I'll watch for a place to pull off."

Fifteen minutes later, Emma had pulled over on the shoulder just before an exit ramp. Ray had found the Owner's Manual in the glove box and thought he had read enough about the GPS to figure it out. After three tries entering his Kansas street address, he finally got the system to say 'Calculating'. Emma said, "Do you think it's ready?"

"I think so, let's give it a go."

There was a long silent period while Emma concentrated on driving in heavy traffic. Also, she kept glancing at the GPS screen to see if anything important had changed. Eventually, she was satisfied that it was working, so she decided to start conversing again. After all, she had just met this guy that morning. While she was trying to think of a subject to talk about, her mind was thinking of all the things she should have thought about *before* inviting him along on this trip. *For all I know, he could be an axe murderer or a rapist or an escaped convict. Maybe he made all that stuff up about Strong City and the rodeo. And, of all the people, how did he know his wife was one of the first to jump? No, nobody could make that up. He had to have lived there. Besides, it's too late to think of all that now.*

245

Finally, she said, "So, tell me about Vietnam. My uncle was there in '68, Air Force mechanic. What did you do?"

"Grunt. I was a grunt. Army infantry. Sorta like being on the front lines, although there were no lines. You never knew for sure where, or who, the enemy was."

"I don't think I've ever heard the term 'grunt' used to describe army guys before. What's that mean? You almost sound proud of it."

"Well, I guess I'm not ashamed of it. We were the foot soldiers, the ones in the face-to-face battles. Infantry, you know, boots on the ground. That was my job."

"How long were you there?"

"A little over nine months. I was shot and evacuated to a hospital in Japan for recovery. I was there another three months before I was discharged and sent home."

"What was that like? The hospital in Japan?"

Ray started to remember all the bad nightmares about being shot and Camp Zama and responded, "I don't want to talk about it!" Then he realized how that sounded to a nice lady who was giving him a ride home and was just trying to make conversation, so he added, "I'm sorry, that sounded bad. But I really would prefer not to talk about that war. However, I can tell you a funny story about how I ended up in the infantry."

Emma looked over at him and nodded and said , "I'm all ears."

Ray started in, "Basic training, Fort Bliss, Texas, right outside of El Paso. It's an eight-week course. We started on a Monday. I think there was something like 200, maybe 220 guys in our training company. On Friday morning, before we started exercises, we were all out on the tarmac in front of our barracks and there was an announcement: 'If I call your name, fall out and line up over here.' They called something like 35 names, and, of course, I was one of them. None of us knew what this was all about, maybe K.P. duty, maybe special assignment, we didn't know. Some Buck Sergeant lined us up two abreast and marched us away from there over to a group of buildings and inside into a classroom. The room was small, just barely enough seats. The Sergeant said 'Lieutenant somebody will be with you in a few minutes'."

"So this First Lieutenant comes in and we all stand and he says 'As you were, be seated.' Then he asks, 'How many of you know what OCS is?' and about half the room raised their hands, me included." He paused and looked over at Emma and said, "Are you familiar with OCS?"

"No."

"It's Officer Candidate School. This Lieutenant goes on to explain that we were all there because we scored high enough on our first week's tests to show that we were qualified for OCS. Then he said, 'Are there any of you right now who know you are definitely not interested in OCS?' I knew it would mean a minimum of one more year of service - three years instead of the two-year draft commitment. I raised my hand, and so did seven other guys. We were all excused and sent back to our company area and told to report to the office. That took care of that, we thought."

"So you were just in for two years?" Emma asked.

"Yeah, but here's the 'rest of the story', as Paul Harvey likes to say."

Emma looked over at him and gave a slight chuckle.

"On the last day of Basic Training, when we all got our diplomas or certificates or whatever, we were back out front of the barracks and our names were called one-by-one to receive our orders for our next duty station. I got mine, and it was for Fort Polk, Louisiana. Everybody calls it the armpit of the Army. Infantry school - AIT, Advanced Infantry Training. When they finished handing out the orders and we were dismissed, I was listening to everyone, 'Where you goin'?, How about you? What are you gonna be doin?', all that stuff. Out of 200 and some guys in that company, I found out there were only eight of us going to Infantry school." He paused to let that sink in. "It was the same eight of us who rejected signing up for OCS."

Emma seemed somewhat concerned as though it really didn't make sense to her, so she had to ask, "What about all the other 200 or so guys? Where else do you go in the Army for additional training? I thought infantry would probably be it."

"No, I was hearing guys with orders for Communications, Mechanized school, Helicopter Maintenance, Ordinance, Artillery, and so on."

"I guess I never thought about all of that."

"Well, there was one more tidbit of information about this story. We were out in the field in Louisiana undergoing training, and we took a lunch break. C-rations. One of the officers, a Captain, walked over to our area of about six or seven guys, and asked if he could sit with us during lunch. He sat right down on the ground with us and visited about where everyone was from and how we were doing. I told him this story about eight of us being sent to Fort Polk seemingly because we didn't want to go to OCS. You know what he said?"

"I don't think so."

"He said, 'Well, you know, the Infantry needs smart people too.'"

"Oh, that's funny!"

"That's it from me on the Army stuff, I kind of fight a battle with PTSD issues, but I'm not nearly as bad off as some of the guys. I try not to talk about it too much."

"I'm sorry, I shouldn't have asked."

"No, it's all right. I just wanted you to know."

It was nearing 3:00 p.m. and Emma said, "We're going to have to get some gas pretty soon. We're almost to Harrisburg, which means Hershey should be coming up. Do you want to stop there and get your kids some chocolate?"

Ray pondered the question and thought of the news he was carrying home to his children, if they didn't already know about their mother. He didn't think it was a time for chocolates or any other gifts. He simply said, "No." Then he added, "But you can stop if you want."

Ray looked at the GPS screen and noticed they were now on I-81. "What happened to Interstate 78?"

"I guess it ended a few miles back, merged with 81. I'm trusting this device. That woman's voice said, '*Stay left and merge onto I-81.*"

"Okay," Ray agreed, "It shows we're still headed west."

"Yeah, but it's an odd number designation, which should mean it's a north-south highway. Eventually, we should be turning more south and then we'll cross I-70.

They stopped for gas at the Hershey exit. Ray used the restroom and got a cup of coffee and a candy bar. He asked Emma if she wanted anything and then offered to drive. She replied that she liked driving, but maybe after dinner, she'd let him take it for awhile.

Back in the car and back on the road, Ray asked Emma about her life. He hadn't noticed any wedding band but he asked anyway - married? kids? Her answers were short. Divorced, one daughter, sixteen, currently living with her father. Then there was an awkward pause and Ray wished he hadn't asked.

Ray could tell Emma was about to add something to the conversation, so he waited. Then she opened. "Actually, my daughter's a good kid. Honor roll, a cheerleader, you know. But she's at that age where she knows everything and I can't tell her anything that she doesn't already know. So, earlier this year, she asked her dad if she could live with him and his second wife. I don't think the new Mrs. Strong was real happy about it, but Savanna says they get along just fine."

A long conversation ensued about raising kids, and they both agreed on many issues. Then Ray said the inevitable, "I just don't know how I'm going to manage it now without Mari."

Emma reached over and tapped her hand on Ray's knee and said, "You're a smart man. You'll figure it out."

Now it was Ray's turn with the negative thoughts. *What makes her think I'm smart. I could be a rapist, or a serial killer. We just met this morning. Maybe she's a serial killer. No, doesn't seem to be the type.* While he was having these thoughts, he realized he hadn't let anyone in Kansas or at his office know where he was. They wouldn't know when to expect him. He wondered if Jennifer had told the kids about their mother. They had to be wondering why we weren't home yet. And, of course, they surely saw the news of the Twin Towers. He decided he needed to call.

Just outside of Akron, Ohio, Emma said, "What sounds good to eat?"

Ray shrugged his shoulders and said, "Whatever sounds good to you. I'm easy to please."

Emma pulled off the interstate at an exit with a large truck stop and several fast food restaurants. "What d'ya think? Truck stop, Wendy's, Arby's? Think about it, I need the restroom." She got out and headed into the truck stop.

Ray got out and stretched. He needed a break from the car. He pulled out his cell phone and called his home number. He was surprised when a man's voice answered. Then he realized it was Ralph. He must have driven up to be with his wife and grandkids at such a horrible time in their lives.

Ray filled him in on his status and said he would be there sometime tomorrow, most likely late afternoon if they decided to stop and sleep. Ralph suggested that was a good idea; it wasn't smart to drive tired. Ray told him they would switch off, although that hadn't happened yet. He asked about the kids and Ralph said they know about their mother and obviously, they're pretty upset. They're staying home from school and they'll be glad to see you tomorrow.

Ray's thoughts were both sadness and relief. At least he didn't have to be the one to break the news to them. He saw Emma coming out of the truck stop and he told Ralph he would call with an update in the morning. He walked towards Emma and said, "How about a blue plate special? Truck stop food okay with you?"

"Fine," and she turned around, leading the way to the restaurant entrance.

During dinner, Emma gave Ray an update. "There's a large midwest map on the wall in the restroom lobby. We're about two hours from Columbus where we'll hit I-70. Then it's probably another three hours to Indianapolis. I'm getting tired, so, if you don't mind driving from here, we could stop at either of those cities or at some interstate motel anywhere in between to get some rest. What do you think?"

"I'm fine with driving. Don't mind at all. And you can pick when and where we stop."

"Well, I'd kinda prefer Columbus. I'm tired now and I'm an early morning person. So, maybe we can get an early start tomorrow?"

"Sounds good to me."

When they finished their meals, Emma asked for a refill on her coffee. Ray picked up the check and said, "Enjoy your coffee and take your time. I need to call my sister. I've got the check," he added, and threw a five dollar bill on the table for the tip. "I'll meet you at the car."

Ray went outside over to the parking area and stood by the car as he called June. She was so glad to hear from him but devastated about what happened to Mari. Ray said he was on his way home by car with a lady he had just met that morning at the hotel. He described the 'madhouse' with all the travelers trying to get out of New York, and how this lady had lost two business associates in the attack. They talked briefly about the building's collapse and Ray wanted to change the subject. June apologized and asked him when he would be home.

He said, "We're in Akron now and heading on to Columbus where we will hit I-70 and maybe on to Indianapolis, depending on how tired we get. So, either way, we should be there sometime tomorrow afternoon."

"Okay," June replied, I'll check on flights, but with the kids, it will be easier if we drive. We'll see you tomorrow evening. Okay?"

"That will be great."

"Who did you say this woman is?"

Ray saw Emma walking out the door of the restaurant. "I'll fill you in more tomorrow, but she was just a strange coincidence, a business woman from Lawrence who lost two associates in the towers. We're driving the company attorney's car back. She's been to Strong City. Grew up in Missouri and used to come to the rodeos as a kid. Gotta go. We'll talk tomorrow!"

"Okay. Love you, Ray!" He could hear her voice crack.

"Love you too, Jude!" He felt a lump in his throat and had to fight to hold back tears.

Emma walked up to the passenger side and unlocked the car. She checked again, "You okay with driving?"

Ray responded by nodding his head and said, "No problem. I'll take it."

Off they headed towards Columbus and I-70. Ray felt good behind the wheel. Emma had found the recline button for the passenger seat and had made herself comfortable. She asked Ray if he was sleepy, or had any questions about the car's controls. He replied that he was fine.

When they neared Columbus less than two hours later, Ray estimated that they still had another hour of daylight. He was going to ask Emma if she still felt like stopping in Columbus but looked over and saw that she was sleeping soundly. He drove straight through headed for Indiana. When Emma awoke a half hour later, he told her of his decision and she said, "Fine."

After a little pause and Emma raising her seat back upright, she said. "You know, I'm sure you're very anxious to get back to see your kids and other family, but I've sort of been stalling. Tomorrow's Friday and I don't want to get back so early that I will feel guilty if I don't go to the office. I think I really need the weekend to get prepared for all the questions and sympathy that I'll be faced with. You know what I mean?"

"I do, and I can understand that. We can stop anytime if we see a decent looking motel, or Dayton is coming up in about fifteen minutes. Otherwise, we will certainly stop in Indianapolis and then we can have a leisurely drive tomorrow and get in sometime late afternoon."

"Sounds good. I'm even dreading getting this car back to Carl's wife. I don't think I've ever met her before. I can imagine her thinking 'How did *you* survive?'"

"That'll be awkward." It was quiet for a minute as both of them thought about that. Then Ray asked, "Tell me about your business. What were you guys doing in New York? I think you said something about a merger?"

"Yeah," Emma answered, "We're in the real estate business, but we're in a specialty field. College towns. We specialize in picking up properties near campus, the closer the better. You know, after awhile dormitories, frat houses, sororities, all become old. And, privately held rentals, apartments, well, after awhile, the owners get old. and those properties also fall into disrepair. We try to get them at the right price and rescue them for another ten, fifteen, twenty years. Then, depending on the property, we may flip it or manage it. We have a small office in most of the Big 12 towns and others in the midwest. Oklahoma City, Lawrence obviously covers Manhattan and Wichita. Our Denver office covers several Colorado schools. Then there's Lincoln, Columbia. Some of these are one-person managers who work out of their homes. We try to stay low key and we try to make an offer before a property goes on the market. We were in the Big Apple to see if our major competitor in this market would consider a merger. If so, we wanted to find out how that might work out. Right now, they are primarily east of the Mississippi, but we've seen evidence that they are creeping westward. My job as Human Resources Manager is mainly keeping all these regional managers happy. Our thought was that with a merger and more employees, we could get better insurance rates and possibly improve on our financing rates with more equity and a bigger footprint. Now we won't know, will we?"

"That's interesting. And, too bad. Will your company survive their loss?"

"Oh yeah," Emma replied. "I'll have to get busy searching for a new Sales Manager. Rex, the one who died, was really our Procurement Manager, but again, we try to keep a low profile so 'Sales Manager' doesn't sound as intimidating as someone in charge of buying property. Rex would get leads from the regional guys. He would do an analysis, check the markets in that area and try to find a way into the property without the owner's knowledge. Then he would assess the physical problems, structure, layout, necessary repairs and so on. So I'll look for an experienced engineer or construction guy."

"What's the company name?"

"We operate under 'Campus Constructors' and our sales side sells under 'College Real Estate'."

"The more you described your operation the more it sounded somewhat familiar to me. Do you have a guy there in Lawrence named Thompson, Bill Thompson, I think?"

"No, it's *Will* Thompson! Yeah, how do you know Will?"

"It's been a few years ago. I'm in the cabinet business and he contacted us about an apartment remodel in Lawrence. If I remember right, you guys backed out of the deal because you discovered some serous structural problems, termites or wood rot, or something like that."

"That would be Will's job."

"Oh my, it's a small world after all."

Make sure I have your card before we part. I'll tell Will about our ride together. We have another potential project coming up in Lawrence, a forty-unit apartment that needs complete updating. They haven't replied to our offer yet. We'll need cabinets if we get the deal to work."

"We can do that."

Ray pulled into the Holiday Inn on the east side of Indianapolis just after 9:30. They each grabbed a suitcase from the trunk and headed inside. Ray went to the counter first and Emma caught up and elbowed him aside. "Ladies first," she said, then turned to the desk clerk and said, "One room, two queen beds." Then she turned back to Ray and said, "Remember, this is still a business expense for me. Save your money."

Ray felt his face flush and he slowly put his credit card back in his wallet and the wallet back in his pocket. *This will be awkward*, he thought, and then he said a silent prayer to Mari. *This was not my idea, I hope, if you're watching, you will see that this is all just the fastest way to get home to our kids. Nothing will happen between this women and me, you can rest assured. I have no desire and neither does she. If she does, I will stop her. We just need to rest.*

They were given a room on the fourth floor. Ray laid his suitcase on the far bed, closest to the window. He walked over and looked out and could see the silver 300M below. His thought went to the view Mari must have had just before she jumped. *Oh crap*, he thought and tried to erase those thoughts as quickly as possible.

He turned around and noticed Emma's suitcase on the other bed and the bathroom door was closed. She came out a few minutes later with a freshly washed face and said, "Well, this will work, don't ya think?"

Ray nodded and said, "Yeah, I guess so, but I sleep in my boxers."

"Okay. I won't peek."

"Sounds fair. Do you want to catch some local news?" Ray reached for the remote and turned on the TV. When he found a local channel, they were advertising. Then the commercials ended and the first scene was of the firefighters and national guardsmen and others searching through the huge pile that was once a proud building. Ray clicked the off button.

"Do you need the bathroom?" Emma asked as she rummaged through her suitcase.

"Not right now."

"Okay, I'm gonna change for bed. Then you can have it."

Ten minutes later, Emma emerged wearing pajama bottoms and an oversized night shirt. Ray pretended to be staring at his phone, so that her promise of not peeking would be reciprocated. Then he moved his suitcase to the desk, opened it and pulled out a KC Chiefs T-shirt and his shaving kit, and headed for the bathroom. After brushing his teeth, he returned wearing the t-shirt and his polo shirt draped over one arm. He folded that shirt and tucked it back into the suitcase, then walked to the far side of the bed and slipped out of his khaki slacks and tucked himself in under the sheets and comforter. He said, "Good night," to Emma, and she responded in kind.

At approximately 2:30 in the morning, something woke Emma. She rolled over on her back to listen and realized it was Ray making unintelligible sounds and almost screaming about the window.

"I have to get out, break the glass!" Ray's words were becoming more clear.

Emma rolled to that side of her bed and sat up on the side and reached over to touch Ray. "Ray, It's all right. It's Emma. I'm here. Are you okay?"

Ray's eyes flashed open in the dark. He could see someone leaning over him and it startled him. He pulled away and tried to jump out of bed but was tangled up in the bedding. He looked again as Emma turned on the bedside lamp between the two beds and, again, the light startled Ray. Then he shook his head in disbelief and realized where he was and recognized that Emma was not Mari.

"Oh, I'm sorry." He shook his head and sat up still startled. He looked around the mostly dark room and paused, then added, "I told you I had issues with PTSD. I thought I was better, but not now, not with the Twin Towers coming down and losing Mari!'

"It's okay. Can I get you anything? A glass of water? I've even got a small flask of bourbon in my suitcase."

Ray's ears perked up. "That might be good about now. I am really sorry I woke you up. What time is it?"

"It's going on 3:00."

She grabbed a plastic glass from the bathroom and poured less than two fingers. Ray sat up against the headboard and downed the alcohol. He coughed slightly and then wheezed. "I think I needed that!"

The next day, Friday, during quiet windshield time, Ray's mind wandered back to the night before and his prayerful promise to Mari. *I told you it would be uneventful. If it hadn't been for the nightmare, it was totally uneventful. I would never lie to you. I love you.*

After witnessing Ray's troubled sleep, Emma decided she wouldn't say anything to Ray about it unless he brought it up. She also decided she would not offer to let him drive. Somehow, she felt safer behind the wheel. Just outside of Indianapolis, she began fooling with the radio. She quickly skipped past news stations unless they were giving weather updates. She didn't want to hear about the World Trade Center, but she did hear that the low overnight had been in the mid 50's, and the high there in Indiana was expected to reach into the 70's. Perfect driving weather. That was all she needed to know. She gave up on finding a station and asked Ray if he would try to find some good music, maybe country and western.

"Okay." he said, but before he reached for the radio controls, he turned towards Emma and said, "I'm really sorry about waking you last night, and I hope I didn't scare you. I scared *myself!* I didn't know where I was and I couldn't figure out who was standing over me. I appreciate your help. I haven't had one of those for quite awhile. I think the last was back in May or June. They used to hit me three or four times a month, way back when. I still go to PTSD meetings occasionally. I think it helps, and I kinda enjoy the camaraderie of the other guys. Oh, and women. Again, thanks for being there and I hope you understand."

"I'm glad I could be of help. I wasn't really sure what to do except to try and wake you."

"That worked. Just took me a minute to come around. Or, was it longer than that?"

"No, a minute was about right. It just *seemed* longer at the time."

Ray began searching the radio dial for something worth listening to and stopped on a station where the Whitney Houston version of Dolly Parton's song 'I Will Always Love You' was just beginning. He turned up the volume. The surround sound in the car was incredible. When the song ended, Emma glanced over at Ray and saw tears running down his cheeks. When she saw that, she felt the tears rising in her eyes also and wondered if she was going to have to pull over to dry them. Instead, she used the back of her hand to blot her eyes and checked her mirrors to make sure she didn't have any close traffic to contend with.

Ray left that station on, but turned the volume back down to a normal level. He pushed the recline button on his seat and laid his head back on the headrest.

Mid-morning, west of Terre Haute, Indiana, Ray called his home to update them on the anticipated arrival time. His son Matt answered.

"Oh Matt, it's so good to hear your voice," as Ray's voice cracked with emotion on the last two words and he hoped Matt didn't notice. But then, he thought, *What difference does it make; he's old enough to understand.* He went on to tell him that they were still in Indiana and would be stopping later for lunch, but should be home by 4:30 or 5:00.

After an Arby's fast food lunch on the western side of St. Louis, there was a long boring spell of un-scenic highway. Ray asked Emma if she remembered the Burma-Shave signs. She shook her head and said, "No, what are they?"

So Ray began to tell her the whole history, including some of his favorites that he could remember. She seemed to like the *'periscope'* one the best and the one Ray quoted, *'Don't lose your head to save a minute. You need your head, your brains are in it.'* She laughed as Ray recited them. He seemed genuinely excited to be telling her about these tidbits of American history. Then, he admitted proudly how he had used the same term paper about the Burma-Shave story for three different courses in college, American History, Creative Writing, and his major in Marketing.

Emma laughed and congratulated him on his creativity. Then she asked whatever happened to Burma-Shave.

"They got bought out by the Philip Morris Company in the early 1960's and that was the end of the signs. They sent crews out around the country to take them down, but a few got missed and remained for several years. There were some along Highway 50 close to Strong City that got me interested. My dad told me all about them when I was young."

"That's interesting," Emma said, and waited to see if he would recite any more of the sayings. But that was the end of the story.

CHAPTER 53

When Emma pulled up to the curb in front of the Reynolds' house, it was just a matter of seconds before Matt and Fran came running out the front door to greet their dad. They were immediately followed by their grandparents, Ralph and Jennifer, and all were there to give Ray hugs as soon as he stepped out of the car onto the green, green grass of home.

Emma stayed behind the wheel to give the family time to embrace and welcome home their son-in-law and their father, and to shed the tears over the loss of their loved one. When the emotions began to subside, she pushed the trunk lid release button on the dash and stepped out to make sure Ray got his luggage and to say hello to the group.

Ray introduced Emma as his savior from New York City. They both needed to get out of there and things just worked out when planes weren't flying and car rentals were all gone. Ralph walked over and shook her hand, and Matt did the same. Jenn smiled at her and said, "Thank you. It's nice to meet you." Fran just stood back and stared at Emma. She still wondered why her mother had to be gone.

Ray went to the trunk and pulled out three suitcases. Fran immediately knew the two light blue ones belonged to her mother and she began to cry. Jennifer stepped over beside her and put her arm around her. Fran turned and buried her face in her grandmother's side. Luckily, she didn't see her father go over to Emma to give her a hug and say thanks and good-bye, but she did watch solemnly as Emma closed the trunk and got back in the car to drive off, headed for Lawrence.

Just before 6:00, the front door swung open and Ray's sister June, husband Bill, and the two kids came rushing in. Ray stood to greet June and she threw her arms around him and they hugged for a long time.

One Tough Son of a Gun

Ray thought to himself that the only other time he held his sister that long was that last day at the ranch when she had been on the swing and he sang to her. *Here I go again with the tears. I really don't want my kids watching me cry, but then, what difference does it make? They'll certainly know I loved their mother.*

Ray had closed his eyes to try to hold back the tears which didn't work. When he opened them as they began to separate, he saw his mother, the last one through the door in the group from Colorado. Then he quickly stepped away from June and rushed over to his mother for another long hug and more tears.

All of a sudden, Matt remembered something he was supposed to tell everyone. "Oh, hey, Chip called earlier and said they would be here by 6:30 or 7:00."

Before the Keys went back to Cottonwood Falls on Saturday, they helped Ray with plans for Mari's funeral. Ray needed to contact the morgue in New York and let them know the funeral home that would be taking care of the remains so she could be shipped home. Ray agreed to let Ralph take care of that and they also agreed on burying Mari. No way was she to be cremated. Ralph said he would take care of contacting the county and the caretaker of the cemetery.

They couldn't finalize plans for a funeral until they knew when they might have Mari's body back in Cottonwood Falls. The Prairie Grove Cemetery, just west of town, same place Ray's father was buried, was awaiting her arrival.

CHAPTER 54

Wednesday, October 10, 2001
Kansas City VA Medical Center
Kansas City, Missouri

Ray had called Dr. Zehr the week before and filled her in on the loss of his wife on 9/11. He told her how that had triggered his nightmares to return, only now they often included fire. He described his latest nightmare from the night before. "It started with Mari and me in a plane on our way to New York. That seemed so real since we had just done that." There was a pause and Dr. Zehr could hear a sniffle and then heard Ray blow his nose.

"Sorry, I'll try again. Then I was in the plane with the hijackers and they had taken over the cockpit and killed some passengers in their way. Several of us on the plane decided we weren't going to allow this. Then I heard the words of that one guy on the Pennsylvania flight that said 'Let's roll!' and we all headed to the front of the plane. When we got to the cockpit door and busted in, it was just, . . . me, m, m, me, all alone with the hijackers. The others had disappeared. I see the pilot," Ray paused and cleared his throat, "on the floor with his throat slashed and the co-pilot still in his seat with *his* throat slashed. The hijacker standing behind him started to attack me with a box cutter. Somehow, I had grabbed a fire extinguisher and swung it at him while I tried to pull the other hijacker out of the pilot's seat. I had an arm around his neck and managed to knock the other guy down with one good swing. I, I, I looked up out the windshield and saw the Twin Towers coming up fast. I jerked hard with all I had to get the guy out of the pilot's seat and looked up again," There was another long pause, "and saw Mari in her new blue dress, standing in the window watching us just before we hit. I woke up screaming. My daughter Fran was in my room trying to calm me down. I don't know how I can make these nightmares stop."

He was having trouble concentrating on his story to Dr. Zehr. As he was reciting this dream sequence, Ray again felt there was another dream he was trying to remember. It was like many times before that he was on the outside looking in, or was it on the inside looking out? Out of where? *Someday*, he thought, *I'm going to remember this one. It's not right that these other scary dreams are so realistic, but there's one out there that I can't remember. Maybe it's even worse.*

"Oh, Ray, that's horrible! I am *so* sorry!" She paused, absorbing the fact that Ray had lost his wife. A victim from the Kansas City area brings the whole attack closer to home. Then she added. "I know you've never liked the idea of prescription drugs, but I've told you before I can get you to a doctor who can prescribe some medicines that should help."

"I know, I know. I still don't like the idea of taking some kind of mind-altering drug for the rest of my life. But, I think I'm going to have to consider it."

Again, there was a pause, and then Ray asked if he could go first in the PTSD session the following week because he would lose his concentration during the other guys' reports if he sat there stewing over what he was going to say. Dr. Zehr told Ray again how sorry she was to hear about Mari and she understood how much this would affect Ray. She said to call her at anytime if he needed anything that she could do to help. As promised on the phone a week earlier, Dr. Zehr allowed Ray to be the first speaker, and she gave a brief introduction.

"Good morning, everyone." She started in, "For many of you, war has been the common denominator. The trauma of seeing battle up close and watching friends die on the battlefield is what brings many of you here. I have to always hope that these sessions will bring each of you some comfort knowing that you are not alone in your suffering, and that being able to describe your emotions, your anger, your fears, allows you to have hope for the future. All of us here want the best for each other. The trauma of war or the loss of a loved one is very difficult for many humans to cope with. Now, I've learned of a recent tragedy that has befallen one of our veterans here today. Losing a friend is always hard to accept, but there is seldom anything worse than losing a child or losing your life partner unexpectedly at a very young age. Ray Reynolds has asked to go first today to express his emotions over a terrible loss. Ray was extremely nervous. He pushed his chair back and stood. "I'm sorry," he began, "I think I need to move while I talk so maybe I won't cry. I can't just sit here and have you all stare at me today. You know me and my anger. It's the nightmares that make me angry, and it's being upset about something that causes the nightmares. I thought I was getting over it. I really don't want you all feeling sorry for me. It's something none of us can change. It happened and I'm pissed about it. I know my anger won't change anything." He was now pacing slowly back and forth on his side of the table. Several people on his side turned their chairs and their bodies so they could watch as he spoke.

"After the events of last month, I think all of us veterans are ready to re-enlist and go fight these dirty rotten Commie bastards that killed so many people," he paused, not because he wanted to, but because he had to in order to compose himself enough to force out the next words, "including my wife!" His voice cracked and his hand went up to his right eye to wipe away the start of a tear. "We'd been married 26 years, but our life together goes back much further than that. We were in New York because Mari was invited to an interview with a large national company. She was really excited about it. Their offices were in the Twin Towers, high up, near the top. Mari hated fire, just terribly frightened by it. I'm sure the prospect of fire was what made her jump."

He paused and took some deep breaths. "I thought I could overcome this PTSD crap, and that I was in control of my life. I'm telling all of you this just to let you know that no matter how bad we all can feel with our emotions and war wounds, physical or mental, things can be worse. It's life! It's our lives and we have to live with it. Mari doesn't get the chance to suffer with PTSD. Her life is over. I'll never find another like her, and I don't even want to try. I felt like you needed to hear this so you'll understand me better in the future."

He reached in his rear pocket and pulled out a handkerchief, dabbed at his eyes, and returned to his chair. He noticed a few others were wiping tears from their eyes. It was quiet for some time. Finally, one veteran on the other side of the table asked, "Ray, did you drive to New York?"

Ray responded, "No. We flew." And the veteran then wanted to know, "How did you get out of there? All the airlines were grounded and I heard all the rental cars were snatched up right away."

Ray took a deep breath and put his handkerchief away. "It was a strange coincidence. Two days after, I was in the hotel lobby hoping the concierge could help, but there were like ten or twelve people ahead of me. A lady walked up and asked me how fast the line was moving and I had to tell her I just got there. Turns out she was from Lawrence and had a car that belonged to one of her business associates who also died in the attack. She was working on getting permission to drive that car back to his family in Kansas. We left later that day."

Another veteran piped up, "Oh man, there's your guardian angel! Don't lose track of her!"

There was a pause after that statement and Dr. Zehr then said, "Ray, you have all of our sympathy. We are so sorry for your loss."

One veteran spoke up and said, "Right! Hear, hear."

Another said, "So sorry, Ray! That's horrible!" And others nodded in agreement.

CHAPTER 55

Wednesday, February 13, 2002
O.P. Custom Cabinets & Hardware
Overland Park, Kansas

Ray was in the middle of designing a kitchen for a large custom home under construction in Hallbrook Farms when his desk phone rang.

"O.P. Custom Cabinets," he answered.

"Ray?"

"Yes?" He thought there was a familiarity to the voice, but he couldn't place it.

"Emma, ...Emma Strong."

It took him a few seconds for the surprise to sink in. He hadn't heard from her since she dropped him off at home five months earlier. This time he couldn't resist responding to her 'Emma, ... Emma Strong' introduction by saying, "Bond, ...James Bond," He paused a few seconds to let her absorb the humor and then said, "Hello Emma, my savior! How are you?"

"I'm fine. Fine. How are *you?*"

"I'm getting along. I have some good days and some not so good. But, I'm doin' okay."

"That's good to hear. I think about you often and wonder how things are going for you and the kids."

"We're getting by. Thanks for asking. How's your business doing over there in Lawrence?"

"Well, that's part of my reason for calling. We're looking at an apartment complex over here that needs some significant updating. I told Will, our construction estimator, remember him? I told him about your company and he wants to come over to show you the concept plans and get some help on cabinet pricing. I thought I'd come along to re-introduce him and say 'hi'."

"That sounds great! When?"

"How about tomorrow? Say 11:30? I'll buy lunch if that works with you?"

"Great! Still using that expense account, huh?"

"Only for special occasions."

After he hung up, he couldn't stop his mind from recalling his road trip with Emma. Back then he was totally lost in the horrific events of 9/11 and the loss of his wife. Now, after hearing her voice again, he was remembering the drive, the motel stop with a strange woman, his nightmare that night, and her efforts to comfort him. He tried to think about other details of those thirty hours together, and wondered what he should mention during their lunch coming up the next day. As he thought about it, he remembered her take-charge attitude at the motel, and the brief glance he had of her in her pajamas. As he thought about that, he remembered she had shoulder length blond hair, was fairly tall with a pretty face and a pleasant smile, especially under the circumstances. Try as he might, he could not remember the color of her eyes and wondered if he ever looked at her that closely. Surely he had when they sat across the table from each other at breakfast, or at the truck stop for dinner. He decided he needed to check out her eyes.

The next day, Emma and Will showed up right on time. Ray shook Will's hand and said it was good to see him again. Then he offered to shake Emma's hand but she bypassed that and greeted him with a smile and a hug. "Good to see you again," she said.

Ray replied with, "Likewise." He hugged her back. He showed them around their office and expanded showroom. Then he suggested they could just walk a block down the street to the local Mexican restaurant if that was okay. They agreed and headed for lunch.

When Emma took off her coat in the restaurant, Ray noticed her slim-line slacks and commented on her colorful sweater. He almost asked her if she had lost weight and decided against it because he really didn't remember her physical appearance that well. But looking at her now he thought she was much prettier than he remembered.

Will listened to Ray and Emma re-live their trip out of New York, and then he finally got a chance to discuss his cabinet needs for the apartment complex. As they finished their meal and Emma reached in her purse for her credit card, she also pulled out a red envelope and handed it to Ray.

"I was hunting for a card for my daughter and I saw this one and it made me think of you."

Ray felt his face was probably turning red and it was at least the fourth time he looked directly into her green eyes. He was pleased, but very surprised to be getting a valentine from a woman he barely knew, especially in front of a guy he barely knew. "Oh, thank you!" He laid it on the table.

"Oh, go ahead and open it. It's not a big deal. Like I said, it just made me think of you."

Ray opened the envelope and pulled out the card. The cover had a picture of a cartoon character sleeping in bed with a series of 'Z's' above his head, and a caption saying *'Wishing you nothing but sweet dreams!'* The inside verse was a simple *'Happy Valentine's Day!'*

"You see why I couldn't pass it up?"

"Yes. Thank you! I can see why that would make you think of me."

They walked the one block back to the cabinet office and showroom and sat down to look at the apartment plans. Ray had his marching orders for an estimate and said he could have something put together by the end of the following week. He could mail it over or deliver it in person.

Emma quickly suggested "In person. I'd like to show you *our* offices."

Thursday, February 21, 2002

On his drive over to Lawrence the following week, Ray remembered the valentine card and looked forward to seeing Emma again. But his real focus was on winning a new customer and possibly obtaining what would be a lucrative cabinet contract. There were twenty-four one-bedroom units with the exact same kitchen layouts, and another eighteen two-bedroom units which he had tweaked a little to save them some money, plus the manager's full-size unit.

Emma met Ray at the front desk and showed him around their offices and introduced him to their president. Then she took him to a conference room and called for Will. The meeting went well and Ray left feeling assured that he would get the project if the purchase offer was accepted by the current owner of the building.

Driving back to Overland Park, he thought about Emma and felt like he owed her a lunch for bringing him the business. Then, he thought he should wait to make sure they got the contract so he could expense the lunch and not have it come out of his pocket.

He figured if O.P. Custom Cabinets & Hardware didn't get the job, he would most likely never see her again. Even if they did get the job, her role in H.R. wouldn't require her involvement.

His mind wandered from that to an old Chuck Berry song, *'C'est la vie' say the old folks, it goes to show you never can tell.'* He couldn't remember the rest of the song and he had no clue why that came to mind. His brain just kept repeating those lyrics.

C'est la vie' say the old folks, it goes to show you never can tell.

When he pulled in the parking lot at his office, another line from the song finally popped into his head, *'It was a teenage wedding and the old folks wished them well.'* But he still couldn't remember anymore. *That's life,* he thought.

CHAPTER 56

Tuesday, August 20, 2002
O.P. Custom Cabinets & Hardware
Overland Park, Kansas

Ray answered his phone and was somewhat surprised to hear from a project manager with Campus Constructors. He had almost forgotten about the project in Lawrence with Emma's real estate and construction company. He barely remembered meeting Joel Wilson when Emma gave him the office tour over six months earlier. Joel informed him that, after a lot of haggling over price issues and problems with the title search, College Real Estate finally closed the deal and Campus Constructors could now get started. Joel said he would be preparing a subcontract for Ray's company and asked him to look it over when he got it and give him a call if there were any questions.

Ray said thank you and said he appreciated the vote of confidence and looked forward to working with Joel on getting the cabinet order placed. Then he asked if Joel could transfer him over to Emma.

"No," Joel responded, "She's out this week. Her mother passed away late last week."

"Oh no. I'm sorry to hear that. When's the service? Do you know?"

Joel responded, "Not sure, but I think it's today. Like maybe at 2:00. Our boss went down to be there."

"There? Where is that?" Ray hoped maybe he would still have time to get there.

"Buffalo, Missouri. That's all I know. I think you can find the obituary online."

"Okay, thank you. That's sad to hear.. Emma's a good friend."

"Yeah, I know, I've heard her talk about you."

"Really?"

"Yeah, we all heard about your trip out of New York. I'm sorry to hear about your loss back then."

"Thanks for the information. I'll be watching for the contract."

Ray hung up the phone and thought to himself, *So, Emma talks about me. It sounded like more than just once.*

He immediately got online and looked up 'Obituaries, Strong, Buffalo, Missouri'. He found the funeral home and called to verify the time of the services and asked if it was too late to order flowers. The funeral director gave him the name of a lady to call at a local flower shop and said she would probably still have time to fill an order. Ray called the number and asked if he could get a large house plant, something Emma could keep as a remembrance. They agreed on a peace lily, and Ray was assured she would get it to the funeral home in time.

Ray said to simply sign it, "Ray from Strong City".

Three days later, Ray received a call from Emma thanking him for the peace lily and telling him how surprised she was to see it was from him and how much she appreciated it. Ray told her he learned of her mother's passing when he called to schedule a lunch as a means of thanking her and her company for the business. He said, "That offer still stands. I just didn't know when you might return to work."

"You don't need to thank me. That was our construction guys that gave you the contract, and that was only because you earned it. They carefully vetted your company before awarding any contract."

"Yeah, but they wouldn't have known about us, if it wasn't for *you*."

"Okay, lunch offer accepted. I'll be back to work next week. Why don't you call me then and we'll schedule something? I'll look forward to your call."

"Sounds like a plan. Good to hear from you. And I'm very sorry for your loss."

CHAPTER 57

Friday, August 30, 2002
Bristol Seafood Grill
Leawood, Kansas

Ray and Emma had settled on Friday for their lunch together, continuing a friendship born out of tragedy. Emma said she would like to meet Ray in K.C. as opposed to Ray driving to Lawrence. She said she wanted to take Friday afternoon off and pick up some additional back-to-school outfits for her daughter, and she wanted to shop at the Country Club Plaza. They agreed to meet in Leawood at the Bristol adjacent to the new Town Center Plaza. During lunch, Emma told Ray maybe she could just do her shopping right there and not have to drive towards downtown. Their lunch conversations that day seemed to center on their children. Emma's daughter Savanna was now a senior in high school. Ray's two, Matt at 22 was now a senior at K-State, and Fran, about to turn 18, was a freshman at Johnson County Community College. They were never at a loss for words until Emma asked Ray how he was doing with the nightmares.

Ray didn't answer right away, but looked at her with a face that suggested he wished she hadn't asked. He held up a hand with his index finger pointed up suggesting just a minute. He looked down at his plate and took a bite of his salmon. After several seconds, and before he took another bite, he responded, "It's like this: I don't like to talk about them because it just brings back mostly bad memories and that makes me angry. I can't really say they're getting better, but I think I can say they aren't getting worse. Or, maybe it's just that I've learned to live with them. I know, at times, it scares Matt and Fran. And when I wake up and see one or both of them standing there, it scares *me*. One thing I've realized from these nightmares and the PTSD sessions at the V.A.

is that I can understand why so many veterans commit suicide. I don't think I could ever do that, but I can see why some people might want to."

"Oh Ray, I'm sorry! I shouldn't have asked. I wish there was something I could do. Aren't there medications that would help, maybe reduce the intensity or the frequency."

"Yeah, supposedly there are. But I don't want to be taking something that has the ability to change me, how I think, how I act, you know, mind-altering drugs. I believe many of the veterans who go that route become reliant on the drug and then what? I also wonder how many of those veterans are on other drugs, you know, self-medicating. I've never tried that."

"I admire your reluctance to stay off drugs, but ..." Emma didn't really know what the 'but' was going to be, so she just stopped that sentence.

"Over the years I've learned how to control my anger, or at least hide it. I guess that's just another form of control. My anger is usually the result of a nightmare and it takes a few days to go away after one of those '*dreams*'. I use the term loosely. I try not to talk much after an episode and, I've learned talking about them does not stop them from coming back."

Emma knew she had touched a nerve and would never bring that subject up again. She wondered about the anger issues Ray mentioned. She needed to change the subject and asked Ray what he thought about the Kansas City Chiefs Ray nodded his head in a response and continued eating his lunch. He asked Emma if she ever comes over to Arrowhead for a game. Then suggested he'd see if he could get some tickets if she'd like to go. Emma thought that would be fun.

When lunch was over and Ray couldn't talk Emma into dessert, they parted company in the parking lot. They agreed they needed to do this more often and both said they enjoyed it. Ray said he would check on some Chiefs tickets, and then returned to work.

CHAPTER 58

Two Years Later

Thursday, December 23, 2004
Kansas City VA Medical Center
Kansas City, Missouri

Dr. Zehr had convinced a few of her session attendees into coming to help with Christmas celebrations at the hospital, and Ray was one of them. A group of carolers from a local church, including some veterans, were making their way through the hospital floor by floor. Ray was one of three people pushing a cart full of gifts behind the singers. As they paused and then passed by a room, Ray or one of the other veterans would take a gift bag to the patients in that room and thank them for their service, and wish them a Merry Christmas.

Once they had completed all floors, there were Christmas cookies, punch and coffee in the cafeteria for the volunteers and carolers. The group arrived on the lower level just before 9:00 p.m. to meet the other volunteers who had filled all the gift bags. The group was excited about their event and very happy to have this time together. Ray had a nice visit with some of the carolers and another Vietnam veteran that he knew from the PTSD sessions.

By the time the group broke up and Ray ended his conversation with his Vietnam pal, it was going on 10:00 p.m.. After pulling out of the parking lot, Ray thought the quickest way home would be to get on the I-435 loop and take it around the east side and south side back over to Overland Park and then north to Prairie Village. As he entered the on ramp, his mind was on the veterans he had just visited laying in hospital beds which reminded him of his time at Camp Zama. He was also thinking about how much worse off some of these guys were than he was. He should be thankful, especially at this time of the year.

He started up the hill towards Eastwood Trafficway, just west of the stadium complex ,and started worrying about celebrating Christmas with his kids. Had he done enough? Did he really get what they wanted? They weren't really 'kids' anymore. They had been through a lot. They were now young adults. Something seemed wrong. He was sensing it.

As he neared the crest of the hill, something was really bothering him. *Was it the gifts? Did I forget something? No! No! There it is!* A vehicle was coming straight towards him. In his lane. No headlights! *Oh Jesus!* He started to swerve to the right out of the left lane, but it was too late. It was almost a direct head-on collision.

The next thing Ray could remember was watching the first responders trying desperately to remove him from his vehicle. He was looking down from above and recalls one of the first responders saying, 'We're losing him!' Ray found himself trying to turn his foot back and forth hoping that would help them get his body loose from the crashed vehicle. Other firefighters showed up with the jaws of life to pry open the drivers door for better access.

Something felt like he had been there before. Looking down on the medevac chopper as Bill Bill ran away yelling something. That seemed so long ago.

Now he no longer saw what was happening on the ground. Everything went dark, but he could hear voices in the distance, and music, soft soothing music. Then a light appeared, soft low light at first which then turned bright and distant. He felt like he was in a tunnel and was drawn to the light which kept getting brighter and brighter. The brightness turned into a beautiful garden area with all kinds of flowers and trees and people in the distance. There was laughter and music and some singing in the background. It sounded like the carolers he had just heard at the hospital. A dog barked.

He didn't remember walking but found himself getting closer and closer to the people. Then he saw Mari. *Oh, Mari!* She came up to him and said hello and gave him a warm hug. She took his hand and walked him closer to other people. There were his grandparents and his father and, and, was that Jesus sitting there on a large stone with young children around him? There was a gray-haired lady who looked familiar. She was smiling and waving at him from behind Jesus. He didn't know her, but felt like he should and he waved back.

It was so bright and colorful and peaceful there. He couldn't believe it. The colors of the flowers and the aroma of the air. His senses seemed to be on high alert.

Mari walked him up to Jesus and said, "This is Ray, my husband."

Jesus reached out and held Ray's hand and said, "I know. I know you've had a troubled life, but you are going to be okay. You need to go back. You'll be fine. We need you back on earth. You have your mother and children to care for. It's not your time yet."

Ray replied, "I think I like it here. My wife, my father. It's so nice."

"Not yet, Ray. Your time will come. I'm sorry you've had to put up with so much."

Mary pulled on Ray's arm and turned him around and started to walk him in the opposite direction. He heard his father say, "Write it down, Ray. Write it all down. It'll be cathartic."

Then his grandfather added, "Good to see you, Ray. You've turned out to be a fine young man!"

Mari leaned in on him and kissed his cheek and she was gone. The bright light was gone. He was being loaded in the life-flight helicopter. The EMT told the life-flight nurse, "He's back. Take care of him." The chopper lifted off.

Ray stared up at the nurse. She said, "What's your name?"

He responded as loud as he could over the noise of the helicopter, "Ray."

"You're gonna be okay, Ray! We're taking care of you!"

"I know. I know!" He said it louder the second time.

In the hospital, after all the vitals were checked and the IV was hooked up, Ray was wheeled down the hall for an MRI. An hour later, the ER doctor came in and asked him some questions to check his mental condition. Ray had a large bump that was starting to turn color on the side of his forehead, but he answered the questions perfectly. The physician finally said, "Except for the bump on your head and the ankle sprain which had you pinned for a while, we don't find anything wrong. This is kind of strange, because we lost you for a short time back there on the highway."

Ray interrupted and said, "Yeah, I know."

The doctor paused after Ray's comment and looked at him to see if he was going to add anything else, and then said, "It's good to have you back. There are indications you have a slight brain bleed from the blow to your head and we want to keep an eye on that. We're going to keep you overnight, maybe two, at least until that clears up and just to make sure we haven't missed something."

Ray said, "Okay. I think I feel okay. How is the other guy?"

The doctor shook his head as a show of disbelief and said, "You know they always seem to survive. Must be the alcohol which allows their body to relax. They took him to another hospital." He paused, looked at Ray's chart and made a notation or added a signature, and then said, "Get some rest."

Ray asked, "Will I see you tomorrow?" He wanted to tell him about his near death experience, but wasn't sure if he was ready. He really wasn't sure he wanted to tell anyone, but he thought a doctor might be a safe person to tell. He thought they at least wouldn't make fun of him.

The doctor left. A nurse came in and said. You don't have any restrictions except they don't want you getting up and walking around right now. So please buzz me if you need the bathroom. Is there anything I can get you?"

"Yes, I need a phone to call my kids."

The nurse walked around the bed over to the night stand and picked up the phone and placed on the bed so Ray could reach it.

Matt was home for the holidays from K-State. Naturally, he didn't answer; Fran did. As the father of a daughter, Ray wasn't sure how she might react, so he asked to get Matt on the phone. He told Matt the circumstances and said he was all right. He wanted to tell him he saw their mother but somehow knew that would freak him out, and he'd tell Fran and they would both think their dad was totally screwed up.

He did tell Matt that their family car was totaled and said they were going to have to rely on Matt's car for a few days, and they would have to celebrate Christmas a little late, but he wanted him to bring Fran over in the morning to see that he was okay and they could then make adjustments in their lives for the next few days.

After talking to his son, he got on the phone with his sister in Colorado and filled her in assuring her he was all right, even to the point of no restrictions on his diet. He asked if she could call their mother and brother, and then he would talk to all of them as soon as he got out of the hospital, which he said might be tomorrow.

Then, for some reason, he thought about calling Emma, but decided against it. He didn't want her to feel obligated to help him with anything, even though he didn't know what it might be that she could do. Besides, it was getting late.

When he finished with the phone, he just laid there, wide awake, staring up at the ceiling thinking about what had happened and his steps into heaven. He couldn't believe it. *Was this a new kind of dream?* He had heard stories about people having near death experiences and remembered that it happened often enough that medical professionals had an abbreviation for them, NDE. He wondered how many people had such an experience and were then too afraid to tell anyone.

He couldn't think about anything else and he couldn't think about sleeping. He started to recount the people he saw: his father's parents, his father, Mari, Jesus. *It was so good to see Mari. What about his maternal grandparents; where were they? Maybe there just wasn't enough time? And who was that smiling little gray-haired lady standing behind Jesus?* That one puzzled him because she looked familiar and he remembered her as someone positive in his life. *Was that the widow Swanson? No, couldn't be, Mrs. Swanson was much taller.*

Then he remembered that his father had said something, more than once. *What was it? It was like instructions. Yeah, instructions. Write it down. That's what he said. Write it all down. What could he be talking about? It was right after Jesus said I had to put up with so much. But he added something else, a word I've never heard him say before; cathartic. What did he mean? I need to look that up.*

Ray looked at the clock on the wall. It was going on 1:30 a.m. and he was still wide awake. He wondered if he had something to eat, a full belly might make him sleepy. He buzzed the nurse's station. The nurse came in, and he told her he thought maybe he was a little hungry.

"You hit the jackpot! With Christmas just a day away, we have all kinds of store-bought and homemade treats in our break room." She grabbed his plastic water pitcher to refill it and said, "Be right back!"

In less than three minutes she came in with a pitcher of ice water and a plate full of fudge, cake, and cookies. Ray looked at that and thought it was more than he needed, but he was going to enjoy it.

After a brief visit, the nurse turned to leave and Ray blurted out, "I got it!"

The nurse turned around and said, "Got what?"

"Oh, nothing. I've been trying to remember someone I saw in a dream and I finally figured it out. It was from a long time ago." He started to wave her off, but then said, "Hey, got a question."

"Okay. What?" the nurse responded

"What's the word 'cathartic' mean?"

"Oh," she hesitated to think and then said, "I believe it means 'you'll feel better,' or like 'it's good for you,' Something like that."

"Okay, that's kind of what I was thinking."

"I think it has something to do with your emotions, or your emotional state of mind, maybe."

He thanked her as she left and Ray went back to the other issue he had solved. He had pictured the little gray-haired lady long enough that it came back to him. She was the nice lady on the flight home from Camp Zama that had thanked him for his service. She was the only one who did. *That* was cathartic!

For the next fifteen minutes, Ray enjoyed a piece of spice cake, a really rich chunk of fudge, and two sugar cookies. He wondered how he would ever go to sleep after that. He took the plate off his lap, set it on the bedside table, and then found the bed control and leaned the bed back towards flat. He shut off the overhead light and laid there. Now, with a sugar high expected to kick in, his mind was working overtime.

I've been in a terrible accident. I'm sure my car's totaled. I'll need to get hold of my agent in the morning. I'm not seriously injured. I can't believe it. Can that near death experience be real? It seemed so real. So clear and such a positive thing. I wanted to stay there. What was 'cathartic'. I still don't ever remember my father using a word like that, but laying here right now, something feels different. I can't believe I'm not pissed about the guy going the wrong way on the highway. He totaled my car and almost took my life. Well, he did take my life, for a few minutes anyway. Normally, for me, I'd be really angry. But I'm not. I hope he's all right. And, I hope he gets some help with his drinking problem. Maybe this will wake him up to his problem.

It was so good to see Mari. She kissed me and sent me back. She's with Jesus. I know what heaven is like. Well, sort of. I only saw a portion very briefly. But, I had Jesus's blessing. Do I tell anyone about this? Will they believe me? Can I just keep this to myself? I don't know.

What was my father talking about? Write it down? Write it all down? What? Write what down? How am I supposed to know? And what do I do with it when I write it down? Maybe it's just for self-satisfaction. I should try it, but where would I begin?

The night nurse checked in on Ray just after 3:00 a.m. and found him sound asleep. She thought he really looked comfortable and peaceful, not like most people she had experienced after a life-threatening accident.

The other thought that kept running through Ray's mind was the fact that he had never been a real religious person. Why should something like this happen to him? As a child, his parents would take him and his siblings to Sunday school, and they would sit through sermons on many Sundays, but after his time in the Army, especially after Vietnam, that pretty much killed his involvement in religious services. When he and Mari and the kids would go back to Strong City at Easter or at Christmas, they would usually go to a church service with either his parents or with Mari's folks, but that was it. When he thought about religion at various times in his life, he almost always ended the thoughts with the idea that you can be a Christian without having to be a devout religious person. In other words, he felt like you could be a decent human being without the need to attend church services every Sunday. Was this NDE proof of his beliefs?

Before he fell asleep, Ray realized that the dream he often sensed, but never totally experienced finally came to light as he was leaving heaven. He was so happy to finally recall that one. *That other thing! I now know what that other dream was that I could never remember. I'm sure that was it. It was going to be an NDE, but it never went that far. I was on the medevac chopper when Bill Bill was helping load me. Then I was no longer in the chopper, I was above looking down right after Bill said 'Hang in there, Wildcat! I'll see you back in the Midwest.' There was a bright light starting to shine in my eyes and then I heard more from Bill. Now I remember what else he yelled as he ran away from the chopper. 'You'll make it! You're one tough son of a gun!' Then the light went out and the next thing I knew I was in the hospital.*

CHAPTER 59

Friday, December 24, 2004
Truman Medical Center
Kansas City, Missouri

Just after 8:00 a.m., and just after Ray had finished a big breakfast of scrambled eggs, pork sausages, toast and a cup of yogurt, Dr. Richard Lee walked into his room and introduced himself. He looked at Ray's chart and then announced, "You seem to be a very lucky man."

"Yeah, I think so."

"Those head-on collisions at highway speeds usually produce more serious injuries and worse. How are you feeling this morning?"

"Good. Although I noticed as I was eating that my right arm has some stiffness or a dull ache to it. I didn't notice that last night,"

"That's not uncommon. Most likely you have some bruising and soreness caused by the airbags. Those things save lives but they can also do some damage. Let's see your arm."

Dr. Lee looked at his right arm and had him move it in several directions. He then pointed to an area above Ray's wrist that had a slight bruising color. "It should be fine. Anything else bothering you?"

"I have a question."

"Yes? What is it?"

"Do you know anything about, or do you believe in, near death experiences?"

That really seemed to get the doctor's attention. He squared his shoulders and looked at Ray, "I'm not sure what to believe, but I've heard enough about them that there has to be some truth to statistics.

We have a doctor here at Truman who is studying and tracking cases. Are you asking because you experienced something?"

"Yes," and he paused. "But I'm afraid to talk about it. I don't know how people might react, even my own family."

"Let me report this to Dr. Abrams. I'm sure she'll want to talk to you. Is that okay?"

"Yes, for now. But, I don't want everybody in the hospital to know about it."

"Your privacy will be assured."

"Thank you."

Twenty minutes later, Dr. Annette Abrams entered his room and introduced herself. She asked Ray if it was okay for her to close the door.

"Sure."

After closing the door, she pulled up the one chair in the room to the side of his bed and gave Ray a brief description of the study she was doing on NDE's. She then asked if she could record their session.

"Okay." Ray said, "But will you be using my name?"

"Only with your permission," she said matter of factly. She paused to see if he had any other questions. "So, tell me about your experience. Let's start with what caused the near death, if you have memory of that"

Ray began and filled her in on all the details he could remember, which was pretty much everything that happened. He even mentioned that Mari whispered in his ear as she kissed his cheek. She had said, *"You don't have to be alone. You'll find someone."* It was a detail he hadn't remembered until just then and, as Ray related this to Dr. Abrams, he realized this was a subject that he and Mari had never discussed; what would one do if the other died unexpectedly?

After an hour of questions and answers, Dr. Abrams thanked Ray for his time and his frankness. She assured him he was not alone with this type of experience and she would probably check back with him before he was discharged. She also said she was glad to see that he was okay.

When the doctor opened the door to leave Ray's room, there were two young adults waiting to go in. It was Matt and Fran. They had been waiting for almost half an hour so naturally they wanted to know what that doctor wanted that took so long.

"Ray wasn't surprised to see them, but wasn't ready with an answer to that question. He thought the truth, at least part of it, was probably the best answer. "Oh, it was just an interview to understand how the accident happened and how much I could recall."

"Really? I thought the police would do that," said Matt.

"Well, they also follow-up from a medical perspective." Then he wanted to change the conversation and said, "Merry Christmas you two! Sorry if I spoiled any of your plans."

An hour after Ray had been served his lunch, Matt and Fran headed down to the hospital's cafeteria to get something to eat. Just after they left Ray's room, his mother and June walked in. He asked if they saw the kids and they both said, "No."

Ray said, "You almost had to have passed in the elevators because they just left."

It was beginning to look like their family would be celebrating Christmas in a hospital room this year. Ray wondered if he needed to write it down. He couldn't see why; he surely would remember this.

Late that afternoon, a police sergeant showed up with a clipboard and introduced himself. He said he had the doctor's permission to visit and was surprised to find that Ray was doing so well. "After what we saw out there on the highway, I am amazed you're alive." He said he was there to follow up on his accident report and needed Ray to tell him everything he could remember about how it happened.

Dennis G. Smith

When Ray finished, the sergeant jotted down a few more notes and then told Ray what they often found in these types of head-on collisions with a drunk driver involved. The police theory is that these accidents almost always occur in the far left lane, the 'fast lane', and Ray agreed that was where he was driving. The sergeant went on to say that they believe an inebriated person who unknowingly makes the mistake of entering an exit ramp and gets onto a divided highway, is then determined that they need to pull over to the right lane and hold their speed down so they don't get stopped, a;; the while not knowing they are going the wrong way, unfortunately, until it's too late.

"So, the guy who hit me *was* drunk?"

"Definitely a DUI. He'll be spending some time in court and, I hope, in jail so he learns his lesson."

CHAPTER 60

Eight Months Later

Thursday, August 25, 2005
O.P. Custom Cabinets & Hardware
Overland Park, Kansas

Following the accident and the NDE, Ray sensed a difference in his life. Somehow he felt better about things. Little problems didn't seem to bother him as much. His attitude seemed different, and various things from his brief walk in heaven kept coming back to him. For some reason, even after his conversation with Dr. Abrams, he still had days where he believed that it had all been a weird dream. It couldn't have happened, even though it seemed so real. Then he would remember looking down on the accident scene and hearing one of the first responders saying 'We're losing him.' That definitely wasn't a dream. All he knew for sure was that the whole experience was unforgettable and he certainly felt like it changed him.

Ray had heard from Emma in January when she called to wish him a happy new year and to ask about his Christmas. When he told her about his head-on collision and spending Christmas in the hospital, she was totally surprised. She even asked, "Oh, Ray, how much more can you take?"

He explained that he was lucky and happy to be alive. He felt like that experience had changed his attitude for the better, which even he couldn't understand. "A normal person," he told her, "would probably be totally pissed off at the whole thing."

"You're right! Damn drunk drivers. Oh, God, I'll pray for you Ray."

They agreed they needed to get together for lunch again and that was that. But it had been months since he heard from her until his phone rang in August.

"Ray," she said, "I've missed you and I'm terribly sorry I haven't been in touch."

"Me, too," he said, "What have you been up to?"

"Busy, terribly busy. But I'm headed over to your neck of the woods this afternoon for a meeting and wondered if you'd have time for dinner?"

"I'm sure I can find the time."

"Good. I think I can remember how to find your place. How about I pick you up about 6:00? You choose where we go."

"Sounds good! If you get lost, give me a call."

During dinner that night at J. Gilberts on Metcalf Ave., the two caught up on a lot of subjects since they had last seen each other. Ray wanted to tell her about his near death experience, but was afraid of scaring her off. After all, she had experienced one of his nightmare episodes on their way home from New York. Instead, he suddenly realized that he hadn't had a nightmare since the car accident so he related that to Emma and said he wondered if the knock on the head cleared all those bad dreams away. He thought to himself, *Wow, I don't remember when the last nightmare was, but I know it was last year before the accident.*

Emma thought that was great and asked about the PTSD issues. He told her he was still attending meetings, not so much for the need, but rather for the loyalty to the others. There were a few 'old timers' there that Ray had known for years, and it was always a good feeling seeing them and feeling like their presence could possibly help the new younger guys, and gals.

When Emma asked about the kids. Ray was happy to tell her that Matt had graduated K-State and was working for an engineering company. Fran was with a girlfriend and her parents on a vacation in the Colorado Rockies and would be home Saturday. He'd been 'baching" it all week he told her and laughed.

After dinner, she drove him back to his home, and Ray invited her in. He offered her a drink or a glass of wine. "All I have is a bottle of Merlot," he said.

"Don't open it just for me," she replied, "But if you're gonna have some too, that sounds lovely."

Ray proceeded to open the wine, then had to hunt for some suitable glasses. It had been awhile since he had served wine in his house.

Ray sat down beside Emma on the sofa and he reached for the remote. "What are the chances we could find a good movie?"

She responded with, "What kind of movies do you like?"

"Oh, I'm flexible," he said as he scrolled through channels. While searching for movie channels, he paused for a bit on '24' with Kiefer Sutherland and noticed that didn't get much of a reaction from Emma. Then he stopped again on 'The Office', another weekly episode show, and Emma said that show was pretty funny. They watched it till it ended just ten minutes later, then Ray was back scrolling and discovered the Royals game.

The Royals were not having a good year with a record of 42 wins and 83 losses at that time, but they were ahead of the Boston Red Sox, so Ray asked Emma if she followed baseball, and she replied, "I'll watch the Royals, but I like it better when they win." Then she noticed the score and added, "Oh, they're ahead!" Ray left it on that channel and they continued talking sports, Royals and Chiefs.

Ray went back to the kitchen and grabbed the bottle of wine so he could refill their glasses. When he handed her glass back to Emma and she reached for it, their hands touched and it seemed like a spark. Ray looked at Emma and she stared back. She tipped her glass in the form of a toast, and said, "To happiness." They clinked glasses and both took a large drink.

Dennis G. Smith

The next morning, they both remembered polishing off the bottle of wine, but neither one knew if the Royals won or not.

Ray called for his boss and got his voicemail. He left him a message that said he needed to take care of some personal business and wouldn't be in until the afternoon. Emma heard him leave that message and raised her eyebrows and smiled. Ray proceeded to fix his favorite French toast and bacon breakfast and asked Emma if she'd like an egg or two to go with it. Happiness was on the menu.

After eating and a second cup of coffee, they hugged and kissed and Emma left for Lawrence. Ray thought to himself as he watched her pull away from the curb, *Wow, that was wonderful*. He still really missed Mari, but he hadn't realized how much the touch of another human, a woman, could mean to him. The thought of being *in love* hadn't crossed his mind, but the love making certainly was satisfying. He hoped Emma felt the same, and his sixth sense told him she did.

CHAPTER 61
Four Years Later

Saturday, July 4th, 2009
Home
Prairie Village, Kansas

Ray was up early. He had a new home project he was determined to finish over the holiday. Ray wasn't sure where he was going with his father's words, but he had decided he would start taking notes, both mentally and physically writing things down. *'Write it down, Ray. Write it all down. It'll be cathartic.'*

Now that Matt had his Electrical Engineering degree and his own apartment in Kansas City working for a large architectural engineering firm, Ray was sure Matt would never return to that bedroom. Matt was engaged to a lovely girl who still had one more year to finish her degree in Elementary Education. She planned on teaching.

Fran, named after her distant relative, Francis Scott Key, was all set to graduate from law school the following year. If all went well, she would hope to pass the bar in Kansas and and enter the legal profession. In the back of her mind, she was hoping her far-distant relative's name might help open some doors for her. Her father laughed and wished her luck with that. Then he wrote it down.

Ray was content and very satisfied with how his children had turned out ,and he had no trouble paying for their college educations. The college fund he and Mari had started right after Matt was born had grown and Ray continued to fund it after Mari was gone. He also had a couple of life insurance settlements which had been invested and had grown nicely. He would still have funds left over after Fran's graduation.

As Ray saw it, he would soon have two empty bedrooms and one should be enough for guests. By Monday, he hoped to have Matt's room completed as an office/den. The bed would go to the basement, until such time that he would decide neither of the kids needed it to furnish their homes. He had purchased a small sofa to be delivered later in the week. He had a new desk he needed to assemble and he wanted to repaint the room in an eggshell white. There would be a flat screen TV on one wall so he could watch what he wanted on weekends and summers when Fran was home.

The final touch was to be a new computer which he intended to pick up the next week. His old one was slow and dated. He wanted something that would make using the computer fun again, and less of an arduous task.

Ray and Emma continued to see each other periodically on weekends or for lunch when one of them had to be in the other's city. Ray was very self-conscious of Fran's dislike for "that woman". When he mentioned Emma, Fran would roll her eyes and look disappointed. Once, she even came out and said she was sorry, but she couldn't help herself. She said she still missed her mother terribly and seeing her dad with another woman just reminded her how much she hated the fact her mother was gone.

Ray told Emma he thought things would change for them once Fran got her law degree and began her career. He added that he thought Fran was actually coming around after eight years of their involvement together. He sensed that her legal education may have caused her to realize her father had a life to live. He couldn't forget Mari's whisper in his ear, *'You don't have to be alone. You'll find someone'*.

CHAPTER 62

Wednesday, September 9, 2009
Kansas City VA Medical Center
Kansas City, Missouri

Ray had continued to attend PTSD sessions even though he had discovered his nightmares had virtually disappeared after his accident and NDE. Something kept him coming back. He felt an obligation to his fellow veterans. Even after Dr. Zehr was given a promotion into hospital administration, he still attended faithfully. There were always new patients who might benefit from his experience, although he had stopped with his long-winded arguments about what was wrong with the world and issues with personal things that bothered him. Since the accident, he mainly just listened.

This month, when it was his turn to speak, Ray simply said he was enjoying the beautiful day, even though there was a chance of rain. "We could use it," he remarked. "That's all."

When the new psychologist, Dr. Adamson, who replaced Dr. Zehr asked if anyone had any comments or questions for Ray, Richard Jensen, a long-time attendee like Ray spoke up. "Yeah, I've got a comment." Then he laughed a little.

Dr. Adamson said, "Go ahead."

"Well, Ray, I kinda miss the ol' days," and he chuckled again. "I sorta wonder what happened? Used to be, we could always count on you to have some kind of complaint about something or other. Like the time your bathroom remodeler took twice as long to finish than he had predicted and you complained about all your family having to share a bathroom in the basement. And I remember your tirade about the red lights on Metcalf not being in sync and how it always screwed up traffic. I'm not makin' fun, they were always legitimate complaints. Oh, yeah, and the judges who were giving out light sentences for rapists and murderers. Those were all valid issues, and we'd all sit here and listen and nod our heads in agreement, but we don't hear those from you anymore. What happened?"

Ray saw Richard's smile and nodded. He thought before he responded, then said, "Rich, I guess I just matured. Maybe with age comes wisdom. I still think about stuff like that, but I've learned that bitching about it doesn't change anything. So all of you should feel relieved that I don't waste your time with my issues."

"Do you still have your nightmares?" Richard asked. "You haven't mentioned them in a long time."

Ray had told the group about his accident at his first session after it happened but never mentioned the near death experience. "No. You know that's funny, because after the car accident and the big bump on the head, they stopped. I still have dreams, *normal* dreams I'll call them, but I wake up and most of the time they're gone, can't remember them. But I haven't had a serious nightmare since. Must've been some divine intervention that knocked some sense into me back then." He laughed after that last statement.

CHAPTER 63
Life After Death

Driving back to his office after that VA PTSD session, Ray couldn't shake the thought of his last statement. It was the first time he had actually said that and realized that it was factual. He hadn't had a nightmare since that accident. And, when he blurted out that sentence, he believed he knew that in the back of his mind, but had never actually thought there was a connection. Now, he couldn't stop thinking that there really was a divine intervention.

He wanted to know more about this. Could it be true? Who could he talk to? Back at his desk, he couldn't shake the thoughts and tried to remember the doctor's name at Truman Medical Center who was studying NDE.

That night at home, he dug out his medical records and tried to sort them in a chronological order looking for Christmas of 2004. He finally found the discharge papers and sorted through several pages of information on exams, treatment and recommendations. There, at the bottom of page four, he saw a reference, *Referred to Dr. A. Adams.* That was it, Dr. Adams, Annette was her first name. He would call her in the morning for an appointment.

The next morning when he called the Medical Center and asked for Dr. Adams, he was told she is no longer there. That stopped his hopes real quick, but he had to ask, "Can you tell me where she is now?"

The operator said, "I'm not sure we have that information, and I know I can't give it out. Let me transfer you."

Someone answered the phone where he was transferred and said, "Can you hold?" Ray held for what seemed like ten minutes, when someone came back on the line. He told them what he needed and was asked to hold again. Two minutes later, the lady came back on and said, "Dr. Adams left the V.A. three years ago and is now with the K.U. Med Center."

"Thank you!"

Ray immediately looked up K.U.'s number and finally got through to a doctor's assistant who transferred him to scheduling. The earliest he could get in to see Dr. Adams was three weeks away.

When he got to his appointment with Dr. Adams, she was very interested in what he had to say about divine intervention and the fact that it seemed to him that his physical injury, or the near death trip to heaven, one or the other, or maybe the two combined, cured him of his nightmares. "Is that possible?" he asked.

"Yes, I have some others who've had somewhat similar experiences. Maybe not as exact as yours, but they have reported that certain ailments they had previously were gone after their NDE. One was a cancer patient who found out four months later that she was in remission."

The doctor quizzed Ray. Had he noticed any changes in other health issues or changes in his personality?

Ray was glad to be able to open up to a medical professional about this and said, "Ever since I was shot in Vietnam, I've had anger issues. I've kept most of them bottled up inside, but not always. Even the flight home after being wounded aggravated me. It was bad enough to be wounded and almost killed, but then no one cared. Well, except for close friends and family, and Minnesota Fats. I'll have to tell you about that one. And there was a little lady I saw again in heaven. She cared. But the rest of the country would just as soon spit on you. That started me being pissed at a lot of things."

"Then, years later," he went on, "losing my wife on 9/11 really pissed me off. But what can you do? All of this war stuff was terrible and mostly mismanaged. Politics get in the way. And I constantly let little things bother me. But, you asked, and yeah, I have noticed a change since the accident. I no longer seem to have those kinds of issues with anger."

"Well, that's good! Right?"

"Oh, yeah, I agree."

CHAPTER 64

After that session with Dr. Adams, Ray became more conscious of his thoughts on subjects that bothered him. He started to worry that maybe the anger issues still existed but he was older and wiser now and could put them aside to worry about more important things. Basically, he was trying to convince himself that he really was over having problems with anger. He had always managed to control it around family and close friends, but that didn't mean certain things didn't upset him; he just worked at letting it go.

Fran was away at college, and he could watch what he wanted on TV at night without worrying about her. He wasn't much into politics, but in a sense, he was glad our country had finally cleared the hurdle of having a black person as president. All of that seemed okay with him until he started seeing more and more reports on this new health care plan that was being proposed, Obamacare, or as they liked to call it, the Affordable Care Act. The more he watched and the more he heard, the more it seemed to him that it wasn't just being proposed, it was being shoved down our throats. This bothered him for what it was, but even more so, he felt like his anger was creeping back in over this one issue.

It was a *big* issue, he told himself. Expensive, all encompassing, and sounded like everyone would have to be insured by the federal government. *If they run health care like they run their wars, we're all in trouble. But what can I do about it?* There were comments about how long the wait may be to see a doctor, then the Obama administration would respond with, '*If you like your doctor, you can keep your doctor.*' For some reason, Ray didn't really buy that. Again, he felt like the anger was growing inside.

Then there was the night that the news announced the U.S. had killed Osama bin Laden. Ray remembered his anger over Mari's death

One Tough Son of a Gun

and he finally felt some justice had been served. He laid awake that night for a long time thinking about 9/11, Mari, and the long search for bin Laden. He tried to imagine the Marines that accomplished that mission and thought that they had to be some of the bravest men around.

Ray tried to avoid all the news broadcasts about the Gulf War and our attacks on Iraq. It wasn't so much that he didn't want to know; he just didn't want to see reminders of what war was like. *And, here we go again, the big arm of the United States Military was halfway around the world trying to assist a little country against aggression from a larger neighbor. Why do we keep doing this?* he wondered. *It's all about the oil!* he convinced himself. And he again had to work to convince himself that his anger issues were not coming back.

At night and on weekends, when he was alone, he spent time in his remodeled den working on the task his father had suggested, '*Write it down, Ray*'. He wasn't sure what he was doing with it, but he was beginning to develop quite a manuscript. After adding different events from his past as he remembered them, he would occasionally take the time to review them and place them into a chronological order. Somehow, he began to feel his father's words, '*It'll be cathartic*.' If it wasn't for that fact, Ray thought he probably wouldn't keep going because it was very time consuming, but it did feel good.

CHAPTER 65

With both kids out of the house, Ray could spend more time with Emma without embarrassment or guilt and their relationship continued to grow. They even began talking about marriage.

His old friend Bill Williams, 'Bill Bill', had retired from Army life and was working for a security company in Omaha. He would try to get down to K.C. to visit with Ray at least once a year and they would attend a Royals game or a Chiefs game if they could get tickets. He introduced Bill to Emma, and asked him when he was going to settle down and get married. To Ray's surprise, Bill Bill said he had a nice lady friend in Omaha and maybe he would bring her along the next time he came down.

The prospect for Ray's and Emma's marriage seemed to be getting closer, and they finally said, "Let's do it!" and made plans to get away to Vegas in the next couple of months and have a quickie wedding. In September of 2014, they met Bill Bill and his lady at Caesar's Palace and tied the knot during a long weekend trip.

Ray and Emma thought life was good and they began shopping for new furniture, and Emma started redoing rooms in Ray's house to put her touch on it.

Ray continued his quest to 'write it all down' and would spend time trying to organize his thoughts into a meaningful manuscript. Ray was pretty much a 7:00 to 4:00 workday guy while Emma liked a lazy morning and worked more like 10:00 to 6:00, usually arriving home just after 6:30. That provided Ray with a couple of hours every afternoon to work on his story, or his anger issues, or whatever it was he was going to call it. He wasn't sure where it was going or what it was for, but he had realized that his father's word, *cathartic*, maybe was therapeutic. At least it seemed to him to be on target. He simply felt compelled to continue.

One Tough Son of a Gun

Emma asked him once what he was writing about and he told her it was something his father had suggested at one time to help him overcome his anger issues. He didn't mention that his father was dead and in heaven at the time. He did laugh when he told Emma that it was going to be the next great American novel, then added, "Naw, just might be my life story. I don't know yet. Right now, it's a series of anecdotes about things that irritate me."

Emma replied to that, "I hope my name's not in there!"

One late afternoon at work, Ray was bored and thinking about what he had told Emma about his writing exercise and thought that there was more truth to that than he imagined. He left work early to get home and work on an idea. He wanted to make a list of the things that had always irritated him.

He knew right away where to start:

9/11 - that really pissed him off

Osama bin Laden and his followers

Being drafted into a war where America didn't belong

Getting shot

PTSD and all the nightmares

Gun violence

Crime in America

Stupid politics and politicians

Bill Clinton and Monica what's her name?

The Affordable Care Act

Judges who issue light sentences or probation for serious crimes

Drunk drivers

Stupid people

Over time, he added more things to his list, even mundane things like people who get involved in road rage incidents, nothing to do with him. And people who are apparently homeless and sit on street corners with homemade signs asking for money when there's a McDonald's or a big box store right around the corner with a 'Help Wanted' sign posted. He has heard a lot of other people comment about that.

He even had an item on his list complaining about radio and TV ads where someone, somewhere in an advertising seminar must've told a large group of people that when you give out your business phone number in an ad, make sure you repeat it at least three times, more if you have enough time. God, he hated that. It almost always made him flip channels and guaranteed that he would not buy their product or service. Eventually, he started to refer back to the list and added notes such as:

- 9/11 - It happened, can't change that, still pissed
- Osama bin Laden - At least we finally got him
- Getting shot - It was war; that sniper was only doing his job
- Stupid people - What's the comedian Ron White say? 'You can't fix stupid!'
- Nightmares - At least, at last, I think I'm through with them; thanks to the NDE
- Ads that repeated phone numbers - Shut the radio off, hit 'Mute'

He continued to amass thousands of words, jotting down notes at work when he happened to think of something, and then typing them later into complete sentences and paragraphs on his computer keyboard. He did feel like it was helpful and gave him something to think about as opposed to simply being angry about the world's situations.

CHAPTER 66

Wednesday, January 6, 2021
The Ellipse
Washington, DC

Halfway between the White House and the Washington Monument is The Ellipse, a park-like open space where President Trump's followers had gathered to hear his comments about the election two months earlier which was being contested on several levels. Ray and Emma had decided they wanted to be there to see what the outgoing president had to say.

Ray and Emma couldn't believe the size of the crowd and like almost everyone else, when President Trump suggested they march peacefully down to the Capital, they went along. While Ray wasn't sure what to believe about all the accusations of fraud, he wondered how old Joe Biden, who did very little active campaigning, could beat out Trump. As far as the various issues with ballots and such, Ray always believed that 'where there's smoke, there's fire'.

After following the crowd down to the Capital building, Emma pointed out to Ray where some guys had started to jump the barricades. In just a matter of minutes they saw others, maybe twenty or thirty yards ahead of them, doing the same, plus some of the crowd had already passed through the barriers and were running up the steps. They held their position for another five minutes and then decided to get out of there and go back to their hotel.

Everything that followed for the next several days and then weeks and beyond was upsetting to Ray. He wasn't sure what to think, but he knew this was his country gone bad. The one thing that bothered him most, and he couldn't help it, was the fact that his anger issues were back. He didn't want to see all this happening, and he didn't think he

Dennis G. Smith

wanted to see Joe Biden as President anymore, but there was nothing he could do about it.

CHAPTER 67

Monday, August 30, 2021
Home
Prairie Village, Kansas

Ray was putting together a spaghetti dinner just after 6:00 p.m. so it would be ready when Emma arrived home. He had the small TV in the kitchen turned on to the local news and heard some comments about the updates on the withdrawal of troops from Afghanistan. He didn't pay much attention because he knew President Biden had kept Trump's withdrawal agreement, but had screwed around with the timing which had the Taliban very upset. Then the national news came on, and the situation halfway around the world was the lead story.

Over the next couple of days, everyone learned that thirteen U.S. soldiers had been killed by a suicide bomber at the airport, and video showed pictures of Afghans trying to board U.S. military cargo planes leaving the airport. It was a total disaster of an evacuation leaving behind military equipment, weapons, vehicles, helicopters, U.S. currency and hundreds of U.S. citizens. Ray couldn't stand to watch it. It reminded him of the final days in Vietnam, only much worse.

Yeah, he realized, his anger issues were back.

His language and his comments about the news startled Emma, but she could understand how he felt and she agreed with him. Now she worried that his nightmares might come back.

CHAPTER 68

Weekend, October 28 - 30, 2022
Home
Prairie Village, Kansas

Ray had told his boss on Wednesday that he wanted to take a day off on Friday to take care of some personal business. After Emma left for work, Ray sat down at his computer desk in the den. He wanted to put a couple of finishing touches on his manuscript he had been working on for several years. Ever since the day he received instructions from his father in heaven.

He pulled a thumb drive out of a drawer and plugged it into the USB port and downloaded the manuscript, over 140 typewritten pages. He headed over to the FedEx store and had them print and bind three copies.

He left there and headed to the VA Medical Center where he took one in with him to the front desk. He asked if it would be possible to see Dr. Zehr. The receptionist said she would have to check her schedule and got up and left her desk. She came back and asked who was calling and he said, "Ray Reynolds. Tell her it's 'Wildcat'."

The receptionist returned again and said, "She will be out in a few minutes."

Dr. Zehr appeared from a side door and walked over to the chair where Ray was waiting. "Hello Wildcat," she said, and stuck out her hand. Ray stood and shook her hand and smiled.

"Good to see you," he said.

"Likewise. What brings you around on a Friday afternoon?"

"I just wanted to drop something off for you." He held out the manuscript.

"What's this?" she asked.

"I thought you might find this interesting."

She reached out and took it from him and felt the heft of it. "Feels like a lot of work."

"Instructions from my father. I hope you'll find it worth reading."

They exchanged a little more small talk; then Ray said he had to go. He had two more copies, one for Emma and a spare just in case. He wasn't sure how Dr. Zehr and Emma would react but hoped they would find it worthwhile.

That evening, when she got home, Dr. Zehr was curious and sat down with a glass of wine and opened up the manuscript to start reading. His last comment as they parted earlier that day had her curious. She had said, "It was good to see you, and thanks for the reading material."

As he turned to leave, he said *"C'est la vie"*.

She started to read.

CHAPTER 1

Wednesday, July 14, 2022
Kansas City VA Medical Center
Kansas City, Missouri
United States of America

Ray "Wildcat" Reynolds has anger Issues. They were probably due to the fact he was drafted way back when, or the fact he was sent to infantry training at Fort Polk, Louisiana, the armpit of the Army. He thought he was smarter than that. Maybe it was the way the Vietnam veterans were treated when they came home. Or

Dennis G. Smith

it could have been the fact that we were in the war in southeast Asia in the first place. Or the things that happened to him there. We didn't belong there, halfway around the world. It wasn't our problem. It was the stupid politics of it. Like people said - "If the politicians had to send their children off to fight, the war would be over in no time". And, from what he knew, he thought a lot of the Vietnamese were okay living under communism. Or they were just too afraid to say or do anything. But why should we try to change that? It's their country.

Besides all that, over 50,000 young Americans died, and countless more still bearing the scars of their wounds, like him. Only many of the wounded were a whole lot worse than he was. Then, to top it all, we give up and pull out without winning the war! Us, the U.S., greatest military might in the world and we let little Ho Chi Minh SOB and North Vietnam win! What the hell? And somewhere he read that Ho Chi Minh said, before he died, "If the U.S. had only known how close they were to winning the war, they would never have left. We were down to sending 14-year-olds south to fight the war." Yeah, Ray knew about that! And he had anger issues. But he worked hard to keep the anger under control.

It's possible that 'survivor's remorse' could have exacerbated his problems. That had been suggested by some of his friends. Why did I live through it?, he often wondered. He should just be happy to be alive.

Then again, just last year, the politics of war won out over a military victory in Afghanistan. After twenty years, President Biden ordered an immediate withdrawal of all troops, leaving behind equipment, helicopters, vehicles, weapons and pallets of money for the Taliban - victors without winning the battle. Although they had to get in one last suicide bomber before we gave the country back to them. No wonder his anger wouldn't go away.

It wasn't just Vietnam, and now Afghanistan bringing it all back, and the PTSD, it was also the September 11th attack with the hijackings and the World Trade Center twin towers coming down. That was personal! He certainly had a right to be angry about that! He wanted to re-enlist, but knew he was too old and probably wouldn't pass the physical. He really struggled with keeping his mouth shut at work when these topics came up because he knew his language, cowboy slang and soldier's words would be outside the bounds of reasonable and probably get him fired.

Whatever it was, whatever it is, it's always the same spiel that pours out of his mouth every time he goes to the V.A. meetings to talk with the "counselors" and the other PTSD sufferers. Why does he feel like he is the only one that speaks out with such anger? Why can't he just listen? He used to be able to do that. At least one day out of every month, he has an outlet for his pent-up emotions. That helps. It's almost a joke now. They all laugh when it's his turn to speak, but no one disagrees with him. There's no argument from the advisors, and the other veterans just nod their heads in agreement and sympathy. He even laughs sometimes when he starts in because he knows they all know what he's going to gripe about, so he tries to make it more interesting each month by adding some new legitimate complaint. Lately, it's been the current administration's decision to pull out from Afghanistan, and the issue of Covid 19 and wearing masks. Nobody ever proved the masks actually worked. The others all nodded in silence.

For almost forty years, once a month, he's been seeking help with PTSD. He'd lost count of the number of meetings with the Veteran's Administration years earlier. At first, he thought he was fine, but the problem with nightmares started. Then it got worse. He liked his V.A. doctor, but there didn't seem to be a cure. Drugs were suggested but he didn't like the idea. Too many fellow veterans were suffering from drug abuse and he didn't want to go down that road. He realizes the only thing that will cure him, and probably most of the others in the room, is dying. He just has to live through it. He's been lucky to have these sessions, two supportive wives, and a wonderful doctor available that have helped him keep his sanity.

Maybe he was lucky. At least he can control his anger and his mouth most of the time. If he could only control the nightmares. Staying busy helped. He felt sorry for the veterans who didn't have jobs. That too made him angry. He just had to avoid situations with political discussions and anything else that might get him started.

That was the end of the first chapter. *This may be interesting,* Jane Zehr thought, *I've heard about veterans who write their stories, but I've got to fix some dinner.*

At home in the Reynolds' house that evening, Ray had left Emma's copy on the table for her to see as he fixed dinner. She walked in, saw it, and said. "Is this your great American novel?"

"Not hardly," he replied, "but it's something you may find interesting. It's historical." Then, to lighten the mood, he added, "and maybe *hysterical*. You'll probably think it's bad, and now that I think about it, it's mostly sad. Maybe you shouldn't read it."

"Oh no you don't. I can't wait to get started." She picked it up.

Ray got up the next morning and immediately noticed Emma was not in bed. He went on a search and found her sound asleep in the recliner in the living room. The manuscript was in her lap. It looked like she was over halfway through it. Good thing it was Saturday and she didn't have to work.

Emma finally awoke around 11:00 and said she had to get busy. Her daughter was coming over in the afternoon and they were going shopping. "But," she said to Ray, "I'm gonna finish your story tonight come hell or high water. Is this all true?"

"Pretty much. I had no reason to lie about anything."

That evening was pretty much a repeat of the night before except that Emma tried to crawl into bed without waking Ray. Didn't work. He looked at the clock and saw it was almost 2:30. She noticed him raising his head to see the clock and said, "I finished it. It's very good. I didn't know you had all that in you. I want to hear more about your near death experience."

"Okay, but not now. I'm going back to sleep."

In the morning, Ray shaved and showered and got dressed. He put on a dress shirt, some pressed Dockers, and a navy blue blazer.

Emma was at the kitchen table in her bathrobe having coffee when Ray walked in. She looked at him and perked up. " Whoa! Where you going?"

"Church. Wanna go?"

Acknowledgments

As an author, I really have to thank my wife Carol for allowing me the quiet time needed to put together this, and all my other books. After all, this is also her retirement time with me and I appreciate her patience and understanding. She has been a good sounding board and has offered many good suggestions when I needed help with certain aspects of a book, especially when I needed a feminine perspective,

I again owe many thanks to my trusted eagle-eye proofreaders, my sister Janis Hayes, and a good friend and former neighbor Richard Sophir. I also had another friend volunteer to proofread and help edit, Noah Slabotsky's help was greatly appreciated. All three did an outstanding job of catching punctuation errors, missing words, plus suggestions for edits that might make a sentence, a paragraph, a chapter, or maybe the entire book better. Thank you for your time and attention to detail.

About the Author

Dennis G. Smith grew up in Council Bluffs, Iowa, served in the Army infantry in Vietnam and then returned to his native state to earn a Bachelor's degree in Communications from Iowa State University. Following graduation, most of his career involved reading, writing, editing and checking technical documents in the design/build commercial construction industry. Now retired, Dennis has the time to re-visit his love of creative writing. He has self-published five books prior to this one

His first book *Missouri's Secret* is historical fiction involving *real* crimes that took place in the early 1990's in Southwest Missouri where five missing women are still unsolved cold cases. His fictional characters find themselves in very real-life situations while the story examines how ordinary people discover their marriage falling apart after many years together. The fictional tale may suggest a possible answer to the unsolved secret of these true cold cases. Somebody knows!

Mr. Smith's next two novels, *Night Light* and *The Man in the Van*, are set in the Denver area and feature Chance Jackson, a street cop turned detective. Detective Jackson also plays a major role in his fifth book *One Day at Willow Tree*.

This author's fourth book, another historical fiction novel, is *War is Hell, A Love Story*. The story revolves around a history student interviewing a survivor of World War II for a term paper. The student gets a story from the elderly sailor that no one had ever heard before. It is a unique case of PTSD, back then called shell shock, that kept this veteran mum for years.

www.ingramcontent.com/pod-product-compliance
Ingram Content Group UK Ltd.
Pitfield, Milton Keynes, MK11 3LW, UK
UKHW020245240426
12048UKWH00026B/1613